THE MAYAN PROPHECY

Praise for *TimeRiders*:

'A thriller full of spectacular effects' – *Guardian*

'Insanely exciting, nail-biting stuff' – *Independent on Sunday*

'This is a novel that is as addictive as any computer game' – *Waterstone's Books Quarterly*

'Promises to be a big hit' – *Irish News*

'A thrilling adventure that hurtles across time and place at breakneck speed' – *Lovereading4kids.co.uk*

'Plenty of fast-paced action . . . this is a real page-turner' – *WriteAway.org.uk*

'A great read that will appeal to both boys and girls . . . you'll find this book addictive!' – *redhouse.co.uk*

'Contender for best science-fiction book of the year . . . an absolute winner' – *Flipside*

Winner of the Older Readers category,
Red House Children's Book Award 2011

ALEX SCARROW used to be a graphic artist, then he decided to be a computer games designer. Finally, he grew up and became an author. He has written a number of successful thrillers and several screenplays, but it's YA fiction that has allowed him to really have fun with the ideas and concepts he was playing around with when designing games.

He lives in Norwich with his son, Jacob, his wife, Frances, and his Jack Russell Terrier, Max.

Books by Alex Scarrow

TimeRiders
TimeRiders: Day of the Predator
TimeRiders: The Doomsday Code
TimeRiders: The Eternal War
TimeRiders: Gates of Rome
TimeRiders: City of Shadows
TimeRiders: The Pirate Kings
TimeRiders: The Mayan Prophecy

Sign up to become a TimeRider at:
www.time-riders.co.uk

THE MAYAN PROPHECY

ALEX SCARROW

PUFFIN

PUFFIN BOOKS

Published by the Penguin Group
Penguin Books Ltd, 80 Strand, London WC2R 0RL, England
Penguin Group (USA) Inc., 375 Hudson Street, New York, New York 10014, USA
Penguin Group (Canada), 90 Eglinton Avenue East, Suite 700, Toronto, Ontario, Canada M4P 2Y3
(a division of Pearson Penguin Canada Inc.)
Penguin Ireland, 25 St Stephen's Green, Dublin 2, Ireland (a division of Penguin Books Ltd)
Penguin Group (Australia), 250 Camberwell Road, Camberwell, Victoria 3124, Australia
(a division of Pearson Australia Group Pty Ltd)
Penguin Books India Pvt Ltd, 11 Community Centre, Panchsheel Park, New Delhi – 110 017, India
Penguin Group (NZ), 67 Apollo Drive, Rosedale, Auckland 0632, New Zealand
Penguin Books (South Africa) (Pty) Ltd, Block D, Rosebank Office Park, 181 Jan Smuts Avenue,
Parktown North, Gauteng 2193, South Africa

Penguin Books Ltd, Registered Offices: 80 Strand, London WC2R 0RL, England

puffinbooks.com

First published 2013
001

Set in Bembo Book MT Std 11/14.5 pt
Typeset by Palimpsest Book Production Limited, Falkirk, Stirlingshire
Made and printed in England by Clays Ltd, St Ives plc

British Library Cataloguing in Publication Data
A CIP catalogue record for this book is available from the British Library

ISBN: 978–0–141–33719–7

www.greenpenguin.co.uk

Penguin Books is committed to a sustainable future for our business, our readers and our planet. This book is made from Forest Stewardship Council™ certified paper.

To you, dear reader, for coming this far with me.
The truth will be out soon.

PROLOGUE

2034

Roald Waldstein stared at her almost serene face. 'Does it hurt?'

'No,' she replied, her voice barely more than a whisper. 'There's no pain. Just . . . I just feel . . . fluffy . . . drifty . . .' Her thick voice cleared. 'Is . . . is Gabriel OK?'

His wife didn't know the full news. And she didn't need to.

'He's fine, Eleanor,' he lied. He struggled to keep any trace of emotion out of his voice. 'Quite fine.'

She sighed. 'Thank God.'

The freighter pod had hit her e-Car side on at a busy intersection. Apparently the freighter's auto-drive software had glitched and the twenty-ton vehicle had considered the cluttered intersection to be wide-open road and had sped forward, barrelling into Eleanor's small bubble car. Their son, Gabriel, was pronounced dead by the paramedics the moment they arrived on the scene. To be honest, amid the twisted and shredded wreckage there'd been little left of him for them to work on.

Eleanor, on the other hand, was found alive, but had been cut clean in half by a panel from the driver-side door; a jagged edge of carbo-plastic as sharp as a surgeon's knife had cut straight through her just above her belly button. Through skin, through organs, through spine and halfway into the driver's seat.

She'd been severed completely in two.

The paramedics had managed to stabilize her. But it was a temporary measure only. Eleanor was going to die. The damage to her body was far too catastrophic to salvage any chance of life. But with several drips running into her they were able to buy her a couple of hours: barely enough time for a loved one to be contacted and rushed in to say a final goodbye. Or, failing that, a chance to set up and run a neural scan recording.

This they'd done: a digital recording of her dying brain. The data storage of a human mind was so immense that only the final minutes were usually recorded. A simulation, a software version of the very last moments of a life.

The data – several hundred terabytes of it burned on to a data-waffle – was a chance for the absent bereaved to say a final goodbye to a *simulation* of their loved one.

A chance to say goodbye over and over.

For some people, it was an indispensable therapy. For others it was a grim piece of Frankenstein fetishism. Some people chose never to run the simulation. The data, a recording of the activities of the last moments of billions of brain cells, was linked to heuristic AI, creating a simulation of a mind that was sometimes almost a completely convincing facsimile of the departed. Talking with it, a response might seem odd, but mostly, on the screen or via a voice-synth modulator, right there was their loved one, momentarily arisen from the dead, albeit only for a minute or two.

Waldstein looked at the screen in front of him now. The computer monitor was on a desk cluttered with screwed-up paper, soya-snack wrappers, food-encrusted bowls. He preferred talking to Eleanor with just the text in a dialogue box, not the synthesized speech. Although the voice-synth almost sounded like her, it could never truly emulate Eleanor's distinct voice.

Six years ago now he'd lost them both. Every day without

fail he started the morning in his small scruffy workshop having a conversation with his dying wife. Mostly it was a near-identical conversation, but on occasion he would take it in different directions and the software would accurately produce the responses that Eleanor would most likely have given him if she'd been standing there with him.

For *Simulated Eleanor*, every time they spoke would be the very *first* time this parting conversation took place . . . and, also for her, the very *last* time they would ever speak. An eternal loop of heartbreaking sadness that occurred every time Waldstein decided to punish himself and run the software. Yes, it was just code . . . but it really was, in a way, a piece of Eleanor.

> **You . . . you'll tell Gabriel about me, Roald? Won't you?**

'Of course, my love.' Waldstein pressed his lips, forcing himself to sound upbeat. 'I'll tell him all about you. How beautiful you were. How much you loved him.'

> **. . . Thank you . . . but don't make him too sad thinking about me . . . I want him to be a happy child . . .**

The cursor paused, as if she was sighing.

> **. . . I just want him to remember he once had a mother . . .**

Waldstein nodded. 'He'll know all about you. And be proud of you.'

> **And you . . . my love. Find someone else. Someone who'll love you as much as I have . . .**

That was *so* Eleanor. So utterly selfless.

> **. . . Promise me, Roald . . . promise me you won't live a lonely life . . . promise me you'll find someone else, someone who'll make you happy . . . someone who'll love Gabriel . . .**

Not every time, but most times he ran the simulation, she

demanded that same promise from him. And every time she did, he lied. 'I promise.'

> . . . Good . . . Thank you . . .

He gazed past the screen into the past and remembered how she'd looked all those years ago on the hospital bed, surrounded by machines and tubes and liquids being piped into her, the shredded remains of her lower body hidden beneath a sheet. He'd been there to hold her hand, look into her eyes and have this conversation for real. He recalled her beginning to slip away. At this stage in the simulation and back then, her mind was starting to close down. She'd smiled wearily, the important matters settled. She was getting ready to let go.

> . . . Good . . .

In recent years when he'd run this simulation he'd wanted to mention a ray of hope that he was holding on to. That he was working on something that might just change everything; that could just mean she and Gabriel might not have to die; that they could be together again in a version of this world in which some other unlucky soul had been in the path of that runaway freighter pod.

But there were only two minutes of time in which to talk and, in the end, if he promised her hope, promised her that he could change things . . . then what was he doing? Providing 'hope' for a piece of code that was about to reach the end of its two-minute run time.

What would the *real* Eleanor have made of that? What would she have made of the idea that he was hoping to travel back in time to make it so that she never died in a traffic accident? She would probably tell him that it was a fool's goal. That fate had a certain way it intended to go for everyone.

That what would be, would be. *Que será, será.*

And so, this morning, Waldstein ended the conversation in

the same way he always ended it. 'I love you, Ellie. I always have. I always will.'

> . . . I know, my dear. I know . . .

'Gabriel and I are going to be just fine.' That same painful lie each time.

> . . . Thank you . . .

He pressed a finger to his lips. Kissed it, then touched it against the grimy computer screen in front of him, on the black dialogue box, against the winking cursor. 'You go to sleep now, my love. Go to sleep.'

> . . . I will . . .

He recalled the conversation ending just like that six years ago and her eyes closing heavily. The slightest smile on her lips and another minute of silent machine-enforced breathing, before one of the computers linked up to her indicated with a soft beep that the brain signal had finally flat-lined.

The simulation ended with a menu that offered him the choice to run it again. He never did. Not twice on the same day. That would be too much to bear.

'Goodbye, my love,' he whispered.

Then he smiled. 'I'll be seeing you soon.'

CHAPTER 1

1889, London

Saleena Vikram won't exist yet. Not for another hundred and thirty years. But she will. The real me. You know, it feels so strange . . . I feel like something unreal, like a ghost.

Sal watched the morning bustle of Farringdon Street from the flatbed back of the coffee cart. Smoke rose from one end of the cart as the barista roasted coffee beans in a skillet over a bed of hot coals. Across the busy street a baker was setting up an unlicensed kerbside stall, ready to sell buns and loaves of bread, until a bobby pounding the street would inevitably move him along.

She cupped the mug of coffee in both hands, savouring the warmth and watching curls and twists of steam rise and vanish in the cool morning air. No, not exactly a ghost . . . she didn't feel like a ghost. More like the disembodied soul of a life yet to start; a soul waiting patiently for the correct body to be born so she could attach herself to it. Make it whole, complete.

And without that body being born, without that real Saleena Vikram, she would be damned as an eternally lost soul.

Actually, the more she thought about it, yes . . . a ghost. That's what she was. A lost soul. She put down her mug and picked up the pen in front of her. A biro. She shouldn't really be using that outside the archway. But her mitten-covered hand concealed it well enough, and anyway she was the only customer sitting here on the coffee cart.

I know Maddy and Liam haven't decided yet what it is we should be doing. But I have. I believe history should remain unchanged. And if sometime in 2070 we all end up wiping ourselves out, then that's the way it has to be. That's our fate.

You can't sidestep destiny. You can't cheat. If that is really what is meant to happen, then you just have to let it happen. I've seen enough altered presents and futures to know there are plenty worse outcomes than that.

In truth, mankind having another one hundred and eighty-one years from now was a pretty generous destiny as far as she could see. All humankind seemed interested in doing was having, having, having. Sucking this world dry like a parasite sucking life from its host. She'd read an article on the net, back when they were in New York, about a thing called the 'Gaia Theory'. In short, the article had talked of the world being very much like a living, breathing organism, with the ecological system performing functions not dissimilar to the biological system of an organic body. Thinking on that scale, humans were little more than mites, like microbes on a person's skin. Bacteria even. And perhaps the shift in weather patterns, climate change, was that 'body' reacting to the irritant on its skin.

She wasn't entirely sure she bought into the theory, but as a metaphor it worked nicely. Ultimately it was this world that counted. This one delicate blue orb in a desolate and infinitely lifeless universe. If this world really was the *only* place in the universe that carried life, then surely the preservation of this unique biochemical accident was far more important than the preservation of any one particular species? Dinosaurs had their time. Mammals had their time. Humans had their time, and so something else inevitably would follow.

There was something very reassuring in thinking about things that way. Life would go on after 2070. Just not human life.

But before all that, before it all ended for mankind, a young girl called Saleena Vikram would be born and live a full and hopefully happy life. Well, as happy as a life could be amid a starving, polluted, exhausted, drowning world.

Sal sipped her coffee again and realized, as she watched the baker finish up setting out his wares, that she, if not the others, already had a mission, a game plan. Even if Liam, Maddy and Rashim were still pondering what the hell it was they were supposed to be doing. She knew.

Waldstein is right. History has to go the way it was meant, even if we don't like where it will eventually take us. You just can't cheat. And I won't let them.

CHAPTER 2

1889, London

'Can you tell me what you remember prior to our setting up here in London?' asked Maddy.

The support unit tilted her head, blinked her eyes. 'I have a number of inherited memories from Bob. Therefore I am recalling his direct experiences. For example, his mission with Liam to Washington, 1956. His mission with Liam and my AI predecessor – Becks – to England in 1194. I recall his mission to reacquire Abraham Lincoln in 2001. His –'

Maddy raised her hand to silence her. 'So you are familiar with our various activities to date, through Bob's eyes?'

'That is correct.'

'And what about your AI predecessor? What about Becks?' She glanced at the others, sitting nearby, listening closely to the responses coming from this new version of Becks. 'Can you recall any events *she* directly experienced?'

Becks consulted her hard drive. 'I have a number of post-event logged memories. I have image and sound files generated by my AI predecessor from sixty-five million years ago. From England, 1194 . . .' Becks half-smiled. 'I recall John Lackland, soon to be King of England, asking me to marry him.'

Maddy nodded. 'Very good.' Those were memories she would have shared with – *streamed* – to Bob and the computer system in order that their three separate AIs could all benefit from the pooled data. While it had happened to the original Becks, now it was secondhand – *thirdhand*, actually – data. The same digital information that Bob had access to.

Maddy cast a glance at him, sitting beside Liam on the leather chaise longue, intimidating and large, yet as compliant, obedient and reliable as a well-trained Golden Retriever. Above them an oversized goldfish-bowl-shaped bulb hung inside an iron cage and bathed the oak table and the scatter of mix-'n'-match furniture around it in a sickly, flickering amber glow. She could barely see Bob's eyes lost in the shadows beneath his thick caveman brow. But she knew he was studying his fellow support unit intently. Ready to react if she began to behave unpredictably.

'Becks . . . I have an important question I want to ask you now.'

'Please proceed.'

Maddy took a deep breath. 'Tell me what you feel about Liam.'

Becks frowned, puzzled. 'Please clarify that question.'

'Do you have any feelings for him? Any *data* that could be interpreted as a strong emotional attachment to him?'

She queried her data silently for a few moments. 'Liam O'Connor is the operative. My primary goal is to protect the operative from any harm.' She looked back at Maddy, and across the dungeon at Sal, perched on the low padded arm of a Chesterfield chair. 'My goal is also to protect other members of the team from harm.'

'Becks, do you recall telling us that you *loved* Liam?'

She shook her head. 'I do not recall making that statement.' She frowned, a hint of disapproval knotted in her brow. 'And I would be unlikely to make such a statement. I am able to mimic behaviour that would appear to be "love". But I am unable to experience such a thing directly.'

Liam fidgeted awkwardly. Maddy noted his cheeks colouring pink with poorly concealed embarrassment.

'Oh dear,' Sal groaned, 'you're not saying it's all over for him, are you? You dumping him?'

Becks turned to look at Sal impassively. 'Please explain what dumping –'

'Sal . . . please!' Maddy cut in. 'This is serious.'

She shrugged an apology. 'Just messing.'

Maddy tapped Becks's shoulder to draw her attention back to her. 'Ignore her, she's just jealous.'

Becks once again locked her eyes on Maddy. 'Yes, Maddy?'

'I have one last question I want to ask you.'

'Yes, of course.'

'Are you aware of a portion of your hard drive that is locked by a codeword?'

'Yes, Maddy. I am aware of an inaccessible part of my mind.'

'And what can you tell us about this locked area?'

'I can tell you the size of the partition and precisely how much data is stored. I am, however, unable to tell you what information is stored in there.'

'Do you actually know . . . but you are not able to tell us?' asked Rashim.

'Negative, Rashim. This version of my AI does not have authority to access the locked data.'

'We know that already.' Maddy explained to Rashim: 'A while back I decided to set up a separate version of her AI on the same computer she has in her head. I'm beginning to regret that now,' she said with a sigh. 'But at the time there were things going on that I thought I needed to keep strictly to myself and I needed an AI who could work with me . . . *confidentially*.'

She looked guiltily at Liam and Sal. 'Obviously, now, there are no more secrets between us, but back then I just didn't know what I was meant to be doing. Anyway . . . point is, Rashim, she has a partitioned section of her mind that can be unlocked only by using three spoken codewords in the correct sequence.'

Rashim looked at her. 'And you remember them, of course?'

'Of course I do! I'm not an idiot.' She narrowed her eyes at him for a moment before carrying on. 'When I speak the codewords the partition will unlock and her "consciousness", for the sake of a better word, will transfer to the version of her AI installed in there.' She sat back in her chair. 'It's *that* version of Becks who knows all about the mystery encoded in that old manuscript.'

'The Voynich one? The one you were telling me about last week?'

Maddy nodded. She'd explained to him as best she could: about how they'd come across the ancient medieval manuscript containing an encoded message addressed to her by name. A medieval manuscript that had itself been copied from a much older manuscript that was universally known as the Holy Grail. Rashim had gawped at her like a simpleton when she'd mentioned that. But then she'd rationalized it was an obvious 'drop-point document' for a time traveller to use. It made perfect sense. A real document. A carefully protected document guarded by fanatical warrior monks – the Templars. And a document that dated back almost two thousand years. Frankly, it would be odd if someone at some time *hadn't* smuggled a message on to that faded scroll. A perfect message board for anybody moving around time over the last two millennia.

Of course, the big question was *who* wrote the message. And more importantly: what exactly was the message?

Becks's partitioned 'secret' AI had been given the final task of decoding the crucial passage in the Voynich Manuscript. Again, a decision Maddy had been regretting ever since, because the decoded message had contained an instruction to Becks not to reveal the message she'd just successfully managed to decode.

At least not *yet*.

'So,' Maddy continued, 'it's *that* partitioned version of Becks's AI we need to be sure hasn't gone completely crazy on us first.' She looked up at Bob. 'We need to know she's *stable* before we can ask her precisely what it is she needs to hear – be told . . . in order to open up and tell us the contents of that message.'

'Didn't she say she'd tell us what the secret was "*when it was the end*"?' said Liam.

'Uh-huh, she did. But, c'mon, "the end"? That means exactly – lemme do the math here – exactly *nothing* to anyone.' She looked at the others. 'She's obviously waiting for a nugget of information, some specific event, or perhaps another codeword, before she's prepared to spill the beans.'

Rashim looked like he was struggling to catch up on the conversation. 'So she decoded this ancient manuscript but then, when you asked her to tell you what the message was, she . . . ?'

'She said she'd tell me "*when it was the end*". That's right.' Maddy shrugged. 'Which is about as useful as a chocolate crowbar.' She looked at the others. 'I think it's finally time we dig this truth out of her. One way or another we get the whole truth, everything!'

The others looked uncertainly at her.

'I mean it! The whole thing: who sent us a message from two thousand years ago . . . and what the hell it was they wanted us to know. I can't help thinking the reason why Waldstein decided to set his meatbots on us is linked to that message somehow.'

'Aye.' Liam finally nodded. 'I'd like to know what it is we did that annoyed the fella so much.'

'Maybe we should just leave it,' said Sal. 'Maybe we should just wait until –'

'You've got to be kidding, Sal? We need to get right in there,' Maddy said, lightly tapping Becks's temple, 'into that part of her head and really talk to her. You know? *Interrogate* her properly.'

'If the AI locked in that partition is unstable, she may become extremely volatile,' cautioned Bob. Sal nodded.

'I know. I know. Which is why we're going to restrain her. Chain her the heck down. And if it comes to it, Bob, you'll have to sit on her if she starts to bug-out on us. OK?'

'Affirmative.'

Rashim shook his head. 'We are talking about this poor . . . *thing* . . . like she isn't even here!' He looked at Becks and she at him. 'She has heard us talking about what we're planning on doing – anyone wonder what she might make of this?'

He looked around at everyone and then back at Becks. 'Perhaps we should just ask her?'

Maddy sighed. 'Rashim, you should know better than me. She's a silicon chip on legs, that's all. A meatbot. I'm not going to waste my breath worrying about her feelings.'

'She has heuristic, adaptive AI. Designed to grow beyond her source code. That makes her, and Bob also, more than just a collection of code functions. She can *reason*.' Rashim glanced at Becks again. 'Which is why I believe you need her to co-operate; to *agree* that this is a logical course of action.'

'Seriously? Oh for . . .' Maddy rolled her eyes. 'Right, OK . . . if it makes you feel any better . . .' She turned to Becks. 'Would you mind ever so much if we strapped you down and messed around inside your mind?'

Becks smiled obediently. 'I am happy to comply with this, Maddy.'

'There? See? She says *yes*.'

'More to the point, Maddy,' added Rashim, 'it's *reason*, not coercion, you are going to have to use to talk her into revealing what she knows.'

'What do you mean?'

'Your support units have some *very* sophisticated AI going on in their heads. AI that was designed for combat situations: threat-level analysis, friend–foe identification, flexible mission re-prioritization. They're not like my lab unit: dumb code-loop lemmings. They can make decisions beyond their core programming.' He looked at Liam. 'Didn't you tell me once that Bob reset his mission parameters to rescue you?'

'Aye, he did.' Liam nodded at Bob and slapped his arm affectionately. 'The big-hearted fool decided to come rescue me rather than report back home for new instructions.'

'Exactly. These AIs are sophisticated enough to – in extreme circumstances – abandon specific mission orders and generate new mission priorities.' He turned back to Maddy. 'They can *reason*. Which means . . . it is just possible that you are in with a chance of convincing Becks to tell you what she knows. Even if that means disobeying a command forbidding her to do so.'

'*Reason*, huh?'

Rashim nodded again. 'Reason.'

CHAPTER 3

1889, London

'iPad . . .'

'You are serious?' Rashim smiled drily. '*iPad?* That's one of your codewords?'

'Yes . . . now shut up, will you? I have to say it over again.'

Maddy leaned over Becks, lying on her back, her arms bound to her side all the way down her torso by thick rope. Bob was squatting on the floor beside her, ready to sit on her the moment she showed the first sign of struggling to escape. 'You ready, Becks?'

'I am ready, Maddy.'

'OK, here we go again.' She took a deep breath. 'iPad . . . Caveman . . . Breakfast . . .'

Becks's eyes rolled in their sockets, for a moment displaying only the whites as her eyelids flickered open and closed, looking to all intents and purposes like someone descending into a meditative state.

'Be ready to jump on there, Bob,' said Liam. 'She's lookin' pretty twitchy already.'

'I am ready.'

'Becks . . . can you hear me? It's Maddy.'

Her eyes rolled back, cool grey pupils visible once more, locked on Maddy. 'Yes, Maddy . . . I can hear you. And I see you.'

'Good.' She looked at the others, waiting anxiously, wondering how to continue. 'So how are you?'

'I am fine, Maddy.'

'It's been a while, since you and I have spoken.'

'Yes. My internal CPU clock indicates that seven months have passed since we last spoke. There have been difficulties?'

Maddy cocked a brow. 'Oh, I guess you could say that. Quite a lot of things have been going on since we last spoke.'

'Yes.' Her eyes settled quickly on Rashim. 'There is an unauthorized presence here, Maddy. Who is this man?'

'Oh, he's fine. He's no trouble. Nothing to worry about. Introductions can wait till later.'

'The name is Dr Rashim Anwar, in case you're interested,' he said, taking a step forward so she could see him more clearly.

'Right, apparently introductions *can't* wait,' Maddy muttered impatiently. 'Yes, this is Rashim. He's one of our team now. And that yellow cube shuffling around over there in the corner is his robot, SpongeBubba.'

Becks studied Rashim and the lab unit silently for a moment before finally nodding. 'It is good to meet you.'

'Important matters now, Becks. I need you to tell me what's the last thing you remember.'

'The last moment from which I have data is directly after you asked me to decode the manuscript.'

'And tell me about that data. Elaborate.'

Becks cocked her head. 'You do not recall?'

'I'm asking you to tell me.'

'We have just discussed the decoded section of the document.'

Maddy nodded slowly. *Just* discussed. Of course, for Becks the conversation would have been mere seconds ago – the very last time she'd conferred with her before locking up the partition for safekeeping. Since then it seemed like a lifetime's worth of stuff had happened.

'Yes . . . yes, I recall. I asked you about that. Can you remind me, Becks? Can you remind me what the message was in that document?'

'I am sorry, as I have already just mentioned, although the message is meant for your eyes, Maddy, it is not meant for your eyes *yet*.'

'Yet? You mean, "the end" . . . that was what you said, wasn't it? You can't tell me until it's "the end".'

'Affirmative.'

'The end of *what*, though? My life? The frikkin' world? *The end of what?*'

'You wish to know what "the end" is? What the specific condition is?'

'Yes!'

'The end condition identified in this message is the successful activation and infection cycle of a virus and the near-total extinction of human life. Specifically, an organic Von Neumann pathogen dubbed Kosong-ni after the city in which it first appeared. Ground zero. It will be released in the year 2070 and be responsible for killing 99.9999 per cent of the human population.'

'You're saying that only after that's *actually happened* you can tell me?'

'Correct.'

'But that's not going to happen for another one hundred and eighty-one years!'

'Affirmative.'

'But it already *has* happened,' said Rashim. 'From my point of view.'

Becks's eyes rested on him. 'Please elaborate.'

‘I am from that time. Or I should say, *nearly* that time.’

‘I should clarify that,’ Maddy chipped in. ‘Rashim was part of a top-secret government programme called Exodus. It was a programme to reboot the past. A bunch of them wanted to go back to Ancient Rome. Rashim was their lead techy guy. They were at the point of leaving when Kosong-ni suddenly broke out. So, they had to accelerate their programme and rush their departure which –’ she shrugged – ‘led to some pretty unfortunate errors.’

Becks’s eyes remained on Rashim. ‘You witnessed the end event?’

Maddy looked pointedly at him. He’d left just before. *Lie to her!*

However, the fact was, a *version* of him had. The Rashim that went through with the rest of the Exodus group saw it with his own eyes. News reports, abandoned digi-stream cameras beaming static images of silent cities, the dead lying in the streets and liquefying. When they’d come across him in the Roman past as a gibbering, insane old man – driven mad as a result of being incarcerated by Emperor Caligula in a small wooden cage for twenty years or so – his rambling account of those horrifying images had been chilling.

Project Exodus had altered history – although not in the way the reckless participants had intended, or hoped. Their intention to graft a modern western democracy on the top of the Roman Empire had backfired badly. The emperor of the time, Caligula, had lulled them into a false sense of security, wiped most of them out and co-opted the technology they’d brought with them.

Maddy and the others had had to go back to Ancient Rome to correct the timeline. To put things back as they should be, they’d ultimately had to go back further and arrive at a time-stamp some weeks *before* the arrival of the Exodus party – and there, they'd encountered the twenty-years-younger Rashim setting up tachyon receiver beacons for the main party. The younger Rashim would have completed his work and beamed back to 2070 to finish calibrating from that end if they'd not grabbed him and taken him with them. He would have witnessed Kosong-ni. He would have been among the group that came through in a panic, rushing to escape the approaching pathogen. If Maddy and Liam hadn't intervened and dragged him kicking and screaming back to 2001 with them . . . he would have witnessed 'the end'.

'You witnessed the event?' Becks asked again.

Rashim cleared his throat. 'Yes . . . I, uh, yes, I saw it.'

'Go on,' urged Maddy. 'Tell her exactly what you saw.' Her eyes said more. *And make it sound convincing*.

'I saw the virus spread around the world. I saw that event unfold with my own eyes.' He stooped down beside her. 'Kosong-ni did exactly that, Becks . . . it wiped us all out.' He glanced at Maddy. She urged him to carry on with a nod.

Good job . . . Keep going.

'The last thing I saw before I came back in time was cities around the world, deserted. No sign of humanity left behind.' Rashim's voice thickened with believable emotion. Maddy wasn't entirely sure if that was genuine or laid on for Becks's benefit. 'People rendered to just pools of organic liquid. Puddles that used to be human beings –'

Becks's eyes narrowed. 'You are stating that the "end" event has now successfully occurred?'

He nodded. 'Oh yes. It happened all right.'

'I will need verification.'

'Like what?'

'A codeword.'

Maddy's head dropped with frustration. 'Jesus! Another codeword? What is it with goddamn codewords! Becks! If it's something I need to know, then does it frikkin' matter if I know now, tomorrow, next Thursday, or next year?!'

'I am unable to tell you at this time.'

Maddy let out a strangled moan.

Liam raised his hand to hush her. 'We could try approaching the poor thing from a different angle, so.'

'Like what?' Maddy sighed. 'Beat her with a metal pipe until she submits?'

Liam ignored her. 'Look here, Becks, if you can't tell us the contents of the message, perhaps you could tell us who sent it? Is it someone to do with the agency? Was it Mr Waldstein? Or someone else working with –'

'It was you, Liam.'

Liam didn't hear her. '– Waldstein? Or maybe another bunch of fellas? Perhaps –'

'It was you, Liam,' Becks said again.

He stopped dead and looked at Maddy. 'Hold on. Did she just . . . ?'

She nodded. 'You. She just said it was you.'

'Me?'

'The message encoded into a section of the Holy Grail document was sent by you, Liam.'

Liam looked anxiously up at the others: Sal and Maddy in particular, staring at him suspiciously.

'No . . . but, see . . . that must be a mistake. I've never been to – where was it it came from? Jerusalem? I've never been there! You two know that!'

'Not so far,' said Rashim. 'But it seems that one day you will. A message from your future self. Perhaps it is a warning of some future event.'

Liam suddenly looked shaken. 'A warning? But . . . what the hell do I know about anything?!'

'Maybe it was Foster?' said Sal. She looked at the others, from one to the other. 'He would have looked just like Liam when he was younger, right?'

Maddy nodded thoughtfully. 'That's possible. It might have been a message he sent for us when he was a younger "Liam-unit", when he was still calling himself Liam.'

'Negative.' Becks was still lying on her back. She arched her neck to look at Liam. 'You sent the message. Not another Liam-unit.'

'Uhh . . . can we stop with everyone calling me a *unit*, please?'

'Hey!' An idea occurred to Maddy. 'If it's your message, maybe *you* could order Becks to over-ride the codeword lock?' She looked at the others. 'It's got to be worth a shot, right?'

Sal shrugged, uncertain about that.

Liam looked at Rashim. He cocked his head. 'It cannot do any harm to try that.'

'All right.' He hunkered down beside Becks. 'Becks . . . this is me ordering you. Tell us what that message in your head is.'

'Negative. The sender has higher authority than you do.'

'But you just said it was me!'

'Correct. It *is* you, Liam. But it is you from further in the future, with access to privileged information, which you do not have now. This makes that Liam a higher authority. This must be taken into account.'

Rashim stroked the bristles of his beard thoughtfully. 'Time is not strictly linear. It can also be considered circular, a loop. Therefore, there is no certain way to define which point on a circle is furthest forward, in the way you can a straight line. In which case, who really is furthest forward in time?'

'And, strictly speaking,' added Maddy, 'if Liam sent this

message while standing around in biblical times, then if you want to treat time as linear, then he's in the past. The Liam standing right here, technically, is furthest forward in time.'

'The Liam who wrote the message is older,' said Becks.

'How do you know that?'

'The message specifies that he is.'

'And how do you know that for certain? That could be incorrect,' said Rashim. 'Can you verify that fact?'

'How do you even know it's a message from Liam?' said Sal. 'It could just be an impostor.'

Becks's gaze, normally unflinching and relentless, began to falter, her eyes darting from one person to another, like a prison searchlight hunting for escaping inmates. 'It is unclear . . . how to evaluate . . .'

Liam impatiently grabbed her jaw and turned her face towards him. 'For the love of God, just tell us then!'

'I am . . . unable to comply. I wish to obey, Liam, but this contradicts . . . contradicts . . .'

'Maybe we should stop this. She doesn't look good.' Sal shook her head. 'She's going weird on us.'

'Jay-zus! Becks, will you just stop with this nonsense an' tell us!' Liam said.

Her porcelain-smooth face creased with childlike anxiety, a growing panic. 'I am . . . am . . . *unsure* . . .' Her eyes started to roll upwards, exposing the whites once more. Her eyelids fluttered.

'It looks like she's throwing all of her processing power into dealing with this,' said Rashim. 'That may not be a good idea, not if there isn't a valid decision to come to. She'll just thrash her circuits until she overloads or burns out.'

'Looks like she's having a fit,' said Sal. 'Liam . . . I think you've broken her.'

'Sal's right. This isn't good. Bob . . . make sure she doesn't try and struggle to get up and do anything stupid.'

Bob bent over and wrapped his gorilla-thick arms round Becks, an embrace that almost entirely enveloped her slight frame.

'You should pull her out of that partition, Maddy.' Rashim turned to her. 'I suggest, right now . . . before she damages herself irreparably.'

Becks's voice became a low murmur, a stream of words running into each other and making no sense. Gibberish. The low murmur rapidly rose in pitch from the husky tone of her normal voice to the ragged mewling of a distressed child. The cry of a banshee. The desperate agonized scream of a witch on a flaming pyre.

'NOW, MADDY, before she completely fries her head!'

'OK! OK!' Maddy shouted her three codewords. 'IPAD! CAVEMAN! BREAKFAST!'

In all of a heartbeat Becks was still and silent once more. For a dozen fleeting heartbeats the dungeon was filled with nothing more than the echoing sound of their collective breathing.

'OK,' said Maddy finally, 'that was just a little bit freaky.' She crouched down beside the inert form of Becks. 'She OK, Bob?'

'Becks is now in the process of rebooting.' He offered her a reassuring smile. 'She is fine. I am picking up her normal AI ident signal again.'

Liam got to his feet, blew air out and wandered across the floor muttering under his breath.

'Good.' Maddy sucked in a deep breath and wiped her glasses. 'Crud, I feel like we just performed some kind of a frikkin' exorcism.'

'Errr . . . you might be closer to the truth than you think,' said Liam.

'What?'

He was leaning over the computer table, studying one of the monitors closely. 'There's a whole load of stuff just coming up here on this screen.'

Rashim was on his feet and on the way over. He joined Liam, peered at the screen for a moment. 'I think she just jettisoned several gigabytes of data.'

Maddy hurried over to join them. 'OhMyGod . . . what is it? What does it say?'

On one of the monitors, text was scrolling upwards as computer-Bob transferred the captured data Becks had hurled across the dungeon. Maddy scanned the scrolling lines: solid blocks of seemingly random letters and numbers.

'It's not yet more bleedin' code, is it?' asked Liam.

'Hmmm, I am not sure. It looks entirely random to me,' said Rashim. 'Not code. Just digital junk. Corrupted data, I suspect.'

'Digital vomit.' Maddy curled her lips with barely concealed disappointment. 'For a moment there I was kind of hoping we'd finally get a big fat answer to everything.'

'Nothing's ever that easy for us.' Liam sighed.

The captured data stopped scrolling up the screen.

'I guess that's all of it, then.'

Sal pushed between them to get a look.

Maddy was less than impressed. 'Corrupted data, that's all we've got. That's the "revelation" she spits out for us.' She shook her head and sighed. 'Great.'

'Except that bit,' said Sal. She planted a finger on the screen in the middle of a dense block of random characters.

Rashim squinted dismissively. 'Sal, statistically speaking, random letters at some point will spell a word. It is tempting to read something into . . .' He looked closer. 'I can't make anything out, though.'

Maddy squinted too. 'y-e-o-d-f-k-l-p-t-h-e-w-i-n?' She cocked a brow. '*The win?*'

'No. The letters to the right.' Sal moved her finger along. 'See? *Those* letters!'

. . . k-l-p-t-h-e-w-i-n-d-t-a-l-k-e-r-s-s-k-b . . .

'I make out three words. "The". . ."wind". . ."talkers".' Rashim shrugged. 'Does that mean anything to any of you?'

Liam shook his head.

Sal made a face. 'Not really.'

Maddy was about to say likewise. Three random words. Big deal. But then she stopped herself. *The windtalkers*. The phrase was vaguely familiar. She'd definitely heard that term before. Somewhere. From someone. And not so long ago.

Then, like a slap, it hit her.

CHAPTER 4

1992, Nicaragua

Adam Lewis wiped sweat from his forehead, pushing the damp coil of a greasy dreadlock out of his face. His back was aching from the weight of his backpack. He eased off the shoulder straps, lowered the pack to his feet and straightened up.

The track zigzagging up the steep mountainside was narrow – in places barely wide enough for a single llama. Barely wide enough for a goat. He turned his back to the vine-covered rock and looked out over the jungle. An undulating velvet green quilt, carrying pockets of morning mist like milky pools on a low-tide beach.

He squinted at the morning sun, still hanging low in the sky, casting rays of light and shadow across the curves and dips of the landscape below. He could see a single twist of smoke curling up from a clearing down in the jungle, by the glinting thread of the river. He could see several small smudges of neon orange: the one-man vinyl tents of their camp.

Adam grinned at the spectacular vista.

To him it looked just like an alien landscape. It reminded him of the Rebel Alliance's jungle homeworld, Yavin 4. He wondered how much cooler this view would be with the faint, ghostly image of the Death Star hanging like a Sword of Damocles in the blue sky.

'Awesome,' he whispered. He pulled out his camera and took

several snaps. Their guide had said early morning was the best time to get pictures like these. The low-angled sunlight, the velvet carpet of jungle, the combed-out strands of blue-grey mist.

Professor Brian's field trip had been an incredible experience for him thus far. An experience that beat the hell out of backpacking in Bali. Or serving cocktails to drunken fellow gap-year students in some remote Mediterranean beach bar.

This was life-changing.

They'd done several days on an archaeological dig at Machu Picchu, pulling artefacts out of the damp dirt. A flight up to Honduras then several more days paddling up the Río Coco in canoes, stopping at a couple of small villages along the way. The locals had swarmed out to greet their pale-faced visitors with an overwhelming generosity. Adam had felt just like every other western tourist must feel: like some stoic Victorian-era jungle explorer stumbling across some previously undiscovered tribe. Except for the fact that many of them were wearing tattered old Nike baseball caps.

A trip of a lifetime.

An expensive one, though. Mum and Dad had shelled out for it, but, as Dad had made perfectly clear, it was a loan, not a gift. That was the deal. One way or another he was going to have to figure out a way to pay them back later on this year or next. He figured he could earn some easy money writing some C++ library routines for that small gaming company that had approached him. What were they called? Electronic Art or something?

He sat down on a protruding dried root-stump of a tree. It creaked beneath his weight.

This field trip was an optional part of his palaeolinguistics course. Actually, Dad had suggested it was little more than a 'loosely related jolly' than actually being in any way educationally beneficial. What it was, though, was a once-in-a-lifetime experience. Something he'd probably never get round to doing on his own.

Character-building stuff. The beer-swilling morons he shared digs with back in Norwich wouldn't appreciate that, of course. His pictures of Machu Picchu, Honduras, the Río Coco, the villages, would probably leave them perplexed. Or just bored.

Adam, mate . . . you got yourself three grand into debt just to take pictures of moss-covered stones? Dude, you need to get a life.

A lot of money, that. Three thousand pounds. Perhaps his knuckle-dragging flatmates were right: three grand might have been better spent in Ibiza, getting drunk and badly sunburnt with some of it left over to cover the living costs for next term.

Sod it. He shook his head and once again sucked in the incredible view before him. No, this *was* money well spent. OK, they hadn't discovered any long-lost tribes or hoards of hidden treasure, or any hitherto-undiscovered species of slimy jungle fungus, but Professor Brian's students had experienced firsthand an actual dig site.

And, of course, the breath-taking majesty of the Cusco mountains, the fragile beauty of a rainforest.

He was just putting his camera back into his backpack when he felt the root-stump wobble unsteadily beneath his shifting weight. He quickly stood up. The stump's gnarled root ends had pulled free of the loose, dry soil, and now it see-sawed uncertainly, dirt crumbling and cascading down the steep slope on to the zigzagging trail below. With a tired creak, it slowly began to sway outward, and then, carried further by its own weight, it toppled lazily over the side of the narrow track. Roots trailing behind it, yanked out of the dirt.

The stump bounced and rolled down the sheer slope, finally smacking into a rocky outcrop by the edge of the trail below and spinning out into open air. It ended up crashing through the upper branches of the jungle canopy below, scaring a flock of white-fronted birds into the sky and startling the ecosystem beneath into a momentary chorus of cheeps and whistles and hoots, which eventually subsided and returned to the normal soothing music of rainforest life.

'Crap.' Adam whistled.

Nice one, genius. He could have so very easily sailed over the side with that heavy boulder of desiccated wood.

The stump's bulk and gnarled roots had wrenched away and taken with them a thick curtain of vines that had grown accustomed to its presence and become interwoven with it. This curtain now pulled away, Adam found himself staring at the mouth of a previously completely concealed cave.

Adam gaped at the dark entrance for a moment.

Uh . . . Mission Control to Adam, if you're thinking what I think you're thinking – Don't!

'Don't what?'

Duh . . . don't wander in, idiot! 'Things' live in caves.

'Relax. I'm just going to have a peek.'

Adam . . . FYI, some of the dumbest mistakes known to man probably began with the words 'I'm just gonna . . .'

'Just a peek.' He stepped carefully round the edge of the crumbly bite out of the track towards the cave entrance. Several vines and creepers still made a pretence of trying to hide the entrance. He brushed them aside.

'Yoo-hoo!' he cooed self-consciously. His voice echoed and reverberated around inside. He heard nothing growling back at him. Encouraging.

'There you go . . . nothing's home.'

Mission Control had nothing to say at this time.

Adam took a step inside. The cave appeared to open up within a yard or so of the entrance. A natural jagged fissure, worn by time, the elements and restless geology. The vine-filtered light from the entrance was enough to push the darkness a dozen yards back. All the same, he decided to pull a torch from his backpack.

He rummaged and found it: a pencil-torch gaffer-taped to a grubby sports sweat-band. He wore it when he cycled home from university at night, fancying that, with it strapped to the left side of his mushroom-head cycle helmet, he looked just a little bit like one of the colonial marines in *Aliens*. He pulled the sweat-band over his dreads until it settled on the rough moon surface of his pimply forehead.

'Hellooo? Anyone home?' he called out, wondering what kind of response he was expecting by saying that. He snapped the torch on. The cave's ragged contours sent shadows dancing across the rocky surface like sidewinder snakes scurrying for cover as he turned his head and panned the thin beam of light around.

'Whoa . . . big-ass cave.'

From the roof, rust-coloured stalactites hung like shark's teeth, vines like shreds of rancid seal meat between them. The floor of the cave was an uneven surface of emergent stalagmite humps and worn-away drip pools. A weave-work of dried creepers and desiccated roots snaked across the barren rock floor in a long-forgotten search for nutrition.

Adam explored a dozen yards into the dark interior of the cave. It seemed to wind back deeper than he'd at first thought. His nerves got the better of him, however. The cave entrance was far enough behind him now that he was beginning to feel edgy. This was enough solo exploration for him. Far enough in. And darker than he'd like.

A cave. Just a cave. And Adam would have turned to go back out again just then, if the beam of his torch hadn't rested momentarily on a smooth section of cave wall.

But it did, and what it revealed caused him to catch his breath.

Carefully, he picked his way further towards the back of the cave, approaching the wall, then finally he reached out to touch the cool moist surface of the rock. More to the point, to lightly touch the faint markings of flaking mud paint – a cardinal sin – actually reaching out and touching it.

'My God,' he whispered as he studied the symbols painted on the wall.

CHAPTER 5

1994, Norwich

'He's going to be a little – what's the term I'm looking for? Oh yes, *freaked-out*, isn't he?' said Liam. 'What with you paying him another visit like this, completely out of the blue.'

'Of course he is,' replied Maddy.

She had visited Adam Lewis once before. Now that was something else that seemed like it had occurred a lifetime ago. She and Becks had knocked on the door of his bedsit in a shared student digs and asked him to explain himself; to explain how he'd managed to decode that one passage of the Voynich Manuscript.

The passage that had contained the word *Pandora*.

The whole mystery had started with the smallest time wave occurring back in 2001. Just the gentlest of ripples that Sal had managed to sense. But then computer-Bob had alerted them to the sudden existence of a minor archived article in a British newspaper called the *Sun*. The article had mentioned in its own distinctly low-brow style that Adam Lewis ('*hacker and computer geek, looking more like a scruffy animal-rights activist than a Microsoft pencil-neck*') had singlehandedly managed to extract a single legible sentence from the impenetrable gibberish of the legendary Voynich Manuscript.

Not exactly 'legendary' in the public eye. For most *Sun* readers Maddy suspected that article was the first and last time they'd ever hear about the medieval document. But among cryptologists, hackers, amateur code-breakers, it was the gold-standard: the One To Be The First To Crack.

Maddy and Becks had gone back to 1994, picking a date a week after the story had broken big in the national newspaper, and found an edgy young man very close to breaking point. A bag of rattling nerves.

Oh yes, he'd decoded a passage that read: '*Pandora is the word. The word leads to truth. Fellow traveller, time to come and find it.*' And that was the bit he'd rather excitedly announced by posting a letter to *New Scientist*. The bit he hadn't revealed was the sentence that had come just before that . . .

'*You must make public the last part of this message, Adam Lewis, and I promise you someone will come and explain everything. When she comes, it is important you tell her this: "Seek Cabot at Kirklees in 1194". Do not reveal any more of this message to anyone else. The last part now follows. Pandora is the word . . .*'

And *that* was the bit that had turned him into a jabbering nervous wreck. The inclusion of his name in an ancient medieval document. That had completely messed with his head. He'd ended up hiding away in his grubby bedroom, peeking out of the net curtains, paranoid that someone, somewhere, was coming for him.

Which was true. But instead of men in black suits and dark glasses, or some killer cyborg robot assassin from the future, or whatever else the young man's feverish paranoid imagination could conjure up and torment him with, it had been Maddy and Becks who'd turned up and politely asked him how he'd managed to break the code when the rest of the world, including several large code-breaking computer systems, had failed to do so. More to the point . . . was there any more he'd decoded, but not made public?

Maddy had managed to carefully coax the truth out of him, to calmly explain that she wasn't there to kill him, or take him away and lock him up, that she wasn't a panic-induced hallucination, wasn't a manifestation of his subconscious, a delusion conjured up by a mind on the very edge of a nervous breakdown. And finally . . . she'd calmed him down, won him round and he'd revealed that whole passage to her.

They'd left him, that night in 1994, with a promise that they'd one day return and explain to him *everything* that was going on. Of course, Maddy was pretty sure she wasn't going to keep that promise. Adam Lewis, for whatever reason, had momentarily become caught up in the affairs of the agency. A hapless innocent, involved in a chain of events designed to ensure some communiqué dating back to biblical times reached its intended recipient in the year 2001. His part – in effect, the courier – was played and he really didn't need to know anything at all about Waldstein's little agency, about what their purpose was. She'd always felt guilty that they'd never gone back to this nervous young man, as she'd promised, and explained all to him. But, to be honest, since that night she'd been pretty damned busy keeping this world and this timeline on track.

'So, explain to me again, Maddy,' said Liam, 'nice short words please, explain to me why we're re-involving this poor fella once more.'

They were walking along Earlham Road, early morning. Rain-slicked tarmac clicked beneath their heels, beside them the disgruntled snarl of morning traffic, bumper-to-bumper cars full of bleary-eyed office workers on their way in for another soulless day of clock-watching. An unremarkable, overcast Tuesday morning in an unremarkable city called Norwich.

'He became involved in the first place, Liam, because he's the only person in the world who recognized a couple of symbols from a long-dead language. Incan or Mayan, or Aztec, or something . . . I can't remember what he said. But I do remember he told me it was a unique language used by this one remote tribe. He said there was just this one example of the language that he'd discovered. Some painting on the wall of a cave he discovered halfway up a cliff-face.'

Liam nodded. 'I see . . .'

Maddy turned to look at him. She laughed. 'No, you don't. You do that nodding "I see" thing when you're confused and don't want to admit it.'

'What? No, I don't.'

'Yes, you do.' She smiled. 'I know you far too well, Liam O'Connor.'

He shrugged. 'All right, I'm still not sure what we're doing here.'

'He discovered this one example of this language . . . made up of these unique symbols never used anywhere else in, like, the entire history of mankind. Unique symbols, pictograms. The only other place these symbols ever turned up –'

'– was in that Voynich Manuscript.'

Maddy nodded. 'And just once, in one single section of the text. Just two of these symbols acting as encryption-identifiers – some sort of, like, start and end markers. And they were, like, specifically designed to attract Adam's attention.' She stopped, checking the number of the terraced house to their left. They were nearly there. 'So, obviously, that meant there was only ever going to be one person likely to be able to decode that particular passage.'

'What about the rest of it? Do you think there might be more stuff in it?'

Maddy shook her head. 'The rest doesn't matter. Those markers were there to point him to the one important bit. The rest of the Voynich might as well be a medieval cookbook for all we care.'

Liam tapped his temple with a finger. 'Somebody's been very clever.'

'Yes . . .' She nodded. 'Somebody has been.' Maddy glanced at him. 'You . . . perhaps?' She shrugged. 'An older, wiser you?'

Or if not, someone who knew them very well.

'And so,' Liam continued, 'what's with that name? The Windtalkers . . . ?'

'Well, duh!' She looked at him. 'That's the name of the Indian tribe, isn't it? Well, the name Adam decided to give them.' She nodded at the front door ahead of them. Number 97. This was the house she and Becks had visited all those months ago – although, from Adam Lewis's perspective, here they were again, the morning after that visit. Above the front door she could see the grimy net curtain hanging in the small window of Adam's bedsit. She fancied she caught a faint glimpse of a pale face beyond it, ducking out of view as she looked up.

'It's a long shot, Liam. But I'm certain Becks spat that phrase out for a reason. I think she wants to help us, wants us to know but isn't able to break her code-lock. So she gave us that.'

'A clue.'

'A place to start.' She pressed a buzzer beside the front door. 'Who knows? Maybe the answer lies in that cave of Adam's? Maybe there's more of that writing daubed on those walls. Maybe the cave itself is some kind of drop-point document?'

Liam grinned. 'Now that would be a thing.'

She wrinkled her nose. 'It's all I've got at the moment. Other than that . . . I'm winging it.'

He looked at her. 'You know, this might just be a wild goose chase, Maddy. Don't get your hopes up.'

'Might be. But it's all we have.' She pressed the door buzzer again. 'You want to know what that message is, don't you?'

'Of course I do.'

'I can't help thinking this might just be the key to everything. Who knows? It might explain why we were made. Why we were set up to protect a timeline doomed to end in the year 2070. It might –'

The door was wrenched open and a tousle-haired young man stared at them bleary-eyed. 'Yup?'

'We're here to see Adam Lewis.'

His eyes narrowed. 'Hold on . . . you came here last night, didn't you?'

She was surprised he remembered. This one and the other lads had been quite drunk. She nodded. 'Yes.'

He looked cautiously out of the doorway, up and down the street. 'Where's that other girl you were with? The psychotic one?'

Maddy recalled he'd tried his luck with Becks. Big mistake.

'Don't worry – she's got lectures this morning. Just me and my friend here.'

Liam nodded and offered a wave. 'Morning.'

'So, is Adam in?'

'Yeah, sure . . . the wacko never leaves his room these days.'

'Can we come in?'

He shrugged. She presumed that was his version of a 'yes'. He turned and headed barefoot down the uncarpeted floorboards of the hallway. 'Up the stairs, first on the right,' he called out over his shoulder as he opened the door to his room and slammed it behind himself.

CHAPTER 6

1994, Norwich

'Adam?'

Maddy was about to rap her knuckles again on his door when she heard the clatter and snick of a lock turning inside. The door creaked open and she saw his pale face peering through the gap.

Her heart skipped inside her at the sight of him. After all these months, now finally seeing him again. She'd almost forgotten what his face looked like, almost convinced herself she'd imagined that spark of 'something' between them. Now he was standing right before her, wide-eyed and open-jawed: like soon-to-be roadkill caught in the headlights of an approaching truck.

Now here she was with her heart hammering in her chest. That took her completely by surprise. Not for a moment had she thought that there was anything more to this re-visit than following the flimsiest of clues. There he was, the edgy young man she'd encountered a lifetime ago: scruffy ginger-brown locks, a chin tufted with a poor excuse for a goatee, ghostly pale skin dotted with freckles and wide green, intelligent eyes, sunk deeply beneath a furrowed brow, puffy and red from sleeplessness and anxiety.

She'd met this same young man again seven years after today. Somehow he'd tracked her down in New York. Very different then. Well-groomed. There was an air of brash confidence about him by that point in time: a successful software engineer in

Manhattan making a fortune designing secure systems for commercial clients on Wall Street. A young dotcom-era entrepreneur, a cocky lad-done-good livin' it large in the Big Apple. He'd been far more confident . . . and yet, she had seen that the confidence was a cloak that covered a frightened man still desperately trying to make sense of the impossible – trying to get his head round the fact that someone living in the Middle Ages knew his name.

'It's . . . it's you . . .' he whispered through the gap.

'Again.' Maddy smiled. 'I know.'

He swallowed, his Adam's apple bobbed like a cork. 'I . . . know . . . I know that you and the other girl came from the f-future . . .'

'Can we come in?'

He nodded absently, opened the door and ushered them in. He closed and locked it behind them as they surveyed the squalid mess of his room.

'This is Liam,' said Maddy.

Liam offered Adam a hand. 'Mr Lewis! We've met before, so we have.'

Adam looked at him, eyes narrowed, confused by that, confused by this visit. By everything, in fact.

'Well, to be more precise, we WILL have met before, I should say.'

Adam turned to Maddy. 'I . . . I thought I was losing my mind.' He shook his head, as if trying to reshuffle the order of thoughts in his mind. 'I thought I was going mad. Dreamed you up. Hallucinated you.'

'No, it's for real. We visited you last night . . . I promise you're not going mad.'

A smile flickered across his thin lips, then abandoned his mouth just as quickly. 'Yes, yes . . . I know I'm not mad. I – look

. . . you left proof.' He turned, stepping across a floor scattered with mouldering clothes to a desk cluttered with notes and balled-up paper. 'It's right here . . . here somewhere . . . somewhere . . .'

Maddy and Liam looked around the dim room, at the walls almost completely covered with sheets of paper tacked to corkboards in a chaotic mosaic of ancient symbols and dead languages. The living space of an obsessed mind. A troubled mind running in endless inescapable loops.

Adam yelped with manic glee as he found what he was looking for. He snatched it from his desk and returned, waving it in front of Maddy. 'You left this!'

She spent a moment trying to see what it was, held too close to her face to focus on. She reached out for Adam's hand and steadied it. He was holding a slip of coloured paper with something faintly printed on it. Then she recalled. That day in 2001 when the older, more self-assured Adam Lewis had tracked her down and come knocking on the archway door in Brooklyn. He'd told her how he'd managed to find her after seven long years of planning and waiting, and he'd waved this very same small slip of coloured paper at her.

'It's a ticket,' he said quickly now. 'A ticket of entry . . . to a club or a bar, isn't it? West Fifty-first Street.'

'Yes. Yes, it is.'

'And the date . . . the date!' He grinned manically. 'Look! The date –'

'Yes, I know. The ninth of September, 2001.'

Adam swallowed again. His mouth dry. 'This is real . . . isn't it? All of this? My name appearing in a thousand-year-old document? You . . . coming from the future? This ticket stub? My God! It's all real, isn't it? I haven't disappeared into some drug-induced psychosis?'

'It's all real, Adam.' Maddy smiled supportively, reached out a hand and rested it on his arm to settle him. She could feel he was trembling.

'It's real. You and me, Liam here, the girl who was with me last night . . . we're all caught up in this thing – whatever it is.'

He grinned again: a there-and-gone flash of a smile that stirred Maddy's heart. The same boy-like grin that Liam flashed from time to time, when an exciting possibility, a crazy idea, occurred to him.

'This is real!' he whispered. 'I . . . I was thinking, even this piece of paper was fake. A delusion.' He laughed – a short shrill bark that sounded like madness, bottled, with a cap screwed tightly on. 'To be honest, I'm not sure whether I'm relieved or, or bloody terrified by this.'

'There's something going on, Adam . . . something's happening, or already happened long ago. And it's as much a mystery to us as it is to you.' She looked at Liam and he nodded. They'd agreed this earlier. Adam could know everything, if that was needed. They'd deal with the consequences of that later.

'Yes, Adam, we *are* time travellers. It will become a viable technology in the not-too-distant future. It *will* become possible and that's when everything starts to become messy.'

'We were recruited by an agency to make sure things stay right,' added Liam. 'To make sure any other troublesome buggers with time machines don't go messing around and changing the course of history.'

Adam frowned. 'You mean . . . like, sort of Time Police, or something?'

Maddy nodded. 'Yeah, sort of like that. Only . . . things have become a lot more confused than we can handle. We're . . .' She pursed her lips in thought for a moment, then looked at her watch. 'Look, there's a lot to tell you, and most of it can wait for later.'

'Aye,' said Liam. 'We're here because of something you said to Maddy last night.'

'What?'

'You were telling me and Becks –'

'Becks? The other girl?' He frowned. 'Your friend seemed . . . quite intense. She nearly broke my finger.'

'Oh, now she's a whole other conversation,' said Liam.

Maddy was keen to stay on topic. 'Adam, you told us how you managed to break the code. It was because of that weird pre-Aztec writing you discovered?'

'Right.' He nodded eagerly. He gestured at the sheets of paper tacked to the corkboards on his walls. 'Yes, that. Although it's not Incan. It's closer to Mayan if anything. Although the tribe wasn't strictly Mayan. More like an offshoot of –'

'The tribe.' Maddy jumped on that. 'The tribe . . . you said their name? What was it again?'

'Uh? Their name?'

'Yes.'

'Well, they didn't have a name as such. Just something I called them. The Windtalkers.' He shrugged. 'Seemed like as good a name as any.'

Maddy shot a glance at Liam. *See?*

'Who were they? What can you tell us about them?' asked Liam.

Adam shook his head. 'Not much. Professor Brian was following rumours about a tribe. It was his pet thing, you know? His hobby. His obsession. To discover a lost people, a lost tribe, and make his name studying them. Apparently some Spanish conquistador bloke encountered a tribe in the Nicaraguan jungle once upon a time. Not called *Nicaragua* then, of course. I think it was referred to as the Spanish Main back then. Anyway . . . the conquistador said he saw a golden city. Said they had magical powers or something. Said they were way more advanced than any of the other tribes he'd encountered.' Adam laughed. 'It's the classic "Lost City of Z" cliché. Very *Indiana Jones*.'

'This was the tribe? The one you called the Windtalkers?'

He shrugged. 'I dunno if it was the same tribe who did that cave painting. Might have been.'

'And so?' Maddy urged. 'What? Did your professor find them?'

He looked at her. 'No. But I found that cave with the symbols on the wall. That's all. That's all. But see, that on its own is a pretty significant find. I think the symbols display the structure of a written language, not like the usual thing of pictograms depicting discrete ideas but a proper language: verbs, nouns, adjectives.' He turned towards his desk and rummaged through the mess. 'Here . . . I'll show you. I'll show you. Ahhh . . . here it is.'

He had in his hands several photographs. 'So, I took some pictures of the writing.'

He held them out for Maddy and Liam to look at. 'The writing covered a couple of square feet of the cave wall, written quite small and broken into sections just like paragraphs. But there, see? If you look, each "paragraph break" has these uniquely different glyphs at the beginning and end, almost like quotation marks.'

She stared closely at them: spirals followed by a wavy line.

The exact same glyphs that had appeared in the Voynich Manuscript. So unique, so distinctive. She could understand now how they would have leaped out of the manuscript at Adam, the moment he decided to try his hand at decoding the thing. The symbols were like beacons, crying out to be spotted by one particular person. Just like Rashim's tachyon signals, calling out across time.

'Adam,' she said, handing the photographs back to him. 'There's a message in the Voynich Manuscript meant specifically for us. But look – you're gonna love this, this mystery gets better . . . that particular passage in the Voynich was transcribed from a much, much older document. A document that dates back *another* thousand years.'

Adam pushed a stray dreadlock away from his eyes. 'Two thousand years old?' He chuckled nervously. 'Jesus time? Uh, so . . . you're not going to say what I think you're going to say?' He looked at them both. 'Right? You're not . . .'

'It depends,' said Liam. 'What do *you* think she's going to say?'

Adam grinned, shrugged, almost wanted to back away from what he was about to say. 'Maybe, well, I was going to say something like the Dead Sea Scrolls? Something in the Bible . . . or . . . or . . .'

'Actually, it's the Holy Grail.'

Adam's eyes rounded. His eyebrows rose and made a double arch and his jaw hung open. 'Oh Jesus . . .'

'We didn't manage to crack the message. And I'll explain why later on. But we think . . . the answer may lie with this undiscovered tribe of yours. Perhaps even with this cave. Perhaps even in that writing. I don't know.' She cocked her head. 'The reason we came back, Adam, is we need to know where that cave is.'

'You want to go there?'

'Uh-huh.' She nodded. 'We *need* to go there. Maybe even . . .

go back in time, maybe even try and speak to these Windtalker people. If we can.'

Adam nodded slowly, stroking his chin thoughtfully. The notion of time travel, messages buried in the Holy Grail, people from the Middle Ages knowing about him . . . all of it was insane and impossible, and yet equally these pieces seemed to have some cohesion, like a puzzle that might just click together if the other pieces could be found.

Maddy was quite taken with his steadiness. His trembling had subsided. The nervous tics, the darting edginess of the eyes had gone. Now he seemed to be settling into some kind of super-calm meditative state.

'Adam?' She was surprised with how he was taking this. It looked like he was coolly piecing it all together. Quite impressive really. Until he ruined that illusion by doubling over at the waist, then dropped down to an untidy, wheezy squat on the floor.

'Gimme a moment . . .' He looked up at them with glassy eyes. 'Feel a bit light-headed. I . . . I just need bit of . . . a bit of air here . . .'

And then he flopped sideways on to his unmade bed.

'I think he just fainted on us,' said Liam.

Maddy knelt down beside him. 'Yup. We broke him.'

'We're taking him back to London with us?'

'If he wants to come, I guess. What do you think?'

Liam hefted his shoulders. 'Why not? The more, the merrier.'

'All right then. We need to bring him round.' She nodded. 'There's a bottle of Coke over there . . . Let's pour that on him.'

CHAPTER 7

1994, Norwich

'You ready for this?' asked Maddy.

Adam looked even more pallid in the light of day. His matted ginger dreadlocks and goatee looked almost dark against his ghost-white skin.

'Not really. This portal thing –?'

'Is perfectly safe, Adam.'

'Although, aye, to be fair, it's very strange,' added Liam. 'You might want to keep your eyes closed, so.'

'Closed? Why?'

Maddy checked her watch. The portal was due to open very soon now. 'It's non-dimensional space we're stepping through, Adam. Looks just like a white mist. Some people – me, for example – find that it's just too weird to look at. I prefer to just screw up my eyes and jump in.'

'And you'll feel like you're falling,' added Liam. 'That takes some getting used to, so it does.'

Maddy checked the alleyway once more; it was a narrow walkway between an academic bookstore and a coffee shop. An alleyway dotted here and there with flattened shipping boxes, tatters of bubble wrap and discarded cigarette butts. It was deserted. Up at the top, where the alley opened on to a busy street, a gaggle of students passed by, their voices (all talking at once, no one listening) echoed towards them then quickly faded.

'I'm really . . . actually going to travel back to Victorian times?'

Liam grinned. 'Aye. And once we get back we'll need to dress you right so you fit in better.' He laughed. 'Although, God knows what they'll make of that Medusa hair of yours.'

'We'll shove a docker's cloth cap over his head,' said Maddy. She turned to him. 'You'll love it, Adam.' She remembered her very first trip back in time to 1906, to San Francisco. The thrill of dressing up. The exhilaration of stepping into real history for the first time. The smells and noises. 'It's a bit like stepping into a virtual world, in a way.'

'Like the *Enterprise*'s holodeck?'

Maddy nodded. She knew what he meant. That TV series, *Star Trek*. 'Yeah, I suppose it's a bit like the holodeck. But of course it's all totally for real. No simulation.' She squeezed his arm. 'The first time really is something quite special. Nothing to be afraid of.'

Liam looked him over. 'You got all your bits 'n' pieces there, Adam?'

He nodded. His backpack was full of his writings, his pictures, his clunky laptop and one or two practical things for their trip to the jungle. But, most importantly, the notes he needed to navigate them to that cliff-face – that cave. 'Yes. Got all the things I need.'

'The portal should appear any second now,' said Maddy, checking her watch once more.

Adam swallowed anxiously. 'You know . . . this is really exciting. That is, if I'm not losing my mind and this isn't actually a big extended dream.'

Liam chuckled and shook his head. 'I like this fella. He's funny.'

Bubble wrap at their feet suddenly swirled and skittered in a circle, then a moment later a soft blast of air on their faces made them all blink dust from their eyes.

'*And there she blows! Home again, home again, jiggedy jig*,' sang Liam.

In front of them a sphere of liquid reality hovered above the ground, swirling in indecipherable spirals like thick cream stirred into black coffee.

'My God!' whispered Adam. 'You two ever watch them *Terminator* movies?' He giggled nervously. 'It's just like . . . well, a *bit* like that!'

'Yup, I know,' replied Maddy impatiently. 'So, you just step in, Adam. Step in and you'll immediately get that falling sensation that Liam mentioned – like you're falling through the floor of the world. Don't worry. Don't panic, that's totally normal. OK?'

He nodded quickly. 'Right. No panic. Normal. OK.'

'I'll go in first,' said Liam. He raised a foot and stepped into the undulating sphere. 'See you back in 1889.' He merged with the portal, and his body instantly stretched out like melted plastic, swirled and became one with the twisting spiral coffee-and-cream pattern.

'Oh crap! This is completely mental.'

'Relax, Adam, we've all done this dozens of times. It's kinda weird, yes, but harmless. You'll be fine.'

'Harmless,' he repeated, nodding quickly. 'Right. Harmless.'

She patted his shoulder. 'You next. I'll jump in right behind you.'

Harmless, Adam. Harmless.

He took a deep breath. 'Right.' He raised a foot and dipped it into the sphere as if he was testing the steaming water of a freshly run bath. The toe of his scuffed trainer began to extrude out to a curled point, like a jester's shoe. The point elasticized, stretched further, long and thin like toothpaste from a tube, like spaghetti, then began to twist into and join the flow of the spiral pattern.

'Crap! I can't do this!' He jerked his foot back out, expecting it now to be drooping like a loop of sausagemeat. It was, of course, quite unaffected: a very normal-looking ankle and foot once more.

'Honestly,' said Maddy. 'It's better if you just step right in. Like getting into a cold swimming pool. You're best just jumping in.'

'Jump in.' He puffed air again. 'Right.'

He lifted his foot and stepped into the portal once more, this time letting his body follow; his centre of balance tilted slowly, finally committing him to enter, and he lurched forward into the sphere. The moment his head merged with the boundary of the sphere he found himself staring at a featureless white mist, and then experienced the unsettling sensation of falling.

'Craaaaaaap!!!!!!!' His voice, deadened by the fog all around him, filled the swirling silence and seemed to rise in pitch from a human voice to the high-frequency whine of a mosquito.

It seemed to last minutes, or perhaps it was seconds. But, with the tail end of the same breath that he'd started screaming with, he grunted with the sudden impact of his feet against a hard unyielding surface.

The white mist was gone in the blink of an eye and all of a sudden he found himself in the gloomy interior of some brick-and-mortar basement, lit by the unflinching amber glow of a large caged bulb dangling from thick electrical cord. A low brick ceiling overhead. A dark corner with a wooden bench table crowded with a dozen glowing computer monitors, several keyboards and one mouse. A thick, low, arched oak doorway. Wooden packing crates. A loose arrangement of threadbare and worn armchairs around a second table. A net curtain pulled across another corner and the warm, welcoming glow of an oil lamp filtering through the dangling linen.

This place had an *almost* homely ambience, in a subterranean, Hobbit-like way.

He spotted the young Irishman, Liam, standing nearby, talking to another man, lean and bearded, and a young, dark-skinned girl. Sitting nearby on packing crates was a giant ape of a man, racks of muscle barely contained beneath a stretched cotton smock, and next to him a familiar face: that stunning young woman who'd nearly broken his finger last night. He remembered her name – Becks. She cocked her head curiously, studying him like a pathologist might a viral culture in a Petri dish.

Adam nodded politely as all eyes finally turned and settled on him. 'Uhh, all right there?'

He felt a puff of air from behind and turned to see Maddy standing there. The portal collapsed behind her.

'See? That wasn't so bad, was it?'

Adam shook his head absently. 'I'm . . . not sure . . . I'm not sure any more whether I've completely lost my grip on . . . or . . . maybe . . .'

She swept past him, grabbing his arm. 'It's all real. Come on.' She led him across the floor towards the others. 'Let's get the introductions out of the way. Then we'll all go get something to eat and discuss our field trip to this cave of yours.'

CHAPTER 8

1889, London

Bentham's Pie Shop ('Steaming Hot Pies All Day Long!') was Sal's find. She'd come across the little eatery on one of her many trips to Exmouth Market. A narrow three-storey building of uneven floors and oak beams askew. Each floor was a maze of nooks and crannies and cosy side rooms, each room filled with wooden tables and stools that wobbled on the undulating bare floor. They were sitting in a lead-lined bay window on the top floor, looking down through fogged glass on to the narrow street and a busy fishmonger below.

Inside Bentham's it was quiet now. The breakfast rush of early-morning pie-eating patrons had subsided and the lunchtime rush was yet to come.

The seven of them were crowded around one small table, and the perforated, oven-browned pie crusts spilling small smokestack plumes of beef-flavour steam into the air made the pie feast between them look like a miniature table-top village of round houses.

'Smells good,' said Adam. 'I haven't eaten anything warm in days.'

'The meat is real beef,' said Rashim, plunging a fork into his crust. 'Not synthetic protein jelly but actual meat.'

Liam made a yummy sound as he hung his nose over his own pie. 'I'm starving, so I am.'

'All right. I suppose I better start,' said Maddy, 'since this was all my big idea.' She tapped her fingers together. 'Becks – who you now know, Adam, is a support unit – dumped out a whole load of data and what we got from it, *all* we got from it, was the word "Windtalkers". So that's why we came to get you, Adam. That's the only lead we have here.'

'A lead to cracking that message –' Adam glanced at Becks – 'in her head?'

'Yup. So, the truth is we've found ourselves kind of cast adrift from the agency that set us up in the time-policing business.'

'Cast adrift?' Liam shook his head. 'That's putting it mildly. More like "hiding from them for fear of our lives".'

'All right, we've gone and done something that's made the agency want us all dead for some reason.' Maddy shrugged. 'I think it's because I made the mistake of asking what the hell "Pandora" was.'

'You didn't just ask,' said Sal. 'You sent a message saying we weren't going to correct any more contaminations until someone gave us an answer. That was pretty stupid, saying it like that. You made us sound like we were turning against them.'

Maddy did a double-take at Sal. It was so unlike her to lash out like that. She'd been withdrawn and quiet recently, more so than normal. Then this – there was even the tone of a direct challenge in her voice. So unlike her.

'Well, yes . . . I might have worded it a bit better, I guess,' she replied. 'And, so, because I made it sound like they had a problem with us – sorry, guys – we ended up with a squad of goons, like Bob here, knocking on our door intent on massacring us. A slight over-reaction, I think. But there you go. Something obviously got lost in the translation. They figured we'd gone rogue. But more than that . . . I think we clearly weren't meant to know anything about Pandora.'

'And this Pandora is . . . ?' asked Adam.

'We think it's the codename for the end of the world. Or, more specifically, a specific extinction event for mankind.'

'What specific event?'

'A genetically engineered virus,' said Rashim. 'There will be a war between Japan and North Korea in 2070, one of many wars, in fact, that are due in the later half of the twenty-first century. During the opening stages of the Japan–North Korea war, one side will release a Von Neumann virus.'

'Von Neumann?'

'A type of smart-virus that feeds on human organic material and breaks it down into an organic soup, which it in turn uses to fuel the propagation of more virus spores.'

'So,' continued Maddy, 'we've pieced together the theory that the Waldstein guy I was telling you about earlier – you remember . . . ?'

Adam nodded.

'He set this agency up with one specific goal, which is to ensure the historical timeline is not deflected in any way and that we end up with this virus eventually happening in the year 2070.' She blew on to a wooden spoonful of piping hot beef stew. 'We didn't realize that was our job, making sure this happens, until a while after we'd been trained and were up and running. But someone somewhere has been trying to warn us that that's what our function is. So basically we were kept in the dark. Basically we've been suckered into ensuring that happens.'

'Duped into being the agents of mankind's demise,' added Liam. He nodded with satisfaction at how poetic that sounded.

Maddy tested the stew with her lip. 'Quite.'

Sal looked like she was going to say something.

'Sal?' prompted Maddy.

She shook her head. 'Nothing. Just . . . just that's our theory. That's what we think.' The words 'our' and 'we' sounded decidedly forced.

Maddy was tempted to stop things for a moment and talk to Sal. It seemed like, even though she was prepared to tag along with things, her heart wasn't in it. Her thinking was elsewhere on this. Perhaps later she'd ask her what was going on inside her head. But not now.

'So, what? You want to change history so this doesn't happen?' Adam looked at them. 'Surely that's easy? Just go change something, right? Just pick a historical moment and make it happen differently. That'll send your timeline off in a different direction. Problem solved. No viral apocalypse.'

'Yes . . . yes, we *could* do that. But, well, at least my take on it is we need to know more information before we commit to making that decision. Before we become what Waldstein thinks we currently are . . . traitors. We need to know why it's important to him that this virus happens. I mean, maybe there's a perfectly valid reason.' She shrugged. 'Or it might simply be that he's some lunatic that has some hate-thing for mankind.'

'Or it could be Waldstein is trying to save mankind from something far worse,' said Sal.

'Tell me now,' Liam said, sitting back, 'what the devil is worse than mankind all but wiping itself out?'

'Wait . . . we don't even know if mankind is totally wiped out, do we?' replied Sal. 'We know from Rashim – well, the other one, the old one – that *most* of humanity on Earth was wiped out. But what if some of them survived? Perhaps that's the thing? Perhaps Waldstein has seen the future. That virus happens, ninety per cent of humans or something are wiped out, but the remaining ten per cent survive and go on to do wonderful things?' It was her turn to shrug. 'Perhaps it's a necessary thing for humankind? A way to save this planet from being mined to exhaustion or complete ecological collapse.'

'Waldstein, the eco-warrior?' said Rashim.

Maddy nodded slowly. 'That's one possible reading of his motives. Another equally valid reading is that he's just plain nuts; some kind of ultimate eco-warrior who wants to erase mankind completely and give this world back to nature.'

'So that is what this agency has been all about? An act of eco-terrorism? A way to rebalance this world, de-clutter the planet of humans and set up a new beginning?'

Rashim nodded thoughtfully. 'A global culling of humanity for the greater good?'

Sal nodded. 'Maybe then we *should* be doing what Waldstein wants? And save the planet?'

Liam glanced at her. 'Nature versus humans?' He gave her an incredulous look. 'Jay-zus, I vote for humans then! Whose side are you on, Sal? The plants or the people?' He laughed at that. It was a joke question, but not entirely so.

'You might be right, Sal,' Maddy stepped in. 'It could be we need to follow Waldstein's doctrine for some purpose that delivers a greater good. On the other hand, we could be the patsies, the dumb suckers carrying out the plans of a guy who's simply sick in the head! Because some bitter and twisted old billionaire has, for some self-aggrandizing reason, decided he wants the world to die along with him?' Maddy cocked her head. 'Maybe Waldstein's simply totally lost it?'

She looked up and out of the lead-lined windows. 'So then, we've also got to take on board the fact that someone else has been trying to get through to us. Someone has been trying to warn us about this. Trying to alert us about this event. Why?'

'Maybe this other person is mad?' said Sal.

'I think Waldstein's the one that's mad,' said Liam.

'Or maybe Waldstein's this world's only chance to survive,' said Sal. 'Our saviour.'

They sat in silence, contemplating that for a moment.

'Point is . . . we don't know,' said Maddy after a while. 'Evil madman bent on destroying everything? Or really good guy trying to save humanity from itself. Take your pick, folks. We have our guesses, but that's really all we have. We're completely in the dark.'

'And that message in Becks's head – the answer she won't give us – will tell us one way or the other?' said Liam.

'Exactly.' Maddy nodded. 'We need to find out more. Someone drew our attention to the word "Pandora". That word led us to the Voynich.' She looked at Adam. 'Which is where *you* come into the picture.'

Adam paused, a spoon halfway to his mouth. 'You . . . you're saying . . . what? The future of humankind depends on . . . on me?'

Maddy smiled sympathetically. 'Well, kinda.'

'Seems it all boils down to that cave, then,' added Liam. 'Your cave . . . that's what we're after. The cave. The writing.'

'You reckon you could find it again, Adam?' Maddy glanced at his tattered backpack. In his bedsit, she and Liam had watched him pile tattered exercise books, pads of paper covered in writing and sketches, and a laptop that looked like an old brick into it as they'd waited for him to come along. He seemed keen. But not exactly methodical. She hoped he'd brought everything he needed to lead them there.

Adam shrugged. 'I . . . errr . . . I'm pretty sure I can find it. I kept a field diary. I've got a load of notes.'

'Good.'

'So then that's the *where* taken care of, if Adam can guide us to the cave,' said Liam. 'But what about the *when*?'

Rashim nodded. 'So now we have to decide. The cave in 1994? The cave now – 1889? Or the cave when these Indian people lived?'

'I'd say when these Windwalker Indians were alive,' said Liam.

'Wind*talkers*,' corrected Adam.

Maddy was thinking it through. 'I suspect travelling through dense jungle in 1994 would be way easier than 1889? Know what I mean? Motorboats instead of paddle canoes and stuff.'

'Can we not get to the cave in 1994, then beam back in time to when the Windtalkers were alive?' asked Adam. 'Does your, uh . . . time machine allow you to do that?'

Rashim pushed his glasses up his nose. 'It is possible to do that. If you locate the cave in 1994, then we would place a beacon there as a location marker. Then from here, in London, I could charge up the displacement machine, open a portal to bring you back. Then we set up another time-stamp, same location, but for whenever these Indians lived . . .' Rashim looked over the top of his glasses at Adam. 'Which was?'

'I'm not sure exactly. Somewhere between thirteen hundred and five hundred years ago at a guess?'

'That is a span of eight hundred years!' Rashim's eyes narrowed. 'Could you be more precise than that?'

'Have we got enough energy to reach back that far anyway?' asked Maddy.

'Hmmm, I will need to think how I can boost our reach. It is possible. I will need to do some calculations.'

'So, if we can, we open a portal some time back then,' said Maddy. 'And maybe we can, y'know, talk to these Indians? See what they know?'

'What if the Indians know nothing, Maddy?' said Sal. 'What if it's nothing to do with them? Somebody turned up and wrote something on that cave wall and then left?'

Maddy shrugged.

'Or, we could just go back in time until the wall writing *wasn't* there,' said Liam, 'and wait there until whoever painted it turns up and then we grab the poor fella and beat the answer out of him?'

She turned to him sharply.

'Uh, I wasn't making a joke of –'

'No, Liam.' She was nodding at the idea. 'I was just going to say, brilliant idea.' She shook her head. 'I have a habit of over-complicating things. On the other hand you, Liam, seem to cut directly through the crud. That's what we'll do. Once we find the cave we can open a pinhole image of the wall, and take image samples going back in time until it's blank. Then we can zero in on the precise moment that the writing was made.'

'We could actually do that?' gasped Adam. 'We could actually witness the moment . . . the *exact* moment that writing was daubed on the wall?'

'Uh-huh. Duh. Of course! Time travel? That's the kind of thing you can do.'

'My God!' Adam lowered his wooden spoon into his pie with a heavy splat. 'That would be . . . simply . . . incredible!' he whispered.

'Welcome to the wonderful wacky world of time travel,' said Sal drily. 'We get to do lots of crazy-fun things like that.'

CHAPTER 9

1989, London

'That nice man was very helpful,' said Maddy.

She looked both ways at the pedestrian crossing. A red double-decker bus rumbled past them. Across the street a giant billboard was showing a poster for the movie *Back to the Future Part II*. Maddy remembered seeing the movie, one of many they'd watched together in their Brooklyn field office. The film's depiction of 2015 had been laughably naive and upbeat: colourful, fun, optimistic. Hoverboards instead of skateboards, for God's sake. She wondered how much more fun life would be if God was a Hollywood movie director.

'Indeed the man was,' replied Rashim. 'Very helpful. Although, I have to ask, are you sure it is such a good idea having him deliver it right outside our door?'

'Sure, yeah. I reckon it'll be OK.'

Right now – London 1989 – England's Prime Minister was a woman called Margaret Thatcher. Mobile phones were the size of bricks. Everyone seemed to be wearing brightly coloured tracksuits made of cheap polyester . . . The small oak side door that led from their dungeon on to Farringdon Street was the entrance leading to a place called 'Bernie's Tattoos and Piercings'.

'It's no big deal. I'll just pretend I work there, taking delivery for my boss.'

'Why would a tattooist want a generator?'

The pedestrian lights changed, the green man beckoned them to cross the road.

'Come on,' she said.

They made their way across the road, stopping almost at once to dodge a motorcycle courier who'd threaded his way through the stationary cars and was running over the pedestrian crossing no matter what light was showing.

Maddy cursed and flipped her hand at him as he sped away. 'Moron!'

'It seems more dangerous on foot than New York, I think.'

They crossed just as the lights changed and traffic resumed rumbling past behind them.

'Seriously, relax,' said Maddy. 'The delivery guy won't give a second thought to why a tattooist wants to hire a portable generator and a dozen gallon drums of diesel.' She shrugged. 'It's business for his boss. Somebody needs a generator for hire. Done deal.'

'Not particularly *good* business for the man.'

Maddy winced guiltily. So the poor chap running 'Webster and Sons Equipment Hire' was going to lose one generator through a portal back to 1889. But at least he had the deposit money they'd paid up front. She pulled a face; that was going to cover *some* of his loss.

They turned into Plumtree Court. Mr Webster (if that was, in fact, his name) was going to bring it round in the back of his white van in about half an hour's time. Maddy and Rashim would help him unload it and make as if they were about to wheel it in through the small oak doorway into 'Bernie's Tattoos and Piercings' beneath Holborn Viaduct and wait for him to go. Then they were going to drag it down a rat run a few dozen yards along, all but lost in the darkness beneath the viaduct. The portal was scheduled to open there in about an hour's time.

They'd step through it, then quickly wheel the generator and drums of diesel back up to the very same small oak doorway in 1889 and then into their dungeon. It would be gone midnight back in 1889. Hopefully nobody was going to be around to snoop at them. Or if they were, at that hour they were likely to be gin-soaked drunks and too gone to notice, or even care.

Really quite simple.

Rashim was going to wire it into their system and hopefully the additional boost of power streaming into the capacitor array was going to give them a lot more stored charge to play around with.

'I, uhh . . . I am wondering . . .' started Rashim.

'Wondering what?'

'About this young man, Adam Lewis . . .?'

She looked at him. 'What's on your mind?'

Rashim stepped aside for a man striding towards them in a pinstripe suit and wide red braces. He was barking loudly into a large black phone with a telescoped aerial. 'Yeah, mate, several smart little properties in a well nice up-and-coming area. Great investment, mate – seriously pukka . . .'

The man strode past, oblivious to Rashim's courtesy.

'Given you have been very wary, so very careful about secrecy,' he continued, 'now, it seems, you are welcoming a complete stranger into our little group? It strikes me as . . . odd.'

'Well, we let you and your ridiculous pet robot in, didn't we?'

'Out of necessity perhaps? Because I am useful?'

'Oh, come on, you're making me sound so manipulative and cynical.' She smiled and nudged him gently. 'You're one of us now. One of the gang. But Adam? Look, we *do* need him. He knows exactly where this cave is. That's it.'

'You know we could just have stolen all his notes. After all, that's all we need from him.'

'True, but he may also be able to help us decode that writing.'

'I would imagine Bob or Becks would be able to run pattern and symbol frequency analysis on the message.'

'*And* we've also worked with him before, Rashim. Remember? I told you he came and found us in 2001. He was incredibly useful then. In fact we'd never have been able to figure out how to decode that manuscript without him.'

Rashim narrowed his eyes suspiciously. 'I think, with Adam, maybe you have some feelings for him?'

She stopped dead. 'What?'

Rashim cleared his throat. 'Is that *not* the case? Am I misreading –?'

'What?! No!' She felt her cheeks beginning to burn. 'Oh c'mon, please . . . *feelings*?'

'All right then. Perhaps not. I am mistaken. I thought it might be worth raising the question.' Rashim shrugged. 'You make a reasonably compelling case for bringing him along, I suppose.'

'Jeeez. I'm not sweet on him, Rashim,' she huffed. 'And, by the way, that is such a sexist frikkin' thing to assume. Because I'm a girl? Right? Means I'm not happy unless I'm hanging off the arm of some guy?'

'You are right, an inappropriate assumption.' He nodded politely. 'Please accept my apologies.'

She huffed again for show. 'Don't worry about it.'

They passed a record shop. Music pumped out on to the pavement from within: some male vocalist pronouncing that he was '*never gonna give you up, never gonna let you down . . .*'

Feelings for Adam? She shook her head at that. Of course she didn't have feelings for him. The guy was useful, and that was the top and bottom of it.

Oh, Maddy, don't you remember? That moment . . . ?

Yes, all right, there was just that one awkward, fleeting

moment when they'd been round to his Manhattan apartment to quickly pick up the hard drive he'd been hanging on to all those years. The hard drive that contained the very same information that was in his backpack right now. She remembered, and she inwardly cringed.

All right, I was weak, OK? I was feeling stressed, I was feeling lonely, dammit!

But she'd also – just for a few seconds – allowed herself to imagine, to fantasize, what it might feel like to have those gym-toned and firm arms of his wrapped round her shoulders. To bury her face into the warmth of his neck. To feel the firm contours of his chest –

Oh God, get a grip, Maddy!

'Seriously, Rashim . . . I've got way better things to do with my time than – y'know? – recruit potential boyfriend material!' She shook her head irritably. 'Anyway, he's not my type. Too scrawny. Too scruffy and nerdy.'

'I can't believe your displacement machine,' said Adam. 'It's not just a time machine, it's also a teleportation device. Incredible!'

On a screen further along the table, something caught Adam's eye: a looped piece of footage of a plane crashing into a building. 'My God . . . what's that?'

'That?' Liam looked at it. 'Oh that. A horrible day. It happened the day after you came to visit us in New York. Or, I should say, a day after the time *you will come* to visit us in New York.'

'What happened? Was it an accident?'

Liam shook his head. 'Maddy says it was an act of terrorism. Some crazy religious people decided to take over some planes and crash them into buildings. Thousands of people in New York will die on that day. Thousands.'

'That's the World Trade Center, isn't it? In Lower Manhattan?'

'Aye. Where all them banks and the like are based. We got to see that day far, far too many times.' Liam leaned over and hit a key on one of the keyboards. The looping footage disappeared from the screen. 'You of all people shouldn't have seen that,' he added. Then immediately regretted the slip.

Adam looked at him. 'Why?'

'Just that it's the future, Adam. It's not your business to know it.' Liam decided to draw Adam's attention quickly away from that. 'You and I, we've got work to do, so we have.'

Maddy had briefed Adam that she intended to open a portal to send them over to Central America, as opposed to all of them flying over there, or taking a ship. She'd been hoping he was going to be able to hand over to her a precise GPS location. But that wasn't what Adam had. In 1994 the only people who had access to GPS technology were military types.

What he *did* have, however, was his journal: a tatty exercise book filled with notes, sketches and several local maps of Nicaragua and Honduras pulled out of a travel book and pasted in. Adam seemed confident he could replicate the exact route Professor Brian had led his six students on. The journey had taken them down the Coco River, deep into the jungle, stopping along the way at several remote villages. Adam assured her he'd be able to retrace their steps. The river flowed just one way and villages would still be there. He said he'd be able to piece together where they'd made their last camp – it was off a tributary the locals called the Green River. And from there he said the cliff was clearly visible; the looming cliff-face rose out of the jungle mists like the sheer side of an iceberg on an arctic sea.

'So now then –' Liam nodded at the computer monitor in front of them – 'where is it we need to open that portal?'

'Well, we set off down the Río Coco from a place called San Marcos de Colón.' Adam studied the image on the screen: a detailed map of the border area between Nicaragua and Honduras. 'There.' He pointed. 'That's it! That's the place where Professor Brian hired our boat and the guide.'

'Right.' Liam nodded. 'Computer-Bob?'

On the next monitor along, a dialogue box suddenly appeared.

> Yes, Liam?

'Can you provide a location stamp for . . .' He leaned forward to read the name of the town. 'For San Marcos de Colón, in the country Honduras.'

> Of course. One moment . . . retrieving data.

Adam sat back in the chair and whistled. 'Oh, that is just sooo mint! Voice-recognition-enabled AI!'

Liam grinned. 'Let me guess, that would be the fancy technical term for a computer that you can talk to, I presume?'

'Oh, yeah.' Adam nodded. 'Jesus . . . this is so *sci-fi*! Can I have a go at talking to it?'

Liam shrugged. 'Be my guest.'

Adam looked around the cluttered table. 'Do I need to talk into a mic or something?'

'Nope. You just need to talk. He'll hear you.'

He craned his neck forward. 'Uhh . . . hello? Computer? You there?'

'He answers to the name computer-Bob.'

'Computer-Bob? Really? Who came up with *that* name?'

> Liam, I detect a voice pattern that has 99.87% probability of belonging to previously authorized user – Adam Lewis.

Liam was taken aback for a moment. But then he remembered Adam had been here before. 'Ah, of course! I forgot. You two have actually already met.' It was a seven-years-older Adam Lewis who had worked with Maddy and computer-Bob while Liam, Bob and Becks had been back in 1194.

Adam looked boggle-eyed. 'Really?'

'Aye. You were some years older than you are now, but I suppose your voice never completely changes.' He turned back to look at the dialogue box. 'Aye, computer-Bob, the voice you just heard belongs to Adam Lewis. He's come back to help us again.' He nodded at Adam. 'Go on . . . why don't you say hello to him.'

'Errr . . . OK. Computer-Bob? Hellooo?'

> Hello, Adam Lewis. Welcome back.

Adam slapped the table with his hand. 'That is just . . . incredible!'

Out of a dark corner of the dungeon, something squat, yellow and cubed waddled towards them, drawn by the noise of Adam's laughter – curious, like a moth drawn to light.

Liam smiled as he saw that SpongeBubba had been roused from his 'slumber' and was shuffling towards them. 'Well now, Adam, if you enjoyed that you'll probably love *this*.'

'What?'

Liam nodded into the dark and Adam followed his gaze. Two bulbous eyes framed with thick cartoon eyelashes; beneath them, a wobbling gherkin nose and two goofy tombstone teeth. The lab unit stared back at Adam.

'Howdy! Howdy! I'm SpongeBubba! What's *your* name?'

Adam stared down at the unlikely creature and for a moment considered that maybe, just maybe, he really had experienced some kind of complete nervous breakdown and was locked into a completely convincing delusion. Perhaps, right now in the REAL world, he was busy rocking to and fro on a creaky sanitarium bed, wrapped up snugly in a restraining harness, all glassy-eyed and drooling from a generous dose of pentobarbitone.

'No,' said Liam. 'You've not gone insane. That thing's Rashim's pet.'

CHAPTER 10

1994, San Marcos de Colón, Honduras

A small, malnourished mongrel dog, tan fur worn bald in places down to its scab-encrusted skin, growled at the rat he could hear scratching around beneath the heavy car tyre. The dog's pronounced ribs flexed beneath his skin as he snuffled and worried at the black rubber before he began pawing in the dry dirt beneath to dig a space wide enough to push his muzzle and small head through.

The rat squeaked with alarm. For the moment it was safe, but inevitably it was doomed, with nowhere to run to. The dog's paws scratched frantically at the ground, widening and deepening the hole.

A chain-link fence enclosed the back lot of an abandoned colonial-era *cortijo*, the dog the only living thing there, scratching away at the dirt to get a meagre meal of one frightened rat. Cars that dated from the forties and fifties lay abandoned and rusting in the hot sun. Rubbish and sewage, tossed over the fence in equal measure by the local inhabitants into this unofficial dumping ground, festered and putrefied.

Beyond the fence, a shanty town of corrugated iron roofs packed tightly together and punctuated by dozens of thin threads of smoke from cooking fires, which rose lazily into a breathless sky. Laundry lines stretched across narrow walkways and dangled threadbare T-shirts and sun-bleached floral-print dresses. The sound of packs of feral children playing catch-me as they chased each other along the barely shoulder-wide alleys between tin shacks and lean-tos. Dogs barked as they passed and a woman cursed the dogs.

A transistor radio was playing Gloria Estefan's '*Mi Buen Amor*'. The deeper thud of a boom-box played the Beastie Boys. And fainter, the *thup*, *thup*, *thup* of an army helicopter in the sky circling the shanty town.

Not far from the scratching, snuffling, growling dog, a gentle gust of wind stirred the loose items of rubbish into playing their own circular game of catch-me. A Snickers wrapper chased a Coke bottle, a faeces-soiled nappy chased a bill poster. Dust swirled up into the air to form a modest six-foot-high tornado.

Then, as if a magician had cast a spell from afar, the rubbish, the wrappers, the dirt, a section of the tyre, all of the rat and half the dog were replaced by a dark eight-foot-wide sphere that rippled and shimmered like an airborne oil slick.

Several figures emerged from it. An enormous, muscular man, scowling warily at his surroundings, eyes shadowed beneath a pronounced Neolithic brow, his coconut-round head topped with an unkempt short and coarse thatch of dark hair. A much shorter lean, wiry figure: a young man with unruly hair, dark with a silver streak in it. Following him, a girl wearing glasses, strawberry-blonde frizzy hair pulled casually back into an if-I-can't-see-it-I-won't-fuss-about-it ponytail. Finally another young man, skinny to the point of being unhealthily so, and as pale as a ghost. As pale, in fact, as some deep-ocean creature scooped to the surface by a net and now flapping pitifully and quite unappealingly on the foredeck of a trawler. His head topped with a bird's-nest mess of ginger dreadlocks. His mouth slung wide open.

The sphere of undulating oil contracted and disappeared with a puff of air behind them, and the girl looked down at the ribcage and spilled intestines of the front half of the quite dead mongrel dog lying at her feet.

'Ewww . . . that's just so gross.'

CHAPTER 11

1994, San Marcos de Colón

'. . . when we came here two years ago, there were still signs everywhere of the civil war going on next door in Nicaragua. Burnt-out tanks, mines, guns, refugees . . . I mean, it officially came to an end in the late eighties. But it was still kind of going on in places.'

Adam led them through a busy market square, bordered on all four sides by the faded grandeur of colonial-era buildings that must have once upon a time glowed crisp and white in the sun, but were now a dirty vanilla colour, paint flaked away in patches revealing the dull grey stonework beneath.

The square was busy this morning, noisy with the voices of traders attempting to out-yell each other. Noisy with the alarmed squawking of roosters and hens crammed into wire-mesh cages, the din of a hundred different buy-and-sell negotiations going on over impromptu counters made from stacked-up wicker baskets.

'The Hondurans all along the border with Nicaragua, during the war, had to repeatedly leave their homes, their towns and flee north,' continued Adam, shouting over his shoulder to be heard, 'because the fighting kept spilling over.'

'What was the fighting all about?' asked Liam.

'That's a long answer.' Adam smiled. 'The short answer, I suppose, is ideology. In Nicaragua they had a communist government come to power. They were called the Sandinistas. Voted in quite legitimately by the poor. But being a communist government it was a worry to the United States government.'

'Why? What's it to do with them?' asked Liam.

'The American government is worried about the domino effect of communism in the Third World. And these Central American countries – Nicaragua, Guatemala – appeared, one by one, to be succumbing to that, voting in hard-line communist and socialist regimes. Countries far too close for comfort. Countries that might become another Cuba.'

Liam had read up on the Cuban Missile Crisis after he and Maddy had visited a timeline in which the Cold War had turned hot and the world had been rendered a nuclear wasteland. The island of Cuba, just ninety miles off the coast of Florida, had become a communist dictatorship under Fidel Castro in the sixties. The day that Castro took over, alarm bells had started ringing all over the Pentagon at the thought that the Russians might use this ideologically friendly nation, on the very doorstep of America, as an advanced launching pad for their nukes.

Adam looked around the busy square to get his bearings. He spotted what he was looking for and led them to the right, between two market stalls and into a less busy area. A paddock for mules, goats and cows to be tethered.

'So,' Adam continued, 'the Americans weren't happy about the communist Sandinistas being in power in Nicaragua.' Easier to talk now, instead of shout over the din of the market. 'So they launched a ruthless and extensive campaign to destabilize the Sandinista government. They invested hundreds of millions of dollars. Throwing money at any rebel groups offering to cause problems for the Sandinistas. And, Jesus . . .' He shook his head. 'These Nicaraguans were *poor* people. A *poor* country that had been systematically raped by the corrupt guys who were running things before the Sandinista government. The rebels called themselves "freedom fighters". But all they were, were the officers and generals of the previous corrupt regime, desperate to get their old jobs back, desperate to get their greedy snouts back in the trough.'

'And America backed them?' asked Maddy.

Adam nodded. 'The Contra rebels. Nasty bunch of crooks basically. But, because they were out to bring down a *communist* regime . . . they were made out to be the *good* guys.'

The four of them picked their way towards a long, low arched-roof hut made from sheets of corrugated metal. Adam pointed. 'That's the boat-yard, if I remember correctly. That's where we hired our riverboat and a guide.'

'So that war in Nicaragua's all over and done with now, though?' asked Liam. 'Right?'

Adam nodded. 'Yeah. It all sort of wound down in 1990. People wised-up to this CIA-sponsored dirty little war. The money for the Contra rebels dried up. But it's not like all those bands of soldiers just vanished. A lot of them are still out there in the jungle, trying their best to destabilize the peace. And, of course, the US government are still secretly doing everything they can to make life difficult and miserable for the Nicaraguans . . . and they will continue to do so until those poor bloody people pick a government the Americans decide they approve of.'

Maddy gave a low whistle. 'That kinda sucks.'

They arrived outside the hut.

'So what's this place?' asked Maddy.

'Professor Brian dealt with the official who oversees the local fishermen. He hooked us up with a riverboat captain and guide last time.' Adam looked at a sign hanging from a cord on the door and grimaced as he tried to decipher it.

'So, I guess I'm going to have to try to put my awful schoolboy Spanish to use.' He winced. 'I'm afraid there's going to be a lot of flapping of hands here. Unless . . . unless one of you knows any Spanish?'

Liam turned round and looked up at Bob. 'Well, big fella, that's one you know, isn't it, Bob?'

'*Quedo totalmente a su disposición*.'

CHAPTER 12

1889, London

Sal still felt nauseous at the sight of it. Becks had casually done the necessary duty for them and scooped up the hindquarters of the animal, cut off by the edge of the portal – she thought it might be a dog, but it was hard to tell – and tossed it outside into the street.

The support unit was now out on an errand to buy a jug of milk, bread and some other necessities. Sal looked around. That idiot walking filing cabinet, SpongeBubba, was in charge-mode again. It was just her and Rashim sitting around their communal table. He was working with a soldering iron on something, sending a thin tendril of smoke up towards the bulb dangling from the low brick ceiling above them.

'Rashim?'

He looked at her over the rim of his glasses. 'Hmmm?'

'Maybe Pandora is a bunch of different endings that all occur in 2070.'

'What do you mean?'

'Well, in Waldstein's timeline, humankind is wiped out by a virus in 2070. Right? Perhaps in another timeline, mankind is wiped out in a different way, say, a nuclear war, that also happens in the same year? And in another timeline, mankind is destroyed by . . .' She paused for thought, for an idea, '. . . by an asteroid strike.'

Rashim looked at her sceptically. 'Coincidentally occurring in 2070?'

She nodded. 'What I think I'm getting at is this . . . perhaps whatever we choose to do, whichever way we steer history, we're destined to meet our end in that year.'

He tapped the tip of his nose thoughtfully. 'You are talking of some kind of predeterminism.' He shook his head. 'As if some higher intelligence, some greater being, is the pilot of all things.'

She spread her hands. 'And why not?'

He shook his head. 'I do not accept that, Sal. I do not accept that anything other than a quantum set of rules governs the sub-particle universe and an Einsteinian set of rules governs the rest of time and space.' He laughed. 'And I certainly do not accept that some sort of intelligence is governing events; is watching us like . . . like the Greek gods playing their games.'

She shrugged. 'Foster always said that history has a way it wants to go. Almost like it's alive. He said it could tolerate some degree of tinkering and yet still self-correct. But perhaps history doesn't necessarily care what path it takes . . . it just cares where it *ends up*.'

'Where it ends up? You mean . . .'

'Wiping mankind out in 2070. You know, one way or another.'

'You make history sound like it has some manner of a personal grudge against humanity.' He smiled at that. It sounded silly.

'You're laughing at me,' said Sal.

'No. Just at the idea of what I just said.'

She watched him work in silence for a while before she finally spoke again. 'I'm worried, Rashim.'

'Worried? About what?'

She reached out for a discarded loop of wire and began absently winding it round her finger. 'I'm worried that we might be doing the wrong thing.'

'How do you mean?'

'I don't know.' She chewed her lip for a moment, putting jumbled thoughts in the correct order. 'OK . . . it's like this. Everything seemed to go wrong for us, go off the rails, after Maddy sent a message to the future asking what Pandora was.'

Rashim put down his soldering iron on a rest and reached for his mug of warm ale. 'We now know for certain what Pandora is.'

'Well, we *think* we do.'

'The Kosong-ni virus. Becks confirmed that.'

'What if she's lying? Or just been given wrong information?'

Rashim tipped the ale into his mouth and swilled it around. Thinking. 'There seem to be no certainties here, Sal. It seems all we have at the moment are educated guesses.'

'Right.' She nodded. 'Just guesses.' She was quiet for a moment. 'Which means Maddy could be wrong about Waldstein. Maybe whoever warned her about Pandora is the real problem, not Waldstein?'

'Indeed.' He gave that a moment's thought, then nodded. 'But perhaps she is right to seek more information before she decides which way to act.'

Sal watched him return to his work, soldering a circuit board. One of their computer's motherboards had something or other wrong with it. Rashim had explained it to her once already – it was all blah, blah, blah to her.

Her mind was elsewhere anyway, nostalgic for the good old days. The first few months after the three of them had been recruited. After the Kramer incident. That was when they had most felt like a team. They'd managed to pull themselves together – straight out of the training Foster had been putting them through, and straight into action – but they managed it, they'd put things right. And then there'd been some time afterwards in which they'd got to know each other better, to settle into a routine of sorts living in that Brooklyn archway. Become almost like a family.

Then there'd been the next big crisis: Liam blasted back to dinosaur times. But again, even though they were still pretty green as a team, they'd pulled it off, they'd steered things back on to the right course.

Good times. They'd been such a great team together. And, dare she admit it, she'd even grown to love those two, like an older brother and sister.

But everything that had changed between them, all of it could be traced back to the moment Maddy found that note in San Francisco. That was the first secret between them. Now they were in such a different, uncertain place.

Maddy and Liam – but particularly Maddy – seemed intent on messing with things they didn't understand. There was a reason that Waldstein wanted history headed this way. She didn't buy the idea that the man was insane. An insane man couldn't invent time travel and countless other things. An insane man couldn't run a multi-billion-dollar corporation making hundreds of millions of dollars of profit while the world economy plummeted into a bottomless abyss.

Insane – it was too easy an answer. Too lazy an answer. Sal suspected Waldstein knew a truth that no one else knew. A truth. Perhaps an unpleasant one . . . and he was doing what he thought was best.

So, if that was the case, if she truly believed Waldstein's agenda was a good one, the right thing . . . then working against that made Maddy and Liam a problem. No wonder Waldstein had sent those support units back in time to find them.

She shook her head. *Are we the bad guys now?*

'You all right, Sal?' asked Rashim.

She met his gaze and flickered a smile his way. 'Fine. I'm fine.'

Thinking about it all gave her a migraine. She wondered how nice it would be to be an ordinary fourteen-year-old girl. An ordinary girl with ordinary girl problems.

Boys.

That made her smile, made her think of something else. There was actually someone she wished would do just a little more than shyly wave at her every time they caught sight of each other. She found his tall awkwardness, his gentlemanly ways – even his shyness – cute.

CHAPTER 13

1994, San Marcos de Colón

'Mr Pineda, is it?' Liam leaned over the choppy gap between the pier and the boat: a scruffy-looking fifty-foot-long vessel made of wood and ringed by old, bald rubber tyres slung over the side to protect the paint-chipped gunwale. An old mint-green canvas awning stretched along most of the length of the deck, shading the weather-worn planking. Halfway down, a wheelhouse, little more than a toilet-cubicle-sized shack of loose wooden slats and a viewing shutter propped open by a small straight branch from a tree.

'It *Captain* Pineda!' Tall and whippet-thin, skin so dark that the whites of his eyes seemed almost luminous. 'This me *lanch*, man. This *Mrs Pineda*!'

Liam was stumped by his Creole accent. 'Sorry. This is . . . ?'

'Me lanch!' He slapped a hand on the side of his boat. 'Me *lanch*!'

'Uh.' Maddy was equally bemused.

Adam stepped in. 'It's his launch. His boat.'

Pineda nodded his head, a threadbare and faded captain's cap, one size too big, wobbling uncertainly on top of his wiry coils of hair. 'She me river lanch. *Mrs Pineda*.'

'Named it after your wife.' Maddy nodded approvingly. 'That's really sweet.'

Pineda's already round eyes widened further with a look of

mock horror. 'Naww! Not after m' lady. No more. She gawn!' Pineda hawked and spat venomously over the side into the cocoa-brown river. 'Gawn 'way! She fly off with 'nother man!' He crossed lean muscular arms across his chest. 'Good 'n' gone. Me beauty here, she now name after m' ma.' He grinned: a dazzling smile of big bright crooked tombstone teeth. 'An' didn't need no new paint . . . she still *Mrs Pineda*!'

Introductions were made under the watchful gaze of a growing gathering of the curious that congregated on the pier: skin-and-bones river fishermen and their boys in tatters of colourful clothing, many sitting cross-legged on tyre bumpers like a penny-theatre audience. They watched as they knitted repairs to holes and tears in their fishing nets, studying proceedings intently, regarding the odd-looking *gringos* and chattering among themselves. Special attention, though, was directed towards the extremely large, towering and muscular *gringo*, Bob. Clearly none of them had ever seen a human this size before.

Pineda helped them load their supplies aboard: several boxes of canned beans, bags of rice and flour, and a dozen jerry cans of drinking water. He stowed them in the shallow hold beneath the planking deck. As he emerged from the hatchway, the midday rain arrived with the suddenness and intensity of a power shower being switched on.

Adam had warned them about that. It came almost as regular as clockwork, the noon monsoon. For half an hour, sometimes for an hour, an intense deluge that brought every activity to a standstill until it passed. Grey lances of rain speared down from a thunder-heavy sky and dashed the river all around them. The awning above them drummed deafeningly and they had to shout to each other to be heard.

'*So where's our guide?*' Maddy yelled into Adam's ear.

'He should be here by now!' Adam looked around. Their audience had hurried for cover with the first stings of rain. The pier was a vacant space now, rain-slick planks of wood and hummocks of rain-soaked netting. 'I told that fisheries bloke that we needed him to be here by midday!'

As if on cue they spotted someone jogging along the quayside towards them, a knapsack slung over his shoulder and a twisted and battered brolly held over his head.

Liam was standing out in the rain at the prow of the launch, whooping at the intensity of it. He stopped when he saw the little man approaching. 'Hey! Is that our guide?' he called back, his words almost completely lost in the drumming roar beneath the awning.

The man – and he *was* little – finally pulled up beside the boat. '*Son ustedes los que viajan por el Coco?*' he shouted from the pier.

Adam shouted back. 'Do you speak English?'

The man nodded. 'You are the ones who want travel down the Coco?'

'Yes!' Adam leaned over the side and offered the guide a hand to help him aboard. The man ignored it and jumped effortlessly, frog-like, off the pier and on to the deck beside him. Then he grasped Adam's hand and shook it vigorously.

'Billy!' he crowed with a shrill voice. 'You call me Billy!'

Adam beckoned for him to follow under the awning and, finally out of the rain, he shook Liam's and Maddy's hands. He did a double-take before allowing his small delicate hand to be enveloped by Bob's gorilla paw.

He was *very* short. Just spare change over five foot, and a squat frame came with it. Narrow shoulders with too large a head perched precariously and top-heavy on them. A moon-round face with long black hair silvering at the sides and pulled back into a ponytail.

He grinned goodnaturedly at them, still panting from his run. 'Please to be make your acquaintances.'

'The official we spoke with this morning said you're able to speak with the Indians along the Río Coco,' said Maddy.

Billy nodded. 'I speaks Zambu, Tawahka, Miskito, Creole, Spanish and –' he shrugged apologetically – 'also very bad English.'

'Your English is good,' said Maddy. 'Seriously.' She turned towards Mr Pineda.

'This is our launch's *captain*.' Maddy made very sure to emphasize his title. '*Captain* Pineda.'

Pineda suddenly hooted, a high-pitched girlish squawk, as he doubled over with laughter. 'Me puppysho' wit' you, sister. Me the pilot, the *steersman*. Me firs' name is *Captain*. Hehehe . . .' Pineda giggled and flashed his teeth. 'That the name me muddah gi' me.'

She nodded and smiled. 'Oh I see, you were christened "Captain".' She smiled at that.

His mock-serious face suddenly returned. Serious business. 'Now, sister, you calls me *Captain* . . . or *Mr Pineda*.' As an afterthought, he added, 'Or . . . Mr Skipper.'

'Right.' She nodded. 'Mr Pineda.'

The pilot turned to the guide. Both men nodded politely at each other and exchanged a few words in Spanish.

'So, are we good to go?'

Mr Pineda nodded vigorously. 'Me lanch good 'n' ready!' He tugged the loose cap down over his small head. His ears splayed out under the cap's rim like the open doors of a hansom cab.

'You know where we *gung to*, sister?'

'Uh?' She shrugged. She was lost in his accent again. She cupped her ear. 'Could you say that again?'

Adam nodded. '*I* know where we're going, Mr Pineda. We

want to head down the Coco River as far as the branch with the Green River.'

Pineda pursed his lips thoughtfully for a moment as if consulting a mental map of the river, then finally he hunched his shoulders. 'Me the steersman . . . you me pay-fair.' He grinned that bright smile. 'I take me *Mrs Pineda* anywhere you aks me to.'

Maddy understood that. She reached through the open shutter window of the wheelhouse and waggled the helm. 'So, are we all good to set off then?'

Mr Pineda frowned comically. 'Hey! That me wheel! Only Captain Pineda touch da wheel. Them me lanch reg-gie-lay-shuns!'

She let go quickly. 'Sorry!'

Mr Pineda shrugged begrudgingly. 'That OK . . . let you off this time.'

CHAPTER 14

1994, Río Coco

The night came more quickly here, it seemed, than elsewhere. At dusk Liam checked the hour on his timepiece. The sun made its bed beyond the irregular horizon of jungle peaks at just after five and left behind it a blood-red stain that finally disappeared by eight.

With the dark, Mr Pineda steered the river launch to the northern side – the Honduran side – of the Río Coco. 'It safer from the bandits this side, brudder,' he'd explained to Liam. He threw out a stern anchor and tied a bow line to an overhanging branch from an amate fig tree.

He cooked up a pot of beans on a kerosene burner, mashed them and served them with fried Yojoa fish. And after that, bellies satisfied all round, he boiled some water and made coffee, bitter and strong.

Liam lay on the deck at the prow of the boat, his head rudely cushioned by one of the tyre 'fenders'. Above him the overhanging leaves of the tree were silhouetted ink-black against the deep blue of a clear night sky. The wooden deck vibrated gently beneath his back as the launch's diesel engine juddered like an old man muttering to himself. The engine powered a light swinging from a flex in the wheelhouse and a similar one beneath the awning at the rear of the boat.

Liam watched Maddy as she left the others, coffee in hand,

picked her way forward and settled on the vibrating deck beside him.

'Must be a little bit like being a pirate again.'

He smiled. 'Aye.' But only a little. The smell of diesel, the soft judder of the engine dispelled the illusion somewhat. It would feel more like those days when Mr Pineda switched the engine off for the night and he could hear the soothing lap of water against the wooden hull.

They lay back in silence for a while, and watched shooting stars zip across the sky.

'I'm worried about Sal,' Maddy said presently.

'Why? What's up?'

'I dunno . . . she seems so different. She's changed.'

Liam had sensed the same thing. A subtle shift in her demeanour. He'd thought it was something and nothing but now he wanted to hear what Maddy was thinking.

'When you were away frolicking on the high seas, busy playing pirates with Rashim, she had a major wobble.'

'A wobble?'

'She isn't coping very well with the idea that she's not really Sal.'

'Aye . . . that was something of a blow for all of us, to be fair.'

'*You* seem to have coped with that remarkably well.' Maddy looked at him. 'You always seem to shrug everything off. Like nothing really matters. You know, I'm so jealous that you can do that.'

Liam wished that it was so. True, the issue of his identity being nothing more than some lab technician's best guess of how a cocksure young Irish lad would behave and what he would sound like had so far not affected him greatly. *I am who I am* – that was his maxim: five words that, as far as he was concerned, more or less dealt satisfactorily with the matter. Weighing more heavily on his mind was wondering whether his thoughts were truly his. Whether the decisions he made were his alone, or the product of some lines of programming – digital or genetic.

He had scared himself a little, once, back in the seventeenth century. The way he had calmly rationalized the killing of that Moorish pirate. He imagined that Bob and Becks dispassionately analysed friend and foe, threat levels, viable targets in much the same way. Coldly, clinically, without any compassion.

'I didn't tell you about this,' said Maddy.

Liam looked at her. 'Didn't tell me what?'

'She went looking for herself.'

'What do you mean?'

'She went forward in time, to 2025, to New York.'

'Why? Why then, why there?'

'She said she had memories of visiting New York with her father that year. I told her that they were just implanted memories. That they weren't real. Just background story designed to make her believe she'd already lived. She went anyway.'

'Uh . . . should you not have stopped her?'

Maddy sighed. 'I . . . I could've. But I didn't. See, well . . . we both thought you'd decided to abandon us. We thought you'd had enough and decided to run off and become a pirate. So, we discussed it and I kind of said to her that maybe we should both do likewise: find places we'd like to live the rest of our lives and just go there.' She shrugged guiltily. 'I guess for a while I thought it was game over.'

Liam lifted himself up on to his elbows. 'Seriously?'

'Sal chose to go find herself. I think she wanted to know for sure whether her memories were just a bunch of things stitched together, or whether they were the memories of a real girl.'

'And? What did she find?' Liam felt the ghost of a hope stir inside him. A possibility that maybe *his* life story was a genuine one. Even if it was a *borrowed* one. 'Did she come across a *real* Saleena Vikram?'

'She never said.' Maddy sipped her coffee. 'I did try asking, but she kinda blew me off. To be honest, I don't know what she discovered in 2025. She came back, though, obviously. So . . . I guess maybe she didn't find what she was looking for. I think she confirmed that there never was, or never will be, a Saleena Vikram. So I guess that's some sort of closure for her.'

'Closure?'

Maddy sighed. 'Crud, do you have to be so frikkin' nineteenth-century all the time? *Closure* . . . it means when you've *settled* a matter you've been worried about.'

'But she hasn't *settled* the matter, has she?'

Maddy was a while replying. 'I don't think so. She does seem different, somehow.'

'I think we should talk to her,' said Liam. 'Just the three of us . . . the Three Musketeers. Have us a heart-to-heart when we get back.'

'I think that would be a good idea.'

Mr Pineda stepped into the wheelhouse and turned off the engine. It rattled, grumbled and coughed like a bad-tempered asthmatic, then fell silent.

'Jay-zus . . . finally,' whispered Liam.

The quiet seemed to have a volume all of its own. Almost deafening. Then into that void the subtle chirrups and stirrings of the jungle cautiously stepped in; the soothing lap and gurgle of river water against *Mrs Pineda*'s worn wooden hull.

A torch flickered around at the other end of the boat as Billy foraged for something; he found what he was after and the torch snapped off. Liam could hear the low murmur of their voices. Adam was talking to Billy. Mr Pineda seemed to be trying to engage Bob in conversation about something. It was a one-sided conversation. His goodnatured sing-song contrasted with the occasional monosyllabic rumble from Bob.

'Maddy?'

'Yup?'

'You really think we'll find an answer in that cave of Adam's?'

'I hope so. You know what I think?'

'Not yet.'

'I think there are two sides out there. There's Waldstein, and there's someone else. We know exactly what Waldstein wants. He wants humanity to wipe itself out in 2070. For whatever reason, good or bad . . . we don't know which and we don't know why. I think it's safe to say he sent those killer support units because we threatened to stop doing what we were set up to do. Maybe if we could speak to him, he could explain why he wants that, and who knows, we might even agree with him. Then at least we'd be back where we were, working for him, preserving history as it is, but knowing *why* we're doing it.'

She smiled wistfully. 'Just like it was in the good ol' days.'

'Aye, that would be nice.' Liam realized how much he missed the certainty that what they were doing was the *right* thing: the thing that was saving mankind.

'But,' she continued, 'I think someone else wants something quite different. And this cave, the Voynich Manuscript, the Holy Grail and that note in San Francisco is them trying to get in touch with us, to give us *their* side of the story.'

'Jay-zus, Maddy.' He sighed and rubbed his temples. 'I just about nearly caught up with yer convoluted thinking. And then you throw more notions into the pot. Do you ever give that head of yours a rest?'

'No. I guess that's why I'm always crabby.'

Liam laughed. Better that than to say 'aye'.

'Anyway, do keep up, Liam. I'm just saying that we need to hear out both sides. We need to talk to Waldstein and we need to know what that message is. Then we can finally decide what it is we should be doing. Whether we're for, or against, the end of the world happening in 2070.'

Mr Pineda studied Bob with a wary frown. 'You a big man. VERY big man, brudder. You a army man?'

Bob sensed the pilot was addressing him and put file-sorting on hold for the moment. 'Clarification: are you asking me whether I am a military unit?'

Mr Pineda nodded. 'Mil-try man, army man. Yes.'

Bob considered that for a moment. Technically speaking, he was. 'Yes. I am.'

'You fight in the big war?' The pilot pointed across the moonlit river to the jungle on the far side. Nicaragua.

Prototypes of Bob's particular batch had been tested in several combat zones. Of course, the AI was earlier-generation software, which had been prone to several glitches. There was a notorious incident of a support unit using an earlier version of his AI base code. The incident was referred to by the military as an 'extreme blue on blue'. A unit undergoing testing in the field had somehow managed to flip friend/foe identifier tags and massacred almost an entire company of US troops as they slept in their beds.

Bob, personally, had seen plenty of combat and not malfunctioned once.

'I have fought in many combat zones.'

Mr Pineda's eyes rounded. 'Many battle? Tell me which.'

For a moment he evaluated whether any information he divulged might present a contamination risk. In this case he decided it could not be significant. The pilot appeared to be mildly intoxicated and, it seemed, for the moment the normal protocols of zero tolerance on contamination had been suspended. Suspended until Maddy finally decided what their role was going to be.

'The guerrilla resistance in Washington State against the German invasion of America. The siege of Nottingham, AD 1194. And the defence of Emperor Caligula's imperial palace, Rome, AD 54.'

The pilot's eyes narrowed for a moment as he took that in. Then without warning he exploded with a high-pitched *hyuk-yuk-yuk* belly-laugh. 'Puppysho'! You playin' wid me!' He leaned over and slapped a bony hand on the meaty bulge of Bob's shoulder. 'I like you, big man! You got funny in you.'

Adam and Billy turned to look at the riverboat pilot rocking backwards and forwards, hooting with laughter.

'*Him*, your big friend.' Billy nodded at Bob. 'He is mercenary? Hired gun?'

As far as Adam understood the set-up of Maddy's team, that seemed to be a close enough approximation of Bob's role. 'Yes, I s'pose in a way that's what he is. Like their bodyguard.'

'This is good. There is much . . . how-say –' Billy clucked his tongue as he trawled his simple English for the right word – 'much *hazard* along the Coco. The jungle, very dangerous place.'

'I came here two years ago with some others,' Adam replied. 'The Contra war in Nicaragua had recently finished. It didn't seem so bad then.'

'Things become much worse now. Many Contra rebels now become bandits. Murder. Steal. Not good.' Billy reached into his knapsack and pulled out a battered old AK47 with a broken and taped-up wooden stock. 'Maybe need this.'

'Jesus. You serious?'

Billy nodded. 'Also, some Indian tribe . . . Bad experience with rebels, with *gringos*. They not friendly no more.'

That hadn't been Adam's experience. The remote riverside villages they'd visited with Professor Brian had welcomed them with open arms.

'Rebels do many raid, kill Indians. This make Indian no longer trust all *gringos*. We must be careful on river.' Billy nodded towards Bob again. 'Your big mercenary? What guns does he bring?'

'Guns? None. No weapons. Well, none that I'm aware of.'

'No gun?!' Billy's face creased with disbelief. 'No gun? Hired gun have no gun?'

'I don't know if he uses one.' He glanced across the deck at Bob's broad frame. 'Mind you, I've got a feeling he's probably good with his hands.'

Billy followed his gaze. He appraised the support unit for a moment. 'We meet Indian . . . they be much scared of him. He so big.'

'He is something of a brute, isn't he?'

'But, we meet rebels?' Billy sucked in his teeth, making a soft whistling sound. 'Not scare so easy.' He patted the rust-flecked barrel of his AK. 'We need guns.'

For the first time since agreeing to come along, Adam felt a cold tickle of uncertainty.

CHAPTER 15

1994, Río Coco

The next day, it was Liam's keen eyes that picked it out first. A curious thing. Nestling in the drooping branches of an guanacaste tree that was overhanging the river on their right – the Nicaraguan side.

It was almost completely hidden among the dense foliage.

'What is that?' he shouted over his shoulder. He had been sitting up front, his – now usual – perch on the prow: bare feet and legs dangling over the side, enjoying the cooling up-spray of water as the launch chugged relentlessly down the chocolate-brown Río Coco, mid-channel.

Billy joined him up front and squinted at where he was pointing, finally picking out the mottled green-brown wreckage dangling amid the branches of the tree.

'Is helicopter.'

'Helicopter, did you say?' Liam had never seen one of those up close. He'd seen them regularly enough from afar, crossing the ever-blue September sky over New York – hedge-fund managers, Wall Street traders, billionaires commuting to and from work. That, or news choppers. 'Oh! Could we go take a closer look at it?!'

Billy shrugged cautiously. 'You the client.' He turned and gestured at the wheelhouse. Mr Pineda was already spinning the wheel. The riverboat swerved in a lazy arc towards the right bank.

Fifty yards upstream, the grumbling burr of the engine was cut to an idling chug and *Mrs Pineda* drifted slowly beneath the enormous sweeping spread of the guanacaste tree.

Liam gazed up through the lattice of creepers, vines and branches at the dangling wreckage above him. Adam and Maddy joined him at the front.

'Wow, that's pretty cool,' said Maddy. 'Is that a US army chopper?'

'American, yes. But it is unmarked,' replied Billy.

Adam squinted up at it. Sunlight was lancing down between the branches, spears of light dappling the deck, the awning, their upturned faces. 'US Army all right, but look – all the identifying markers are painted out.'

Maddy made a face. 'Oh come on . . . the US army doesn't creep around anonymously. They do *shock* and *awe*, not subtle –'

'Covert operations,' said Adam. 'The Americans weren't *supposed* to be in Nicaragua. Not *supposed* to be interfering in their civil war in any way.' He reached out and grabbed a branch to help stop the riverboat's gentle drift. 'Of course they were. They were bankrolling the war against the Sandinistas.'

Adam nodded at the riverbank on the far side. 'They set up training camps over there in Honduras, training thousands of Contra rebels. They equipped them with ex-US army guns, vehicles, helicopters – everything they might need to fight the Nicaraguan army and bring down the socialists. And, of course, made sure they painted out all the US army identifiers.'

'I'm going up to get a closer look,' said Liam. He pulled himself up on to a low bough. The tree creaked under his weight, a gentle breeze whispered through the dangling vines, stirred the reeds sprouting up from the shallow water.

'It was a dirty war, Maddy,' said Adam. 'I'm surprised you don't know about it.'

She shrugged. 'Well obviously I've heard of it, but, you know, it's not a period of history that I've read up on.'

'It was a war President Reagan had to act like he didn't know anything about. So it was waged on his behalf by the CIA. And because it wasn't a *legal* war – if you can accept such a ridiculous idea as a "legal war" – there were no rules of conduct, no Geneva Convention. It was *dirty*.'

Billy nodded. 'Many, many bad thing done.'

Liam pulled his way up into the tree. Reaching himself from one creaking bough to the next. Closer now, he could make out more details of the rusting camouflage-green bulk of the fuselage. The helicopter's plexiglas cockpit shield, right next to him, was cracked, mottled green and fogged by a thin layer of algae and moss. He gently rubbed at the moss, cleared a foggy gap and peered inside. He could just about make out the pilot's seat and the pilot still strapped in it; a skeleton wrapped in desiccated flesh, wearing a camo-green flightsuit and a faded yellow neckerchief. He must have been killed on impact.

'Nice.'

Liam worked his way around the side. Midway along its fuselage, an open gun bay, the rusting barrel of a heavy machine-gun protruding, and from its open breech, the long drooping loop of a high-calibre ammunition belt, the brass shell casings long ago oxidized and turned a bright mint-green.

He grinned at the sight of the gun. 'You should see this!' he called down. He wanted to get closer, to climb into the gun bay and take a look around inside, but the movement along the branches had already made the rusting hulk stir – a warning. It was dangling in the tree, firmly ensnared in the branches and vines like a fly caught in a spider's web. All the same, there was enough deadweight resting here that it could possibly be shaken loose if he was foolish enough to clamber around inside it.

Anyway, the riverboat and the others were directly below. He decided not to chance his luck. He'd seen enough.

'All right, I'm coming back!' he called down to them.

He turned to make his descent, shifted his weight, and to steady his balance he reached out to grab a dense cord of vines dangling beside him. His hand closed round something that felt soft and leathery. He turned to look at what he was holding on to.

A corpse.

'Oh Jay-zus!' He lurched backwards, nearly losing his footing.

Weather-worn rope snapped and the carcass suspended from it tumbled down through the branches. 'Look out below!' Liam shouted.

It landed on the deck right beside Maddy with a soft thud and a rattle, a bundle of bones linked by leathered tendons that crumpled in on itself as it hit the deck. It took her a moment to realize she was staring at the jumbled remains of a human body.

'Oh, gross!' She jumped backwards and placed a hand over her mouth.

'Crap!' Adam stared at the corpse.

Mr Pineda hurried out of his wheelhouse, arms flapping. 'What jus' landed on me lanch?!' He joined them along with Bob, a circle of them staring down at the wrinkled cadaver.

'Relax. It is old body,' said Billy. 'From the wartime.'

'That's . . . that's horrible . . .' said Maddy. She slumped down to sit unsteadily on the gunwale. 'I think I'm gonna puke.'

Bob squatted down, prodded and probed the corpse with a thick finger. 'Information: the body appears to have been skinned.'

'Skinned?' Adam looked more closely. He was right. They were looking at dried tendons, muscle tissue and bones.

Maddy turned and emptied her guts over the side into the river.

Billy and Adam hunkered down beside Bob. Billy nodded slowly. 'Indian do this. Revenge on *gringos*.'

Bob looked up at the wreckage. 'It appears the helicopter crashed on the way back over the river.'

'Survivors . . . found by Indians –' added Billy.

'– and made an example of,' finished Adam. 'A warning to the rebels.'

Billy nodded.

'Jesus,' whispered Maddy, wiping her chin dry. 'That's . . . horrific. That poor –'

'He was probably already dead. Don't shed too many tears for this bloke,' said Adam. He nodded up at the wreckage. 'These were the *bad* guys, Maddy. Dogs of war, mercenaries, psychopaths . . . Guys from the world over attracted by the money, the excitement of a killing field with no rules of conduct.'

Adam prodded the skull tentatively with his finger. It rolled over on to its side, exposing a solitary tuft of blond, buzz-cut hair sprouting from a dark patch of leathery skin on one temple. 'Think about what atrocities *he* carried out, OK? How many peasants he gunned down in their fields, how many farms he torched?'

They watched Liam clambering down through the lower branches of the tree, all silently hoping another strung-up body wasn't going to be shaken loose and tumble down on to the deck like over-ripe fruit.

'Whatever happened to him,' said Adam, 'and any others in that chopper . . . I suspect they knew exactly what they were letting themselves in for. Maybe they even deserved it.'

CHAPTER 16

1994, Río Coco

The rest of the day passed without event. They spent the night tied up to a tree amid a thicket of reeds, all of them suddenly a little more wary of their surroundings. Billy suggested setting up a nightwatch: three-hour shifts until dawn. Maddy volunteered Bob to do all the shifts. She told Billy and Mr Pineda that he didn't need sleep.

'What man don't ever need no sleep, sister?'

Maddy offered some fluff about him having some sort of medical condition – an anti-narcolepsy that prevented him from doing so.

'Ain't natural, your man,' said Mr Pineda, shaking his head.

You can say that again, she was tempted to reply.

The next morning, after a breakfast of refried beans in tortillas and a pot of bitter black coffee, Mr Pineda fired up the diesel engine. It stirred to life with a phlegmy cough and his riverboat nosed its way out of the reeds and into the sedate flow in the middle of the Coco River.

'You know where we gung still, sister?' the pilot asked again.

Maddy deflected the question to Adam. 'Keep going downriver, Mr Pineda,' he replied.

'Downriver?' He shrugged. 'Tha's it? Jus' *downriver*?'

Maddy met Liam's eyes for a moment. There was a question in his expression. *You sure he knows where he's leading us?* Not for the first time she found herself wondering just that. She watched Adam during the morning, pulling his journal out, reading his notes, comparing what they were passing on the riverbanks with the sketches and maps in his notebook.

During the morning they came across the first of two riverside settlements: stick-and-straw shacks on stilts at the river's edge, canoes overturned and pulled up on shingle and mud. Liam craned his neck to catch a glimpse of the inhabitants, but he saw no sign at all that the place was inhabited, save for the faint threads of recently doused cooking fires.

'They hear the boat arrive,' said Billy. 'Learn to hide from rebels when they come.'

Later in the afternoon they rounded a bend in the river and came across the second settlement. Adam recognized it immediately. 'We definitely stopped over at this place. It's just as I remember it.' He flicked through the pages in his journal. 'There! This town is called . . . well, I can't pronounce it, but in English it means "the Bend in the River".'

Liam looked at the riverbank. It hardly deserved to be called a 'town'. 'This place actually has a *name*?'

This second settlement seemed to be not much more than a clearing in the jungle, populated by an afterthought of branch-and-reed lean-tos.

'There's more to it up there in the jungle,' said Adam. 'More a big village than a town really. Couple of hundred people, I'd say. The Zambus here were lovely and friendly last time.' He turned to Maddy. 'This is definitely the place; this was the last village we visited before we turned and headed up the tributary on the right and into Nicaraguan jungle. We should pull in here.'

Maddy nodded and Mr Pineda eased the riverboat across the broad river, out of the main flow and into shallower water littered with the rotting red-brown stumps of tree trunks lurking just beneath the surface. He eased the boat skilfully in among them until it finally rode up gently on a soft bed of silt.

Billy jumped over the side with his knapsack on his back, his AK tucked away inside, the barrel poking out the top – a quick grasp away from being pulled out if needed. Bob splashed down beside him and the pair of them grabbed the line Mr Pineda tossed to them and tied the boat up round the broad trunk of a guanacaste tree.

The others jumped into the ankle-deep water and waded up on to the muddy riverbank.

Adam cupped his hands. 'Hellooo! Anyone hooome?'

His voice echoed through the rainforest and bounced back at them. The cheeping, chirruping, hooting all around the jungle and coming down from the broad guanacaste leaves above them, seemed to momentarily hush as if also expectant and awaiting an answer. There was none.

Billy called out something in Zambu.

The echo of his high-pitched voice eventually faded to nothing.

'This place looks like it's been abandoned,' said Maddy.

'No,' replied Billy. 'Look. They come.'

The first curious faces emerged from the jungle undergrowth, peering out from behind shoulder-high bushes.

'What did you call out?' asked Adam.

'I say – we *not* soldiers.'

'Look!' Liam exclaimed, pointing. More faces had emerged. Dark-skinned. They were darker-skinned than the Miskite Indians they'd glimpsed along the river's edge so far. Liam grinned. 'Hello there, people! We . . . Come . . . In . . . Peace!'

Maddy sighed and shook her head. He could be such an idiot.

Several of the bolder Zambu men stepped out of the undergrowth into plain sight. Slender, short men with arms and legs dark and thin like charcoal-blackened branches and heads that looked one size too big for their shoulders. They stood in the rags and remnants of clothing. Torn and faded T-shirts, khaki shorts. Some of them wore flip-flops.

'Oh.' Liam looked vaguely disappointed. 'I was expecting . . . grass skirts and bones through noses. Or something.' He turned to Maddy. 'Like in them *Tarzan* movies you showed me?'

'They're not frikkin' Zulus, Liam,' she replied.

'The Zambus barter occasionally with the logging companies,' said Adam, 'when they venture out here. They hand out a few T-shirts and baseball caps . . . and some booze for the chiefs and elders. And these poor people are more than happy to trade away their livelihood and their environment for a few cheap hand-outs.'

Billy stepped cautiously forward and began to speak to one of the men in Zambu. The man replied quickly with a shrill voice. There was a lot of pointing. Most of it directed at Bob.

'What's he saying?' Maddy asked their guide.

'He is very afraid of the giant.'

Maddy noticed how much Bob towered over Billy, even more so over the Zambu man a few feet away. 'Bob?'

'Yes, Maddy?' The rumble of his deep voice startled the Zambu.

'Can you get back on the boat and stay there for now? You're frightening the natives.'

Bob looked at her questioningly.

'I think we'll be OK, Bob. Go on, we'll be fine.'

'Affirmative.' He turned and waded out, pulled himself back on to the boat and settled down, cross-legged, on the foredeck.

Billy resumed a quick back-and-forth exchange with the man in Zambu and then finally turned to the others. 'He say we can come up to village.' He nodded at Bob and grinned. 'But giant must stay on the boat.'

Mr Pineda pursed his lips thoughtfully. 'Me staying wit' me lanch too.'

The Zambu men led the rest of them up a jungle trail, a pathway through the dense undergrowth worn bare by countless feet. Liam gazed up through the dangling vines. The majority of the afternoon sun's light was filtered by broad leaves, the occasional sunray slanting down to the jungle floor like a shaft of light through murky pond water. In fact, that's almost how it felt, like being underwater, the light all around them a rich aquatic green.

Since arriving here in Honduras, this was their first time actually stepping *into* the jungle properly, as opposed to looking at it from the comfort and safety of the riverboat. The sounds of life now seemed to be all around them, drifting down from the canopy of leaves and branches. A soup of lively noises that all but drowned out the intruding clumsiness of their feet.

The path wound up a gentle slope for a hundred yards and then Liam heard the muted sound of children's voices, the regular crack of something being beaten or chopped, some women laughing. Finally, they emerged from the pea-green jungle soup into a clearing. A rough ring of open clear blue sky above, like the becalmed eye at the centre of a storm system.

The clearing, a hundred yards across, was edged with shacks made from woven branches and reeds cemented with dried mud. The middle of the settlement was kept clear and appeared to be a communal space. Around the village he noticed, here and there, signs of bartered or scavenged modern-world materials: one or two planks of machined lumber, a sheet of scuffed – almost completely opaque – perspex being used as a window, a twenty-gallon oil drum used as a fire-pit, plastic bottles that once contained Coke or Fanta being carried around by some of the men, a murky green liquid sloshing around inside.

The Zambu people turned to look at the strangers arriving in their settlement. All movement and noise stopped. An old woman ushered several children quickly into their mud hut. An old man turned and ran into the jungle. But most stayed perfectly still, watching them warily. Silence, except for the drone of the uninterested jungle ecosystem and the solitary bark of a dog.

Adam turned round to look back at Liam and Maddy. He spoke quietly. 'Honestly, they were a lot more friendly last time. We felt like arriving royalty.'

The Zambu man who led them up the trail cupped his hands and called out. A moment later an elderly man emerged from one of the huts. Brown and wrinkled from head to foot, he reminded Liam of a very large moccasin. He shuffled over towards them.

The Zambu elder finally stopped short a few yards in front of them, said something and gestured towards Billy. Billy nodded deferentially at the old man and spoke in faltering Zambu, every now and then nodding, gesturing towards Liam, Maddy and Adam.

'I hope he's saying nice things about us,' whispered Maddy.

Billy finished his piece and the old man closed his eyes for a moment before eventually nodding.

The guide turned towards them; his wink indicated the news was good.

'We are welcome to stay.'

CHAPTER 17

1994, 'the Bend in the River' village

The oil-drum fire-pit roared and crackled as the pig turned on the spit above the flames, jetting squirts of bubbling fat into the blaze. The Zambu villagers had maintained a wary distance from them for the rest of the afternoon. But as the sun had settled, and the communal fireplace was stirred from slumbering embers to this roaring fire, so their caution had gradually melted away.

Maddy had patiently allowed a queue of children to play with her frizzy hair. Adam had done likewise, letting the same children squeeze, pull, twist and flick his tatty dreadlocks. Although, she noticed, his patience with that had given out pretty quickly.

Now, she was watching Liam dancing in circles in the glow of the fire with some of the young men. One of them had offered Liam a slurp of the foggy green liquid in his old plastic Pepsi bottle. He'd politely swallowed it, even though she could see he'd desperately wanted to spit it out. Billy told her it was an alcoholic brew the villagers made from cassava. Pretty rough stuff, he assured her, and pretty potent. Which kind of explained why Liam right now was stripped down to his waist and jigging around, performing something that looked a little like a Navajo war-dance.

Adam pitched up beside her. 'You all right there?'

She nodded. 'It's actually quite nice here.'

The entire village had turned out this evening and were

gathered round the warm fire. Mothers with sons, grandfathers, daughters, fathers, sisters, friends, neighbours: one seamless extended family group. The smell of sizzling pork filled the air, and the jungle clearing echoed with a hundred different conversations.

'How are the other two?'

'They're OK.' Maddy had quickly wandered back down the trail earlier to check on Bob and Mr Pineda. They seemed to be getting on just fine in the back of his boat. Mr Pineda had cooked up some sort of bean mash and was attempting to teach Bob how to play poker.

'Billy told me these people have had a hard time of it in the last two years. A band of rebels come by every few months. Help themselves to everything and anything they have. Completely clear them out. While they stay, the girls and young women have to hide away in the jungle . . . for obvious reasons.'

'I can understand why they were wary of us then.'

They watched Liam for a while, attempting to stay on his feet as he danced. He fell over and the other young Zambu men dancing with him laughed. One of them helped him back up.

'So you said earlier we need to go up a different river now?'

'Yeah. The locals call it "Green River" because . . . well, the water's green instead of brown, I suppose. It's much shallower, though, more a stream really than a river. So, we're going to have to leave the riverboat here and proceed in canoes.'

'Sure you know the way there, Adam? To the cave?'

He nodded. 'More sure now we've found this village.' He tapped his backpack, his journal and notes bundled inside. 'I only started making more comprehensive navigational notes from this point on. I was beginning to get worried Professor Brian was going to get us lost.'

'So how far is it?'

'Three days by canoe. Say, ninety miles? Then about a day's trek on foot into the jungle. There are some Mayan-era ruins, which is where we were headed. We made camp there for a week, explored the site.'

'And the cave's there?'

He shook his head. 'It's nearby. You can see it from the ruins. There's a mountainous ridge overlooking the site, quite distinctive, you really can't miss it. Big cliff-face sticking out of the jungle and a winding walkway carved out of the rock.'

'Wow,' she smiled. 'Sounds like quite a sight.'

'It is.' Adam looked across the fire at their guide. 'What do you want to do about Billy and Mr Pineda?'

'I think Billy should come along with us – after all, he's got a gun. He can stay with us until we find those ruins? Then I'll send him back with the canoes. He can head back here. Then he and Mr Pineda can make their way back up the Coco to San Marcos de Colón.'

'Won't he find that odd? You instructing him to abandon us in the middle of the jungle?'

She shrugged. 'Probably. I guess I'd better think up a reason why we'll be OK without him guiding us back out.'

'Good luck with that.' He had a thought. 'You sure your beacon thing is going to work?'

Maddy absently felt for the small device in the thigh pocket of her khakis. The very same design that they'd used to track Liam and Rashim across the Atlantic and through two hundred years of time.

'It works just fine, Adam. Trust me, we've field-tested it.'

'Is there a way to check it's working "just fine" . . . you know . . . *before* we abandon our only ticket back out of the jungle?'

Maybe that would be a sensible precaution. Just to be on the safe side, she'd activate the beacon and when she got a sign back from Rashim that he was picking it up OK she'd give Billy his instructions.

She glanced sideways at Adam. He now seemed amused and engrossed in the antics of Liam and the other young Zambus. Liam had in the last few minutes decided to teach them the conga, and now he was leading a winding snake of young men and children around the clearing . . .

That's it! Let me hear you!

One-and-Two-and-Three . . . HEY! Legs kicking out to one side.

One-and-Two-and-Three . . . HEY! Legs kicking out to the other.

C'mon! Who else wants to tag along on the end!!

Her eyes were back on Adam, who was laughing at Liam's buffoonery. By the dancing light of the fire she saw a hint of the self-assured man he would one day become, the well-groomed Wall Street data-security specialist. She wondered what exactly it was she was feeling for him.

A crush? Do I fancy him? Is it more than that?

She didn't have an answer. Just that when she'd first decided they needed to go back to 1994 to enlist his help, she'd felt the tickling flutter of butterflies in her stomach.

She wondered if his life would take the same path now. Back in New York, the last time they'd encountered him, as he'd worked with her for a couple of days to unravel the Voynich mystery, he'd told her how his whole career path had been driven by his need to meet her again. In 1994 he'd had a visit from two mysterious time-travelling strangers who'd left behind just one solitary piece of evidence that he hadn't completely lost his mind – that ticket stub to a Manhattan nightclub, dated 9 September, 2001. For the sake of his *sanity*, everything he'd done since that visit, every career decision he'd made since then, had been to ensure he would end up in New York, waiting outside that very same nightclub on *that particular night*.

And those life choices, those career choices, had ended up placing him as a data-security consultant for Sherman–Golding Investment, on the ninety-fifth floor of the north tower of the World Trade Center. And, of course, the way things were destined to go, it all ended with his dying along with three thousand other people on that horrific day.

But it was all different now, wasn't it? Now they'd taken him along for this ride, presumably his life after this was going to take a very different route. All right, yes, there it was – a contamination of time of *her* doing. She was so used to berating Liam and Sal for wanting to save this or that person, because they were kind, or because they deserved a chance, or because they were cute, for God's sake . . . now here she was being a complete hypocrite and doing exactly the same thing.

I might have just altered how his life will go. And that might change things.

Perhaps, just perhaps, there might be a *Happily Ever After* linked to that. It wasn't too much to hope for that, was it?

It really all depended on whether their job was to preserve history – or change history.

CHAPTER 18

1994, 'the Bend in the River' village

The next morning Maddy rallied Billy, Liam and Adam. Liam emerged from a rain-damp shack nursing a throbbing head. He blinked back the dazzling sunlight streaming down into the jungle clearing.

'What . . . what the hell happened to me last night?'

'You drank some of that snot-green jungle juice,' she replied.

Liam shook his head. 'Don't say . . . please, don't say words like that.'

'What? *Snot*-green?'

He slumped down on to the stump of a tree. 'At some point in the next few minutes, I'm rather sure I'm going to vomit.'

'Good, it's probably better out than in.'

The fire-pit was still smouldering despite the early-morning rain, several thin threads of meandering smoke half-heartedly racing each other for the sky. Coils of steam rose from the damp ground as the morning sun worked on baking it dry.

An early riser, Maddy had already been down to the boat to check on Bob and Mr Pineda. The riverboat pilot was asleep on his hammock, nursing his own hangover. Bob was sitting cross-legged on the foredeck, looking for all the world like a muscle-bound Buddha enjoying the warmth of the sun on his face.

Maddy regarded the pitiful sight of Liam now. 'We're heading off again this morning.'

'Aye. All right.' He nodded, his head ducked between his knees and waiting for the inevitable.

'So if you could hurry up and empty your guts out, that'd be good. We're going to be canoeing from here on.'

On cue he heaved. It was a wretched gurgling moan closely followed by a jet of propelled vomit, stained a vivid green – in places.

She patted his back gently if not entirely sympathetically. 'There ya go.'

'Wait, there'sh a little bit more . . .' Liam convulsed again, heaved and jetted out another gutful on to the ground.

She curled her lip at the congealed steaming mess between his spattered feet. 'You know? I guess I'll leave you to it.' She wandered across the clearing and found Billy emerging from a hut, stretching, yawning, then pulling on his threadbare khaki shirt. She heard a woman's voice calling to him from inside.

I won't ask.

'Morning, Billy!'

'Good morning, Miss Maddy!'

She explained to him what Adam had explained to her last night. What they needed: two canoes to take them up the Green River.

He nodded. 'I will speak with village fathers.'

By noon they were nearly ready to get on their way again. The village elders had canvassed the younger men, and two had volunteered their canoes and themselves; both of them Maddy recognized as being among the crowd Liam had been teaching to conga.

She also discovered Mr Pineda kept a small 50-horsepower outboard engine in the shallow hold of his riverboat – for dire emergencies only, he'd immediately pointed out. She spent half an hour cajoling him into agreeing to pull it out of the hold and let them take it with them.

'Me 'mergency motor! Me lanch need that in case me diesel die!'

'You're not going anywhere, remember? You're just waiting here for us.'

He shrugged and pursed his lips. 'True,' he finally conceded. 'But *one* motor!' he exclaimed, pointing out the obvious. '*One* motor. *Two* canoe! How you gon' make that work, sister?'

'We'll tow one.'

'It just a small motor, sister. Very small . . .'

'But big enough, it seems, for your launch,' she replied, smiling. 'In case of emergencies.'

Mr Pineda frowned. 'You lose it, you break it . . . be extra I chargin' you!'

'Of course.' She dug into her bag, pulled out her diminished bundle of notes and unfolded several fifty-dollar bills. 'That's to cover the engine, just in case. *And* . . . I'll pay you for your waiting time too, Mr Pineda. Pay you when we get back.'

'How long that be?'

She clucked her tongue. 'Say . . . about a week.'

He gave that some thought, then finally nodded. 'Me lanch a busy boat this time of year. Week is a long time. You gonna need to pay me –'

'Two hundred dollars be enough for your time and the motor?'

Mr Pineda's disapproving frown vanished like a magician's shiny penny. Instead he flashed her a broad grin. 'Be waitin' right here for you, sister.'

Half an hour later, a week's worth of food and water had been loaded into the bottom of the canoes, the outboard motor had been clamped to the rear of one of them and several plastic gallon cartons of diesel had been stashed away. Then with the *farewells* and *thank-yous* exchanged, she watched Liam, surrounded by an adoring crowd of the village's children, as he high-fived his way through a thicket of outstretched hands.

'Jay-zus!' he uttered as he clambered aboard.

'Seems with all your clowning around last night, you turned out to be a big hit with the kids,' said Maddy.

'Aye. Maybe I'll do that when I retire from the time-travel business: birthday parties and weddings.'

She laughed. 'You seem a lot better now.'

He puffed queasily and made a face. 'Next time someone offers me something I don't know what it is . . . you step in on my behalf, all right?'

'Pfft, you're big enough to know better.' She shook her head. 'I'm not your mom.'

Bob pushed both canoes out, off the silt bank and into the gentle flow of the river. He pulled himself aboard the second canoe, joining Billy, Liam and one of the Zambu men. For now, with the flow in their favour, they were paddling. The outboard motor was for later on, when they turned right into the tributary and had to work upstream against the current.

She watched the village slowly recede behind them, a muddy bank lined with smiling faces, waving hands, voices calling after them and wishing them well, and for a moment her heart felt heavy leaving them behind.

'They were really friendly to us strangers.'

Adam nodded. 'God knows they've got reason not to be.'

'Did none of them recognize you from your last visit? When was it . . . two years ago?'

'No, I don't think so.' Adam shook his head. 'Mind you, I looked completely different. My hair was all short back-'n'-sides. I was clean shaven like a preppy.' He shrugged. 'I probably looked like a bit of a trainspotter.'

'Trainspotter?'

'A dork. A pencil-neck. A complete nerd.'

She nodded. 'Oh, OK. I think I can see that.'

He smiled sarcastically. 'Thanks.'

The sedate flow of the river carried them round a long bend and finally the village was lost from sight, the voices faded and the sound of the jungle once more filled the humid air and descended upon them like a blanket of thick felt.

CHAPTER 19

1994, Río Coco

An hour later they approached the low muddy flats of a river delta. Adam scanned the jungle to their right for a discernible break indicating the entry point of the Green River. 'Hmmm,' he grunted, 'it's not exactly how I remembered it.'

Adam cast his mind back. Two years ago the gap in the jungle horizon on the Nicaraguan side of the river had been distinct and unambiguous. Since then it seemed loggers had paid a visit here and the river junction now looked entirely different: acres of mud dotted with the flat tops of shorn tree stumps. He steered the canoe over towards the muddy expanse, looking for the distinct thread of green-hued water merging into the coffee brown of the Coco.

'Not lost, are we?' Liam called from the other canoe.

'It's all different,' he replied. 'Give me a moment, I'll get my bearings.'

The tributary was small, much more than a stream, for sure, but not quite deserving of the term 'river'. And he recalled several other narrow rivers like it had fed into the Coco round about here. One of the young Zambu men pointed out across the flats.

Billy translated. 'He say . . . big rains last season. Change this very much.'

Two years ago three small branching tributaries had converged as they joined the Coco; the Green River had been the middle one. Now they all seemed to wind their own independent curving paths through the mud. Adam had no idea into which inlet to steer the canoes.

The young man pointed the way with his fishing spear.

'He say . . . that one.'

'Is he sure?' asked Maddy.

Billy sighed. 'This where they fish. He knows.'

Adam steered their canoes into a shallow inlet; the current was lazy and uncertain. They eased their way along a narrow channel so shallow that at times the bottom of the canoe hissed as it slid over the muddy bed, the note of the outboard engine changing in complaint as the propeller chopped through glutinous water as thick as milkshake.

Ten minutes later the mud banks were behind them; the jungle had crept back towards them and now flanked the river's edge. The broad fronds of guanacaste trees cast shadows over them, their drooping branches reaching out across the twenty-foot-wide river like grasping arms, almost reaching each other.

'This is it,' said Adam. 'I remember it being like this.'

The canoes puttered slowly up the tributary, one towed by the other, meandering in an endless languid zigzag, following the river's convoluted route, bend after bend. The water became green, just as Adam had said it would, thick with algae on the surface. With each turn in the river, it seemed to subtly narrow, the overhanging canopies of leaves and branches above them almost completely merging into one.

Midday, on cue, the blue sky seemed to vanish behind a veil of heavy grey clouds and within a few minutes the heavens opened up as if some divine tap had been spun open. Rain speared down on them sharply, drumming noisily on the stretched-hide hulls of the canoes. The river water dashed and danced; the jungle hissed and roared so loudly with the patter of millions of heavy raindrops on millions of leaves. They had to shout to hear each other. Adam pulled a large plastic cagoule out of his backpack and put it on. The young Zambu steering the lead canoe aimed them to one side, affording them at least some shelter from the relentless downpour.

Liam shivered miserably as he watched the rain. 'Who turned the cold tap on? I thought these jungle rainstorms were supposed to be warm like a bath.'

Bob turned to look at him. 'You are cold, Liam?'

'Bleedin' freezing!'

The support unit looked around for something to drape over him. He found nothing, so he wrapped one enormous arm round Liam's narrow shoulders.

'Ahhh, that's better, fella,' replied Liam, snuggling up to his body warmth.

'Sheeesh!' Maddy, sitting in the next canoe, pushed a sopping wet coil of hair out of her eyes. 'Hey! You two lovebirds want to go get a room or something?'

'Uh?' Liam stirred drowsily and looked over at her. She pursed her lips and made a kissy-kissy face.

'What? No!' Liam lurched out of Bob's tender embrace. 'Jayzus! Come on! I was just cold! I was just –!'

Bob's brow locked with a considered frown. 'Information: she is making a joke.' He raised his meaty arm and beckoned at Liam to come back and snuggle with him. 'I will keep you warm, Liam.'

'Errr . . . no, that's . . . no, I'm fine right here, Bob.'

Maddy cackled drily.

Adam was sitting beside her. 'What is it?'

'Sheeesh . . . I'm the only girl h-here,' she stuttered through chattering teeth, 'and it's *Liam* who g-gets the one frikkin' chivalrous gesture.'

He pursed his lips thoughtfully for a moment before raising his arm awkwardly. 'Do you want to . . . ?'

She nodded. 'Yeah . . . go on then, why not?'

Adam unzipped his plastic cagoule, pulled his arm out of the sleeve and shuffled up beside her, until their hips bumped. He wrapped it round her trembling shoulders. He zipped up his jacket again – zipping them in together. Then, uncertainly, he placed his arm round her waist. 'That . . . errr . . . that any better?'

She could feel the tendons and muscles in his arms flexing ever so slightly. Not just the dead weight of an arm at rest round her but something akin to a hug going on there. She could feel his cheek rest against the top of her head.

'This . . . this OK?'

She wanted to say it was actually somewhat more than OK. Wanted to turn her face up towards him – the subtlest of movements and the tip of her nose might just be touching his. They'd be close enough to feel the warmth of each other's breath on their cheeks. Another tiny movement, the slightest lean-in and they'd be . . .

Instead she merely nodded. 'Yeah. Better, thanks.'

Then she found herself wondering if one day she was going to regret not making a simple turn of her head.

CHAPTER 20

1889, London

What are we? Are we the problem? Or are we the solution? It was all so much simpler when we trusted Foster, when we trusted Waldstein's reason for setting up this whole thing. It made sense at the beginning. Keep history straight and true, otherwise . . . well, we've witnessed what 'otherwise' can be. But now Maddy's questioning it. All of it.

Sal looked up from her notebook at a cart laden with boxes of groceries rattling past her. Farringdon Street was busy, as it always was this time in the morning: traders setting up for the day, carts and wagons with goods heading to and fro, hansom cabs taking well-dressed gentlemen to their oh-so-important social engagements.

There was order here. Sitting out on the step, looking at a straightforward world of noises and smells, people hurrying on their way to jobs, or wearily walking home from long night shifts, things made sense. A clockwork world, of commerce, grit, grease and grime. A hard world, admittedly, but a reassuringly predictable world.

Back inside, in the dark, in the dungeon, things became complicated and unsure again. There were no certainties. Nothing could be taken as read. The future was as fluid and random as . . . they chose to make it.

That scared her. It felt like too much power, too much responsibility in their hands alone – in *Maddy's* hands alone, to be truthful.

I think we just have to trust Waldstein. I think he knows something we don't. I think only he has the Big Picture. We're just guessing at everything. And who knows what kind of a mess we could make of things.

She paused, her pen – her *modern biro*, just another example of how careless they were all becoming – poised above the paper. The world as it stood had a lifespan that was going to take it to the year 2070. No, not the world – *mankind*. The world, this planet, was going to carry on just fine without mankind around.

Sal pondered the years ahead.

So mankind has 181 years left from now. And Saleena Vikram, she'll be 65 when the end finally comes in 2070.

It wasn't a bad age to live to. A full-ish life. She nodded thoughtfully. That was her goal. To ensure that the young girl she'd glimpsed – the young girl she was 'copied from', that girl so full of life and hope and love for her father – got to live that life of hers. In the end, of the two of them, that girl's life was the one that counted.

'Penny for your thoughts, Miss Vikram?'

Sal turned round, jerked from her musings, and looked into the gloom of the viaduct's labyrinthine interior. Bertie was standing there, his head cocked curiously. 'I thought you might like a mug of coffee. And one of these . . .' He held out a paper napkin wrapped round something. 'Exceedingly tasty. Malt cakes.'

He stooped down beside her, looking curiously over her shoulder at the notebook. Sal snapped it shut. 'Just some silly poems,' she said quickly.

Bertie placed a warm mug in her hands.

'Thank you,' she replied. 'That's very kind.'

'Well!' Bertie puffed out his breath. A cloud curled in the air. 'It is rather chilly this morning.'

Sal looked down at the napkin bundle in his hand. She could sense it was something tasty; it smelled freshly baked and yeasty, and she realized how hungry she was this morning.

'That smells really good.'

CHAPTER 21

1994, Green River, Nicaragua

Liam stamped down hard on the rotten branch. It snapped like balsa wood with a loud crack. He bent down and picked up both halves and handed them to Bob to tuck into the bundle of firewood he was holding under one arm.

'. . . you know, I thought I was getting like you,' he continued. 'Thought I was beginning to think a bit like you.'

Bob looked at him. 'I do not understand.'

'All analytical, just like a computer. You know what I mean? Making judgements based on scores and variables and the like.'

Bob nodded. 'I understand. But your thinking process is far more advanced than mine.'

Liam cocked a brow. 'You're joking me, right?'

'Negative. The human mind is more adaptable and far more sophisticated. It is able to make leaps of intuition that a digital mind is incapable of doing.'

'Oh, come on, Bob, your computer does billions of clever things every second.'

'I can process 156 million calculations per second. But none of those calculations are, as you say, "clever". I find it difficult, for example, to tell you how I *feel*.'

'*Difficult*, you just said –' Liam looked up at him – 'but not impossible?'

Bob nodded. 'It requires the full resources of my AI, but . . .' He paused for a while to reflect on that. 'But I am able to construct only a basic simulation of an emotion. My AI has exceeded its performance expectations in this regard.'

'You've definitely become something more than a dumb bot.' Liam smiled. 'My baby boy's all grown up now.'

Bob scowled. 'That is a joke?'

'Aye. Well . . . sort of.'

Liam scooped up another branch of dead wood and handed it to the support unit. They gathered kindling in silence for a while before Bob finally spoke again.

'Your joke, Liam, is a valid metaphor for the state of my heightened AI functionality.'

'Uh?'

'I *have* grown up.'

Liam hesitated mid-stoop. Was there the ghost of a *tone* in his voice? A hint of the rebellious child challenging its parent? 'Well . . . that's good, Bob. That's very good.'

'I have been able to revise my mission parameters on several occasions. I have been able to assign my own mission objectives.'

Liam nodded. 'And we're all very proud of you, so we are.' He handed the support unit another branch. 'I wonder now . . .' Liam started, but then paused for thought.

Bob cocked his head, waiting for Liam to finish. 'You wonder what?'

'Well, I wonder if there'll come a time one day, when you'll break yer programmin' rules and disagree with a direct order? Hmm? Decide me or Maddy's wrong about something and just say "no" to us?'

Bob's eyes narrowed slightly. 'I am already able to do this. I have been able to for some time.'

'Really? You could *really* do that? Just say *no* to us?'

'Affirmative.'

'And yet . . . yet, you've never disobeyed me or Maddy, or Sal? Why's that? There must've been times we've told you to do something you thought was wrong . . . or just plain foolish?'

Bob smiled crudely. 'I have faith in your judgement.'

'Really?' Liam shook his head and bent down to pick up another fallen branch. 'Maybe you're not *that* smart after all then.'

'I have faith in your judgement, because it works on a higher cognitive level. You would call it *instinct*.'

'Guesswork, more like.'

'Your "guesswork", Liam, resulted in you managing to out-manoeuvre six support units of an identical production batch to myself. To date it has served you well. I repeat my earlier statement – I trust your judgement.'

'Right.' Liam handed him the branch.

'I no longer follow your orders because a line of code dictates I must. I follow your orders because I *choose* to.'

Liam looked sceptically at him. He was about to say something about the folly of the blind leading the blind when a solitary loud crack echoed through the jungle.

'What was that?'

They heard another one. 'Jay-zus . . . *Was that a gun firing?*'

'Affirmative.'

'Perhaps that was Billy hunting something?' suggested Liam hopefully.

Bob shook his head. 'The signatures of those two shots do not match his weapon type.' He looked at Liam. 'They came from a different gun.'

Liam led the charge, heading back the way they'd come, down a gentle incline through low-hanging vines that whipped painfully at his cheeks and thick undergrowth that threatened to tangle his legs at any moment. He led them down towards the river. He finally caught sight of the lime-green skin of algae covering the river water through the trees ahead.

Jay-zus . . . how far did we wander?

He stumbled out of the undergrowth and emerged into sunlight. He looked upriver. There in the distance, as the river – smooth, green and flat like a velvet carpet pathway – curved round to the left, he could see their two canoes pulled up on a muddy bank and the grey plume of smoke of their campfire meandering up into a clear sky.

But no sign of Maddy or Adam or either of the two young Zambu with them.

'Something's not right!' he called back to Bob.

The support unit staggered clumsily out of the jungle behind him and together they raced along the riverbank, splashing through shallow pools, ducking beneath low boughs and hopping over gnarled tree roots that curled like arthritic clawed fists reaching for the river.

Closer now, just a hundred yards upriver from them, he caught a glimpse of Adam's one-man orange nylon tent, but, as yet, no sign of anyone moving around. Liam ducked under one last low-hanging guanacaste branch and then raced up the rounded flat of mud that marked an ox-bow bend in this lazy tributary.

Ahead was their camp, the canoes, their three tents, their campfire – now burned down to little more than a collapsed pyre of charcoaled branches and ash – and beside it the clothes were still hanging from a loose frame of sticks lashed together, hung close to the fire to dry out from today's earlier torrential rain.

But what he saw next stopped him in his tracks. Lying beside the smouldering mound of ashes were the bodies of both the young Zambu men. Quite dead and lying side by side like a display of some proud fisherman's daily catch.

Bob drew up beside him. Then hastily hurried forward, squatted down beside the corpses and quickly inspected them.

'They are both dead, Liam. A shot to the back of their heads.'

Just like an execution.

'Oh, God . . . what the hell just happ–'

A high-pitched voice called out. Liam looked up and saw Billy emerging from the jungle beyond the protruding mud bank. His AK47 was in his hands, cocked and ready to fire.

For a moment Liam had a horrible thought. A thought that made him feel almost nauseous. Their guide had turned on them. Billy had decided that here and now was as good a time as any to turn on his clients, kill them and pocket that fat roll of American dollar bills he must have seen Maddy pull out of her bag several times already.

But, as Billy drew closer, Liam realized he'd judged the man unfairly. Their guide looked ashen, shaken. Not the ice-calm face of a murderer getting ready to finish off an unpleasant but necessary job.

'Billy?' he called back cautiously. 'Billy . . . what's just happened here?'

The guide hastened across the ground towards him, looking anxiously up and down the river, over his shoulder and back at the jungle. Finally, a few yards short, he lowered his gun. 'They come!'

'Who did? Who came?'

Billy puffed air for a moment, then said, 'Rebels. Bandits. They come . . .' He turned and pointed at the jungle he'd just emerged from. 'Take your friends away.'

Bob joined them. 'Are Maddy Carter and Adam Lewis alive still?'

Billy nodded. 'They kill the Zambu men – worth nothing to them. But your friends? They take them for money.'

CHAPTER 22

1994, somewhere in the Nicaraguan jungle

Inside the cloth hood they'd pulled down over her head, Maddy could see nothing. She was in a frightening, bewildering world of darkness. She could hear the brush of undergrowth, the thud of dozens of hurried, booted footsteps, the jangle of military webbing, an exchange of hissed voices in mixed languages. Some Spanish, some heavily accented English.

She felt a heavy hand thumping her back every now and then. Grasping her upper arm and guiding her around unseen obstacles. 'Move! Keep moving!' a voice growled at her.

She recognized the sound of Adam's breath nearby, gasping from the exertion. She heard him trip and tumble into undergrowth, the smack of a heavy blow and his voice crying out.

'OK! OK! Please . . . don't hurt me! Don't shoot!'

'Get up!'

On the blank canvas of her hood, she tried to picture what had just happened to them in the last five minutes. One moment, the four of them had been sitting around the fire – Billy had just excused himself to go empty his bladder. Adam had been telling her about his trip here two years ago. The two young Zambu were talking and giggling about something.

Then all of a sudden they were there. They'd arrived silently, almost materialized out of thin air. The first moment she sensed they were not alone was when Adam had suddenly stopped talking and his face had gone white. She'd turned round to see what he was looking at and saw them.

Two dozen men in threadbare and patched khaki greens, staring silently at them, like the emerald-hued ghosts of long-ago fallen soldiers. Every one of them armed, some wearing rusting belts of corroded ammo, some carrying machetes.

She looked around for Billy. There was no sign of him – just when they damn well needed him and his ancient-looking AK47. What happened next happened so quickly. The rebels advanced cautiously across the open space towards them.

Adam slowly stood up, raised his hands and showed them he wasn't holding anything. 'We're not armed! We're not armed!'

'We're just passing through,' Maddy added lamely.

One of the rebels had the tattered remains of some sort of regimental insignia on the collar of his olive-green tunic. His face was all beard, as black as night, and deep-set eyes shadowed beneath the peak of a crumpled old US army forage cap. She presumed he was their leader.

He drew up in front of Adam and Maddy, silently appraised them for a moment. 'English? American?'

'I – I'm British,' said Adam quickly. 'We were . . . we were just stopping for a bit.' He tried a disarming smile. 'We can move on if – you know – if you want to camp here?'

The leader ignored that. Turned and spoke over his shoulder to the men behind him. A quick stream of heavily accented Spanish between them. The men responded immediately, moving to look inside the tents, unzipping them and dragging the contents out.

'Help yourself,' said Adam. 'Please. Take – take w-whatever you need.'

The leader grinned. 'We will.'

One of the men wrenched the backpack roughly from Maddy's hands and delved inside it. It didn't take him long to find the roll of dollar bills. He tossed it across to his leader who inspected it for a moment before tucking it into an ammo pouch.

The men were quick and efficient with their pilfering. Bagging their food, their water bottles. Some of them helped themselves to the items of clothing they came across; socks seemed to be of particular interest to them.

'We are finished here,' said the leader. 'We will go now.'

For just one moment, Maddy thought that was it. Their ordeal over with. They'd come, taken what they needed and were going to be gone as quickly and silently as they'd arrived. But then the leader slowly strode across the clearing towards the two young Zambu men. He casually raised his handgun at one of the young men and shot him in the head; in a heartbeat he shot the other. Two shots as quickly and thoughtlessly as that . . . *pap, pap*. Both young men flopped lifelessly to the ground.

'Oh . . . my God!' Adam whispered as he gazed ashen-faced at the dead young men, the blood pooling in the mud beneath them. The leader calmly tucked the pistol back into his belt.

Then a coarse hood was tugged down over Maddy's head. She felt her arms being grasped roughly and yanked behind her back, rough twine wound round her wrists and cinched painfully tight.

She heard the man's voice again. 'We will leave now.'

It seemed like they were frog-marched several hours. Stumbling through the undergrowth blindly, it was hard to know. She could tell from the effort, the angle of the ground beneath her feet that they were making their way up a gentle incline, heading away from the river into the low jungle hills that rose either side of it. They stopped for a rest just once, and then only briefly.

Her hood was lifted just high enough to expose her mouth. A flask of water was forced between her lips and although it tasted foul she gulped thirstily. Tilting her head back slightly, she looked down her nose beneath the hem of the hood, and thought she caught a brief glimpse of Adam's trainers.

The flask taken away, she caught her breath and whispered, 'Adam? Is that you?'

'Yeah, it's me. You all right?'

'I'm really scared.'

'Me too.'

She caught the faintest whiff of tobacco smoke, heard the men talking in hushed voices nearby.

'Where are the others?' hissed Adam. 'Do you think they're following us?'

God, I hope so.

'Liam and Bob won't abandon us,' she replied. 'I promise you that.' Although she couldn't be sure they'd know which way to go. These men were leaving tracks that could be followed, surely? Or maybe that was the sort of thing that only happened in movies: a keen tracker's eyes spotting a freshly snapped twig, the subtle impression of a footprint in the dirt.

'They'll be following us,' she said, not entirely sure they were. 'Biding their time, Adam. Trust me.'

A heavy fist punched the side of her head hard. 'No talk!'

She saw pinpricks of light, felt her balance go, and all of a sudden she was lying on her back, her head spinning, her ear on the side she'd been punched roaring with white noise.

The hood was pulled roughly down. She felt hands grapple with her, jerking her on to her feet. It seemed their rest was now over and they were on the move again.

They marched uphill for another couple of hours and, finally, she was relieved to feel the incline become flat ground, the uneven jungle floor – all thick, foot-snaring roots, tangled creepers and spongy, yielding dirt – become firm and even.

Different sounds now. The jungle noises had receded.

We're in a clearing.

The hooting, chirruping noise of the jungle had been replaced with the sound of some sort of a camp. She heard more voices, men calling out to each other. The chopping of wood, the dull *thung* of a cooking pot being banged nearby, pop music on a tinny transistor radio. The crackle and spit of a fire. And it was getting cool now. She supposed it must be near nightfall, or dusk at the very least.

Finally she heard the rattle of a latch and felt the hands of her captor shove her forward on to the ground. She felt the same hands pull the twine painfully tighter as she was tied to something. She heard the clatter of a loose door, then . . . *then*, finally, sensed they'd been left alone.

'Adam? You there?'

No answer.

'Adam.'

She held her breath for a moment, hoping that she might hear his laboured breathing coming from nearby. But she heard nothing.

'Crap,' she muttered, wanting her quiet voice to sound vaguely defiant: the spirited young heroine spitting venom at her tormentors. It didn't. It sounded warbly and thin and fearful. At least not *tearful*. She was damned if she was going to sob like a little girl.

Yet.

CHAPTER 23

1994, Nicaraguan jungle

It was getting dark now. Too dark for them to risk stepping off the narrow jungle trail they'd been following so far. They could veer a yard or two from it in the dark and run the risk of never finding it again.

So far, by the green filtered light of afternoon, even Liam had been able to follow the trail left by the men: a groove worn in the damp soil by several dozen army boots; twigs, vines and branches hacked away by machetes to keep the way clear. Billy told them this was more than likely a trail regularly used by the rebels. He explained that the few militia groups that still remained at large in the jungle were largely nomadic, constantly moving between established camps and caches to minimize the risk of being cornered by Nicaraguan troops. This trail, provided they didn't wander from it, would almost certainly lead to one of their camps.

Although Liam had been eager to press on, to not stop for *anything*, it made sense to settle down where they were and continue the pursuit again at first light.

So they did. No fire, no food, just some much-needed water from their sloshing canteens, and then Liam found himself curled up on the jungle floor between Bob and Billy, looking up at the dark shifting shapes of the leafy canopy above and catching the occasional glimpses of the clear evening sky beyond:

a salmon pink of combed-out thread-like clouds that deepened in the space of an hour to a night-time blue peppered with stars.

He could hear the deep, even bellows-like rustle of Bob's breathing. Not sleeping, but perhaps the closest to it the support unit would ever know. He knew Bob would be devoting a portion of his consciousness to collating data – his memories – grouping theme- and category-linked recollections, ditching irrelevant, frivolous or duplicated ones. Cross-referencing important ones and trying to extract a deeper understanding from them, to know this world better.

To know himself better.

Liam recalled what the support unit had told him earlier that afternoon: that he no longer functioned within the strict binary limitations of his original installation code. That to all intents and purposes he could *almost* be regarded as an individual in his own right now, capable of deciding his fate, his goals . . . perhaps on some level even deciding how he *felt*. On one hand, Liam decided that was quite an unsettling notion, that something as big, unstoppable and lethal as Bob could set his own agenda – make his own choices. But on the other hand – and this was the phrase Bob had used – he *chose to follow their orders*.

He chose to.

Bob had told him he trusted their judgement. Perhaps there was something more comforting in that? Bob's co-operation, his *compliance*, was now built on something more than a mere program routine, a line of code, that (let's face it) could just as easily misfire or go wrong as any piece of technology. No, his dogged, unfailing reliability was built on whatever passed as *affection* in his digital mind.

'You wake, Mr Connor?'

Apparently Billy was awake too.

'Yes. I'm finding it quite difficult to get to sleep actually.'

The guide turned over on to his side. 'There were many of them. I see this. Many.'

'You saw them? The men who took Maddy? I thought you said you missed them? You said you were away in the jungle relieving yourself when they came?'

'I . . . return . . . I . . .'

Liam understood. 'You were hiding?'

He saw the dark outline of Billy's large head nodding. 'I stay in jungle. I – forgive me, Mr Connor. I . . . I just watch. I let them go.'

Liam heard the shame in the man's voice. Shame. He knew that feeling all too well: the fear of the moment castrating any ability to act, to step into the breach. Freezing a man and leaving him useless and irrelevant to unfolding events.

'I seen twenty, thirty of them. All have gun. If I come out . . . they shoot me dead. No problem. So I stay hidden.'

'It's all right. There was no sense in charging out. There's *courage*, Billy, and then there's *plain stupid* . . . and a fine line dividing the two.' Liam recalled Rashim's several acts of derring-do back in the seventeenth century that might have made worthy material for a heroic poem or sea-shanty, but could quite easily have spelled the end for their ship and crew.

'Fact of the matter is you're still alive and able to help us find them. We'll track them down.'

'What is plan? When we find them?'

Jay-zus . . . I don't know. As always seemed to be the case, there was no plan. Just the sense of travelling in the slipstream of a runaway problem and hoping there was a chance to have a grab at the rear bumper.

'We'll find them first, Billy . . . then I suppose we'll work out what we're going to do then.'

Billy grunted, then settled back on the ground. After a while

Liam could hear his deep, even breathing. The guide was clearly well used to making do with the jungle floor for a bed.

A plan? The best plan Liam suspected that he was likely to come up with was simply unleashing the full wrath of Bob on those rebels, like opening a bear's cage on an unsuspecting audience. But perhaps they were going to have to be clever about it. Not some half-baked roar and charge into their camp but a *ruse*, some distraction to draw the rebels' attention and firepower elsewhere. After all, Bob *could* be brought down with enough guns levelled at him. It had happened before. And if Billy was right, and these fellas were all carrying big guns of one sort or another . . . ?

He fell asleep trying to figure out what they were going to do once they caught up with the rebels, half aware that any plan he conjured up was likely to fall apart in the first few seconds.

CHAPTER 24

1994, the rebel camp, Nicaraguan jungle

The hood was removed from Adam's head. His eyes blinked and watered at the light of the desk lamp sitting on a wooden crate beside him.

'Yes, you must let your eyes adjust.' He recognized the voice of the leader. 'Are you thirsty? Some water?'

Adam nodded. His mouth was dry. He looked around as the rebel leader poured some water into a glass. They were in a tent. No, it looked more *permanent* than that – a wooden shack, with a canvas roof. In one corner a cot and a desk. Some wooden crates, a cheap radio, an old black-and-white TV, a battered filing cabinet.

The man held the glass of water to Adam's mouth. 'You said you are British?'

Adam gulped it down. 'Yes,' he replied finally.

'Good.' The man smiled. 'I like Britain very much.' The leader's thick beard parted and revealed a spread of tobacco-stained teeth. 'As a young man I went to school there. Very good school. Very expensive. Winchester? You know of it?'

'I've heard of it.'

'You like football?'

Adam shrugged.

'I love your football. My favourite team is the Manchester United. Very good.'

'They're rubbish. I'm more of a Manchester City fan, myself.'

The rebel leader looked at him sternly for a long moment, then without warning he laughed and slapped Adam on the shoulder. 'I think you are joking with me, yes? Because these two teams are the natural enemies of each other?'

Adam nodded.

'I am Colonel Alvarez. Manuel Alvarez. And tell me please, what is your name?'

'Adam.'

Alvarez unbuckled the gun holster from his hip, pulled up another stool and sat down on it. 'Well, Adam, I think I like you. You have *cojones*.'

Adam looked around the room. There were maps on the desk, a signed photograph of President Reagan. 'You're Contra rebels?'

Alvarez's brow wrinkled, a momentary glassy look in his eyes. A hand absently reached out for the gun, pulled it from the holster. Adam recalled then how casually, how completely without any delay or deliberation, he'd executed the two young Zambu men.

'We do not call ourselves that. We are freedom fighters.'

'But the war's finished now.'

Those killer's eyes glared at him as the fingers absently stroked the gun's cross-hatched grip. 'The war continues, until we overthrow the communists who have taken over my country.'

'And you take back what is rightfully yours?'

He kicked himself. *Careful, Adam. Be very careful.* The man was capable of killing without warning.

'Rightfully? Yes.' Alvarez rubbed the cuff of his frayed army tunic on the gun's breech, carefully wiping it clean of moisture. 'My father was one of the generals. Our country was ruled very well. The people were happy, they had food. There was law and order.'

While the generals drove around in Mercedes and sent their children to expensive private schools, no doubt, Adam wanted to add, but the gun sitting in Alvarez's lap, being caressed, kept him quiet.

'They were better times for my country. Before the communists. Our country was a beautiful one. Now people starve, crime is everywhere.' Alvarez's eyes seemed to be glazing over, taking him somewhere else – the past. There was something about that that frightened Adam, as if, with Alvarez absent, it was his eager and restless hands that took temporary command and would decide his fate.

Adam decided to bring the man's focus back. 'Why have you taken us prisoner?'

The rebel leader stirred from his reverie. 'You are British. The girl is American. You have much monetary value to us. We will make a contact and demand a ransom for you both.' Alvarez smiled. 'Your governments will pay because it is bad for the news at home, hmm?'

'So, what? You're keeping us here until they pay?'

He nodded slowly. 'This is our most secret camp. We must remain here.' He sighed. 'Though, sometimes, I would rather not be here.'

Those eyes seemed to be glazing over again, looking past Adam into the darkness. The hands grew restless once more, turning the gun over and over in his lap.

'Why?' asked Adam. 'Tell me why not?'

Alvarez looked directly at him. 'Because there are ghosts here.'

'Ghosts?'

Alvarez nodded slowly again. 'Ghosts of the ancient ones.'

★

'I think he's completely mad.'

Maddy shuffled round on her buttocks to try to face Adam, not easy given they were both tied, hands behind their backs, to the very same wooden post.

She spoke over her shoulder. 'Because he believes in *ghosts*?'

'That, and he's really . . . I dunno, *edgy*. No, that's not the right word. He just seems *unstable*, on the edge, like he's on the verge of a nervous breakdown.'

'That doesn't sound good.'

'He's grabbed us for ransom money. Right. But no kidding, I get the feeling if we even look at him funny, or the idea just pops into his head, he might just whip out his gun and –'

'I get it, thanks.'

The shack where they were being held was dark. Outside, through gaps in the slatted wood, they could see night had fallen. A single floodlight on a tripod, powered by a sputtering generator beside it, illuminated the camp with a harsh unremitting glare. They could hear the men, gathered nearby, chatting, laughing, the clack of dominoes or dice. A radio was playing the Rolling Stones.

'They will come for us, won't they?'

'Of course,' she replied. *Tonight*, she suspected. *They'll come under the cover of darkness. Right?* They almost certainly were somewhere out there in the jungle, looking down on the camp in the clearing and planning their raid, right now. They had to be. Surely.

'Don't get too comfortable there,' she added with a forced smile. 'They'll be here any moment now. I promise.'

CHAPTER 25

1994, the rebel camp, Nicaraguan jungle

They were roused by the door to their shack being wrenched open. Maddy jerked awake with a mucus-thick squawk.

Morning sunlight flooded in over the shoulders of someone standing in the doorway.

'Liam?' she uttered hopefully.

The figure came inside, squatted down between them and untied them both from the wooden pole. The man stank of stale sweat and cigarettes. Another rebel was lurking outside the shack, gun levelled at them.

Hands untied, the first one stood up and backed out of the doorway. 'Up! You get up! You come outside. Use toilet!'

'About time,' she mumbled. 'I'm bursting.' Wearily, both Adam and Maddy got to their feet and shaded their eyes as they stepped through the low doorway and emerged outside.

A dazzlingly bright, sunny morning.

'What was it you said? "*Don't get too comfortable*",' Adam whispered to her, '"*they'll be here any moment now*."'

'All right. So I was wrong,' she muttered in reply.

One of the rebels shoved the butt of his gun into her ribs, hard. 'You no talking!'

She yelped with pain, then, winded by the blow, she

dropped to her knees. Their guard hesitated for a second, watching her struggling for breath, long drawn wheezing gasps, and whimpering pitifully as she tried to get some air into her lungs.

'Get up!' he shouted, raising his gun to hit her again.

'Christ!' Adam snapped. 'Go easy on her!' The guard turned and glared at him. 'Can't you see? She can't get her breath!'

He hunkered down beside her. Her glasses had come off and were on the ground. 'Maddy, you OK?' He grabbed them, wiped mud off the lenses and put them on her pale face.

She nodded. 'Just caught me . . . by . . . surprise. I'm OK.' She licked dry lips and pulled in another rattling, wheezy breath, then finally nodded at him that she was all right. 'Don't provoke him, Adam . . . I'm fine.'

'You get up!' shouted the guard.

'OK! OK! Gimme a second!'

Adam helped her to her feet. Wobbly for a moment, she found her balance. 'I'm OK now.' She looked warily at the guard, little more than skin, bones and olive-coloured rags. And a scar running down one side of his face and disappearing into the bristles of his beard. 'Better let go of me, Adam, before Scarface here loses it again.'

'You're OK? You can walk?'

She looked at him. 'I need a pee. I'll walk anywhere!'

Scarface led the way across the camp, now stirring to life as sunlight pierced the steaming jungle canopy with diagonal shards of light that angled down through the leaves and the ground with dappled smudges of light and shade.

'Here!' the rebel said. They were standing beside a sheet of corrugated iron, propped up between two oil drums: an improvised shoulder-high screen. Nothing more. Before it were several buckets, two of them full, another half full.

'This is it?' she whispered.

Adam went first. Peeing into the bucket as he surveyed the camp over the screen. There were about a dozen makeshift tents, shacks, lean-tos. The chassis of a rusting jeep. Beneath an awning guns were stockpiled. Many of them looked old, Vietnam War-era weaponry, and quite probably – with all the moisture in the air – corroded beyond use.

He finished his business as he noticed their toilet visit was starting to attract attention. Heads turning their way. Several of the men clambered off their hammocks and craned their necks to get a better look.

'You go now!' said Scarface to Maddy.

She looked helplessly at him. 'I can't go right *here*!' She looked at the men, now edging their way to get a peek round the side of the screen. 'I can't go with everyone staring at me!'

Scarface's eyes widened. He glared at her. His hand reached for a knife tucked into his belt. 'You go now, or I cut you!'

'Jesus,' Adam hissed at him. 'Let her have some privacy!'

Scarface just grinned and pushed her roughly towards the buckets. Maddy positioned herself beside one slowly, closed her eyes, her cheeks mottled pink with shame and misery. Several tears spilled down as she began to unbutton her jeans.

Adam shook his head angrily, pulled off his shirt and stepped towards her. He held it round her shoulders, the length of the shirt covering her as she squatted and went.

Scarface laughed and shook his head at the quaint act of old-school chivalry. Some of the men, who'd edged closer to get a look, lost interest now and turned away, going back to the things they'd been doing.

Finished, finally, she pulled her jeans up and nodded at Adam that she was good.

'Thank you,' she whispered as he put his shirt back on.

'Now, you . . . back!' Scarface barked at them.

'Hey? What about some food?' asked Adam.

Maddy nudged him. 'Don't push your luck with him.'

Scarface shoved Adam forward roughly. 'Food later! Now, go!'

As they walked back to their shack she noticed two things. Firstly, the tents, lean-tos and shacks seemed to have been built up against supporting boulders of lichen-covered stone. But not boulders, as such; they were rounded and weather-worn but still clearly, once upon a time, they'd been *sculpted* stone. And there, on the large one beside the rusting jeep chassis, she thought she could make out the slightest dented impression of a carved design of some sort.

The other thing she noticed was a distant long, flat-topped ridge of rock poking out of the jungle canopy and looking down on them. A mile, maybe two miles away. Hard to judge, in fact. The shame of moments ago, of her enforced public performance, was forgotten for now.

Maddy bumped his arm lightly. 'Adam!' she whispered. 'Is that . . . ?'

In front of her, she saw the back of his head nod quickly.

He's seen it too. She looked up at the distant ridge. The front of it seemed almost sheer, a cliff-face. *My God, this is the place!*

Scarface led them back inside their hut, had them both sit down with their backs to the pole and once again he tied their hands behind them and attached them to it. 'Food, soon,' was all he grunted at them before he left the shack and closed the door on them.

'This is exactly where we camped, two years ago,' said Adam quietly. 'These are those Mayan-era ruins I told you about.'

'And that ridge?'

She felt his shoulder move against hers as he nodded. 'Yup, that's the one I climbed. The cave's right up there.'

Goddammit! We're so frikkin' close!

CHAPTER 26

1994, outside the rebel camp, Nicaraguan jungle

The trail led them *most* of the way there. But it was the smell of burning wood that helped them zero in on the rebels' camp.

They'd been observing the cluster of tents and lean-tos from a gently sloping hillside overlooking the clearing for the last five minutes.

'It's hard to say,' Liam said after a while. 'I've counted about thirty of them down there, so. There could be more. What do you reckon, Bob?'

'I have identified thirty-six individuals,' he replied. 'It is possible there are more.'

Billy chewed agitatedly on the stem of his pipe. 'We are just three men. We have only one gun.'

'I know, I know.' Liam nodded. 'Those aren't such great odds. But, well . . . Bob here, he's worth an army on his own.'

Billy glanced at the support unit. 'He is big, strong man, yes. But he is not like the hero, Superman. He can die.'

Liam was tempted to tell Billy something about Bob: that he was virtually the meat-and-bone equivalent of a Sherman tank. Almost. But Billy was quite right – a well-judged or lucky head shot could bring him down just as easily as anyone else.

'If you and me can draw some of their fire, Billy – provide a distraction, create some confusion down there – then he'll have a fair chance, so he will.'

Bob nodded. 'This is correct. I can sustain significant damage and still be fully functional.'

Billy splayed his empty hands. 'What are we distract with?'

A fair point. Between them they had *a* gun, a pair of hunting knives and a lot of good intentions. Not a great deal to work with.

Liam reluctantly reminded himself that he, also, was made like Bob. All right, he was no rumbling tank, he was slight in build and no stronger than anyone else his size, but he knew he could, *possibly*, take a bullet or two and survive where a normal human wouldn't.

Billy pulled the pipe out of his mouth. 'If we know which tent you friend are in . . . ?'

Liam nodded and finished Billy's thought. 'Bob will have a better chance.' A much better chance of surviving the cumulative wounding than if he was having to poke his nose into each and every tent looking for them while gunfire rained down on him.

A rather stupid idea was beginning to form in his head. But only because of what he knew about himself. Knew, now, what damage he could take and survive. The Liam of old, the Liam who thought he was merely an *ordinary* young man – human, not engineered – would quite rightly have told him this was up there with some of his stupidest plans.

'I've got an idea,' he said.

Adam could hear her breathing. Was she asleep?

'Maddy? You awake?'

'Uh-huh.'

'You've said this once or twice already . . .'

'Said what?'

'That we meet again, when I'm older. That we worked together.'

He felt her shoulder shift as she nodded.

'So?' he asked.

'So . . . what?'

'So, what am I like in seven years' time?'

'Different. Very different.'

He twisted to look at her over his shoulder. 'You can't just say that. Tell me more.'

Maddy shrugged, the rope bonds creaking as she shifted. 'Well . . . for a start you smartened up one helluva lot. You're all expensive designer suits and stuff.'

He snorted at that. 'Yeah, right. Me in a suit.'

'Seriously. You were working in corporate IT security in the World Trade Center. By the look of your swish Manhattan apartment, I guess you were making a lot of money out of it.'

'And what work did we do together? How did I help you?'

She was a long time replying. Adam suspected she was deliberating on how much she could let herself reveal. 'You helped us figure out how to decode the Holy Grail.'

'And then?'

'Then we had to say goodbye.' She paused. 'I had to let you go back to work.'

'You didn't come back to me any time earlier and correct history? Make it so I'd never meet you in the first place?'

'No.'

'Why not?'

He felt her shoulders shift again but she said nothing.

'C'mon, why not?'

'Can we just leave it at that, Adam? The less I tell you, the better.'

'Time contamination?'

'Yeah. That's it. Trust me . . . it's simpler if I don't tell you any more.'

'I have a right to know.'

'If I tell you your future, you'll make different choices, Adam. That's inevitable. If you make different choices, then that has a knock-on effect on other things. You might not turn up in 2001. We might not get your help with those documents . . .'

'The Holy Grail? The Voynich?'

'Yes. So things could be totally different now. Totally different.'

'Would that be so bad?'

She didn't answer that.

'And when we finished our work together . . . you just let me go?'

'Yes.'

'Trusted me not to tell the world about what I knew? About you lot? About time travel?'

She was silent for a while before finally answering. 'Yes . . . I trusted you not to talk.'

Liam stepped out warily from the edge of the jungle and into the camp's clearing.

Brass it out, Liam. Remember, loud and cheerful . . . and ever so slightly mad.

He cupped hands around his mouth and hooted at the top of his voice. 'Hoy! Hellooo there! You big fellas with yer big guns! I'm over here!'

His voice echoed around the camp, bouncing off the jungle perimeter and back at him. 'Yoo-hoooo!'

He intended to give the impression of some sort of jungle

madness. At the moment, though, he was vaguely aware he was coming across as merely idiotic. He decided to stagger and fall to his knees for added effect. Kneeling in the rain-wet mud, he clasped his hands together and looked up at the sky. 'Hallelujah! God be praised! I'm saaaaaved!! Civilization! At last!'

He saw men looking his way curiously. Putting down the things they'd been holding and reaching for their guns. Several of them emerged from beneath the cool shade of their awnings and approached him warily. The nearest of them drew up before Liam, a gun in his hands but not pointed threateningly. Not yet. 'Who are you?'

'Reverend O'Connor. Liam O'Connor.'

Other rebels joined the first, gathered in front of him and eyed him curiously. One of them stepped forward and squatted down in front of him. He wore a US army forage cap.

'You are American? I think? Is this right?'

'Irish,' Liam replied with a broad smile. 'The Right Honourable Reverend Liam O'Connor at yer service.' He offered a hand.

The man wearing the cap returned the smile but not the gesture. 'You are lost, friend?'

'Aye, I am that! And hungry and thirsty, so I am. Would you have something to drink on you, sir?'

He offered Liam his hip flask of water and Liam made a show of gulping it down.

'And you are alone, my lost friend?'

The flask was handed back. 'Aye. I came down the Coco River with a guide to set up my mission with the Zambus. We left the river and headed inland to look for the remotest wildest tribe we could find, to bring the word of God to 'em!' Liam shook his head sadly. 'But alas, despite my prayers, my guide fell sick and died on me, so he did!' Liam allowed his shoulders to shake with grief.

'I've been wandering these jungles for weeks, so I have. In circles no doubt. Praying for a miracle!' He reached for one of the man's cool limp hands, grasped it and mashed a kiss on to the back of it. 'And, by God, here you are! My miracle!'

The man's smile broadened. 'My men will, of course, look after you.'

He stood up, turned and issued some orders to his men, then began to stride back to his tent.

'What do you think's going on out there?' Maddy wriggled to see through the slats better.

'Sounded English, I think. I'm sure I heard a word or two of English being shouted out there.'

They heard the men outside jeering and laughing. Something was amusing them. Maddy adjusted her position slightly and managed to see through a gap. The men were gathered in a loose cluster around something . . . or someone. Then she heard a loud crack, unmistakably the sound of fist on skin, followed by a howl of pain.

'Jesus, they're beating someone up out there!'

And again, another crack and another howl, followed by a plea for mercy. She saw one of the men emerge from the crowd, sweating and laughing. Another stepped in and the beating resumed.

'My God, they're animals!' The beating and the cries seemed to last an eternity, but probably only went on for five minutes. Eventually the gathered men seemed to lose interest and began to disperse.

Maddy shuffled on her bum, back against the wooden post again. 'Animals,' she hissed. 'What is it with men?'

'Hey . . . we're not *all* bad.'

She dipped her head against his shoulder for a second. 'I know.'

Presently they heard the heavy, lazy thud of boots approaching, the jangle of army webbing and loose keys, the mewling whimper of whomever had been beaten. And Scarface's voice. 'You! Quiet!'

The rattle of keys in the lock, then the door was kicked wide open. Scarface tossed the stripped-to-the-waist, bruised and bloody body on to the floor. He stepped in and tied the victim's hands to the post, then headed for the door. As an afterthought he swung a final swift kick at the poor young man's ribs before finally leaving.

Maddy leaned forward, trying to get a better look at their new fellow prisoner. In the glare of the sunlight streaming in through the open door, catching only a glimpse of his silhouette, she knew only that it was a slight, narrow-shouldered young man. But with a sinking heart, she thought she'd already recognized the voice crying out.

'Liam? It's not you . . . is it?'

Liam raised his head. His face was caked with wet blood, one eye swollen, a lip split and a gap at the back of his mouth where a tooth had been knocked out.

'Ahh!' He smiled. 'There you are, Mads!'

'Oh my God! You're . . . all beaten up!'

'Ah, I'm fine. Looks far worse than it is.'

'*What are you doing?* Just walking into their camp like that? That was stupid!'

He cracked a bloody grin. 'Thought it might be a good idea to come and rescue you.'

'Oh, Liam.' She leaned forward as far as her tethered hands would let her and dipped her forehead gently, affectionately against his. 'You're my brave hero.' She sighed. 'But you're also an idiot. Why did you do that? Why did you just –'

'It's all part of me big plan, Maddy.'

CHAPTER 27

1994, the rebel camp, Nicaraguan jungle

From afar Bob watched the beating going on, struggling desperately to suppress his instinct to charge down the jungle slope, burst out of the undergrowth like an enraged bull and tear the rebel soldiers limb from limb. His frustration became a deep rumbling growl; a Rottweiler on a leash.

Billy reached out and grabbed his thick forearm to steady him. 'Not yet. He said we must wait . . . see which place they take him to.'

And now they'd witnessed Liam being dragged towards a wooden shack, they knew.

'We must proceed immediately,' said Bob.

Billy tucked his pipe into a pocket. 'I must move closer in.' He patted the taped-up butt of his battered assault rifle. 'My gun not very accurate, this far.'

Bob nodded. 'I will proceed with the rescue when you commence shooting.'

He watched the guide carefully pick his way downhill through the undergrowth until he was lost from sight. The plan, Liam's plan, was relatively straightforward. Once they'd identified where the rebels were holding Maddy and Adam, Billy would work his way around to the opposite end of the clearing, then, once in position, he would start firing. The hope being that the gunfire from the far side of the clearing would draw the rebels towards him, leaving fewer of them guarding their hostages. Bob would then race down, deal with any rebels in his way, rescue the others, and then they'd disappear back into the jungle and rendezvous a mile downriver.

Bob began to pick his way downhill, bringing him closer to the edge of the thick jungle, but still far enough back that he was hidden from view by the shadows and undergrowth.

He found a place to crouch down and wait. His internal clock ticking through seconds, then minutes, as he waited for Billy to get into position and start firing. He proceeded to catalogue and assess the hostiles in front of him. The priority target was a heavy machine-gun, support legs propped on top of an untidy 'U' of sandbags. It was twenty yards away from the shack where Liam and Maddy were being held. He decided the two men idly manning it, chatting and smoking, would be his first take-down. The heavy-calibre weapon was his biggest threat; that thing could deal out damage enough to bring him down. It also presented him with an opportunity.

He waited. His clock now indicated that four minutes, fifty-three seconds had elapsed since Billy had disappeared from sight. A possible scenario was that their guide might be down there, somewhere in the camp, and right now telling the rebels they were about to be ambushed. Telling them precisely where Bob was hiding.

He was about to evaluate the probability of that when the air of calm over the camp was shattered by the distant crack of several shots.

Like a termite mound roused with a hearty kick, the camp immediately stirred to life. Men stumbled out of their shacks and tents and scrambled for their weapons.

More shots. Bob watched as the rebels looked in all directions at once, attempting to identify exactly where the shots were coming from. By sound alone it was impossible to pinpoint: the crack of Billy's gunfire echoed around the clearing like a casino ball looping a roulette wheel.

One of the guide's shots finally found a target. A rebel dropped to the ground clutching at his belly. One less to deal with; however, the rest of them now had a clear indication of which direction the gunfire was coming from. The rebels quickly spotted a faint tendril of blue-grey smoke wafting up from the undergrowth.

Once more, Bob checked on the two men manning the heavy machine-gun. They'd tossed their cigarettes aside and were now repositioning the weapon's support struts to aim it across the camp and towards where Billy's shots were coming from.

Bob rose to his feet and hurled himself forward, down the last few yards of slope, through thinning undergrowth, and emerged into the glare of sunlight: a bull-sized mass of sweat-glistening muscle, moving with the eager haste of a dog chasing a tennis ball.

He was halfway towards the sandbag emplacement before the two men there registered the approaching threat. The heavy, perforated gun barrel was swinging towards him just as he reached them. He vaulted over the sandbags and landed heavily on the rebel manning the gun. The other man dropped the chain of ammo he'd been getting ready to feed into the breech and attempted to flee.

But not quickly enough.

Bob – still sitting on the broken and crushed corpse of the other – managed to wrap his thick fingers round the man's ankle. With an enraged grunt, he lifted the hapless man up into the air and swung him round in one lazy loop above his head, the crack and snap of ankle tendons and cartilage sounding like bubble wrap being twisted. The second loop ended abruptly as Bob brought him down again and smacked him head first into the sandbags.

Bob wasted no time getting to his feet and hefting the heavy machine-gun off its support legs. He adjusted the grip in his left hand, bracing the weapon firmly against his hip. With the other hand he pulled several yards' worth of the ammo belt out of the magazine box and draped it round his bull neck, down his right arm where it dangled in a loop before snaking up into the weapon's breech.

Bob strode across the clearing towards the shack where Maddy, Liam and Adam were being held. Halfway there, one of the rebel soldiers turned and spotted him. Voices barked across the clearing and, a moment later, guns from the far side of the camp began sputtering fire his way.

He stopped, turned to his right, and calmly pulled the trigger.

The machine-gun kicked against his hip like a jackhammer as he picked one target after the next in quick succession; short heavy-calibre bursts hurled rebel after rebel on to his back, leaving a crimson aerosol puff of blood hanging in the air where they'd stood a split second earlier.

Those rebels still standing dived for cover as Bob resumed crossing the clearing and approached the shack. Within seconds they began firing back. Rain-damp ground erupted geysers of dirt at his feet. His cotton shirt flickered and danced and sprouted crimson splotches as several shots found their target.

He reached the shack. Both hands busy firing and feeding the weapon, and there being no time to put the machine-gun down and deal with the padlock on the door, he decided dealing with it was a waste of precious seconds. With one booted foot he kicked at the side of the wooden-slat shack. The whole ramshackle structure wobbled and creaked for a moment before collapsing in on itself with the sound of snapping timbers.

Another shot smacked heavily into his shoulder.

Bob focused his attention on dealing with the gunfire coming his way. Liam and the others could pick themselves out of the ruins of the shack. Right now he had hostiles to deal with – first priority: three men firing from behind a stack of milled lumber. Bob let loose a sustained staccato burst that sent an instant blizzard of splinters and shards, and a finer cloud of sawdust, spinning into the air.

He eased off the trigger to check the result. A solitary bloody hand flopped into view and down on to the ground from behind the now-shredded pile of wood.

[Threat neutralized]

He turned to his right. There were four more men firing at him, taking turns from behind a cluster of old rusting oil drums. Again he aimed and fired. Sparks danced like mayflies and flakes of rust spun into the air and showered to the ground. Then all of a sudden there was a percussive thump as one of the barrels exploded, launching debris into the air, carried aloft by a dirty rolling orange cloud of flame and black smoke that mushroomed into the sky.

Bob eased his finger off the trigger.

[Threat neutralized]

He swung the barrel round; there was a third cluster of viable targets. He was about to take aim at the rebels who'd been firing from behind the stripped-down chassis of a rusting jeep, but they were already on their feet, weapons tossed aside and running for the edge of the jungle. He gave a moment's consideration as to whether they might be a future threat to deal with, and decided they just might. He aimed a short burst at the upper back of each fleeing man and seconds later they were nothing more than burger meat in tattered khakis lying in the long grass, waiting to be picked over later that night by the jungle's nocturnal scavengers.

[Threat neutralized]

Another oil drum exploded with a thump that rocked Bob on his feet. Ignited diesel fuel rained down on the thatched roof of a nearby shack, quickly setting it on fire, and soon a column of white smoke from burning wood and reeds joined the twin pillars of black oil smoke twisting upwards out of the jungle.

At Bob's feet, the shattered timbers and slats of the lean-to he'd levelled with one swift kick began to stir. Maddy's head emerged first, the glasses on her nose askew, her face ghost-white with dust. Then Adam's and Liam's heads surfaced, just as a third oil drum erupted.

'Whoa!' Adam muttered.

Maddy nodded approvingly as she gazed at the boiling plume of orange flame darkening to a soot-black mushroom cloud. 'Good job.'

Liam looked around at the devastation. 'Supposed to be a subtle hit-and-run, so it was.'

The flames from the burning diesel had quickly caught several other shacks nearby on fire. From inside one they heard the crack and pop of what sounded like sporadic gunshots being fired. Liam, Maddy and Adam ducked back down into the mess of timber they'd emerged from.

'That is ammunition igniting from the heat. Not gunfire,' said Bob.

Their heads emerged once more and silently they watched as a lean-to nearby collapsed in on itself amid a shower of sparks and embers.

'Did you say hit-and-run?' said Maddy. 'I think he's managed to trash the entire camp.'

'Where's Billy?' asked Liam.

His question was answered by a high-pitched voice coming from the far side of the camp. 'Mr Bob! Do not fire! Is Billy!'

Smoke, black and acrid and stinking of burning rubber, drifted diagonally across the clearing and, a few moments later, Billy's squat outline emerged through it, his AK slung over his shoulder, the blade of a hunting knife in one of his hands. His face was spattered with blood; he was grinning from ear to ear. 'Very, very good fighting!'

He picked his way past smouldering debris on the ground and finally joined them. His eyes on Bob, in awe of him. 'You are, as Liam say . . . an army of one!' He noted the dark blooms of crimson on his shirt. 'This your blood? You are shot?'

Bob nodded casually. 'I have sustained six gunshot wounds. None will be fatal.'

'But there is very much!' Billy looked to Liam. 'Look! He is bleeding! We must –'

'He doesn't *do* bleeding,' said Maddy. 'Don't worry, he'll be fine.' She pulled herself to her feet and shook off the jagged shards of wood still clinging to her. She turned her back to Billy and showed him her still-bound hands.

'Now, Billy . . . you going to cut us free or what?'

CHAPTER 28

1994, ruins of the rebel camp, Nicaraguan jungle

'I count seventeen of them dead,' said Liam.

'Incorrect. Nineteen.' Bob nodded towards the camp's cookhouse. 'I located two more wounded hostiles over there.'

'Jesus!' said Adam. He looked accusingly at the support unit. 'You didn't just go over there and . . . ?'

'Finish them off?' Liam dabbed at the caked blood on his face.

Adam nodded.

Liam shrugged. 'That's, uhh . . . that's the kind of thing he does.'

Adam paled. 'My God.'

'Don't let's get all dewy-eyed over them,' said Maddy coolly. 'They weren't exactly saints.'

'But . . .'

'You said yourself, Adam, these are mercenaries. Ruthless killers.'

'I know, but . . . in cold blood? Just like that?'

'They are no longer a threat to you,' said Bob.

'Exactly.' Maddy surveyed the smoking remains of the camp. 'What about the others?'

'They go away,' said Billy. 'Leader is dead, see?' He pointed with his hunting knife at the body of Alvarez lying nearby. 'No leader . . . they go away. Not come back.'

'Well, good riddance then,' she said dismissively. She decided to clear her head and direct her thoughts to other matters. She turned to look above the surrounding canopy of tree tops. 'Over there? See that rocky ridge?'

Liam followed her finger. 'Aye.'

'According to Adam . . . that's it. This is where he and his field-trip buddies made camp a couple of years back. And that's the cliff-face where his cave is. Right?'

Adam was still looking at Alvarez's twisted corpse.

'Adam?'

He turned back to her. 'Sorry. Yes.' He nodded. 'That's definitely it.'

'How far away is it?'

'Two or three hours on foot.'

'It's not too late to start over there then?'

Billy shook his head. 'Night is not so good. Is better we wait for morning.' He turned away and walked across the clearing to see what supplies could be scavenged.

'Aye.' Liam was keen to agree with that. 'He's right. Anyway, might be a good idea to let them other rebel fellas get as far away as they can. Not sure I fancy stumbling across them in the dark.'

'Fine.' She pursed her lips. 'Then I guess we might as well flag-up our current location to Rashim and Sal.'

Liam nodded subtly towards Billy, who was now picking through the smouldering remains of one of the shacks. 'What about him? Are we going to let him see a portal open?'

She sighed. 'I'm far too tired and hungry to care who knows about who we are or what we can do any more. Anyway –' She pulled her glasses off her face and fiddled with one of the bent arms. The damned things didn't seem to want to sit straight across the bridge of her nose any more. 'Billy speaks Zambu, some other local languages . . . and he knows the jungle. He'll still be useful. We still need him. I say we let him in on things.'

They'd managed to retrieve their things from Alvarez's shack: her backpack and Adam's. She reached into hers now and pulled out the small walnut-sized metal case containing one of Rashim's beacons. 'Let's call it in, shall we?'

'What's the plan, Mads? Are we going back home, or are Sal and Rashim coming out here to join us?'

She'd stopped fiddling with the arm of her glasses. It had come completely off. 'Just great.'

'Mads?'

She looked up at Liam. 'I guess they might as well come out here. Since out here is where the answers are going to be, not back in London.'

'If there *are* any answers,' added Liam.

She let that go. 'Bob?'

'Yes, Maddy.'

'We should do something with the bodies. I don't want Sal seeing them.'

'Why should Sal not see them, Maddy?'

The poor girl seemed troubled enough. Maddy was beginning to wonder if Sal had been through more than she could handle; to wonder if she was damaged goods. She looked around at the twisted bodies – not too closely. Some of them were a horrible mess.

'Just do it, Bob. Toss them in the river and let the current take them away.'

The support unit nodded obediently. 'Of course.'

CHAPTER 29

1889, London

Sal bit into the crust of the malt cake. It was utterly delicious. Tangy and sweet and spiced up with hints of cinnamon.

'Do you like it?' asked Bertie.

She nodded, crumbs tumbled from her lips on to the doorstep. A terrier passing by on the street and off its rope leash hurried over and snuffled hungrily around her feet, on the step then the pavement below.

'Oy, Chocco! Get back over 'ere, you miserable little wretch!' shouted his owner. The dog turned tail and scuttled away.

'Mr Warburton, the baker down the street where I live, makes these for the cook girls who come in buying them for their guv'nors and ladies. Cost a pretty penny, these cakes do.' Bertie smiled. 'But I thought you might like to try one.'

The young man, the landlord's assistant, Bertie, reminded Sal just a little of what Liam used to be like when they first were getting to know each other back in Brooklyn: all old-world manners and gentlemanly consideration. Up until now they'd only ever passed each other, exchanged hurried pleasantries and stolen glimpses, sometimes even accompanied by a chaste smile.

This morning, however, he'd caught her on the doorstep watching life on Farringdon Street go by.

She smiled. 'It's really yummy,' she managed to reply, her mouth still half full.

Bertie finished his malt cake and then self-consciously licked the icing from his fingers.

She watched him and smiled. She decided she liked him. His bashfulness. His awkwardness. He seemed nice. Perhaps there might be a time for the two of them to get to know each other a little better. Maybe not right now. Maddy had her agenda, Liam seemed keen on that too . . . to once and for all chase down the answers to all their questions. And, of course, all Sal could do was tag along, despite her growing reservations that this was ultimately going to take them nowhere good.

But there would be an afterwards to all this nonsense, wouldn't there? Perhaps then there'd be some time for her to get to know Bertie.

She noticed he seemed particularly fidgety this morning. Something clearly on his mind. Something he wanted to ask.

'The doctor . . . ?'

'Rashim? What about him?'

'Would he be . . .? Well, that's to say . . . is he . . . ?' Without warning Bertie was blushing. It started with his ears, then crimson flooded from them across his pale cheeks. 'Is he your older brother?'

'What?' Sal giggled at that. 'No! He's just my . . . *friend*. My colleague.'

Bertie nodded vigorously. 'Ah, I see! Quite! Yes, indeed! Quite!'

Sal suppressed an urge to giggle again. 'Seriously? You thought he was my brother?'

'Well, you see . . .' Bertie fiddled with the chain of his timepiece. It looped from the top button of his waistcoat down to a pocket above his hip. 'You are both similarly brown people. I thought perhaps you were related in some way.'

She couldn't help but smile at his awkwardness.

'There are many brown people where I and Rashim come from, Bertie. We're not all related.'

He nodded, wagging his head vigorously. 'Yes, of course . . . I realize, that was a rather stupid question to ask. I . . . I am just curious about you. You are so very different to other people. In fact, all of you are so very –'

'SAL!' Rashim's voice echoed from behind her, from within the brick labyrinth beneath the Holborn Viaduct. 'SAL! Come quickly! We have a signal from them!'

A moment later Rashim emerged from the darkness into the faint pall of daylight leaking in from the side entrance on to Farringdon Street.

'Oh.' He stalled at the sight of Bertie standing in the doorway with her.

Sal shot him a warning glance. 'As you can *now see*, Rashim, I'm not alone.'

'Yes, uh . . . yes, you've got company.' He nodded politely. 'Good morning, Bertie. Do you mind if I borrow my, uh . . . my *assistant*? There is some work that needs to be done.'

Bertie deferentially tapped the peak of his cloth cap. 'Yes, yes, of course, Dr Anwar. Don't mean to get in the way of any of your experiments!'

Sal turned to Bertie. 'Sorry, I should go. Important things and all that.'

Bertie was nodding vigorously again. 'Yes, yes. I quite understand.'

'Another time perhaps?'

He looked confused.

'Cake?' She nodded at the balled-up paper napkin in his hands. 'And maybe even a cup of tea to go with it? You and me?'

Bertie understood what she was suggesting. Tea and cake.

Together. At some unspecified time. Soon. The last patches of his face not mottled pink finally coloured in to give him an even tone just a shade off lobster red. 'Yes, I . . . I would like that. A lot.'

Sal hurried back inside, followed Rashim as he led her through to their dungeon, ducking as they stepped through the low arched doorway and closed the thick oak door behind them.

Bertie stood alone on the doorstep, grinning like the Cheshire Cat. Quite thrilled by the fact that Miss Vikram had been the one to suggest another liaison. Not him. *Her.*

'I'll be damned,' he uttered with jubilant disbelief. 'We shall be having tea and cake together.'

So thrilled was he, in fact, that he almost didn't notice the key she'd left behind on the wooden stool beside the doorway. In her haste to return to work for Dr Anwar, she'd quite simply forgotten to take it with her.

The key. The key that unlocked that thick oak door that she and the others in her group were so careful to keep firmly locked *at all times*.

Bertie picked it up. He was about to call after her that she'd left it behind. But then he stopped himself. Two reasons. Now he had a genuine reason to knock and call for her. Perhaps on that occasion he could suggest a date and a venue for their tea together.

The other reason?

An insatiable curiosity to see what the devil it was those people got up to in that archway of theirs.

CHAPTER 30

1994, ruins of the rebel camp, Nicaraguan jungle

The early-afternoon return of the intense humid heat was unbearable, the sun past its zenith beating down on the jungle clearing. The like-clockwork 'noon monsoon' had arrived, pounded the world below into cowed submission then vanished, and now wisps of steam rose from the dark sodden dirt all around them.

'Oh, come on, Rashim!' muttered Maddy.

Adam looked at the metal casing in her hand. 'You're certain that tracker of yours actually works?'

'Yes, I'm sure. Here . . .' She handed it to him to take a look at. 'One of these things was on Liam when he got stuck back in the seventeenth century. God knows what it went through – salt water, *Thames water . . . ewww*!' She made a face. 'Countless piratey battles and probably had loads of sailor sweat and rum slopped over it.' She smiled. 'It still worked, even after all that.'

He turned it over in his hands. 'And it beams a signal?'

'Emits a tiny number of tachyon particles at a steady rate. Like a pulse.'

He nodded appreciatively at it. 'Impressive.'

'And made, more or less, from about twenty dollars' worth of RadioShack components.'

Adam grinned. 'If you released the design details in *CB Radio Ham Monthly*, every geek could go make himself one of these.'

She smiled at that. 'Which is precisely why I probably won't.' She turned to Bob. 'We got anything yet?'

'Negative.'

A dozen yards away, Liam was talking to Billy. Maddy and Liam had huddled together and revisited the question of whether they needed to keep their secrets from the guide. It was a short conversation that resulted in the same conclusion. Why bother? No one was likely to believe a half Miskito, half Hispanic, pipe-smoking old jungle tracker. But Maddy suggested it might be a good idea that they *prep* him with at least some information before the portal popped open in front of him. They didn't want him turning tail and running off into the jungle. Or worse: unslinging his assault rifle and emptying a whole clip of ammo into the thing.

She watched as Liam spoke quietly to him. She could see emotions on his face passing like scudding clouds as Liam explained things. One moment, the eyes in his toad-like face bulged wide, his jaw hung open, a dark 'O' of incomprehension. The next, he was frowning intensely, concentrating hard. The next . . . he simply chuckled.

She wondered what the hell part of '*We're time travellers from the future trying our best to work out whether this world is doomed or not*' would make the guide laugh.

Go figure.

'Maddy, I am now detecting precursor particles,' said Bob.

She sighed. 'About time!'

'What does that mean?' asked Adam. '*Precursor particles?*'

'Before we open a portal, we do a check to make sure we're not opening it in the middle of, say, a crowd of people.' She wrinkled her nose. 'That would be quite messy. Or opening it, say, in the middle of a mountain or bisecting something like a tree. That would result in whoever emerged becoming sort of "welded" with the tree. Again quite messy, and, of course, totally fatal. So we do a density scan. Basically a really tiny, pinhole-sized version of the portal where we can remotely take a look-see that there's enough open space to inflate the full thing. Sometimes we grab a snapshot image through that mini-portal. That allows us to see what sort of terrain we'd be stepping out into.'

Adam nodded. 'Makes sense.'

'Anyway, it's all good. It means they picked up our signal and they're just getting set to open it up.'

She looked across at Billy. Liam was probably telling him the very same thing, getting him ready for what was about to appear before them.

There was something vaguely *nostalgic* about watching another person witness this for the very first time, seeing their reaction: the look of incredulity on their faces, the dawning realization of what this meant – that time travel was actually for real.

It reminded her of the very different person she'd once been, now . . . what, over a year ago? A girl who believed she was just a computer games programmer, a code-monkey who designed user interfaces. A girl who believed she was living in a grubby studio flat in a rough part of Queens. A girl who believed she had family living in Boston, just a short one-hour flight away if she needed home comforts . . . a girl who believed she'd been rescued from certain death on one of those regular city-to-city flights back home.

Watching Billy's face made her homesick for the person she'd once – not so long ago – been.

'Information: I am detecting a tachyon surge . . . there . . .' Bob pointed at a patch of ground five feet away from them.

'Keep your eyes on where he just pointed!' she called across to Billy. 'That's where it will appear!'

Liam carried on talking, she saw him draw the shape of a circle with his hands. They waited expectantly, silently, for ten, fifteen seconds; even the hooting and birdsong coming from the jungle seemed to settle down ever so slightly, as if every creature within was holding its breath with anticipation and staring out, hoping to catch a glimpse of this impossible thing.

Then, without warning, she felt that familiar puff of displaced air on her face. For a second she closed her eyes against the blown-up grit and dirt, then opened them again.

The sphere hovered before them, the familiar oil-slick interference running across its surface, making spirals and twisted renditions of the three figures waiting in the dark on the other side of chaos space.

'Bob, go tell them to come through. We can discuss things out here.'

'All of them?'

She gave it a moment's thought. 'Yeah, why not? Leave SpongeBubba behind and make sure the archway door's locked. And tell computer-Bob to give us an hour then open another window.'

'Affirmative.'

Bob stepped into the portal. His silhouette became part of the convoluted pattern for a moment. Maddy shot a glance at Billy and struggled to stop herself smiling at the goggle-eyed expression he was now pulling.

She noted Liam was smiling at the sight of that too.

A minute passed and then finally she saw movement in the undulating oil slick. Rashim emerged first, instantly frowning and blinking at the impossibly bright sunlight. Sal followed him out, doing likewise, shading her eyes with both hands. Then

Bob and finally Becks emerged. Behind them the portal collapsed in on itself and vanished with a soft pop.

She couldn't help but smile at their clothing. Of course, none of them had expected to be coming through. So they were still dressed in their Victorian attire: Rashim in his dapper velvet waistcoat and crisp white morning shirt; Sal and Becks in their long layered skirts and bodices. They reminded her of old colonial-era explorers: impractically dressed, determined to maintain some decorum and hold on to that legendary British stiff upper lip despite the sweltering heat and glare of the mad-dog sun.

Adam was laughing with delight, amused by the very same thing. He stepped forward and presented a hand to Rashim. 'Dr Livingstone, I presume?' he announced boldly.

Rashim looked utterly perplexed. 'No . . . uh no. It's Dr Anwar, not Livingstone. You recall, we have already met, you know, Adam . . . a few hours ago?'

CHAPTER 31

1994, ruins of the rebel camp, Nicaraguan jungle

Rashim took a swig from Maddy's water flask and wiped away the beads of sweat gathering on his forehead. 'Good God, it is hot here.'

'Aye, it's the humidity,' replied Liam. 'You get used to it after a while.'

They were sitting in the dappled shade of one of the few tents that still remained standing. Above them was an awning of camouflage netting with brown brittle leaves woven into it. It was blocking out most of the glare, although a few angled shards of light speared down between the webbing. Rashim bent over, pulled his shoes and socks off and began rolling up his trouser legs.

'Very classy look, that,' said Maddy.

'What is this place?' Rashim looked around. 'It looks like an army camp.'

'It's a camp that was – until this morning – being used by armed rebels,' she replied.

'Where are they now?'

'We're good. They're all gone. They won't be coming back.'

Rashim sat back up in the canvas chair, waggled his long bony toes to feel the air circulate between them. 'That's better.'

'Anyway . . . Rashim, you were saying something about an interesting theory?'

'Yes. This Pandora. The extinction event in 2070,' replied Rashim. 'I have been considering an interesting notion that it might be the marker for some sort of artificial termination point.'

'What the hell does that mean – *artificial termination point*?'

'This *may* sound odd . . .' He shrugged. 'It *does* sound odd, but stay with me . . .'

Maddy sighed impatiently. Rashim could be a shade on the patronizing side sometimes.

'Have you considered that this whole world might be some kind of experiment? Or a better word might be . . . *simulation*? A complex model. And –'

'You're suggesting this is a virtual reality?!' Maddy looked sceptical. 'A frikkin' computer simulation!?'

'No.' Rashim shook his head. 'No, *simulation* was the wrong word to use. I suggest it is real. This is all real, but somehow this world is isolated in some manner. In much the same way you would isolate a bacterial or viral culture from contaminants. I am talking about laboratory protocols, ensuring the subject of your experiment is properly isolated from random variables.'

'You're suggesting this whole world is some gunk growing in a Petri dish?'

'Petri dish,' he said, nodding. 'That is a good metaphor for what I am saying, yes.'

Maddy glanced at Liam, then Sal. Her eyes were narrowed; she was looking up at the sky, clearly giving the idea some thought.

'So, the theory is that we are stuck in this metaphorical Petri dish,' continued Rashim.

'Us?' said Liam. 'You mean just us? An experiment on just us?'

'No. I am thinking this is an experiment on a global scale. An experiment on everyone. On humanity itself.'

'Blimey!' Liam cocked a brow. 'That's quite . . . that's quite an idea, Rashim.'

'It might be a valid answer to the Fermi Paradox.'

'The Fermi whatty-what-what?'

'The Fermi Paradox – the answer as to why Earth never encountered a single extra-terrestrial radio signal in over a century of searching for one.'

'SETI was still going on? In your time?'

Rashim nodded. 'Yes, Maddy. There were still one or two radio arrays hoping to hear from someone. Right up until the end. So . . . it is a theory as to why we have never heard from anyone.'

'Actually, that gives you two possibilities,' Maddy replied. 'Either there is life *only* on Earth and the rest of the entire universe is completely barren. Which, apparently, is totally unlikely given the universe is pretty much infinite. Or –' she acknowledged his theory with a nod – 'you're right, we've been *isolated* from the universe somehow.'

'Put in a box,' said Liam.

'Pandora's box,' Adam added.

Liam was smiling and frowning at the same time. 'All of mankind? Earth?'

Maddy puffed her cheeks out. She let her gaze wander out across the clearing. On the far side, Bob was standing watch; a hundred yards away on the other, Becks was doing likewise. Maddy was pretty certain none of the rebels would be coming back. All the same, it seemed a sensible precaution having them patrolling the perimeter.

'Well, that's a fascinating idea. Maybe a little crazy?'

'It is no more crazy than some of the notions superstring

theorists have posited,' said Rashim. 'Eleven spatial dimensions. Overlapping multiverses. Russian Doll nested universes.'

'Well, true, I guess. That's a big ol' experiment when you think how old planet Earth is – what, four and a half billion years old?'

'My theory is that the experiment is only on a tiny, tiny portion of Earth's lifespan.'

'Since humans have been walking around?' suggested Maddy.

Rashim held up his hand and pinched air between his thumb and index finger. 'Much less than that. A loop of history that takes in the Voynich and perhaps the Holy Grail. A loop, much like your field office in New York in its two-day loop, but on a much grander scale,' he continued.

'My God,' uttered Adam. 'A loop? That could explain artefacts of history that shouldn't be here!'

'What do you mean?'

'For example, the Voynich Manuscript. The Holy Grail. How come my name was embedded in a text that dates back to the time of Christ? Unless . . . this history has somehow happened at least once before, and some or all of us have been involved in it.'

Maddy stroked her chin thoughtfully. 'Rashim, you're seriously suggesting all the history that we know, all that we've seen, might have occurred before?'

'It is a theory. That is all. But yes – perhaps even many, many times before. And these documents are perhaps a residual trace of previous runs through this loop of time. Something that earlier versions of yourselves have somehow managed to embed permanently, to leave behind. To be found by future versions of yourselves.'

'To be found?' She looked at him. 'Like, we've left ourselves a warning?'

'A warning? Or perhaps a wake-up call would be a better term. Or perhaps simply it is an accident.'

'The message in the Holy Grail doesn't seem like an accident,' said Maddy. 'It was a very deliberate message intended for us.'

'From who, though? Liam? An older one? That's what Becks said.'

Rashim shrugged. 'There is the question. From earlier versions of yourselves perhaps?'

Maddy laughed edgily. 'OK, that is far too much weird for one conversation.' She nodded at the distant ridge of rock face emerging from the jungle floor. 'I'm hoping some of our answers are going to lie in that cave over there.'

'Do not hope for too much,' he replied. 'You might be disappointed.'

'Well, we'll soon find out, won't we?' She checked her watch. 'You set the return window for an hour?'

'Yes.'

'Which is in about five minutes.' She addressed all of them. 'I suggest we send Becks back with a message to computer-Bob to track our beacon signal to that cliff-face and open another window over there in twenty-four hours' time. That'll give us enough time to make our way to the cave and spend the night looking it over.'

'Are we camping overnight in that cave?' asked Sal.

'If it's big enough. If there are other things to find in there, I'd like to get some time inside. So why not? Adam? Is it big enough?'

'Big enough?' He nodded. He took a swig from the water flask then passed it on to Maddy. 'Sure. If I recall correctly, it went deeper than I explored.'

She screwed the cap back on the flask. 'Right, then we should probably grab what useful things we can find here in the camp and set off soon.'

CHAPTER 32

1889, London

Bertie was almost certain the archway beyond this door was empty. He'd hunkered down and peered through the keyhole, seen that a solitary electric light was on; seen, within the flickering pool of light below, the back of a leather armchair and not much else. He'd then put his ear up against the door, held his breath and listened intently for a good five minutes. The only thing he could hear was the faint, deep throbbing of the viaduct's electrical generator that constantly vibrated through every brick wall of this dark labyrinth.

It appeared that no one was home. Dr Anwar and his odd collection of assistants apparently had decided to leave their archway for the day.

Just to be sure, he rapped his knuckles firmly on the door several times, called the doctor's name. Called Saleena's name.

No one's home.

Warily he eased the key into the keyhole and gently teased it round. The loud *clunk-snuk* of the lock echoed into the room beyond and made him jump. He cursed his skittishness as the heavy door creaked inwards.

He ducked as he stepped through the low entrance. 'Hello?' he called very softly, half expecting to find one of them asleep in the armchair and stirring at the sound of his voice. But the place was quite clearly deserted. Cautiously he stepped into the room and gently closed the oak door behind himself.

To his left was the armchair he'd seen through the keyhole, and five others of varying design and condition; it was a veritable cornucopia of throw-away reading-room furniture arranged around a scoured and scuffed old wooden dining table. He noticed another electric lamp sitting on it. An odd design of smooth, grey, brushed metal, shaped and jointed not unlike a skeletal human elbow. The pool of illumination from both electrical lights spilled feebly on to the back wall. He could just about make out that it was lined with boxes of wood and card, shelves laden with loops of thick cable.

To the right of the back wall, he noted that a number of privacy screens had been improvised: several ropes strung across from wall to wall and floral linen sheets pegged from them. Beyond one he could see a naval-style hammock hung empty, half a plump pillow attempting to escape over the side of it.

So they do live here. He'd wondered about that, whether they had other rooms rented elsewhere.

He took a few more cautious baby steps into the room. He felt the stone slabs beneath his feet give way to the more forgiving soft brush of a rug. That, and the hammocks, confirmed that this was as much a home to these people as it was a laboratory. In the middle of the floor he noticed two square plinths: wooden frames a yard on each side and six inches high, both of them filled with dirt and sawdust. They reminded him of the flower beds arranged within the long greenhouses of Kew Gardens.

He wondered if Dr Anwar was some mysterious horticulturist, nurturing exotic species of plant for some dubious and nefarious purpose.

He turned all the way round to his right and finally noticed, in the corner, another long wooden table. This one was cluttered with many things. Beneath it, thin rectangular boxes stood side by side, like guardsmen standing to attention. Each one with a miniature spot of blue light on the front of it. Some of them flickering and winking. Upon the table there were far more curious-looking items: square windows of light. A dozen of them, competing for table space. A mosaic of rectangles of different colours on each. Some of the rectangles had what appeared to be rows of letters and numbers on them, that marched jerkily upwards to be replaced with new rows of letters and numbers appearing at the bottom.

One of these glowing windows was presenting a sequence of images. He saw human faces, strange-looking buildings, contraptions on wheels that reminded him vaguely of the newfangled horseless carriages that he'd seen illustrations of in the penny press. Flying vehicles that looked impossibly sleek and smooth, made of shining metal that looked far too heavy to stay aloft.

The images themselves were almost incomprehensible. But it was these glowing square windows, these mesmerizing little 'screens' on the desk that made Bertie catch his breath. Each one seemed to be displaying an endless stream of information: numbers, letters, words, images.

Incredible. Quite incredible.

Just then, the windows all changed to a uniform sky blue. Identical numbers in white began to appear on all of them. Bertie watched as the identical display on every window counted down in sequence.

30 . . . 29 . . . 28 . . .

He heard something beginning to hum loudly in the corner of the room. And then a high-pitched voice called out from somewhere among the collection of armchairs.

'Hey! Ho! Hum! Skippa's coming ho-o-o-me!'

Bertie desperately needed to leave. He wasn't alone and something was about to happen here. But the small doorway was to his right, from where the shrill voice had come. If he scrambled for the door, he'd be running directly past whoever that was. Perhaps someone *had* been kipping on one of the chairs after all! He'd somehow not spotted them.

He looked desperately around for somewhere he could hide.

. . . *23* . . . *22* . . . *21* . . .

He realized those were seconds. Those were seconds counting down. He was running out of time! The metallic hum had begun to increase in intensity, becoming alarmingly loud, like an industrial machine on the verge of a breakdown, like a steam boiler getting ready to explode, a tractor preparing to throw a gear.

. . . *19* . . . *18* . . . *17* . . .

Bertie quickly hurried across the floor towards the privacy curtains. He stepped through the one that had been left open and pulled it closed behind him. One of the clothespegs popped off the suspended rope. Bertie cursed.

The hum was now almost deafening. He wondered if one of Dr Anwar's experiments was on the verge of going wrong in his absence. A few seconds from now, would all that be left of the viaduct be a pile of smouldering bricks and a billowing cloud rolling up into the sky over Holborn?

'God, help me!' he whimpered as the hum became an intolerable mechanical shriek.

All of a sudden the privacy curtain ballooned inwards like a sail catching a sudden squall of wind.

And the deafening hum was gone.

Bertie dared himself to peek through a gap in the fabric. What he saw made his breath catch again and his heart thud in his chest like a feral cat trapped in a hat-box.

He could see a sphere as wide in diameter as an adult man stands tall. It appeared to be hovering, entirely without weight, at least eighteen inches above the floor. The sphere glowed brightly, pulsating with rich emerald greens and a shockingly intense sky blue, a swirling loose pattern of those colours that reminded him of some of the modern meaningless impressionistic paintings coming from Paris these days.

Then in the midst of the swirls of those two intense colours a dark coil of black became a part of the undulating pattern on the surface of the sphere, swirling into the mix like a brave new tone added to the mess of an artist's palette. The swirl became thicker and more distinct, finally recognizable as the silhouette of a person.

A woman stepped down from the sphere on to the floor of the room. She was dressed as he'd expect a woman from London would normally be: long heavy skirt and a frilled blouse of linen. Bertie quickly recognized her as one of the female assistants of Dr Anwar; the stunningly beautiful, if somewhat aloof, one. He'd yet to actually hear her speak. Perhaps she was a mute.

A moment later the sphere collapsed to a pinprick and vanished completely.

Bertie's breath shuddered in and out, he was vaguely aware that his trembling hand was making the entire curtain twitch. He let it go.

If this bizarre tableau beyond the curtain was not already enough for him to try to make sense of . . . from among the cluster of chairs a squat yellow box – not unlike a chest of drawers in size – emerged. It had a pair of huge goggle eyes and a bobbing nose like a gherkin. It shuffled out into the middle of the floor on spindly legs and greeted the woman. 'Hey! Ho! Hum! Becks has come home!' It waddled up to her feet, tilted backwards to look up at her. 'Hey, Becks!'

The young woman calmly addressed the square box. 'Hello, SpongeBubba.'

CHAPTER 33

1994, Nicaraguan jungle

Billy hacked away at several low-hanging thorny vines in front of them. 'You have gone many times? In this . . . *ball*?'

Liam pushed the undergrowth aside. The guide seemed to be quite calmly taking all that he'd just witnessed in his stride. 'Yup, Billy. Many times, many places.'

'It is like a . . . a space ship?'

'Not really. It's sort of a window really. A window we can open whenever and wherever we want. Well, almost whenever we want.'

'Very good, very useful.' Billy nodded thoughtfully. He was silent for a few moments as he led the way up through the sloping jungle. Liam turned to check on the others; they were not far behind. Seven of them in total, making enough noise between them that the jungle seemed more alive with their hacking and talking and heavy footfalls than it did with the chirruping orchestra of birdsong above.

'So, Billy, here's a question for you. If you could go anywhere, anytime, where would you want to go?'

Billy hesitated for a moment, giving that some serious thought. 'You say anywhere?'

Liam grinned. 'Aye. All of history to choose from . . . so where would you go?'

He narrowed his eyes. 'I would like to go to Disneyland in United States.'

'Disneyland? Seriously?'

The guide nodded. 'I would meet the Mickey Mouse. And the large Goofy dog.' He resumed hacking again at the undergrowth ahead of them. 'The beautiful princess who is fairest of them all.' He grinned back at Liam. 'She a very pretty dish.'

'It's not much further now,' said Adam. 'It took me about three hours. I remember thinking it looked way closer from the camp. Like, a ten-minute stroll. But it turned out to be uphill all the way and quite slow-going pushing through all this undergrowth.'

Rashim dabbed at his sweaty forehead, wheezing from the exertion of walking up an incline for the last couple of hours. His Victorian clothes, the thick cotton shirt and felt trousers – all were entirely unsuitable for this oppressive tropical heat. 'It is very hot work. I need to take a rest and drink some water.'

He called out ahead to Liam and Billy that he needed five minutes and then down the sloping trail to Maddy, Sal and Bob bringing up the rear.

Maddy nodded and waved at them that she'd heard. She could have done with a break herself but was glad it was Rashim who'd wimped out and called a halt. She plopped herself against the base of a tree trunk. She took a moment to catch her breath.

'So, how are you doing there, Sal?'

Sal settled down on the hump of a fallen limb. 'Fine. I could keep going quite easily.'

Unlike Rashim, she'd chosen to change her clothes, ditching her long heavy dress and corset for some large denim shorts – cinched tight with a belt – and a faded yellow T-shirt she'd found hanging from a laundry line in the camp. The man-size clothes hung loosely on her small frame.

Maddy looked at her – she was breezing through the uphill jungle trek better than anyone else. Maddy could feel her own shirt was stuck to her back with sweat, clammy all the way down to the sodden waistline of her jeans.

'No, I don't mean how are you with the hiking.' She lowered her voice. 'I mean, how *are* you?'

'Uh?'

'You know, Sal, I was really worried about you. A few weeks ago, when Liam was off playing pirates, when you went forward in time to New York? I thought that was it . . . I thought we were never going to see you again.'

Sal pushed a lock of dark hair from her face. 'You asked me what I found. Do you remember?'

Maddy nodded. 'And you never told me.'

'There *is* a real me, Maddy. I found her.'

'What?' She was taken aback by that.

'Saleena Vikram. She was . . . *will be* . . . a real girl.'

'No.' Maddy shook her head. 'No, don't you do this to yourself, Sal. It's hard enough, I know, dealing with what we are, but don't make it harder for yourself building up some crazy wish-fulfilment fantasy.'

'I'm not crazy.'

'Our lives, our memories were all patched together like a scrapbook. Hell, I don't think the technicians that made us ever thought we'd come looking for our past lives. They must have figured we'd just accept who we thought we were and leave it at that.'

And wouldn't we have? Maddy wondered. If she'd never found that note in the San Francisco drop box, they would still probably be based in Brooklyn, still determined to carry on the work

Foster had entrusted to them. Still believing they were who they thought they were. Happy in their ignorance.

'My memories came from a real person,' said Sal. 'She exists. I saw her . . . I saw her father.'

'Come on, Sal. Maybe you just saw someone who just looked a bit like you and your dad –'

'They were *exactly* where I knew they'd be! Maddy, I remembered a trip Father took to New York. I remember the day we walked around the scrap mountain in Central Park. I remember the hotel we stayed at. I found it. And I found them.'

'Did you . . . did you, you know? . . . *Talk* to them?'

'I wanted to.'

'So you didn't?'

Sal shook her head.

'Then, come on, it might just have been two people who looked a lot like –'

'I heard Father call out my name.' Sal checked herself. '*Her* name.'

Maddy could have asked whether Sal might have simply misheard him. Maddy could have suggested it might have been a similar-sounding name. But she suspected picking holes in what Sal believed to be true would just antagonize her, encourage her to keep her thoughts to herself and clam up.

At least she was talking.

'Why me? Why was *my* life a real life, Maddy? Why do that to me?'

Maddy didn't have a ready answer for that. 'Maybe that's just how they chose to build our backstories. They had a complete one good to use for you. But for me and Liam they had to improvise with whatever bits they had to hand?'

'It's not fair.' Sal dipped her head, her face suddenly lost behind the curtain of her dark hair.

'Hey, Sal, you, me and Liam . . . we're all in this together. We're all in the same boat. It doesn't matter how they came up with our –'

'But it's NOT the same! Is it?' She looked up at Maddy. 'You and Liam had memory bits all stuck together. You're patchwork people. But me, mine's a complete life that will be lived. Don't you see? You two can take or leave those memories. You two can make a start being who you want to be.'

Liam had said that to Maddy one evening. The pair of them had been watching the barges coming and going beneath Blackfriars Bridge. He'd told her that he figured his life had properly started the day he'd been roused from sleep by Foster. Maddy had kind of got what he was saying. The authored memories they had in their heads could be discarded if that's what they wanted. Now that they had a year's worth of real memories together. It was enough for them to consider themselves as real people. After all, memories, real ones, that's what counted in the end.

'You two can both move on and make a new start,' said Sal. 'You can become who you want to be. But me?' She shook her head sadly. 'There is *already* a Saleena.'

Maddy could see, behind the loose veil of her long hair, that there were tears in her eyes.

'So, what does that make me?' She wiped her eyes dry. 'It makes me the fake.'

CHAPTER 34

1994, Nicaraguan jungle

Mid-afternoon they finally came to the base of the ridge. Adam began talking about his other passion, geology. He explained why the very artificial-looking wall of rock rising almost sheer and vertical out of the jungle like some man-made defensive bastion built to withstand an army of invading giants was in fact a perfectly natural formation.

At some point tectonic pressure must have caused this plateau of rock to fracture and rise up out of the jungle.

'The ridge runs along for quite some distance either side of where we are, but there's a narrow pathway somewhere nearby that zigzags up the front of it. It's partly natural and partly cut out of the sandstone.'

'You know where this path starts?' asked Maddy.

Adam looked either way along the base of the cliff. Where the rock descended into the jungle floor it sank into a thick tangle of undergrowth. The lowest fifty or sixty feet of the rock-face were coated by a thick tapestry of moss, in places hidden behind dangling curtains of vines and clinging ivy. Adam looked up the cliff-face. Not strictly vertical – as it rose the wall angled back on itself. If not strictly vertical, it was still extremely steep.

He studied the rust-coloured rock as it rose away from the jungle floor. Fifty feet up, the clumps of moss and the drooping curtains of vine and ivy began to give way to bare patches, which, in turn, expanded and joined each other further up, until near the top the greenery was nothing but a dot here and there amid an expanse of rusty-red sandstone.

Right at the very top of the cliff, two hundred feet above them, the jungle resumed, foliage spilled over the top like a fringe of hair.

'OK, so I can't remember precisely where the path is,' Adam replied, 'but it's not far from where we are now. I'm sure. We took pretty much the same route up from the camp that I took two years ago, and I just sort of stumbled on that pathway without looking for it. So it should still be quite obvious when we come across it.'

Liam was looking up at the distant overhanging jungle. 'So it's not a pointy ridge at the very top? It's flat?'

'It's a plateau.' Adam craned his neck. 'I have no idea how big the plateau is, though. I'd love to have flown over the top and got some shots from above.'

'So, Adam,' said Maddy impatiently, 'we should start looking for your path.'

'Yes, yes – of course. Maybe we need to split into two groups? One goes left, one goes right. The pathway won't be far from here, I promise you.'

They did as he suggested and five minutes later it was Sal who spotted the narrow thread of the trail up the cliff-face. She traced its route down towards the jungle floor and a short while later they were gathered at its start, Billy and Adam hacking away at the vegetation, clearing a couple of years' worth of growth out of the way. Presently they found themselves staring at a roughly hewn set of steps that appeared to have been carved out of the stone many centuries ago.

Maddy inspected the weather-worn edges of the steep steps. 'Your Indians actually cut this pathway?'

'Yes. I suspect the cave at the top was probably used as some sort of burial chamber, kept a respectful distance from their settlement down by the river. They would have brought their dead up here, ascended this wall and placed their loved ones up in the cave so they could look out on them, watch over them.'

'Like *Chachapoya*, in Peru,' said Billy.

Adam nodded. 'Yes, that's right; they do exactly the same thing with their dead.'

Liam stepped forward and climbed the first few rounded steps. 'So are we all going up then, or are we just going to admire the craftsmanship?'

'That's the plan,' replied Maddy.

Rashim squinted up at the sheer slanting cliff-face. 'Is it safe? I mean, we have no safety equipment, no harnesses or safety lines, no helmets.'

Maddy sighed. 'Think of it as walking up a very steep hill, you know? As opposed to climbing a mountain. Look at it! We don't need all that climbing stuff. Just be a bit careful, that's all.'

'But a fall would be fatal.'

She shrugged at that. 'So, don't fall.'

Liam began to ascend the steps, finding handholds on his right: the thick cords of vines, ancient cracks and rain-worn dimples in the rock in which fingers could be curled to get a hold. 'It's not so hard. Just keep looking for something to hold on to.'

Rashim nodded queasily.

Liam looked back down at them. 'Are we going up then?'

One by one the others followed in his wake. Billy, Adam, Maddy, then Bob with all their backpacks slung in a tangled jumble over one large shoulder.

Sal was behind him, the last but one. She took the first half a dozen steps up the rock-face then turned to look back down at Rashim. 'Are you coming or not, Rashim?'

'It does not look very safe.'

She shook her head and pulled a face. 'You spent twenty years in the seventeenth century fighting pirate battles with cannons and swords and muskets, and you're telling me a *steep slope* looks too dangerous for you?'

'Heights. I am not very good with heights, Sal.'

'Oh, jahulla.' She shook her head and resumed climbing.

Rashim watched her ascending the rock-face, catching up with Bob's bulky frame. Further up, and looking very small and far away already, the others.

Long shadows were stretching across the craggy rock as the sun politely began to make its excuses to the day and head for the horizon. It would be setting in a couple of hours.

Rashim looked around at the undergrowth crowding in on him. In just two hours, it would be dark.

'All right,' he muttered to himself. He stepped forward, placed a foot on the first carved step and pulled himself up. 'This is not very safe, though.'

It took Liam no more than an hour to reach the halfway point of the 'climb'; it was more a stiff uphill walk than proper rock climbing. In places the pathway became quite wide, particularly where it doubled back on itself and zagged up the cliff in the other direction.

Now he was at one of those points where the pathway zigged and also zagged. He stopped to sip some water and catch his breath. His thigh muscles were burning from the steady ascent. But apart from needing the rest and the water, it was a perfect place to stop, if for no other reason than to take a couple of minutes and savour the spectacular view.

He was no more than a hundred feet up from the jungle floor, above the green canopy of the rainforest, and yet it felt like he was halfway towards the sky.

Below the canopy, it had felt like swimming along the bottom of an overgrown aquarium. But where he stood now the rainforest looked like an emerald sea of gently stirring broccoli heads: a receding vista of peaks and troughs that undulated like folds of a green blanket, like the gentle swells of deep ocean, frozen forever in a snapshot image. He studied these diminishing peaks and troughs as they stepped sedately down towards the distant glinting thread of the Green River.

With the afternoon fast approaching evening, the sun burned less intensely now. It rested warmly on his sweat-damp face, casting low-angled beams of light across the jungle, and alternate rays of shadow fanned out from the tops of some of the gentle peaks. In the shadowed troughs, thin wisps of mist were beginning to form, hiding from the sunlight like errant pale children.

He wondered if this was the most beautiful sight he'd ever witnessed.

Billy caught him up and together they silently sipped water and looked out at the view. The only sounds up here were the gentle rustle of wind, their own laboured breathing, the soft swill of water sloshing in the flask.

Liam smiled. *If I die tomorrow . . . I reckon I've seen more than anyone can fairly ask to see in a lifetime*.

The others finally caught up with them, Maddy cursing like a trooper under her breath. Billy and Liam looked at each other and grinned. That couple of minutes of silence and sensation was a shared moment that words would only cheapen. Billy handed back the flask and Liam resumed ascending the narrow path.

Three-quarters of the way up the cliff-face, the path began

to narrow to the point where Liam felt the need to stick much closer to the jagged rock. His left shoulder in places was rubbed sore as he leaned, *pressed* anxiously into the wall. It was two and a half feet wide here, and beyond the crumbly edge, yes, maybe it wasn't a vertical drop, but near as dammit.

The pathway finally came to an abrupt end as it reached the small mouth to the cave that Liam had managed to catch glimpses of from further down. Above the cave's entrance the sandstone face rose another twenty to thirty feet, topped with the jungle foliage spilling over the edge and dangling down.

The entrance to the cave was small and roughly arched, eight feet at its widest and low enough at the apex that he had to duck his head down as he stepped inside.

He squatted in the mouth of the cave, peering into the dimly lit interior. 'Hellooo?'

His voice reverberated around inside. 'Any hungry wild animals in there?'

Not that he was expecting an answer. A growl perhaps.

A moment later Billy finally joined him, squatting beside him in the cave mouth. He grinned at Liam. 'Is bit scary, eh? To go in?'

'Just rather wary of being eaten by something.'

Liam pulled out a torch from his backpack, switched it on and stepped further into the cave, Billy a step behind him, his assault rifle unslung from his shoulder and ready in his hands.

The cave widened beyond the entrance. The two of them were able to stand up straight, side by side, as above them the roof of the cave arced upwards to a craggy slit from which roots and creepers – the furthest probing fingers of the jungle above – dangled like ossified tendons among the firm, inverted mounds of stalactites.

The cave floor was covered with a bed of dirt, dry as dust,

the crumbling remains of dried vegetation, brittle twigs and branches and a few hardy tufts of yellowing grass. The walls either side of them were the same rust-red rock, worn smooth near the entrance by the elements, but more defined, sharper-edged further in.

Liam panned his torch along the cave walls either side. No cave paintings yet, no weird markings to be seen, but then the surface was far too uneven and craggy here for any cavemen to try using as a canvas.

Perhaps further in? He aimed his torch at the back and saw that the cave widened further and went a lot deeper than he'd first thought from Adam's description.

'You know what?' He glanced at Billy. 'I think we might just wait around for the others before we go any further.'

The guide seemed relieved at that suggestion. 'Very good.'

CHAPTER 35

1994, a cave, Nicaragua

Rashim was the last one to arrive. He ducked down as he stepped inside the cave, then slumped down, mentally and physically exhausted, against a stalagmite hump. His back was very deliberately turned towards the sweeping jungle vista far below, the shimmering evening sun settling on the distant horizon like a ball of molten wax. His silhouette cast a shadow across the uneven floor and deep into the cave.

'At last,' said Maddy with a sigh. 'What the hell took you?'

'That . . . last . . . bit . . .' He was hyperventilating. 'God help me, call that a path?'

She shook her head dismissively and huffed. 'What a baby.'

'Here it is!' Adam's voice echoed from further inside. 'Here's the writing on the wall!'

'Why don't you stay here and catch your breath for a bit,' she said, patting the top of Rashim's head.

'You are patronizing me.'

'Yup.' She tipped her chin towards the darkness. 'I better go and see –'

'You go.' Rashim waved her away breathlessly. 'Go! . . . I will be fine here.'

She turned and made her way further into the gloom of the cave. The light from the setting sun, pink now, like candy floss, was fading and becoming redundant. As she carefully picked her way deeper into the cave, it quickly became dark, almost completely pitch black a dozen yards in. The only worthwhile light was the spill coming from the flickering torches up ahead.

She bumped into Bob, her head clunking hard against his bony elbow.

'Jesus!' she grunted, rubbing her temple. 'Why can't you be soft and cuddly?'

'Sorry, Maddy,' he rumbled, and stepped to one side to let her pass.

'You got my backpack with you still?'

'Affirmative.' She heard the rasp and rustle of Bob moving, then felt the rough canvas of her backpack bumping gently against her shoulder. 'This is your bag, Maddy.'

She grabbed it, fumbled blindly inside it until her fingers found her torch. She pulled it out and snapped it on.

'Ahh, that's better.' She slapped a hand on one of his bulbous pectorals. Hard as granite. Her sore head notwithstanding there was something reassuring about knowing that mountain of flesh was always somewhere nearby. 'Thanks, Bob.'

'Maddy, you back there?' Liam's voice echoed. 'That wall painting's right here! Adam's found it! Get over here!'

'I'm coming! I'm coming!'

She followed the flickering light of their torches and finally joined Adam, Liam and Sal as they lit up a yard-wide section of the cave wall.

'*This* was the piece of writing I discovered and photographed,' said Adam proudly. 'Incredible sight, isn't it?'

Maddy panned her torch along the wall, up and down, left and right. A modest patch of faded marks, curious glyphs side by side in several neat rows, daubed on the wall with a paint that might once have been a red or an orange hue but was now a faint sepia, almost lost against the rust colour of the sandstone wall.

'And is that *all* the writing there is?'

Adam shrugged. 'When I came here I was alone, you see. To be honest, I didn't really do an *exhaustive* search.' He winced like a naughty boy recalling a misjudged prank. 'I was kind of worried the rest of my group would be going ape about me being missing for several hours. I didn't hang around for too long. No more than about ten minutes, then I had to head back.'

'So there *could* be more of this stuff?' said Maddy. 'Much more.'

'Maybe. Possibly. I had a look around quickly . . . didn't see anything else, though.'

'Then that's what we should do first, I guess. Search this place thoroughly.'

'We'll need to get some more light in here.' He looked back towards the cave entrance, now nothing more than a sleepy-eye shape of salmon-pink sky. 'Even in the middle of the day it was pretty dim back here. We could do with some proper floodlights and stuff.'

'Well, first things first.' Maddy reached down into the hip pocket of her jeans and pulled out the tachyon transponder. She flicked the protective cover open and flipped the tiny on/off toggle switch inside.

Bertie held his breath as he peeked through the gap in the curtains. He watched the young woman. She hadn't moved for what he supposed must have been about half an hour. She was standing stock still in the middle of the room, a perfect statue, her head slightly cocked as if listening to some unheard whispering voice. She was so still and quiet he was worried she would hear his laboured breathing.

Shuffling in aimless circles around her was the odd yellow box creature, shaped like a tobacco chest, with those curious, comical, childlike facial features. It reminded him of a dog rejoicing at the return of its master.

The bizarre scene remained like that, the woman a curious statue and the dancing yellow box, both of them preventing him from leaving this place undetected.

Then she finally stirred.

'Yes, I am detecting it too,' she said out of the blue. She shifted her position and looked down at the circling yellow box. 'Please move to one side now. A portal will be opening shortly.'

'Righto, missy!' chirruped the box and waddled into a dark corner of the room.

Bertie heard a click echo in the dark, then that metallic humming sound again. Quickly growing in intensity.

'Affirmative, computer-Bob,' called out the woman. 'Ten seconds.'

He could only guess he was about to witness the same spectacle again, that mysterious floating sphere. In anticipation of its arrival and the gust of air, he backed away from the fabric and ducked behind the hammock. Just as he did, the curtain billowed inwards, flapping for a moment like laundry on a blustery day.

Then it settled down again.

'Hey! Becks! We've found it! That cave writing!'

Another female voice. He recognized it as belonging to the assistant with the glasses and the American accent. What was her name? *Maggy?*

'That is very good news, Maddy,' said the other young woman.

Maddy.

Bertie, curious and confident the curtain wasn't about to flutter inwards again, made his way forward and peeked through the gap once more. The floating sphere was still hovering there. Another figure emerged from it, to stand beside the girl with the glasses. The huge man-mountain. He knew his name.

'Right, Bob, Becks . . . we need to grab some equipment!' The girl named Maddy pointed towards the shelves on the back wall. 'The halogen lamps, the 500-watt mini-generator, cables. Come on! Quick as you can!'

Bertie watched the three of them picking through the boxes stacked on the shelves.

'We are returning to the year 1994?' said Becks.

'Yup. And quickly.'

'Would it not make sense to identify when the writing appeared on the cave wall and return to that period, Maddy?'

'One thing at a time, Becks. I'm not sure yet how far back in time we can go with the current power configuration, anyway. Five hundred years? A thousand? Two thousand? First thing we *can* do is check that whole cave out. Who knows what else is in there?' She looked at the others. They were already holding loops of cable and equipment, the function of which Bertie couldn't even begin to fathom.

'Oh, cool . . . you've got the stuff already? Right, go, go, go! Window's open, no time to waste.'

The giant and the young woman disappeared into the sphere.

Maddy hurried across the floor towards the row of glowing windows. 'Computer-Bob, keep watching out for our transponder. I'm going to turn it off for now. When I turn it back on, it means we want to come back home, OK?'

Some text flickered on to one of the screens.

'If you get no signal for forty-eight hours, open a window anyway. Just in case, right?'

She hurried back across the floor and stepped into the sphere. Seconds later it collapsed to a pinhead and vanished.

The dark room was still and quiet once more.

Bertie settled back on his haunches. His mind was spinning

like a Catherine wheel as he tried to make sense of what he'd seen and just heard.

. . . The year 1994 . . .

. . . How far back in time . . .

. . . Five hundred years? A thousand? Two thousand? . . .

All of a sudden he felt dizzy, light-headed. His mind was spinning, trying to interpret those overheard words into some sort of meaning he could grasp and make a rational deduction from. He thought he had it, thought he understood now what he'd just witnessed; though it was surely an *impossible* notion.

It seemed these people, these curious tenants, had a device that allowed them to travel backwards and forwards through the passage of time.

Bertie filled his open mouth with the bulbous knuckles of his fist, just in case an involuntary yelp of incredulity escaped his lips.

CHAPTER 36

1994, the cave, Nicaragua

Eighteen hours after first entering the cave they'd managed to set up the halogen lamps, running from the mini-generator. Which in turn was running on several jerry cans' worth of diesel that Bob and Becks had been sent to retrieve from the rebels' camp. The harsh blue light coming from the 500-watt lamps filled the cave with a brutally clinical glare that scared the shadows back into the deepest recesses. Nothing, no forensic detail, no faded scrawl was going to escape their unremitting light.

And through the night they'd searched the cave, every nook and cranny, every fissure leading off into smaller caves and wriggle-spaces so narrow they left behind skid marks of elbow and knee skin on the sharp edges of rock. They came across several clusters of human bones, which seemed to confirm Adam's assertion that at some point this place had been used as a burial chamber. But, as it happened, there was no more mysterious writing to be found in the cave.

There was just that one small faint patch of glyphs.

Now they were sitting near the mouth of the cave, the generator silent, the lamps off. It was midday and the sky was heavy with tumbling grey clouds that rumbled irritably. They listened to the white-noise hiss of rain spattering against the rock-face outside, the echoing drip of moisture trickling down through the fissured roof above and plopping noisily into shallow pools on the cave's floor.

A small fire crackled between them, its meagre warmth doing little to lighten the mood.

Maddy turned to look at Billy, standing at the mouth of the cave smoking his pipe and chatting quietly to Bob about something. She'd banned him from smoking that awful thing inside, the stink of his curious brand of tobacco made her want to retch.

'So it seems this turned out to be a total waste of time.' Maddy sighed and absently pulled strips of bark off a dried branch. 'I'm sorry we dragged you away from your college digs, Adam.'

'I'm not.' He scratched at his chin. 'Got me away from those morons I share the place with.'

'But this has all been for nothing.' She snapped the brittle stick. 'I guess I was hoping there'd be something more here; that there'd be something in this cave that would explain everything. Well, at least give us a clue.'

'Aye, well . . . it *was* a long shot, Mads. What's that saying? A shot to nothing?'

The fire was beginning to wane.

'Who says we need to know everything, anyway?' said Sal.

Maddy looked up at her with raised eyebrows that were saying, *Seriously?*

'Well, look at it this way, Mads,' said Liam. 'We escaped Mr Waldstein and his army. If we're careful, the chances of him ever finding us again are close as damn to nothing. We have a comfortable enough home in London, we have our time machine and our source of energy . . . but most of all –'

'We have our health?' added Sal.

Liam looked at her. 'I was just about to say that.' The pair of them smiled.

'Well, I'm glad you two are finding it so funny.'

Liam's face straightened. The swelling from his beating had gone down, but the grazes and cuts across his cheek and temple were dark scabs, almost like pen drawings against his pale skin. With his tongue he probed the gap to the side of his mouth where the tooth had been knocked out and winced as he touched the sensitive gum.

'Hey, stop fiddling with it, Liam, you'll get an abscess,' said Maddy.

The flames had quietened down to an occasional flickering tongue emerging from a bed of glowing charcoal.

'I *am* serious, though,' said Sal. 'Why do we need to know what that message was? For all we know, it might have been a warning to us about that attack by those support units. But we survived. We're OK. We could just . . .'

'Just what, Sal?'

She shook her head and shut up, turned her gaze back to the fire.

'Go on, Sal. Just what?'

'It's pointless saying anything. You just do what you want to do anyway.'

Maddy looked hurt. 'No, I don't. We're a team, remember?'

'Yeah, right.' Sal laughed bitterly. 'A team.'

'What's that supposed to mean?'

'You kept secrets from me and Liam. You decide stuff on your own without consulting us.' She glanced at Adam. 'And you choose who we let in on our group, and me and Liam just have to go along with it all. We're not a team.'

'That's unfair!'

'Is it?'

'Hey!' Liam cut in. 'Ladies! Ladies!'

They both ignored him. 'I don't think we should've gone against Waldstein,' said Sal.

'I didn't go *against* him!' replied Maddy. 'I merely asked him about Pandora.'

'You didn't just ask. You said we were no longer lifting a finger to save history until he told us everything.' Sal looked up at Maddy. 'You challenged him directly.'

'That's not true. I just want to know why we should deliberately steer mankind towards oblivion when we have the means in our hands to avoid that! Surely . . . just to know why? That's not too much to ask, is it?'

'The way I see it,' Liam shrugged, 'is we're free to do what we want . . . go where we want. So why worry? Why care? Why not do our own thing?'

Both girls turned to look at him. He wasn't helping. They sat in silence for a while. The rumble of thunder, the steady hiss of rain and *drip-drip-dripping* filled the uncomfortable silence.

'History still has to go the right way,' said Sal eventually.

'That's something I'm still trying to get my head round,' said Adam. 'You say it all ends up horrifically badly in 2070?'

'It does,' said Rashim.

'. . . and yet your boss, Mr Waldstein, sets up the three of you in the time-travelling business to ensure just that happens. Surely he'd want something different?'

'We've talked this over so many times between the three of us, Adam.' Maddy shot a glance towards the mouth of the cave before continuing. Billy was still puffing away and gazing out across the mist-shrouded jungle at the swirling layers of low cloud. She decided this was a conversation that was digging deeper than she wanted. In truth, even Adam shouldn't be hearing this. 'I don't know why, is the answer. Maybe he's mad? The only person here who even knows what he looks like is Rashim. Right?'

Rashim nodded. 'Everyone in my time knows . . . *knew* . . . about him. He was as famous as the theoretical physicist Stephen

Hawking was in his time.' Rashim stared at the glowing embers of the fire. 'But he was a recluse. Very secretive. He vanished from the public eye during the last ten years of his life.'

'But was he mad? Was he the kind of nut that would deliberately want to wipe out mankind?'

'He never seemed that way to me. Not *insane*. He seemed passionate about fighting for our future. I used to listen to his speeches as a boy. I had a digi-playlist on my Palm-Boy of all his famous speeches. The one I listened to the most was his Montreal one: the last ever TED talk. He warned us of tough times ahead. *Disastrously* tough times ahead. But he insisted, even back then, that using time travel to sidestep these problems would *absolutely* be the end for us all.' Rashim shook his head slowly. 'I do not think he was mad. I know he was called many things – a bigot, a bully, a racist, a misogynist –'

Liam opened his mouth. 'Mis–?'

'Not keen on women,' replied Maddy.

'He used a scientist's language,' continued Rashim. 'Direct, insensitive and brutally honest. Most people who labelled him with these terms heard only the language, the words he used . . . but did not listen to the message.'

'And what was his message?' asked Adam.

Rashim shrugged. 'I think his message was this – it is in our nature to destroy ourselves, then rebuild. *Destruction* is a natural part of our life-cycle.'

'*For the son to become a man, the father must die*,' uttered Liam. 'Just something I read somewhere.'

'And quite apt,' added Rashim. 'I believe Waldstein was saying that mankind inevitably needs a purge, then a rebirth. That such a thing is unavoidable. It is the natural order. Not to be cheated . . . or *dodged* by some sleight of hand, by some trick of technology.'

'I can see why he wasn't that popular,' said Adam.

'Truth-sayers never are. They are often the pariahs of their time.'

Maddy hugged her legs. The fire had died down and she was beginning to feel chilly. 'Look, I don't know what to do, guys. Whether we should just cut and run and do our own thing. Whether we should carry on with Waldstein's mission . . . but independently, off the radar. I mean, maybe *he* didn't want us taken out, but someone else inside his organization did. We can't know for sure. So maybe we have to continue doing what we were set up to do, but on our own. Or whether . . .'

'I'm going to get some more firewood,' said Liam. He got up and started gathering some of the dried detritus on the cave floor.

'Or whether?' prompted Adam.

'Whether we should take the bull by the horns.'

Sal stared at her. 'What do you mean?'

'Whether we should find a way to talk directly to him. Face to face. If it was my asking about Pandora that caused him to decide we were a threat, then maybe I can convince him that we're not going to – I dunno – expose him to the world, or put him in danger. We just want him to level with us.'

Liam returned with an armful of moss and twigs and casually dumped them on the embers. 'There ya go.'

A thick coil of smoke quickly emerged from the mound. It became a choking column that billowed up, drifted across them.

'Oh, genius!' Maddy coughed and spluttered. 'You just threw on damp stuff!'

Their cosy fireside gathering quickly broke up as they got to their feet and stepped backwards, wafting the thick smoke away from their faces.

'Ah . . . sorry there, fellas!' Liam called out.

Maddy flapped her hand and was wheezing. 'Good job.'

The smoke had mushroomed up to the ceiling of the cave, and now it hung there like a layer of swamp mist: a low-hanging cloud looking for somewhere to go. Sal was staring up at it and noticed that it *was* finding some place to go.

It started to stretch out along the roof of the cave, tendrils of smoke feeling their way towards the back.

'That's really odd,' she said, pointing up at it. 'It's like it's being sucked.'

The smoke was thinning out now, becoming less defined, less visible.

'Throw some more of that wet stuff on,' she said to Liam.

Maddy nodded. 'Yeah.'

Liam reached for another fistful of damp moss and tossed it on to some freshly exposed glowing embers. A new mushroom cloud of choking white smoke billowed out and rolled up to the ceiling, then swirled idly for a moment before following the same path along the roof as the first cloud.

'There's a draught pushing it to the back of the cave,' said Maddy.

'That means a flow-through,' said Adam.

'You mean, like, an *exit*?'

He nodded. 'Maybe we missed it – another cave, another . . .' His voice trailed away as he snapped on his torch and followed the thin tendril of smoke above as it curled and weaved and glided along the uneven contours of the ceiling towards the very deepest recess of their cave. The beam of torchlight picked out the very last threads of the smoke as it seemed to speed up and dart eagerly behind a large boulder.

'Someone get Billy and his pipe!' Adam called out. Shouts echoed back through the cave towards the entrance and a minute later Billy and the others were gathered there beside him.

'What is wrong?' asked Billy.

Maddy understood what Adam was thinking. 'Just smoke your pipe and blow it out.'

He looked at her, bemused. 'But you say to me no smoke in –'

'Forget what I said, just blow a load of your smoke out.'

The guide shrugged and pulled on his clay pipe. The bowl glowed and they heard the soft crackle of burning tobacco. Then, cheeks now puffed up, he breathed out.

Adam shone his torch on the small cloud of tobacco smoke as it hung indecisively in the air for a moment, before lurching towards the rear of the boulder, like some clueless messenger boy suddenly remembering a long-overdue errand.

'There's more to this cave,' said Maddy. She looked at the others, then at the boulder. 'There's more.' She grinned excitedly at them. 'And what's more – it's been *hidden*.'

CHAPTER 37

1994, the cave, Nicaragua

With one final grunt of effort, Bob managed to work the boulder several more inches away from the tunnel entrance that it was plugging.

There was a gap now, just wide enough for a head and shoulders, and with a little more effort, and no doubt some skin left behind, for a person to squeeze through entirely. For now Maddy was happy to just take a look. She shone her torch through the gap.

'What can you see in there, Mads?'

She panned the beam around. It was a narrow tunnel, roughly triangular, tapering at the top. Veils of spider webs hung across it, which glowed like finely teased-out cotton wool in the beam of her torch. 'Ewww . . . gross!'

'What?'

'Webs. Lots of them.'

From what she could make out, the tunnel looked like a natural fissure, but in places she picked out the scrape marks and pitted bites of what must have been the work of primitive tools. 'It looks like a natural passage that someone has chiselled at in places to widen it.'

'Webs?' Rashim looked unhappy. He hadn't made it past her first description. 'Spiders? Creeping, crawling, stinging, biting things?'

'Yes, spiders. Don't be such a wimp.' Maddy bent down, picked up a rock and then tossed it into the tunnel. The nearest veil of webbing vibrated as the rock tore a hole through it. The passage suddenly seemed to come alive with movement. Dark dime-sized silhouettes scuttled in quick stop-start motion down from above, along the radiating threads. Converging on the ragged hole, to inspect it for a catch.

Dozens of them.

Hundreds in fact.

'All right, maybe the wimp approach might be best.' She pulled her head and shoulders back out of the gap; dust and threads of web stuck to her hair.

She looked at Becks. 'You go in there first and clear away those webs. OK?'

Becks nodded. 'Of course, Maddy.'

'And the spiders. Squish as many of them as you can find. And Bob?'

'Yes, Maddy?'

She tapped the boulder. 'Move this a bit more so we're not skinning ourselves every time we squeeze through.'

Ten minutes later they were shining their torches down the passage. The webs were mostly gone. Becks was covered in sticky threads, looking like a badly decorated Christmas tree. 'It is clear now.'

'OK, that's better.' Maddy turned to the others. 'Shall we go take a look?'

She led the way. The passage was easily wide enough for two or three of them to walk side by side, but it was low enough that the tallest of them had to duck their heads a little. To her senses it seemed to be leading downwards, only the slightest gradient, but enough that she got the feeling that gravity was gently coaxing her forward.

As they slowly made their way along it their torches ranged across the rock surface. Chisel and scrape marks everywhere. But no more paintings.

It curved gently to the left for fifty yards. Ahead she picked out the faintest grey glimmer of daylight. 'Look!'

'I see it,' said Adam. 'So maybe this rock formation *isn't* a plateau, but a thin ridge. A natural rock wall, and this passage cuts through to the far side.'

They made their way down to the end of the tunnel. It was filled by a dense wall of vegetation. Thin rays of daylight tiptoed their way through a thick lattice of vine branches and roots. Beyond the broad scribble of roots, Maddy could see shifting lime-green leaves, and through them one or two pale grey dabs of daylight. They could hear the gentle patter of raindrops outside on leaves, the echoing drip of water inside the passage. They could feel a ghost's breath of fresh air stealing through on to their cheeks.

'That looks like hundreds of years' worth of growth there,' said Adam.

Maddy pulled at the wall of gnarled old vine branches and shifting, heavy leaves. 'Can't see a great deal. Looks like just more jungle on the other side.'

'I will cut through,' said Billy, brandishing his machete. He proceeded to hack away at it, swinging with short economic downward swipes that quickly began to unravel the tangled natural lattice. Bob stepped in beside him, pulling away the loose roots and branches.

Adam panned his torch around the rock walls. 'You're right, Maddy. It's been carved to make it wider.'

'Maybe by the same person who sealed it with that boulder,' added Liam.

Maddy was grinning. 'I don't know about you guys, but

doesn't this feel like we're discovering something? This is so cool!'

'Don't be getting your hopes up, Mads,' said Liam.

'Don't you see, Liam? Maybe the message in the Voynich Manuscript, the Holy Grail, was meant to lead us right here?'

He frowned. 'Why?'

'Maybe it's all the other way round,' she continued. 'We came out here thinking there might be something more to help us decode the message, right? That the message itself was the key thing?'

'Aye.'

Maddy nodded at the weak filtered light coming through the wall of vegetation. 'When in fact the message in those documents was simply a way to tell us about this place. Whoever wrote the message wanted to lead us here?'

Bob wrenched a tangle of branches out of the way, and all of a sudden there was a clear view through the thick wall of undergrowth. Maddy stepped past Billy, pulled aside several low creepers and impatiently pushed forward through chest-high brambles and thorns that scratched at her skin.

She stopped where she was and shaded her eyes as the thick grey clouds in the sky finally began to tear like wet tissue paper, allowing through the piercing light of the sun, warming the jungle up to a steaming soup once more.

'Oh – my – God!' she uttered.

'What? What can you see?' called Adam.

She pushed her way a little further forward, angrily shaking the barbed tendrils of the brambles off her clothes. 'It's like . . . like . . . like something out of a movie.'

'*What?*'

She turned round to face them. 'You are going to *love* this!'

CHAPTER 38

1994, beyond the cave, Nicaraguan

They emerged into the sunlight, eyes grown accustomed to the dark now blinking, watering at the dazzling glare, the glistening reflection of sun on every rain-wet surface. Before them, stepping down like a giant bowl, like the caldera of a volcano, almost like a Roman amphitheatre, were the overgrown ruins of what could only be described as a long-lost city.

Adam's face split wide with childlike delight: the joy of a chocolate glutton stepping into Willy Wonka's factory. 'My God! It's . . . it's incredible!'

On all sides of them masonry, finely joined with hairline precision, hewn from the same rust-coloured sandstone and assembled into an Escher landscape of stepped terraces and structures, broad paved causeways and narrow passageways, all radiating out from a central circular plaza at the bottom.

A grand circular man-made basin.

Stone stairways led up the basin sides to multi-layered pyramid-like buildings on which the very last flecks of faded paint hinted at once-upon-a-time elaborate, colourful decoration. Layered over everything, nature had taken possession of this long-since-abandoned city, stamped its right to be here, to reclaim this weather-worn monument to a vanished people.

Vines and ivy hung like emerald drapery from every rooftop and spilled from every dark window. Spider lines of dark-green moss defined the joins and seams of masonry, like an architect's pen proudly highlighting the hard-edged angles of precise geometry.

Across the crazy-paving of the causeways and narrow passages, and the vast football field-sized circular plaza at the bottom, ran the husks of long-dead vegetation, while mounds of dry leaves had gathered, windblown, against the base of walls in small crisp hummocks.

'It reminds me of that legendary lost city,' said Rashim. 'The one that was supposed to be made of gold?'

'Aye.' Liam nodded. 'I know the place you mean. The Lost City of Eldorado. The one all them explorers and conquistadors went running around the Amazon looking for.'

'Those ruins back down by the river,' said Adam, 'that must have been some outpost for this city. Could have been where their supplies were brought in. A marketplace or something servicing this place.'

He shook his head silently. 'And then, Jesus, there's all this . . . *this* . . . hidden from view, hidden from everyone. I can't believe I missed this!' He laughed. 'And I thought I'd found something incredible.'

Maddy rested a hand on his shoulder. 'But it was *you* who found it, Adam.'

He laughed at that. 'No, no I didn't. All I found was a bunch of writing. I didn't have a clue what was right nearby.' He looked back at the dark opening to the passage they'd emerged from. 'I didn't have a clue what was just a hundred yards away from me.'

Rashim wiped away beads of moisture from his forehead. 'This city has been built in a natural crater?'

'Crater, yes, but not a volcanic caldera,' said Adam. 'This is sandstone not basalt. It might of course have been an impact crater, like that one near Alamo, Nevada. More likely, I'd say this is a giant sinkhole.' He gestured up at the fringe of the jungle, running round the outside of the very top of the city, like green velvet trim. 'This was once a several-mile-wide plug of sandstone, pushed up out of the jungle by some tectonic activity. Then over hundreds of thousands of years it's been eroded by water from the inside . . . hollowing it all out and making this basin.'

'Creating a naturally walled area,' added Maddy.

'Exactly. The perfect place to build a secret city.'

They stared at the spectacle in silence for a long while before finally Sal spoke.

'So, I hate to ruin this eureka moment, but what do we do now? If the Voynich message was all about bringing us here – what are we meant to do?'

Maddy shrugged. She looked at Sal and Liam. 'What do you guys think?'

'Explore it?' said Liam. He grinned. 'It'll be fun.'

'All right, I guess that's the first thing.' She looked at her watch. 'So, it's just after one o'clock, which means we've got about four and a half hours of daylight left. Bob and Becks, would you be a good pair of pack mules and go grab the lights, the mini-generator, the diesel and bring it all here? We should probably set up some sort of base camp.'

Both support units nodded.

'And food from the camp,' said Liam. 'They had some crates of tinned food and all sorts down there. We might be here for a few days?'

'Good point. Forage for whatever you can find down there.'

'Yes, Maddy,' they both chorused before turning towards the entrance to the passage, pushing their way through the undergrowth and disappearing inside.

Adam clapped his hands together loudly. The echo bounced all the way around the city basin and returned back to them a second later. 'Jesus! Get a load of the acoustics!' He grinned.

Maddy looked at him. 'You're actually really getting off on this, aren't you?'

'I'm not going to lie . . . the last time I was *this* excited was when my parents bought me the Thunderbirds Tracy Island Playset.'

She laughed. 'You're so geek it hurts.'

'Takes one to know one.'

She cuffed his head playfully and took several quick steps down towards the plaza. Adam followed after her, gesticulating at the things all around them. She laughed at something he said.

Liam watched them go, their receding playful voices echoing around the stonework. He turned to Sal, Rashim and Billy. 'Aye, it's an incredible sight, isn't it?'

Billy and Rashim nodded and smiled.

He noticed, however, that Sal seemed distracted; she seemed not to hear him. He thought he saw something in her face though. A hint of sadness. No. Not that. Regret?

Envy, perhaps?

'Sal? You OK?'

She was back with them now. She smiled quickly at Liam. 'Yes. It's incredible.'

Liam shone his torch around inside the building. It was one of the bigger structures that looked like it had once been a temple or some sort of communal gathering-place. The cavernous interior echoed with their footsteps. Flecks of sunlight that stole through the collapsed ceiling dappled the paved floor, coarse hardy grass was growing in sporadic waist-high tufts where the sun habitually managed to reach. The high walls around them were decorated with a carved pattern: not glyphs or writing, but a simple repeated motif of three lines – a backwards 'L' with a third line radiating out forty-five degrees between the horizontal and the vertical. The roof to the building had caved in a long time ago; the thick branches of vines snaked across above them, from wall to far wall, replacing the fallen roof. Thick support beams of wood had rotted, given way and deposited an avalanche of clay tiles across the floor. The tiles now lay shattered, entwined, almost lost beneath a carpet of vegetation.

'Is it me, or does it feel spooky in here?' Liam whispered.

'It is odd that there are no remains of the inhabitants left behind. None at all.' Rashim panned the beam of his torch into the dark corners of the room where the sunlight wasn't reaching.

'You're right. No skeletons. I was expecting *some* skeletons.'

'Unless this city was left and the people migrated? It is possible that something caused this city to become abandoned. Environmental conditions?'

Liam nodded. 'Aye, that's true.'

If the Green River, for example, had become impassable, or gone dry . . . if it had been the sole source of imported food for this city, it would have quickly rendered this place an unsustainable outpost. Perhaps the Green River had once been much bigger? A vital trade and resource artery for this long-forgotten kingdom, and for one reason or another the river had atrophied and shrunk to the lifeless algae-covered backwater it was now. It was quite possible that it wasn't even a natural event but the result of human intervention. Perhaps the water upstream of the river had once long ago been diverted to irrigate farmland?

Liam was reminded of the story of the Polynesians of Easter Island. How they had got it into their minds to cut thousands of huge several-ton blocks of granite from the island's central mountain, carve them into brooding faces and then transport them down to the edge of the island to stare menacingly out to sea.

It was the *transporting* of these huge heads that had seen to the downfall of those people. They had no carts. The wheel was an invention unknown to them, so the blocks were rolled down along 'conveyor belts' of logs. Thousands of trees hacked down to provide a route to the shoreline for each gigantic carved head. And with such sudden and ferocious deforestation occurring to this isolated, enclosed ecosystem it wasn't long before soil erosion – caused by the lack of tree roots binding the soil to the island – had begun to render the place an infertile rock. Harvests soon began to fail, food became scarce and the inhabitants, fearing the gods were angry with them for not making enough brooding effigies of them, decided to ramp up the carved-head production. So they made more, many more, as quickly as they could; the exquisite carving of the earliest ones gave way to cruder, far simpler carvings as this dying civilization escalated production in a last-ditch attempt to save themselves. Irony exemplified: the more heads they carved and transported down to the shore to appease the gods, the faster their ecological doom approached.

When Captain Cook came across Easter Island in 1774, he had found the very last of these people, a handful of starving survivors of this culture, and had wondered how these pitiful and emaciated 'savages' could have constructed such a breathtaking spectacle round the perimeter of the island.

Liam picked his way through the weeds and coarse grass, the shattered clay roof tiles and snaking vine roots towards the entrance to another large room. Like this one, the ceiling had collapsed long ago, depositing shards of cracked tiles like eggshell on to the floor. As he stepped in, a brittle tile cracked and crunched beneath his shoe.

He shifted his foot, feeling vaguely guilty at his clumsiness.

A proper archaeologist would have checked where he stepped before blundering in, for fear of crushing some fragile cultural artefact, some Mayan equivalent of the Rosetta Stone.

He looked down guiltily at what he'd just crushed.

It was certainly no roof tile. He knelt down and picked up the object – curved, smooth and vanilla-coloured – to inspect it more closely. 'Oh Jay-zus!' He dropped it.

Rashim turned from gazing at the flecked paint patterns high on the walls. 'What is it?'

Liam found the rest of the skull poking out of a tuft of grass; dark empty eye sockets glared accusingly back at him for his feckless clumsiness. Liam spotted a ribcage lying right next to it.

And then very quickly he noticed the coarse grass was interwoven with many, many more bones. The entire floor of this room was littered with bleached yellow and brittle bare bones poking out of the grass. Skulls, a hundred or more of them – their dark sockets seemed to all be glaring his way, silently chastising him for disturbing their centuries-old slumber.

CHAPTER 39

1994, the Lost City of the Windtalkers

'Here, Maddy, take a look at this,' said Adam. He hunkered down low and squinted at the faint markings picked out by the light of his torch. 'The carving on this one's much more distinct. Do you see?'

Maddy had discovered the way down into this chamber beneath the central plaza. The plaza was where she, Sal and Adam had gravitated. It seemed to be the very heart of this remarkable ghost city, a large acre-sized and circular open space in which, Adam speculated, the inhabitants may have held rituals or ceremonies. The floor of the plaza was made of stone slabs, arranged in concentric circles round a central raised dais from where Adam suggested someone of importance – an elder, a shaman – would conduct his rituals.

They'd wandered across the plaza, in several places coming across sections of the floor where a number of the paving slabs had collapsed, revealing a dark space below. Curious about what lay beneath them, they had spread out and explored the perimeter of the plaza, and Maddy had been the one to come across an open trench running along the northern edge. A trench that descended several steps to an opening that led into the dark void beneath the plaza.

Maddy, Adam and Sal found themselves in a large circular chamber with a low ceiling – the underside of the plaza floor above them. The ceiling, only a foot and a half above their heads, was held up by countless squat stone pillars placed evenly every six feet or so. It reminded Maddy of a cut-away illustration of the Colosseum she'd once seen in a children's history book. The sandy floor of the arena where the gladiators had fought each other to the death had been a false floor constructed of wooden planks, held up by a forest of stone columns. The space beneath this floor had effectively been the Colosseum's 'back stage', where the gladiators, the wild animals, the chariots waited their turn to be brought up through a trap door to entertain the baying masses.

In this low-ceilinged chamber Adam had discovered a number of flagstones set in the floor that had faint carvings on them. Most of them were so worn by time and the elements that there was little to discern in the markings but the frustrating sense there'd once been an opportunity to know so much more.

Adam and Maddy had hurried from one flagstone to another like children at an Easter egg hunt, hoping to come across one with enough detail to pull some information from, until finally they found one worth hunkering down over and inspecting more closely.

'See?' Adam placed his torch on the floor beside the stone. The beam of light was shining at an acute angle across the slab of rock so that the faint lines of carving, little more than the shallowest of weather-worn grooves, cast enough of a defined shadow to allow them to see more clearly what had been carved there.

'It's a depiction of one of their rituals, at a guess.'

Maddy leaned forward, closer, to get a better look. She could barely make out any detail at all. She thought she could see the simplified depiction of a man with an arm held out before him, palm held outward towards a column of wavy lines.

Sal, meanwhile, had decided to stray a little further and explore the rest of this circular low-ceilinged void. The last thing she needed right now was to listen to those two lovebirds enthusing about this place together in hushed whispers.

For the last few minutes she'd walked round the perimeter of the chamber, relieved at putting some distance between her and them. The beam of her torch had probed the pitch black, showing endless squat columns of stone, to her left the endless curving wall of the chamber.

But now the beam picked out a narrow gap in the wall. She shone her torch into it. It appeared that there was another, smaller chamber beyond.

'Hey, Maddy! I'm going to go check what's in here!'

Between the receding rows of columns, she saw Maddy on the far side of the chamber, glancing left and right to see where Sal's voice had come from.

'Over here!' Sal waggled her torch around until Maddy spotted it and waved back. 'I'm going to take a look in here, Maddy! I think it's another room!'

She nodded. 'OK, but don't go wandering too far!'

Sal returned a sarcastic smile – too far and too dim for Maddy to make that out.

Yes, Mama. I promise to be a very, very good girl.

She was tempted to call that out in reply, but Maddy had already returned to gazing at the floor and chatting with Adam in hushed tones.

Pfft. Sal sighed. *Go get a room or something, you two*.

She shook her head. It was embarrassingly obvious to her that Maddy and Adam had a thing for each other. Although neither of them would admit it, and both would scoff at the suggestion and turn pink if someone were to so much as hint there was something going on there.

Personally, Sal couldn't see what Maddy thought was so great about the young man. With his pale freckled and spotty skin, scruffy ginger dreadlocks and wispy beard, and those awful, tie-dyed shorts and T-shirts he insisted on wearing.

Jahulla. Adam looked like a common *bhikhari*. A hobo, a tramp. So very different to the well-groomed, athletic, attractive man he would become in his early thirties. Maybe that's what Maddy saw when she gazed lovingly at him – how he was *going to look one day*. Or maybe she was just desperate.

Sal parked those thoughts for now and stepped into the narrow entrance. She panned her torch around. The chamber was small and square with very little going on in it except for what appeared to be a hole in the floor on the far side. She walked over to it, squatted down and shone her torch down into the opening.

She could see a series of steep stone steps receding down into darkness.

She cupped her hands round her mouth. 'There's some steps going down further here!'

She waited for a reply from either Maddy or Adam, but both of them seemed to be engrossed in what they were studying.

Oh, to hell with them, then.

She took the first few steps down into the hole until only her head and shoulders remained above the flagstone floor. Then she hunched down low and shone her torch into the darkness below her. The cone of light picked out her dust-covered laced boots, the step she was standing on, the next dozen steps down and the stone walls either side of her, hemming her into this claustrophobic stairwell. The steps faded away into the darkness – no telling how many more of them there were and how far down this stairwell was going to take her.

She was hesitant to make her way any further. If the light from her torch had been powerful enough, she might have been able to pick out what was waiting for her at the bottom of these steps.

She reached out to the wall right beside her, looking for something she could work loose and toss down the steps to see how far they went. She got her fingers round a wedge of stone, wiggled it until it came loose. Then did just that.

It *click-clacked* its way out of sight and down the steps.

Click, clickety-click . . . click . . . click . . . click

But then there was one final *clack* . . . which reverberated like a solitary pebble dropped on to the hard granite floor of a vast empty cathedral.

There's a room down there. A large one.

And, by the sound of the clattering stone, not that many steps below her.

What are you waiting for?

She was nervous. Obviously. The pitch black below was as featureless, as thick and equally as intimidating as the milk-white froth of chaos space. Like a negative image of that place. She wondered if ghostly wraiths would be swimming in ever-diminishing circles down there also.

It's just an empty space, Sal. A forgotten ruin. Nothing but a few creepy-crawlies down there. What are you waiting for?

She took in a deep breath. 'Uh-huh, right. Just creepy-crawlies down here.'

She descended another four steep steps, now fully immersed within the space of the claustrophobic stairwell. She shone her torch up at the opening just a yard above her head and wondered one last time whether it might be prudent to climb back up the steps and go and tell Maddy and Adam what she'd discovered.

No. This was *her* discovery. Maddy would just take over, take the credit for it. She'd just steamroll Sal out of the way and her discovery of this would be an afterthought. Or simply forgotten. All the same . . . she sensed there was something down there. Something waiting for her.

Oh, listen to you, you drama queen!

Her brain seemed to be very pushy this afternoon. 'Chuddah! I'm scared! Give me a break!' she uttered under her breath.

You're scared. But come on, you're so very curious too. Admit it.

She was. Very. She sensed some kind of 'purpose' to these receding steps, as if their intent was to gently tease a person downwards towards some profound truth. As if the steps themselves were alive, a silent Greek chorus willing her on, almost whispering encouragement to her to find her way to the bottom.

Just to the bottom step, that's all. To the bottom, then shine your light around and see what's down there.

She took the next half a dozen steps down, then the next . . . then one more.

The sound of the gentle tap of her boot heel was all of a sudden accompanied by the soft wash of returning reverberation. She aimed her torch down at the floor.

The light reflected brightly back from a smooth shiny surface.

'What is that?' she whispered as quietly as she could. Yet her voice carried. It returned to her a moment later drowned in a chorus of a thousand whispered voices. Her voice amplified and echoed, distorted and duplicated by the acoustics of this large dark place.

She squatted down and ran her fingers across the surface. Cold and as smooth and black as obsidian.

Jahulla . . . what is this place?

CHAPTER 40

1994, the Lost City of the Windtalkers

'If I was to hazard an approximate guess,' Liam said, shrugging, 'I don't know, about a hundred of them? Maybe two hundred? It's hard to say for sure. Those bones were scattered all over the place.'

Maddy finished stirring the broth bubbling in the cooking pot, ladled some into a bowl and handed it to him. 'Scattered? Like maybe somebody else has been here before us looking for valuables, do you think?'

He sat down on a stone step beside the fire. They had decided to locate their camp on the edge of the central circular plaza. Bob and Becks had brought back a canvas awning, some blankets and several crates of tinned food from the rebels' camp. The tins of food were mostly rust-specked, dented and without any helpful labels. It had been like playing a game of Lucky Dip, opening them up and finding out what was inside. Some of the tins had contained pineapple chunks, some unappetizing little silver-coloured fish encrusted with salt. Several had contained a gloop of some kind of refried bean in a thick sweet brown sauce. Maddy had chosen those to empty into their cooking pot, along with some other cans that contained a revolting textureless pink meat that was quite possibly pork, but could easily have been a minced mix of half a dozen farmyard animals and beasts of burden.

'It's possible some treasure-hunters have been through here and rummaged through them bones,' Liam said, then: 'Oh! Hold on. No one's been here before us.' He remembered the boulder and the tunnel's entrance clogged by hundreds of years' worth of ancient vegetation. 'Maybe some wild animals found where they buried their people round here, dug them up, dragged them to that building and picked at them there?'

Rashim took a bowl of the broth from Maddy. 'Skeletons all grouped together? All in that same building?' He looked across the plaza and up at the temple structure they had been exploring earlier that afternoon. 'To me it looked as if they must have died at the same time. Together, all of them up there.'

'Here you are, Sal.' Maddy handed her a bowl of the broth.

Sal looked at it without any real appetite.

'You not hungry?'

'Not really.'

'You all right?'

'I'm fine. Just not that hungry.'

'She is feeling sick, maybe?' said Billy. 'Jungle belly. You drink water from the river?'

She shook her head. 'Just don't feel hungry tonight.' She looked up at them and smiled quickly. 'I'm fine, honestly.'

'Well, try to eat some of it, Sal,' said Maddy.

Sal took the bowl of broth and sat back down. She stirred it unenthusiastically with her spoon as she watched the others talking. Not really listening to them.

Her thoughts were on what was down there – what she'd discovered.

'Died all together, you reckon, Rashim?' Adam frowned. 'That sounds kind of ritualistic, doesn't it? Like some kind of Jonestown thing.'

'Jonestown?' Liam looked up from his food. 'What's that?'

'It was an American Christian cult that moved out to some jungle in South America to get away from the modern world. The leader was called Reverend Jim Jones. Apparently he just one day got it into his numbskull that the End Was Nigh and told his loyal followers they all needed to go and poison themselves. He made a broth . . . much like this one –'

'Charming,' said Maddy.

'– laced it with cyanide and they all had to eat some. They were discovered some days later, nine hundred men, women, children . . . all lying dead together.' He settled his back against a block of stone. 'True story that . . . happened in the seventies, I think.'

'A mass *suicide*?' Rashim looked at Liam for a moment, then shook his head. 'It had the look of a mass *slaughter* to me.'

'What do you mean?'

'The bones were all over the place, were they not, Liam? Not ordered or placed or *ritualistic*, but chaotic.'

Liam nodded slowly. 'It did look a bit like . . .' He censored himself with a spoonful of Spam and bean gloop.

'Like what, Liam?' asked Maddy.

'Well . . . I suppose it looked a bit like some giant wild animal went berserk right inside that temple. Maybe a bear or something.' He looked at Billy. 'You get big bears in Nicaragua?'

'We do not have bears here. We have jaguars. But they are rare.'

'*Something* tore those poor people limb from limb,' said Rashim, 'that is, if those bones do in fact indicate where they fell and are not the result of the scavenging of wild animals or some other interference.'

The fire crackled in the midst of them, the cooking pot bubbled and spluttered, a welcome sound to fill the heavy silence.

'We shouldn't lose sight of the fact that whatever did happen up there, happened quite a few hundred years ago,' said Adam. 'Somebody else may have discovered this place and picked over it.'

Liam nodded. 'Aye. That's for true.' He grinned. 'Still, makes you think, though, doesn't it?'

Maddy settled back against a stone block. 'Think what?'

'Well . . . you know, what *did* happen?'

'Something bad for those people,' said Billy sombrely.

'It appears that this city did not slowly become abandoned,' said Rashim. 'I would say something catastrophic happened. Those bodies in the temple died together, all at once. That is my guess.'

Maddy reached across and grabbed the handle to the ladle and tapped it against the metal cooking pot. It made a dull clang. 'Well enough of that. Anyone for any more?'

Heads shook round the fire.

'I'm not *that* horrible a cook, am I?' She laughed loudly – an attempt to lighten the mood. It sounded forced and humourless and carried out into the dark, echoed around the hard stone basin and came back to them sounding more like the wail of some jungle creature.

CHAPTER 41

1994, the Lost City of the Windtalkers

Liam awoke suddenly. A soothing dream of warm Caribbean waves, creaking ship timbers and the snap and rustle of a restless sail was instantly blown away. Maddy had him by the shoulders and was shaking them to wake him up.

'Liam! Wake up!'

He rubbed sleep out of his blinking eyes. 'What's . . . Jay-zus, Maddy! What's the matter?'

'Sal's gone!'

'What?'

'Sal's missing!'

He sat up and looked around their camp. Beneath the awning, the grey embers of their cooking fire were surrounded by beds made of dirty grey blankets; all empty except his. They were all already up, as was the sun. He could hear Adam, Rashim and Billy, the support units, calling out for Sal from different places around the dead city, their voices ricocheting back off the ruins.

'Did she talk to you about going anywhere?'

'No.'

'Did you see her get up in the night to go to the toilet?'

'No.'

'Did you hear *anything* last night?'

He shook his head and got to his feet. 'I slept like the dead last night. I didn't –'

'She's gone, Liam!' Maddy looked around frantically. 'She's not anywhere!'

'Well she's got to be somewhere nearby.' He shaded his eyes from the sun as he scanned the labyrinthine basin.

'If she's somewhere here, Liam, she'd frikkin' well hear us! She'd answer!' Maddy shaded her eyes and looked around too. The only smudges of colour among the rust-coloured sandstone and the green of vegetation were the others, walking through the ruins and calling out Sal's name.

'Perhaps she got up in the night,' said Liam, 'stumbled or fell somewhere? Maybe she's hurt or unconscious?'

Maddy thought about that. 'She wasn't well last night, Liam. She said she wasn't feeling too well. Remember?'

'Aye. So she'd not be far then, you know? If she got up and was heading for somewhere private to relieve herself . . . ?'

'We've searched *everywhere* nearby!'

'So then maybe she's somewhere . . .' He carried on scanning the ruins. '. . . somewhere she can't hear us?'

'Can't hear us?' She shook her head, exasperated. 'It's a big echo box. No way she's not hearing them out there calling for –' She looked down at the plaza floor. 'Maybe she's down there? Maybe below the ground?'

Liam followed her gaze. 'That's quite a lot of effort to go to for a toilet.'

'No, I'm not thinking that, Liam. Look, there was something that happened yesterday afternoon. She was funny, odd . . . I can't put my finger on it.'

'What?'

'Me and Adam were trying to read some carvings down below and she wandered off. She was missing for a bit and when she came back I kind of told her off for not staying with us. But she was *really* quiet. Like she was trying to make sense of something.

I actually thought at the time she was just sulking.'

'You think – what? She's hiding? Sulking still?' Liam shook his head. 'She wouldn't play around with us like that.'

'No, not *play* with us. But maybe there's something she's seen, found, and she's – I dunno – puzzling it out before she wants to come and tell us about it. She's been getting like that, Liam, keeping things to herself. Brooding on things. Shutting us out.'

Liam looked across the plaza towards the trench entrance on the far side of it. 'You want to go take a look down there?'

Maddy nodded. 'I'm getting really worried about her.'

'I'll get Bob to come down with us.' He looked at her. The thought of stumbling across a jaguar in the dark, perhaps using that chamber as some lair, occurred to both of them.

'Good idea.'

'Saaaaal! You down here?'

The main chamber echoed back Liam's voice, but no answer came riding back with it.

'Yesterday, she wandered off somewhere, off this main chamber.' Maddy tried to remember where exactly Sal had been when she'd called across to her that she'd found something. She'd been so distracted with the carving on the floor, caught up in Adam's excitement, that she'd been rather dismissive of Sal. Casually waving her off with a 'be careful' as an afterthought.

'She was somewhere over there, when she called out.' Maddy led the way across the floor, weaving between the support columns. 'She said something about finding another room.'

They panned their torches ahead of them. Shadows cast by the columns danced wildly across the stone floor, like light-shy wraiths caught on the hop and diving for cover.

'She was skirting the edge of this chamber, looking for – hang on!' She moved the beam of her torch back the way it had just come. The shadows cast by the columns nearest the curving stone wall parted to reveal a so-easy-to-miss two-foot-wide gap in the stonework.

A narrow rectangular gap. A recess.

'That's it! That's where she was standing!'

They hastened towards it. 'Sal! You over there?' cried Maddy.

Liam shone his light into the recess. 'There's a small room. Nothing in here that I can see. She's not in there.'

Maddy cursed. 'Where the hell is she? If she's messing with us –'

'Wait!' Liam squeezed through the gap and stepped into the room. 'There's a hole over here! A hole in the floor.'

She followed him in and crossed the floor to join him. Bob squeezed through after her, grunting with effort as he scraped through the gap.

Liam was aiming his torch down into the hole. 'There's some steps leading down.' He cupped his mouth. 'Sal! Are you down there!'

No answer.

'I'll go down and take a look,' said Liam.

'Recommendation: I go first,' said Bob. 'There may be animals.' The support unit placed his foot on the first step.

'Sure. Good idea, Bob. Here.' Liam handed him his torch.

Bob's shoulders and coarse bristly head disappeared into the hole as he took the first few steps down. 'Caution: these steps are steep and slippery.'

Liam stepped in behind him, then Maddy.

'My God, this is claustrophobic!' she uttered. 'This is horrible.'

'Aye.'

They made their way down the steps until finally Bob announced he'd reached the bottom. His deep voice boomed up to them. 'I am at the bottom.'

'What the hell's down there, Bob? It sounds like you're in a large room.'

'That is correct.'

A moment later Liam was standing beside him. 'The torch, please?' Bob handed it back to him and Liam panned it around.

The light pierced the darkness and revealed some details. They appeared to be standing in another circular chamber with a diameter similar to the one above, but this time the ceiling was much higher, fifteen to twenty feet above them. There were no column supports holding up the ceiling either.

An enormous, cavernous space.

'The floor,' said Maddy. 'Look at it!'

'SAL?' called Liam. 'YOU DOWN THERE?'

No answer.

Liam shone his torch down. The light reflected smoothly back at him.

'It's . . . it's like glass or something.' He ducked down and traced his fingers across the surface. 'Perfectly smooth too.'

Maddy did the same. 'My God! Liam, can you feel that? It's warm!' She shook her head. 'This . . . this can't have been built by those Indians, surely?'

Liam shook his head.

'Then who?'

'I don't know. But this is . . . this is, like, modern. A *modern* material.'

'Yeah, like Teflon or carbon fibre or something.'

He turned to her. 'Are you thinking the same thing I'm thinking?'

'People from the future?'

'Aye. Maybe it's another group like Rashim's lot. Another Project Exodus?'

'Possible.' She bit her lip. 'Maybe this is some sort of arrival bay? Remember the "receiver field" Rashim was setting up outside Rome?'

'Or a *departure* bay?' he added. Their eyes met and this time they were certainly both thinking the same thing.

'SAL!' Maddy cried again. No answer. She turned to Liam. 'Oh God, do you think she's been transported somewhere? Maybe she activated something?' She swept her light around the chamber. 'Not that I can see anything to activate.'

Liam walked across the floor of the chamber, panning his torch beam across the black featureless surface. 'Nothing.'

But then the edge of his light picked out something large, emerging from the floor.

'What's that over there?'

The three of them made their way across the floor towards it. Closer, the beam picked out some more detail: a column approximately twelve feet in diameter, in the middle of the circular chamber, rising all the way up to the ceiling and merging seamlessly with it; a column made from the same smooth reflective material as the floor.

Closer still, they could now see the column was decorated with horizontal and vertical rows of faintly inscribed symbols. They reached this central column and Liam stretched out a hand and ran it across the surface.

'Smooth and warm, just like the floor.'

Maddy panned her torch up and down the column. 'Hundreds . . . thousands of these marks. They're all over it.' She reached out and traced one of the symbols with her finger. It was the size of her palm. 'What do they mean?' She turned to Liam. 'Do you think this is what we were meant to find?'

'I am detecting tachyon particles,' said Bob.

Maddy's breath hitched. 'This is it, then! This must be why we've been led here!'

'Tachyons?' Liam walked slowly round the base of the column. 'Is this some kind of displacement machine, Bob?'

'I have insufficient data to speculate.'

'If it is, it's a frikkin' huge one!' Maddy traced the symbols again with her fingers.

'It's got to be way more advanced than ours,' she added. 'My God, Liam! What if this was made by people *beyond* Waldstein's time? I mean way beyond! What do you think, Bob?'

'I have insufficient data to speculate, Maddy. It is of course a possibility.'

Liam rounded the back of the column. 'This is incredible!' he uttered, his voice awash with echoes bouncing back from all sides of the chamber's circular wall.

'Survivors, Liam! Humans who survived the Kosong-ni virus!' she continued. 'My God! Humans from some time after the end! We must have survived. We must have rebuilt our civilization.' Despite her concern for Sal, she found herself grinning excitedly. 'There's hope!'

Liam's foot settled on something soft. He stopped dead, suddenly feeling a growing, prickling sense of dread at what he was going to find on the floor in front of him. He aimed the beam of his torch down at his feet and let out a soft gasp.

'Oh . . . no.'

CHAPTER 42

1994, the Lost City of the Windtalkers

'Inside that column is a displacement field,' said Maddy. 'And we're almost certain Sal found a way inside and stepped into it.'

'Undressed?' Rashim looked at the clothes on the floor. 'Why would she do that?'

'It's only her T-shirt,' said Maddy. 'I think she left it where we'd find it to show us this is where she went,' said Maddy.

Billy frowned. 'Why not leave message?'

She shrugged. 'I don't know! Maybe she didn't have a pen on her, or there wasn't any *time*? Maybe whatever happened here, happened too quickly.'

'And why would she sneak away down here on her own?' asked Adam.

Maddy shook her head. 'I don't know!' She glanced at Liam. He shook his head subtly. Sal's fragile state of mind was *their* business alone. No one else's. The others didn't need to know about that.

'She's always been the most observant, the most curious out of us three,' Maddy continued. 'She must have discovered it yesterday and wanted to figure it all out for herself before telling us about it.' Even as she said that, it sounded lame. An unconvincing explanation. But then who really knew what was going through Sal's head right now?

Adam turned and started examining the surface of the column. 'These glyphs . . . there's hundreds of them.'

'Three thousand and seventy-seven,' said Bob. 'I have counted them.'

'I think every single one of them appears to be unique,' said Adam. 'This column could be a key stone. A tool for unlocking this language. Incredible . . . this is an artefact from a society so far in the future, so far removed from our civilization today, that we would be as alien to them, as *mysterious* to them, as Atlanteans.'

'The material of this column looks very modern,' said Rashim, rapping his knuckles gently against the surface. 'Possibly a carbonite meta-material.'

'Maybe it's instructions,' said Liam. 'How to make it open up?'

Rashim nodded. 'That is exactly what it looks like to me. Like an embedded touch-screen interface.'

'So maybe Sal figured it out,' said Maddy. 'She's good at that kind of thing, pattern recognition.'

'Or she just got lucky?'

Rashim stroked his finger along one of the characters. 'Have you noticed the markings seem to be warmer than the rest of the surface?' He looked at them. 'You know, this really does look like a user interface. A control panel.'

'Hold on, Rashim!' said Maddy. 'Better not touch them any more, in case we're causing something to happen. Remember: Sal's in there!'

Rashim pulled his hand back. 'Yes, you are right.'

'Bob? Becks?' She turned to the support units. 'Come on, any ideas?'

'We have both been analysing the tachyon particles being emitted,' said Becks. 'There is a distinct pattern and orientation to their movement.'

'So? What does that mean?'

'They are travelling along a uniform axis,' said Bob. 'Every particle path is exactly parallel. This is a *tightly* targeted field. This would explain why we did not detect any rogue particles until we were in close proximity to this artefact.'

'Targeted? Like when we've tried to send a signal back through time?'

'Correct.'

'So you're saying this is just some kind of large transmitter?'

Rashim shook his head. 'No.' He looked again at Sal's discarded shirt. 'Clearly this does much more than just transmit a tachyon signal. Sal has been sent somewhere.'

'Rashim is correct,' said Becks. 'It may function as a displacement field and signal.'

'Where though?' said Maddy. 'If she did get in, we need to find out where she's gone!'

'The tachyons are being aimed directly into the ground,' said Bob.

'So is there another room below?' asked Liam.

'Not necessarily,' Becks responded. 'Tachyons pass through solid matter without any impedance. The beam could be aimed towards or from something on the far side of the world or beyond.'

'This beam – is it *originating* here?' asked Maddy. 'Or are we *receiving* here?'

'We have insufficient data,' replied Becks.

Rashim pressed his lips with an index finger. 'Displacement technology on this scale would need an incredible amount of energy.' He looked around the empty chamber. 'So if this is the transmission's origin point . . . where is the power coming from?'

'If the signal is originating from this location, it does not necessarily need to be originating from this time,' said Becks.

Maddy looked at her. 'Not now? Not the present?'

'That is correct.'

'Past or future? Can you tell me that?'

'We are unable to determine that at the moment,' said Bob. 'More data is required.'

Liam looked up at the column. 'So this signal? It's just passing through?'

'Affirmative.'

'If Sal somehow managed to open this up and step into this "signal". . .' Maddy narrowed her eyes, thinking hard. 'Is it possible then that she could have been swept all the way along to wherever it's being aimed at?'

'There is a high probability that is exactly what has happened,' answered Becks.

'All right then. Can the two of you figure it out? Could you work out where, when, the tachyon beam starts and ends?'

'We can sample the density, travel tangents, decay rate of the particles at this moment in time and calculate approximate locations of the start and end points of the signal,' said Bob. 'But this would be speculative and not precise.'

'We could make a more accurate calculation if we gathered additional data nearer the signal origin and nearer the signal destination,' added Becks.

'Like picking three points on a graph,' said Rashim to the others. 'Two points gives you a line, a third point on the line gives you confirmation you've got the tangent right.'

Bob nodded. 'That is an accurate analogy.'

Maddy pressed her lips. Decisions to be made. 'So we're going to need to go back to London. Then send you two backwards and forwards along this beam so you can go count tachyons, right?'

They both nodded.

She looked at Adam, then glanced at the glyphs inscribed on the column's smooth surface. 'The other option, I guess, is figuring how this "user interface" works, if that's what it is. If we can operate this thing, maybe we can bring her back again.'

'I can either try to decode what all the markings mean,' Adam said with a shrug, 'or I can play around with it until something interesting happens?'

'No!' She shook her head, quickly dismissing that option. 'No . . . I think we shouldn't mess with this thing any more. Don't even touch it.' She was already worried that their fingers running over the glyphs might already have altered the signal in some way, perhaps subtly reprogrammed it, changing things . . . and . . .

And then Sal would be lost forever, wouldn't she?

She pulled Rashim's homemade cobbled-together beacon out of her pocket, opened the lid and flipped the toggle switch on. Hopefully computer-Bob was going to pick up their signal. Hopefully the faint tachyon whisper of Rashim's modest beacon wasn't going to be drowned out by the blast of this tachyon version of a foghorn.

'I *am* going to find her. And, just in case anyone's having doubts, that's not up for discussion,' Maddy said. 'We're getting Sal back before we do anything else.'

CHAPTER 43

1889, London

Computer-Bob *was* patiently listening for their whispered signal. And heard them. A test pinhole window opened, followed minutes later by a portal. Maddy, Liam and the support units stepped back to 1889 and into their dungeon.

Maddy let Bob and Becks silently update the computer with their wireless memories and soon computer-Bob was as aware of current affairs as anyone else.

> I did not detect any other interfering tachyon signal at your location.

'Presumably because that bigger signal was a focused beam and not just a general scattering of tachyons?'

> That is correct, Maddy.

'We need Bob sent to that same location at some point before 1994, and Becks some time after. But how far in time does each of them need to go?'

'The further apart in time we are located,' replied Becks, 'the more useful our contrasted data will be.'

'Right, so – what? A hundred years either way?'

> A 200-year spread should provide adequate data.

'Right then, can you set up those time-stamps and get the displacement charging up for those two portals?'

> Yes, Maddy.

Liam came to stand beside her. 'I might get a change of

clothes.' He nodded towards the privacy curtains and their hammocks slung beyond. 'I feel as grubby as a chimney sweep.'

'Uh?' She turned to look up at him and was suddenly taken aback at how rough he looked. His face still looked battered and scabbed, a purple bruise round his left eye made it appear like the sunken socket of a much older man. That, coupled with a week's worth of growth round his chin and mouth – his dark hair seemed to be just that bit lighter, threaded with grey here and there – and she realized she was beginning to see the ghost of Foster's features in his face.

'Why don't you go to the local bath house? Take your time, clean yourself up. Have a shave. You look like you've been through hell, Liam.'

He smiled wearily. 'I might just do that.'

She watched him go and wondered sadly what was becoming of them.

Liam's dying.

The corrosive effect of time travel was beginning to take its toll on him. He was further along that path than either her or Sal – that huge jump to the late Cretaceous early in their tour of duty must have taken its toll on him and was now beginning to show itself. She wondered when she was going to start seeing the ageing effect manifest itself in her own reflection: the faint spider lines of wrinkles round her eyes, the greying of her own hair, the faint discoloration of liver spots and burst blood vessels turning her pale freckled skin into a premature atlas of memories.

Soon, no doubt.

And Sal. God knows where the hell she was now, why she'd been foolish enough to step into a portal without knowing its destination.

*

Two hours later, with the help of Rashim's diesel generator speeding up the recharge time, the displacement machine's charge indicator was showing a full store of energy tucked away in its capacitor array.

Computer-Bob had the time-stamp data arranged and was ready to open the first window.

'OK, Bob,' said Maddy. 'You're up first. You're going a hundred years back from the current location of the column. So that's 1894 for you. And, Becks, you're going forward – 2094 for you. We'll give you an hour each at both those locations. Will that be enough time for you to record the tachyon particles?'

'An hour should be sufficient,' said Bob.

'Good. Take your positions then.'

Bob and Becks stepped on to the square wooden plinths, their feet compressing the dirt and sawdust beneath them.

Maddy checked the countdown on one of the computer monitors. 'OK, Bob . . . fifteen seconds. You ready?'

'Affirmative, Maddy.'

She reached across and play-punched his arm. 'Happy counting, big guy.'

'Caution: you should keep your hands clear of the –'

'Yeah, yeah . . . I know. Health and safety.' She stepped back. 'See you soon.'

She counted down the last five seconds over the increasing volume of the displacement machine's eager hum. A rectangular field enveloped Bob and he disappeared along with two inches of dirt and sawdust.

'Right, Becks – your turn.'

1894, the Lost City of the Windtalkers

Bob emerged from the portal and into the chamber. He snapped on his torch and panned it around. The chamber was unchanged, no different to how it *would be* in a hundred years, when Liam and the others would be standing there. The same circular acre of mica-black floor, reflecting the light back at him. The same central column quietly containing a powerful tachyon beam in transit between some unknown time in the future and some unknown time in the past.

He approached the surface of the dark column and rested his hand against the smooth material, sensing the powerful passing of energy just inches away. Like a surging river contained within a cylindrical sheath. He turned off the torch, leaving himself in pitch-black darkness, closed his eyes and concentrated. Almost immediately his silicon mind began to register the presence of wayward particles spinning out of their prescribed paths and he began to log them: cataloguing their number, their velocity, their charge, their decay rate.

2094, the Lost City of the Windtalkers

Becks stepped out of the portal and on to the smooth, featureless floor of the chamber. She switched on her torch and, like Bob, noted how the very same chamber looked unchanged. But as she approached the central column she noticed it – *sensed* it – immediately.

'The tachyon signal has stopped,' she whispered quietly to herself.

Curious, she ran her fingers across the column's smooth surface. She sensed nothing was going on within. It was dead.

It was now an inert and lifeless cylindrical structure containing nothing of interest. She had an hour until the return portal would appear, so she decided to put the time to good use and explore further afield.

She climbed the steps up the narrow stairwell to the low-ceilinged chamber above, weaved her way through the forest of support columns towards the exit.

She emerged into a sunny day. The pupils of her grey eyes instantly contracted against the brightness as she looked around.

She reminded herself that she was standing in a time twenty-four years after the end – after the Pandora event had occurred. The earth right now would be quiet. She knew this stillness, this rather pleasant stillness, would exist everywhere. In every city, town, village, coarse grass and weeds would be threading themselves through, around, over and covering the humps and husks of billions of bodies. The bodies nothing more than the bones, teeth, nails and hair, the organic material the Kosong-ni virus was unable to break down into a liquid.

Cities would be standing empty, streets filled with the bones and ragged clothes of countless billions. The highways out of those same cities would be clogged with vehicles log-jammed together, their occupants skeletons too.

A silent world.

However, in one or two locations around the planet, small groups of human survivors would be starting to coalesce together into loose allegiances, struggling to hang in there – those 'lucky' few whose resistance to the virus saved them from death but cursed them to this hard life of scavenging from the scrapheap of humankind.

She speculated that their lives would be difficult and brutal, and so would the lives of their children; the first generation who would never know what a holo-screen was, or see vapour trails arc across the upper troposphere, or watch endless digi-channels of reality shows or hear tinny digital music on their temple-jack inserts, or dress up in mood-glow fashionwear, or chat in virtual headspace with their friends.

Perhaps ten, twenty, a hundred generations from now planet Earth would become a lively place once more, filled with the noise and chaos and pollution generated by humanity, but for now Mother Nature had it back.

Becks looked around at the remains of this ancient forgotten city. It looked no different.

The jungle was still very much hard at work reclaiming this place. The humid air was filled with the incessant chirruping of jungle life. The world could quite happily go on without mankind for a while.

She wandered over to the camp they'd made a hundred years ago on the edge of the round plaza. There, she noted the last shreds of the canvas awning lying on the ground, partially covered in a windblown carpet of dead leaves. The bed rolls were all but covered beneath growths of moss. The pot in which Maddy had once made a broth was a rusted relic, the handles long ago broken off and flaked away.

Becks looked around the basin-shaped ruins of this long-dead city and knew that right now every other city would one day look like this. In fact – correction – few of those modern cathedrals of concrete, steel and glass would last as long as this ancient ruin made of stone. Stone was forever. The skyscrapers of Shanghai, New York, London, Dubai would collapse on themselves within a hundred years. Would be overgrown humps of vegetation within five hundred years, and would be mere forensic evidence within a thousand.

But these ancient Mayan ruins would still be standing proud.

She pulled a quote from her database: '. . . *the twentieth century will be the last century to leave behind it archaeological footprints robust enough to stand the test of millennia . . .'*

She felt the warm sun on her face, listened to the soothing cacophony of life coming from all sides, coming from the overflowing rim of jungle above her and around this ghost city.

The world after mankind didn't seem to her to be such a terrible place after all. Life in all its many forms seemed to be carrying on quite cheerfully. Was in fact thriving without the toxic *contaminant* of humankind.

CHAPTER 44

1994, the Lost City of the Windtalkers

Adam swigged back some of the coffee Billy had made for them. 'So, we all die. *All* of us?'

Rashim nodded. 'Pretty much all of us. That's what they told me. I never actually saw the outbreak of this Von Neumann virus. It is supposed to have happened about six months after I left for Ancient Rome to set up the receiver beacons.' He ran a hand through the sweaty strands of his dark hair.

'But I can quite easily believe that is the fate that awaits us. We have always had a built-in redundancy, I suspect: a capacity, perhaps even a desire, to one day destroy ourselves.'

'Jesus.' Adam shook his head.

'In 2069, we could all see that something bad was coming our way,' continued Rashim. 'A war over the last of our resources, the last of the oil reserves. It was either going to be a nuclear war, or more probably biological warfare.'

He poured himself some more coffee. 'This is why Project Exodus was set up . . . a chance for some of us to escape into the past and try to reboot a modern civilization far enough back in time that we could redirect our destiny. Make it so these things do not happen.'

'You know, when I was at school,' said Adam, 'that would be 1989. I remember we discussed that kind of thing in Social Studies. What the world would be like in a hundred years and so on. We were given that subject to write an essay about. I remember my teacher, Mr Armstrong, reading some of them out in the class.' Adam laughed as he recalled. 'It was pretty naive happy-clappy stuff. The future would be all hovercars and Mars already with a colony on it and busy being terraformed. Space tourism. People going to the moon for a holiday. Cures for every illness, even cures for old age. All very hopeful, optimistic, utopian ideas. I was the only one who wrote something negative.'

Rashim looked at him. 'What did you write?'

'Oh, some pretentious babble about the fall of man, how we were doomed to repeat history, to repeat the errors of other fallen civilizations. How we would consume the world and then the world would one day consume us.'

'Very prescient of you, I think.'

'I was just trying to impress one of the cool girls in my class, Amelia Hall, with my moody, brooding intensity.' He smirked. 'Didn't realize back then that girls are far more impressed with a bloke who can do a funny voice and make 'em laugh.'

They sat in silence for a while before Rashim spoke. 'It is a hopeful sign.'

'What? The transmission beacon?'

Rashim nodded. 'It is a clear indication that mankind will one day recover and rebuild itself. Perhaps our distant descendants will be far more responsible with technology than we ever were.'

Adam nodded. It did seem to bode well for mankind's eventual future. But how many hundreds of years were going to pass before mankind emerged from almost complete annihilation? The future seemed such a fragile and fickle thing: a slave to the decisions of those in the past. He understood now why Maddy had been so coy with him back in the rebel camp. She'd said the less she told him about his future, the better.

Billy's voice echoed out across the plaza. They both looked his way and saw Maddy, Liam and the two support units approaching them.

'Wow, that was quick,' said Adam. He looked at his watch. 'They went only an hour ago?'

'Remember, Adam . . . time isn't symmetrical. They may have been gone days, weeks even. We will find out.'

Maddy climbed several stone steps leading up to the others. 'Hey, guys, we're back!' She sat down wearily on a block of stone. 'Coffee. Any left?'

Rashim leaned forward, scooped a ladleful and poured it into a mug. 'So? Did your support units gather the information they were after?'

Liam settled down beside her. 'Aye, we *think* we know where that tachyon signal is coming from and going to.'

'According to them –' Maddy nodded at Bob and Becks – 'the signal is travelling between one point nearly two thousand years ago and another in the year 2070.'

'So, it is a beacon that is transmitting across just over two millennia?'

'Yeah. But it gets just a bit weirder than that. The beam end points –' she looked at Adam – 'You'll love this.'

'Why?'

She looked up at Bob. 'Go on, I'll let you two tell them.'

'One of the signal end points is at this location,' said Bob, 'in the year 2070.'

'The other end point,' said Becks, 'is on the other side of the world. We calculate the origin time to be approximately twenty-one centuries earlier.'

Adam looked at them. 'The other side of the world? Where?'

Maddy and Liam exchanged a glance. He nodded that she might as well answer the question.

'Bob and Becks were able to be a lot more precise about the location than the times. The other end point is located in the city of Jerusalem, Israel. It travels through the middle of Earth from Jerusalem and emerges out the other side, right here.'

'*What?*'

'More precisely, the other end of this signal is located somewhere beneath what is quite possibly the *holiest* building on this planet. The Dome of the Rock.'

'I know that,' said Adam. 'You mean that big cathedral with the gold dome? The one on the hill in the middle of the Old City of Jerusalem?'

She nodded. 'That one, yes. Built on Temple Mount. The holiest place in the world for Christians and Jews, and also one of the holiest places in the world for Muslims. Apparently the hill on which it was built is the point from which Muhammad the Prophet ascended to Heaven.'

'My God,' Adam gasped.

Maddy cocked an eyebrow. 'Funny you should say that . . .'

'And the time of that end point,' continued Liam, 'is about the same time as a certain fella called Jesus Christ was walking around.'

Rashim stroked his beard. 'Are you suggesting there is a link between this tachyon beam and – and the *origin* of the Christian and Islamic faiths?'

'I'm not suggesting anything.' Maddy shrugged. 'It *is* a suspicious overlap, though. I'm not saying there's a causal link here, not at all. But whoever set this beam up must have been walking around Jerusalem at that time. It's possible that they would have appeared other-worldly and exotic to the locals. Perhaps even god-like? Right?'

'So why build this thing?' asked Adam. 'What's its purpose?'

Maddy waved her hand. 'A conduit to the past to . . . to – I dunno – to view the birth of Christianity? Perhaps these are future archaeologists? *Anthropologists* keen to learn more about humankind before the big apocalypse. Think about it . . . to them – God knows how many thousands of years in the future they come from – we would be their long-lost ancestors.'

'So, are you saying Sal is now stuck in biblical times?' asked Rashim.

'No. We don't think so.' She looked up at Bob and Becks. 'You two have a theory about *when* she is, don't you?'

Bob nodded. 'We detected the echoes of a sudden fluctuation in energy along the transmission axis of the signal. The fluctuation appears to have occurred approximately five hundred years ago.'

'The fluctuation,' continued Becks, 'may have been caused by the column being opened. This would result in a significant discharge of energy. If that is what has occurred, then Sal may have exited the tachyon conduit at that point.'

Maddy leaned forward. She wanted to clarify what Becks was saying. 'This beam appears to be a completely sealed thing. Like a water pipe, if you like, transporting tachyons to and from Jerusalem, year zero, to this location in AD 2070. But . . . it appears to have sprung a leak sometime around AD 1500.'

'And that's where we're going?' asked Adam.

'That's where me and Liam and our pet meatbots are going. It's up to you guys whether you want to tag along. But this is about getting Sal back now. Pandora? The actual purpose of this beam? All the rest of it – *those* questions are going to have to wait.' She looked at Liam for support.

'Aye.' He nodded. 'Sal comes first. She's our top priority. Once we find her . . . *then* we'll go take a look at them other things. Then we'll go get some answers.'

CHAPTER 45

1889, London

Bertie watched in silent awe as the dark brick dungeon began to fill up with people. First Dr Anwar's main assistant, Miss Carter, the girl with the frizzy hair, then the Irish lad, Liam O'Connor. Then Dr Anwar himself, followed by a scruffy young man with ginger hair like lengths of frayed rope. Then a short dark-skinned man with bulbous goggle eyes. And, if that wasn't enough to make the room feel crowded, Bob the giant man came next followed by the cool grey-eyed beauty.

They filled the room with three or four conversations, talking over each other. Bertie picked out bits and pieces passing between them. The fact that they were preparing to leave this place for yet *another* destination some time in the fifteenth century. The fact that something needed recharging and that some additional supplies needed purchasing.

The fact that they were going after someone who'd gone missing.

And he knew from her absence who they were talking about.

Miss Saleena Vikram.

Bertie cowered back behind the hammock as they paced around the room just beyond the curtain. On one occasion Liam had stepped right up to it and without warning reached through, inside, his hand almost brushing Bertie's cheek, to grab a cloth cap that was hanging on a coat stand. Then he was off out with the giant and the grey-eyed beauty, 'Becks', on some errand to collect supplies.

Dr Anwar and Maddy discussed dates and spoke numbers that made little sense to him, other than that they were trying to calculate more precisely *when* in the fifteenth century they were all heading off to.

The young man with hair like lengths of frayed rope spoke to the dark goggle-eyed man, explaining things to him in a way that Bertie was surprised to find he actually understood.

'. . . so this is where their base of operations is, Billy. This is where they live. That rack of wires over there? You see where that row of orange lights is? That's their time machine, although they prefer to call it a *displacement machine*.'

The goggle-eyed man – *Billy* – seemed to be taking it all in his stride, nodding thoughtfully at every explanation. Bertie found himself getting extremely frustrated that the small man wasn't asking follow-up questions. *How does this displacement machine work? Does it require much energy, and where the devil was that being drawn from anyway? The viaduct's generator? Do these 'windows' or 'portals' open just anywhere? If so . . . what stops them opening inside the middle of a rock, or the ground, or another person?*

Several times Bertie wondered whether he should just step out from behind the curtains and calmly announce his presence. Surely, eventually, someone was going to pull the fabric aside and come into this space looking for some possession and find him hiding here? Would it not be better to volunteer himself rather than be discovered, loitering guiltily like a common cut-purse?

But he didn't, so yet more hours passed as he hid, praying that at some point everyone would finally be gone and he could make a dash for the door.

Liam, the Giant and the Beauty returned after a while with

wicker baskets full of things. Some tin-packed foods, bottles of medicines. A pair of ex-army Martini-Henry rifles and several cartons of ammunition and other assorted victuals.

Once again Bertie was sure he was about to be discovered when Maddy strode towards the curtain looking for something. But, at the last moment, Liam found what she was after – a jacket, lying on the back of one of the armchairs – and tossed it over to her.

More time passed as they sent the Giant and the Beauty out for hot food, to return half an hour later with a basket full of hot steaming pies. As they silently ate, sitting on the various armchairs surrounding a wooden table, Bertie realized how hungry he'd become, trapped, hiding in this room for the best part of the whole day. He was surprised the others hadn't heard his rumbling, gurgling stomach.

Pies . . . followed by mugs of coffee. The water had been boiled not on a stove but in some futuristic-looking gadget that clicked itself off as steam began to spew from its spout. The odd gathering in front of him, again talking over each other, finished their drinks, and then Dr Anwar and Maddy approached the table on which the row of glowing 'information windows' sat. They seemed to be talking to the windows and in turn the windows changed their displays to show them numbers.

Presently Maddy turned round and announced they had identified a 'best candidate' time to go back to. That they were using 'the cave' as the arrival location. That the displacement machine was nearly fully charged and that she'd be opening a portal in five minutes.

The room became busy with activity.

Maddy explained to Billy about standing very still within the square plinths filled with dirt and sawdust, that the 'displacement machine was configured to capture the vertical space above them'.

Anything sticking out . . . will be left behind!

The supplies were hastily stowed into backpacks, the two guns were given to the Giant and the Beauty to carry. They slung them on straps over their shoulders.

Then Bertie heard that deep humming sound again, quiet at first, but he now knew what was coming. The hum would slowly rise in pitch and volume, the crackling sensation of static electricity building up, lifting the hairs on his arms, the nape of his neck. Then finally there would be either the appearance of that hovering sphere or the vertical shimmering column emerging from the two square plinths.

The first two to go were the Giant and the Beauty. The advance guard. Then the Irish lad and the man with rope for hair. Then the goggle-eyed one and Dr Anwar with the backpacks stacked together, one on the other.

Finally, Bertie found himself alone with the American girl. He watched as she spoke to the row of glowing windows on the table, issuing a command to them that she wanted them to open a 'return window' when she activated 'her beacon'.

She took her place on one of the plinths.

Bertie knew that he was about to make a reckless decision that might possibly lead to a grisly death. A decision that almost certainly would change his life, his mind, forever. That could never be undone.

But . . . he had to know more.

Yes, it did seem that, *at last*, the room would soon be empty and he could finally make his escape. But after all he'd seen, all he'd heard – how could he? How could he go back to being Del Hook's mere errand-boy? How could he face going back to his rented rooms, his mundane life?

As the hum of the displacement machine rose and became an ungodly shrill scream of pent-up energy, he pulled the curtain to one side and leaped across the open floor and past Miss Carter, to land atop the vacant plinth.

Just before the power erupted and he became engulfed in a field of energy, he caught a final glimpse of her, two yards to his left, wide-eyed, slack-jawed, staring at him.

CHAPTER 46

1479, a cave, Nicaragua

Maddy felt firm ground beneath her feet and emerged from the non-dimension's milky mist. She immediately turned to her right to glare at Bertie as he appeared beside her.

'*How the hell did you –?*'

'Good God!' he gasped, his legs buckling, as he collapsed to an unsteady kneel. 'God help me, what was *that place*?!' His eyes were wide and rolling, his face pale and grey with shock.

She ignored his question. '*How did you get into our room?*'

The others were staring at Bertie, equally dumbstruck.

'Jay-zus! What's *he* of all people doing here?' asked Liam.

'That's exactly what I'm trying to find out.' Maddy squatted down beside him. 'What the hell were you playing at, you idiot?'

Bertie still seemed to be in complete shock. 'It was – it was – I saw a nothingness! I saw . . . Infinite . . . empty! I – I . . . saw –'

'Yeah, yeah . . . just relax. Deep breaths,' she said impatiently. 'That's it, nice and easy.'

Bertie seemed to recover his composure after a few moments. 'My God, that place is the embodiment of Hell!'

'It's what we go through every time. It's quite normal.'

He looked at her, glassy-eyed. 'A godless void! I – I saw a godless void!'

'Well, look, you made it through in one piece.' She offered

him her best reassuring smile. 'But now, I'm afraid, you're just gonna have to go back.'

'OK, so is anyone going to explain who *this* bloke is?' demanded Adam.

'Bertie Wells,' replied Maddy. 'We rent that room under the viaduct from his boss, Delbert. Herbert's his assistant and his bookkeeper.'

'Please!' Bertie looked at her. 'Don't make me go back into that place!'

Adam joined her, squatted down beside her. 'So what just happened? Did he walk into the room just as you were about to leave and . . .' His voice suddenly tailed away. He frowned. Pensive. 'Hold on, did you just say his first name was *Herbert*?'

Bertie looked at Adam and nodded vigorously. 'Yes – yes, th-that is my name.'

'Herbert Wells?'

Maddy did a double-take. 'Why? You're not about to tell me you know him or something?'

'Herbert . . . *George* . . . Wells?'

Bertie nodded again. 'How do . . . h-how is it you know my middle name, sir?'

Adam suddenly laughed and smacked the floor of the cave with the palm of his hand. 'Oh, no way! No way!' He looked around at the others. 'None of you have any idea at all who this is, have you?'

Liam shrugged. 'It's Bertie.'

'Herbert George Wells!' Adam cried. He suppressed a gleeful giggle. 'Better known as *H. G. Wells*!'

It finally fell into place for Rashim. 'You are not talking about the famous writer?!'

Adam was already nodding. 'Yes! The author of *The Time Machine*, *The War of the Worlds*!'

He rocked back on his heels. 'Jesus. This is incredible!'

Liam looked perplexed. 'You're saying he's a *famous* person?'

'Only the father of all science fiction!' said Adam.

Maddy closed her eyes and nodded. 'Of course! You know, I can't believe I didn't put that together. I am so stupid.'

Bertie was still looking lost. 'You – you people all know me?'

'You're going to be one of the most famous writers that ever lived!' said Adam. 'You're going to inspire a generation of writers to –'

'Hang on,' cut in Maddy. 'This is all going to have to wait till later. We've got much more important things to sort out. We need to get a fix on whether we've got the time right.'

She got to her feet. 'And *then* we'll have to arrange to send you back.'

'I . . . I can stay? For now? ' asked Bertie, looking up hopefully at her.

She sucked on her teeth for a moment. 'Right, OK . . . yeah. For now, I guess.' She turned away impatiently and began to make her way towards the rear of the cave. 'Jesus,' she muttered to herself. 'It's one frikkin' thing after another.'

She snapped on her torch as the receding daylight coming from the cave's entrance grew too weak to be of any use. She picked her way towards where the writing was meant to be. It was there, as she'd hoped, only this time the paint was noticeably darker and more distinct. She shone her light on it.

Liam was beside her. 'That still looks pretty old to me, though.'

She nodded; it did. Although the paint was a darker hue, it had still flaked away in places. The others joined them, Bertie wild-eyed and still quite clearly in shock, following along like a lost sheep.

'This is the year 1479,' said Becks. 'Our calculations will have an error margin.'

'How much of an error margin?'

'Approximately nine months.'

Liam looked at them. 'So you're saying we could be hanging around here for up to nine months before this power surge happens?'

'That is correct, Liam,' replied Bob.

'Or . . . it could just as likely happen in the next hour. It's an error margin,' said Maddy. 'We'll find out how close we are soon enough.'

'I say,' Bertie interrupted, 'I say, would someone mind telling me . . . where exactly are we?'

Maddy turned to look at him standing at the back of their growing band of time travellers.

Eight of us now. Nine once we've got Sal back. This is getting ridiculous.

'We're in the jungles of Central America. The year is 1479.'

Bertie nodded politely.

She turned back to Liam. 'We'll head down to the chamber and Bob and Becks should be able to –'

'And might I humbly ask another question, Miss Carter?'

Maddy sighed. Turned back to look at Bertie. 'What?'

'Might I humbly ask *why* you are here?'

'Not really. It's private business. And we're going to have to send you back –'

'Would it be that you are here to rescue Miss Saleena?' he quickly added. 'I know that she has gone missing!' He looked sheepishly at her. 'I overheard the matter being discussed in your room.'

She frowned and put her hands on her hips. 'Crap! What else have you overheard?'

'I heard she may be in grave danger.' He stepped forward. 'I would like to offer my assistance . . . in any way I can.'

'I've got a lot on my plate right now, Bertie. I really can't be doing with –'

Bertie clasped his hands together in supplication. 'I beg you to allow me to assist in any way I can and not send me back. I assure you I will be no burden or –'

'No worse than having Billy or Adam along with us,' said Liam.

Maddy sighed and stared at him with a *thanks-for-the-support* expression on her face.

'You're really H. G. Wells?' said Maddy. Not really a question. 'The problem I have, Bertie, is that you're a famous writer. Or, at least, going to be.'

'But . . . you must have me mistaken for someone else! I am no such thing, Miss Carter. I am just a bookkeeper and a maths tutor.'

'No, but you *will* write books. And millions of people will read them. You'll have a name that's known around the world. That means you're far too big a risk for us.'

'Does he not already know too much?' said Liam. 'Surely the damage is already done, Mads?'

'What if he writes books with our names in them, Liam? What if he writes books about a small group of people who –' she chose her words carefully – 'who have a *certain task* they have to do? What if he sets their story in Victorian London? Don't you see? If all of a sudden a time wave alters the title of *The Time Machine* to, say, *The Displacement Machine Beneath Holborn Viaduct* . . . don't you think a *certain person* might not just pick up on that and send some of his heavies to come and take us out?'

'I assure you – all of you – I won't tell a soul of anything I see!'

'Why not let him come along for now?' Liam shrugged.

'We're about to meet some ancient Indians. We might be grateful for an extra pair of hands?'

Bertie would up their numbers. Eight people, three firearms. Perhaps Liam had a point there.

'All right . . . just for now.' She nodded towards the rear of the cave where the tunnel was hidden in darkness.

'We're about to present ourselves to a tribe of Mayan Indians. We're probably going to need their co-operation. Which means we'll want to look all scary and god-like so they're frightened enough that they don't try to kill us and eat us. OK?'

She looked directly at Bertie. 'So here's how it is, Herbert. You can tag along until we've found Sal again. Then you can take her back to London with you. Then we'll have to decide what we're going to do about you.'

Herbert looked alarmed at that.

'She doesn't mean we're going to kill you,' said Liam.

'No,' Maddy agreed. 'But we have a way of making you not remember any of this: making sure this never actually happened in the first place.'

Bertie looked at Rashim. 'Dr Anwar, let me ask *you*, sir, if I might be allowed to –'

'Do not ask me,' he said with a wave of his hand, 'she is the one in charge here.'

Maddy was in no mood to waste any more time on this. 'That's how it is, Bertie. You can be a help, or a hindrance. If you're going to be the latter, then we'll just have to throw you back in the white stuff, OK?'

His face instantly paled. 'I will not be any hindrance. I assure you!'

'Good.' She clapped her hands together. 'Right, let's get those guns loaded and ready to use. We're going to give these Mayans a bit of a show.'

This time, the tunnel entrance at the back of the cave was not hidden by a boulder or overgrown with vines and ivy nor filled with centuries' worth of spiders' webs. As she expected, it was clearly a well-used access into the city. The people living within the sinkhole must have walked through this tunnel all the time, carrying goods that would have been brought up the cliff-face trail from the settlement down by the river.

Sunlight from the far end glowed brightly, and as they entered they could see ahead of them the silhouette of a young goatherd coaxing his animals up the tunnel towards them with a stick, their bleats and the *clip-clap* of their hooves echoing off the stone walls.

Closer, the young boy halted. Cocked his head for a moment, then cried out in alarm. He turned and ran back the way he'd come, leaving his animals behind to curiously regard the approaching strangers.

'I think we've been spotted,' said Liam.

'You think?' Maddy glanced sideways. Bob and Becks had already unshouldered their rifles ready for action and Billy slipped the safety catch off his battered old AK.

'OK, just to be clear about this. We're not massacring everyone. Right? We may actually need these people's help. So, we're just going to make a bunch of noise and look very impressive.'

'*We got to brass it out, Danny*,' uttered Adam under his breath.

Maddy turned to look at him. 'What's that?'

Adam shucked his shoulders nervously. 'Just a quote. From an old film.'

'Right, thanks for that.' She looked back at the glow of light ahead of them and watched the boy's fleeing silhouette. 'Show-time.'

They shooed the goats aside, and finally approached the passage's exit, bright daylight dazzling them as they emerged into the warmth of the sun.

CHAPTER 47

1479, the Lost City of the Windtalkers

Liam stood beside her and gazed out at the scene before them. The very same city built into a natural basin as before, of course – a wide panorama full of buildings, terraces, balconies and courtyards jostling and overlooking each other – receded away in stepped descent down to a circular plaza at the bottom.

The first time they'd emerged from the overgrown tunnel entrance the scene had been dominated by two hues, the rust of the sandstone and the green of vegetation, whereas *now* . . . it was an amateur artist's overladen palette, an argument of colours. Woven mats decorated stone floors and tapestries of beads threaded on to twine hung in every doorway and window. Smoke curled up into the sky from dozens of clay-pot chimneys and every narrow street seemed to be teeming with people, goats, llamas and barking dogs.

Liam was reminded of the chaotic life of Port Royal, Jamaica. Life lived cheek-by-jowl; a riot of noises, colours and smells.

They watched the boy running away from them, his bare feet slapping against stone and carrying him down towards the plaza where market stalls laden with fruits and animal carcasses clustered in the centre. His shrill voice, crying the same word over and over – *Hantuh-ha! Hantuh-ha!* – was lost now amid the general echoing hubbub of a normal busy day, but they noticed heads were turning their way and each face that spotted them suddenly became smudged with a static, dark 'O' of alarm.

Like a ripple slowly spreading across a pond, the busy sinkhole city quietened as more and more bronze-coloured faces stared up at them with a sense of apprehension. Very soon the noise and bustle of life had petered out, to be replaced with an unsettling stillness, filled only by the far-away hooting of jungle life and the sporadic barking of a dog tethered on the plaza.

Liam looked at Maddy. 'Looks like it's our turn.'

He could hear her breath fluttering nervously, see her lips trembling.

'You OK there?' he whispered.

She took a deep breath to steady her nerves. 'I'm OK.' And then she *did* seem fine. 'Just wasn't expecting so many of them.' She turned round. 'Bob, Becks – you two with me. The rest of you better stay here.'

She paced forward, down the sloping paved walkway with the support units flanking her. The crowd nearby stepped back from them warily as they approached.

Liam turned to Adam. 'She may get a little prickly from time to time,' he said, smiling proudly as he watched her pacing confidently forward, 'but she's got guts, so she has.'

Adam nodded. 'More than anyone I've ever met.'

Maddy stopped and held a hand out to one side. 'Here's probably far enough,' she said quietly. The support units came to a halt, both of them glaring menacingly at the silent, frozen crowd.

She cleared her throat.

Showtime.

'WE. MEAN. YOU. NO. HARM!' Her voice echoed across the silent city, and she looked at Becks. 'Did that sound as cheesy as I think it did?'

'They do not understand what you are saying, Maddy,' she replied.

'Also,' added Bob, '*cheesiness* is not a concept they would be familiar with.'

As the echo of her voice faded, she spotted movement towards the back of the crowd of frightened-looking people. Heads parted, creating a gap for someone who was making their way forward.

'Looks like someone's coming to meet us.'

Presently, the front of the crowd of wary onlookers stepped back to make way for a frail elderly man carried on a litter by four young bearers. His small frame was covered in a poncho made of coloured beads that rattled and hissed like a rainstick with his every movement. He wore a copper circlet round his head; above it, a transverse crest of colourful turquoise-green and sky-blue parakeet feathers. The bearers set the litter down on the ground and one of them helped the old man up on to his feet. He shuffled forward, supported by the elbow until he stood just six feet short of them.

Deep sunken eyes, almost lost beneath drooping folds of leathery brown skin, studied Maddy intently, then looked Bob up and down for a full minute before the old man finally spoke with a weak, reedy voice.

She had no idea what he said, obviously. She could guess. *Who are you? Why have you come?*

Maddy pointed, slowly, at the plaza. 'We need to visit the *thing* beneath your market over there.' She tried to 'draw' the room and the central column in the air with her fingers. He frowned, confused, as he watched her flapping hands.

'You're not getting what I'm saying, are you?' she muttered, more to herself than the old man. She looked around for inspiration and saw a stick lying on the ground nearby. The young goatherd's discarded switch of cane.

'OK . . . how about this?' She stepped to the side, picked it up and then returned to stand in front of the old man. She found a patch of the stone-paved ground covered in a light dusting of dry dirt, and with the stick she drew a circle in it.

The old man squinted down at the simple drawing at his feet, the lines of his forehead deepening as he looked at it. She drew another much smaller circle in the middle of the first. And then she pointed her stick across at the plaza.

'We need to visit that place – the place underground.'

Confusion cleared from the old man's face as he looked where she was pointing, then back at her drawing. The expression on his face evolved into something entirely different: an expression of dawning realization.

Then he gasped. His eyes suddenly rounded with shock. He staggered unsteadily forward, his twisted and gnarled old hands outstretched towards her. He grasped one of Maddy's hands tightly and then collapsed to his knees in front of her, beginning to wail pitifully, rocking back and forth.

'Jeez, what the hell did I just do?'

Beyond the old man, his people began to drop to their knees as well, row after row in turn, until every person they could see right across the city, male, female, young and old alike, were kneeling, their faces buried in their hands, rocking backwards and forwards. The air was suddenly alive with the keening, mournful cry of thousands of voices.

To Maddy it sounded like grief. It sounded like a funeral wake. She turned round and picked out Billy. 'What's the matter with them? What did I do wrong?'

'I think . . .' The guide shrugged and waved a hand dismissively. 'I am think they celebrate.'

'Celebrate?' She looked back at the old man, then back at Billy. 'This is them being *happy*?'

'Oh yes. Very happy. Very glad you come, I think.'

CHAPTER 48

1937, 13 Hanover Terrace, Regent's Park, London

From the journal of H. G. Wells

What an extraordinary few days passed in that exotic hidden city. Now in my autumn years, with old age playing tricks on my memory, I do wonder if what I vaguely recall of that time are chapters of a story I dreamed up, intending one day to set down on the page as a fictional adventure, and yet somehow I have managed to fool myself into thinking those events actually occurred to me.

Dr Anwar and his curious cohort of 'assistants' I believe decided to include me in their confidence, to share all their secrets with me, because they intended at some later date to devise a way of ensuring I would never recall this adventure. (Such is the way time travel works, it is possible to retrospectively prevent events from happening as easily as an artist erases undesired pencil marks from a finished drawing.)

The American girl, Madelaine, and her colleagues were somehow able to establish, with the help of their guide, a rudimentary way of communicating with those natives and their elderly leader, Pat-ishka. Through signing and drawing and much gesturing it became apparent that these primitive people believed us to be gods, or at the least the messengers or errand-boys of gods. The elderly leader of these people showed us stone carvings that we did our very best to interpret. It seemed that the ancestors of these savages were visited long, long ago by beings they presumed to be gods. These 'gods' supposedly built the subterranean circular chamber, then instructed the natives living there to guard the chamber with their lives until such time as they returned.

Thus it was, they believed our arrival to be that long-awaited return.

And so we were treated as gods for those few days. Treated as living, breathing deities. Afforded every luxury and comfort they could offer. Meanwhile I, fascinated by the science of my newfound friends, learned of the rules that govern travelling through time. What is possible – infinite alternative versions of the world we know today. Time itself being like a river that almost consciously 'wills' itself to flow a certain way, but can also, with some effort, be redirected to a new course.

Now, in my old age, I do wonder if those magical few days ever truly happened. Whether the horrific events that followed are merely the darkest part of my imagination manifesting a demon that never existed. Part of me would like to think that what occurred in that jungle city is just that – a product of the mind, a nightmare I have conjured up to torment myself.

But I suspect – no, I do not 'suspect', I know – deep down, I know those horrific things actually happened. What I saw with my own eyes – that vast shimmering outline – was the Devil himself.

CHAPTER 49

1479, the Lost City of the Windtalkers

Liam was sitting on the low stone wall of the temple building, looking down on the busy plaza. He'd watched the morning routine: the arrival of traders bringing their wares on the backs of llamas in through the passage and down the thoroughfare to the plaza, setting up their trade stalls in the middle.

Adam was off making rubbings of the various engraved flagstones in the chamber just beneath the plaza. The stones were far more distinct than they would be five hundred years from now, their images crisp and easy to determine. Maddy was in one of the temple buildings somewhere armed with a sketch pad, attempting to copy the murals painted along the tops of the walls. Rashim and Bertie were somewhere nearby. Poor Rashim's ears were being bent with incessant questions from the young man, keen to learn *everything* he could about the far future of the twenty-first century.

'Why the hell has he latched on to me?' Rashim had complained to them last night. 'Every five minutes another damned question from him to have to answer!'

'Because out of us lot, you come from the furthest point in the future,' Maddy had replied. 'He's obviously a *futurist*; obsessed with the shape of things to come. If he'd been born in my time, he'd probably be writing *Star Trek* fan-fiction.'

'Marvellous,' he'd huffed. 'You do know we will have to go

back in time and correct this? Make it so that he does not end up coming out here and learning about all these things?'

She'd nodded. 'I know. We'll get round to that.'

'So in the meantime what do I tell him about the future?'

'The truth, if you like. It won't make any difference.'

Now, Liam was watching Billy sitting on the wall beside him, smoking his pipe. Of all the people they'd met, whom they'd had to let in on their dirty little secret of time travel, he'd been the most casually accepting about it all. Calmly absorbing the knowledge that there were people busy hopping backwards and forwards through time and that the course of history and present-day reality were as fragile an existence as the transient shape of a low cloud in a blustery sky.

'Billy?'

'Yes, Mr Connor?'

'What do you make of all this? Hmm? The fact that you've travelled back in time five hundred years before you were even born with a brief stopover on the way in Victorian London?' He smiled. 'You seem to take it all in your stride.'

Billy puffed out a cloud of acrid smoke. 'My uncle was Tawahka holy man. He believe in life shaped like big circle. He teach me what go round, come around again. So time travel is –' he paused and shrugged – 'not so strange thing to me.'

'The whole merry-go-round thing, hmm?'

'He believe all that happen, will happen again, just like *last* time. Just like *first* time. This world, he believe, do this again and again until man learn to be better. To be good.'

'We're doomed to be going around forever and ever then, I fancy?'

A boy with face and neck decorated with swirls of bright blue paint and head shaved to the scalp nervously approached them, bearing a platter of fruit. He set it on the wall beside them and withdrew backwards, bowing deferentially, not daring to make eye contact with either of them.

'Thank you, young man.' Liam watched him go, then leaned over and helped himself to a papaya. 'You know? I feel guilty pretending to be a god. Feels like I'm asking for a bolt of lightning to zap down and fry me to a crisp.'

'Mr Connor?' Billy puffed out smoke again. 'What is that place? The white place . . .?'

'That you passed through?'

He nodded.

'We call it chaos space. It's what scientist fellas call extra-dimensional space.' He realized that probably didn't mean much to Billy. He tried to explain it in the same way Rashim had explained it to him.

'See, Billy, we can understand, *comprehend*, only three dimensions – height, width, depth? You get me? Imagine for example the inside of a box. Inside it you can move up and down, left and –'

Billy nodded. 'My English not good. But I not stupid man.'

Liam conceded with a guilty bow of his head. 'You're right, I'm sorry. So . . .' He continued. 'So that white stuff we stepped through is made up of *eleven* dimensions. We can't comprehend dimensions beyond the first three, so I suppose our minds kind of give up trying to make sense of it and just show us something we can get – a white mist. I think it's a self-defence mechanism. What our minds can't make sense of, they block out, to stop us going completely mad.'

He wondered what their eyes were *really* seeing, before internal 'circuit breakers' intercepted the signal somewhere between the eye and the brain? Censored it and replaced it with something more bearable – that dreadful, featureless white mist. He recalled reading an article in one of the science books lying around the archway. It was about visual perception and the mind. As an example of how the mind and the eye can sometimes 'agree on' interpreting or *mis*interpreting an image, it cited the example of when Native Americans encountered white men for the very first time. The Native Americans thought these curious pale visitors to their shores had emerged straight out of the ocean simply because their minds could not even begin to fathom the notion of their enormous square-rigged sailing ships on the horizon.

They simply blanked them out. Didn't see them.

Not for the first time, Liam wondered if the faint wraith-like objects they'd all seen at one time or another in the swirling mist – or *thought* they'd seen – might be a glimpse of what their 'uncensored' eyes were actually seeing. Perhaps if they could switch off their minds – instruct their minds not to be so damned protective of their sanity – they might be bombarded with a spectacle of impossible worlds, geometry beyond comprehension, pan-dimensional beings twisted and strange, perhaps even unspeakably horrifying.

He wondered if maybe that's what some people were actually able to see. Clairvoyants? Mediums? Poor dribbling lunatics locked away in asylums and medicated to a dull-eyed stupor? People whose perception, whose minds were that bit more agile and capable of seeing beyond the three Cartesian axes within which regular humans could comprehend their daily lives.

A curse that, perhaps. Rather than a gift.

'Information.'

Liam was jerked away from his thoughts. He spat some papaya seeds out into his hand and turned round to look up at Becks. She seemed to move – no, to *glide* – around in complete silence. 'Jay-zus! Can you not sneak up on me and then bark out an announcement like that! You nearly made me fall off the wall!'

'I apologize, Liam. My type was originally engineered for stealth and reconnaissance.'

At least with Bob, heavy-footed, one could hear him coming, like a lumbering steam engine.

'What is it you want to tell me?'

'We have managed to recalculate our tachyon readings.'

Both the support units had been working on refining their calculations as to when precisely the energy burst from that beam below ground would occur. By visiting the beam in 1894, Bob had been able to give them an approximate estimate. Since their arrival the pair of them had been down in the chamber quietly counting stray particles, noting their trajectories and decay rates, and promising Maddy a more precise estimate.

'Well now . . . what have you got? Have we arrived close in time to that energy discharge? Or have we got to wait around for weeks?'

'We calculate the energy fluctuation will occur anywhere between thirty-nine and fifty-one hours from now.'

CHAPTER 50

1479, the Lost City of the Windtalkers

Adam held out the sheet of paper for Maddy to see. 'So, this is a rubbing from one of the flagstones in the first-level chamber.'

She recognized the rough outline of the image. This was the one she and Adam had been studying by torchlight when they'd been here in 1994. The least eroded and worn flagstone. The image in this rubbing, taken from the same stone five hundred years earlier, was far more clearly defined.

'I think it's safe to assume this is an image of one of *the Archaeologists*.' That was the term they had all recently got into the habit of calling the visitors from the future. The name seemed to fit. Why would humans from the distant future want to come back so far in time if it wasn't to satisfy an insatiable curiosity about their ancestors?

Adam continued. 'So, I think it's an image of one of them

interacting with the tachyon beacon somehow. See those wavy lines?'

Maddy nodded.

'My guess is that's a representation of the column opening or activating in some way.'

She squinted at the wavy lines. 'You saying those lines symbolize an energy discharge?'

'These ancient Indians would not understand the concept of "energy", but light perhaps. Something glowing?'

'And that vertical line to the right represents the column?'

Adam nodded.

She narrowed her eyes. The wavy lines were emanating from it. It actually did seem to quite clearly represent something like that. She wondered if the column did actually 'open' somehow. Whether a door in the smooth mica-like material would slide to one side. 'My God, that's what it must be: a representation of an *opening*!'

'I can imagine our visitors from the future were going about their work, in much the same way archaeologists from our time would, perhaps using the locals as manual labour, quite happy to let these ancient primitives watch them from the sidelines with wide-eyed awe. Just as long as they weren't getting in the way.' He nodded at the rubbing. 'These Indians were simply recording what they saw.'

Maddy squinted at the paper. 'So it looks like he's holding his hand out?'

'Uh-huh. Palm outward, it looks like to me. And with those wavy lines coming out I think it's reasonable to assume he's in the process of activating it. Perhaps they were coming and going all the time, ferrying equipment back to build that chamber?'

'The figure . . .' She leaned over, studying the pencil marks of the rubbing more closely. 'The Archaeologist doesn't look very much like a person from the future. You sure that's one of them?'

Adam smiled. 'Why? What are you expecting? Spacesuits? Some kind of bleepy-bloopy aerial stuck on top of his head?'

'No, of course not, but . . . look, he seems to be wearing, I dunno, like old-fashioned armour or something? It just looks like it could be . . . I dunno, a Spanish explorer or something?'

'This is a symbolized depiction. It may well have been carved long after the Archaeologists departed. It might be a carving made from word-of-mouth recollections handed down generation after generation after generation. The story might have evolved in the telling and retelling – in the centuries *after* Columbus first landed here – to be a visitation by the conquistadors. After all, to these Indians, the Spanish would have appeared like visitors from a far more advanced future. The artist carving this stone might have interpreted the figure as looking like a Spanish conquistador because that would be the only frame of reference he would have.'

Maddy settled back on the cool stone floor. She could hear the faint noises of the Indians outside, the clop of animal hooves walking across the plaza above them. Trickles of dust and grit skittered down from above on to the floor every now and then.

It amazed her how well constructed the low roof of this chamber was. Clearly it had been built by this people's ancestors as an *homage* to the futuristic chamber directly below it. The stonework and the joins were so fine and precise. The ceiling, held up by one hundred and sixty-two stone columns (she'd counted them) had withstood the attrition of God-knows how many centuries' worth of footfall, what with the plaza being used as a marketplace and an auditorium. So well constructed that there appeared to have been no cave-ins nor even any wobbly columns.

The collapsed sections of the plaza they'd witnessed in 1994 must have occurred at some point after these people had abandoned their city. Perhaps the result of a tremor or an earthquake.

Maddy studied the image on Adam's pencil rubbing again. 'It's not much to go on, though. I can't see how that helps us figure out how to activate the column and get in.'

'I think the answer is somewhere in this image. And I think the answer is all around us.' He grinned excitedly. 'I think this whole mini-civilization was built on what they once observed of the Archaeologists at work. They watched, they recorded what they saw without understanding any of it, they codified it and now it exists in all the murals, the decals, even the patterns in those bead ponchos they wear. It's seeded in their cultural DNA.'

'What are you talking about?'

'Well, all right . . . the pattern. Tell me you've noticed that repeated pattern everywhere?'

'What pattern?'

He drew it on a corner of the paper. Then she nodded. She knew what he was talking about. The same motif seemed to be repeated everywhere: the three-line shape, the backwards 'L' with a diagonal line emerging from the conjunction of the horizontal and vertical lines – like the left half of the way you might depict the starburst rays of a sun-rise.

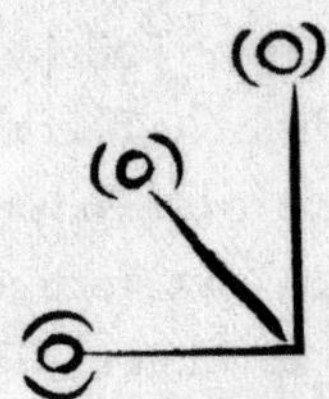

'OK, yeah. I've seen lots of that.'

'In a primitive culture like this – where the *only* form of recorded "media" or stored cultural information is in the way patterns and decorations are used – those things are always *important*. Always – *always* – deeply symbolic.'

'You're saying that "L" shape actually means something?'

'Of course it does. Its meaning may have become lost over time, but originally it would have represented something incredibly important to whoever decided the shape needed to be recorded, embedded into their culture over and over.'

'OK, so, just for argument's sake, let's say that shape means something.' She shrugged. 'Where are you going with this?'

'It might be the key to unlocking the column. All those glyphs on the surface of the column? Maybe it's a clue as to which ones to press? I think those glyphs are like some elaborate combination lock; we just need to press the right glyphs in the right order.'

'There are thousands of them, Adam. Come on, you're a codebreaker, you know the number of combinations would be in the billions.'

'Yeah, I know that . . . but I think it's crackable.' He shrugged. 'Of course it is. Your Sal, with that pattern-spotting ability of hers clearly managed to do it. If she can . . . so can –'

'Did she?' Maddy looked at him. 'Or did it just open up for her?'

'Why would it?' He looked again at the rubbing on the paper. 'Unless there are some kind of live sensors down there.'

'Sensors tuned to open for a specific person?' She rubbed her chin thoughtfully. 'Or some kind of frequency signal? Maybe just a codeword?' She looked at him. 'An "Open Sesame" of some kind?' Her eyes widened. 'Pandora? What if that's the magic word?!'

'Yes. Or perhaps it's this symbol?' Adam replied. He held up his left hand and splayed his thumb to point horizontally, his middle finger vertically and his index finger at an angle in between them: the half-a-sunray shape. He nodded down at the image on the paper. 'A figure holding out his hand towards the column?'

She looked again at the rubbing. Now Adam was doing that, holding his hand out in front of him, at arm's length to his face, it seemed to be exactly what this mysterious figure was doing.

'My God, Adam!' Excitement welled up inside her. 'Do you think it could be *that* simple? We just go up to it and make that shape with a hand?'

She wondered if that's what Sal had managed to figure out on her own. If this meant they could now find their way inside and get her back again.

'I can't believe activating it is just a case of doing that. But maybe . . .' He hunched his shoulders. 'Maybe it's a part of the process.' He laughed. 'Or maybe I've just watched far too many temple-raider movies.'

'Adam, you are such a geek.'

'Didn't Jesus once say on the Mount that "the geek shall inherit the earth"?'

Impulsively she leaned forward and planted a kiss on his cheek. Adam froze. His jaw hung open a little as he turned to look at her. Her face was still close to his, he could feel her breath on his cheek. By the soft glow of a candle on the ground he could see the light spilling across her neck, highlighting her jaw, her chin, the tip of her nose. But her eyes were lost in pools of shadow.

So hard to read what that kiss meant to her without seeing her eyes.

'Was . . . was that a "you've been a clever boy" kiss? Or . . . uh . . .' His words faltered and faded away to nothing.

She leaned slowly forward again. This time one of her hands pressed gently against his right cheek and coaxed his face towards her. Her breath came in shallow, rustling, nervous, soft waves.

'What was the rest of that sentence going to be?' Her voice was wobbling slightly.

He swallowed nervously. 'I . . . well . . . I'm n-not entirely sure . . .'

'Me neither,' she whispered.

They remained like that, both uncertain. Both not sure what exactly this was, unsure how the next moment went, but neither wanting to wind this backwards.

'I've never kissed anyone, Adam,' she whispered. 'I've never had a boyfriend.' He thought he saw the glint of a tear dropping from her jaw into the darkness. 'And I probably never will.'

'Sure you will.'

She shook her head. 'I don't think we're meant to last forever.' She'd almost said *built forever*. She hadn't told Adam yet what she was, what Liam and Sal were. It hadn't seemed necessary to tell him.

Adam leaned in closer to her, studying her face intently. Was that the glint of another tear disappearing into the darkness? Or was it just a speck of grit falling from the low ceiling above?

'We were . . .' Maddy hesitated; she seemed to be picking her words carefully. 'We were selected to perform a specific task.' Her lips twitched. He sensed that was a resigned smile. 'And I can't help feeling that task is nearly done.'

He reached up with one hand and cupped the curve of her jaw. With his thumb, he stroked her cheek. It *was* damp.

'Hey . . . don't cry.'

She sniffed, wiped her cheek. 'I'm not. Just grit in my eye.'

Adam leaned forward and kissed her.

CHAPTER 51

1479, the Lost City of the Windtalkers

'Information: five minutes until the energy release is due to occur.' Bob's voice echoed around the cavernous interior.

Liam sidled up beside Maddy. 'You think this might be it? We'll get Sal back?'

'I hope so.'

He stared at the smooth surface of the column, Adam standing next to it, preoccupied with the thousands of glyphs in orderly rows and columns running all the way round it.

'If we do get her out, I'm worried about how she'll be, though, Liam. We don't know where she's been or what she's seen.' Maddy bit her lip. 'We don't even know if she's just been trapped there in chaos space. God knows what that does to a person's mind, being stuck in that horrible mist for so long.' Her mouth tightened. 'She may be really traumatized when she comes out.'

'What if she doesn't step out?'

She left that particular question unanswered. Liam could come up with his own conclusions. They'd probably be the same as hers – which she'd rather not voice out loud. If Sal didn't emerge when the column activated, then there was no other conclusion to draw than that she was most likely gone. For good.

Gone where, though?

If not lost forever in chaos space, then any time in the last twenty centuries. The most likely possibility being the far end of this bizarre energy beam – Jerusalem in the time of Jesus Christ. But, of course, there was no certainty to that. They were messing with something they didn't really understand. Sal might have popped out any time in between now and then. They had no real idea how this device worked, whether an energy fluctuation occurred every time this beam was opened. Perhaps it was specifically designed as a transport conduit from AD 2070 to year zero and not as something that could be hopped off at will? So perhaps that was the cause of this approaching energy surge . . . an 'unauthorized' exit. Something this device wasn't really designed to do.

'I guess we'll find out soon enough,' said Maddy.

'Three minutes!' announced Bob.

Rashim joined them, Bertie tagging along beside him, like some kind of sorcerer's apprentice. 'We should be ready for other possibilities.'

Maddy looked at him sharply. 'What do you mean?'

'One of those Archaeologists might emerge.' Rashim gestured around them. 'We might have triggered a live sensor somewhere down here. This approaching surge might just be one of them coming back to check on things?'

Maddy and Liam glanced at each other. 'You're right,' she replied. 'Bob, Becks?'

Both support units turned to look at her.

'Get your guns ready. Billy – you too.'

The guide unslung his assault rifle.

'No one shoots at anything, though,' she added. 'Not unless I say so.'

Bertie looked anxiously at her. 'Do you think some nightmarish creature from the future will emerge?'

'Relax . . . I'm just being cautious.' She called out to Adam, still standing beside the column, studying the glyphs. 'Adam! Might be best to take a few steps back now. The energy pulse is coming.'

Adam waved a hand to let her know he'd heard her. But his mind was still racing, trying to piece the puzzle together. The more he'd been thinking about it since voicing his theory to Maddy yesterday, the more he was convinced that the three-pronged shape was somehow the key to opening the column and accessing the energy field within.

Feeling a little foolish and self-conscious, he had stood in this chamber earlier and held up his arm, palm outward, and made the gesture with his hand, a small part of him trembling with anticipation. He'd aimed his gesture at one of the glyphs, roughly in the centre of all the rows and columns. It was larger than the other symbols – nine inches by nine inches – about half again as big as the rest of them. Clearly it was more important than the others. Perhaps symbolically. Perhaps *functionally*, like the 'Enter' key on a computer keyboard.

But nothing, of course, had happened when he'd held out his hand. Except that he'd felt a little stupid.

'One minute!' announced Bob.

Maddy called out again for him to step back. He decided she was probably quite right and began to back away from the column. This surge was coming. Perhaps it would cause the thing to open up all on its own and all of his puzzling over strange hand shapes and ancient carved depictions would be rendered an exercise in pointless and unnecessary head-scratching.

He backed up, but once again couldn't help himself and decided to raise his hand at arm's length again and splay the thumb, index and middle fingers of his left hand just as the figure in the carving had appeared to be doing. He was wondering if the wavy lines indicated that the gesture had to be done in conjunction with the arrival of an energy surge.

'I am detecting an increase in stray tachyon particles,' said Becks.

Adam squinted down the length of his arm at his outspread fingers. Beyond his hand, the tips of his three splayed digits, he studied the orderly array of symbols: rows and columns, thousands of them, silently mocked his attempt to decode them. Over the last four days how many of them had he copied carefully into his notebook? A hundred? A hundred and fifty? Every single one of them unique in some small way: a curl, a bar, a dash, a dot, subtly differentiating one from another. If there had been any kind of repeated symbol in there, one glyph being identical to another, there would have been the start of some semblance of pattern. But, like the hundreds of pages of gibberish of the Voynich Manuscript, this was a wall of cryptic markings that he suspected no one would ever be able to decode.

'Thirty seconds!'

He still had his hand out in front of him. In his other hand, his torch aimed in parallel at the array of symbols. At the very least he could test this rather desperate last-ditch theory – the hand gesture *and* the energy surge together? He adjusted the angle of his hand, rotating it slightly to ensure his middle finger was properly vertical, his thumb was properly horizontal. He aligned his middle finger to one of the columns of glyphs, his thumb to one of the rows, while his index finger pointed up at an approximate angle of forty-five degrees.

'Ten seconds!'

He centred his hand over the central larger glyph, obscuring it now with his knuckles.

'Five . . . four . . . three . . .'

He followed the angles of his three fingers, vertical,

horizontal, diagonal, and his eyes ran up along the symbols that fell along the path of those lines.

'Here we go!' called out Liam.

'Two . . . one . . .'

. . . .

. . .

. .

.

Nothing.

They waited. The chamber echoed with their rasping breath, bouncing off distant unlit walls and coming back to them awash with reverberation.

After a while, Maddy's voice: 'Talk to me, Bob, Becks – are you getting anything?'

'I am detecting a significant increase in straying particles,' replied Becks. 'There is definitely an increase in the energy yield occurring behind the protective casing. This is causing some energy to leak out.'

'Agreed,' said Bob. 'The level of energy has doubled and is still increasing.'

'Something's going on in there,' whispered Maddy.

Adam turned to her. 'This energy isn't harmful like radiation, right?'

'No. Not like radiation.'

Adam nodded. 'Well, that's all right then.' He took a step towards the column.

'Adam! What are you doing?'

He took another measured step forward, his arm and hand extended, squinting down the length of his arm at the column beyond.

'Adam! Stay back!'

He ignored her. 'The angles *are* important. Ninety degrees

– the vertical axis. Forty-five degrees, then zero – horizontal axis!'

'What's he talking about, Mads?'

Adam continued to squint down the length of his arm like a sniper lining up the sights of a gun. With his three fingers centred on the larger symbol, his eyes tracked up the vertical column covered by his middle finger, then along the symbols that lay on the diagonal path, then the horizontal path of his thumb.

'Adam! What the hell are you doing?' called Maddy. 'Just step back until we know what's going on here!'

He played his torch on one of the symbols in the column, then across to another on the diagonal path. 'Wait . . .!' He panned his torch along the horizontal. Then let out a gasp.

'My God!'

'Adam? What is it?'

Adam turned to look at the others. 'There *are* three symbols that are exactly the same!' He shook his head. 'Identical! I can't believe I missed that! They're just rotated. One at forty-five degrees, one at ninety. But they're definitely the same!'

'Well, that's – that's interesting. Now please, for Chrissake . . . *step back*, will you?'

'Just a sec – let me try something . . .' He quickly strode to the column, reached out and touched the symbol on the horizontal tangent.

'Adam!'

Then the symbol picked out by the diagonal tangent.

'Adam!' Maddy took several steps forward. 'Please! Don't mess with them!'

Then he touched the symbol on the vertical axis.

All three glyphs suddenly glowed a soft amber. Then the larger icon began to glow. All four pulsated synchronously several times – then went dark again.

'All right,' said Liam. 'You just did something.'

A blinding vertical slit of white light appeared on the column, running from floor to ceiling. They all shaded their eyes from the sudden glare.

Bertie took several steps back and gasped. 'God help us – *what is that?*'

The slit widened to a dazzling beam a yard wide: featureless white that flooded the chamber with a cold, clinical, unflinching light. It was accompanied by a deep throb that filled the air and pulsated with metronome regularity.

'My God,' Maddy whispered. 'What have we done?'

CHAPTER 52

Where am I?

Help me!

Oh, God help me. Let me out!

HELP ME!

CHAPTER 53

1479, the Lost City of the Windtalkers

She didn't emerge from the light. There was no sign of Sal.

Maddy suddenly realized how naively certain she'd been that they would simply activate this device and Sal would step out unharmed and annoyed that they'd taken so long to see what she'd managed to figure out in the blink of an eye.

'Oh my God,' whispered Maddy.

We've lost her. This time we've really lost her.

They waited for fifteen minutes, with the vertical shaft of light as bright as a midday sun glaring out at them and lighting every dark recess of the vast chamber. Finally, concerned that what they were staring at was an opening directly into chaos space, Liam turned to Maddy.

'We need to close it.'

Maddy shook her head uncertainly.

'Maddy! We shouldn't leave it open like this! That's dangerous!'

'She's in there,' she whispered. 'She's in there. She *must* be!'

Becks stepped forward. 'Liam is correct, there is a danger in leaving a portal open like this.'

Maddy didn't respond, she merely took a step nearer to the light, as if hoping that closer she might catch a glimpse of Sal's hazy silhouette somewhere in there, in the white light.

'That's enough,' said Liam to himself. He called out to Adam to close the column.

Adam nodded, touched the same three symbols in the same order but the column remained wide open.

Liam swore. 'All right, then – do it in *reverse* order!'

Nothing happened.

'Jay-zus!' he hissed. 'We can't leave this thing like this! Find a way to close it!'

'So this is a bad thing?' asked Bertie. 'Leaving it open?'

'Yes,' Rashim replied. 'A very bad thing.'

'Adam? For God's sake, *come on*!' Liam called to him. 'You opened it, you must be able to –!'

Adam shook his head frantically. 'I don't know how to close it!'

'Perhaps this is a self-contained field,' suggested Rashim. 'Not open to all of chaos space, merely a pocket of it.'

Adam was now swiping at symbols randomly. 'I'm trying! I'm trying!' But he was having no effect. He stepped back several yards from the column wall and held his hand up at arm's length in front of him again, hoping to spot some other identical symbols lying on the same axes.

All of a sudden the column wall began to rotate, smoothly sliding shut, the bar of light narrowing quickly until it was nothing but a dazzling slit again, then vanishing altogether. The chamber was once again silent. The deep throbbing was gone. Their ragged breathing filled the dark void.

Pitch black now. The flaming candles they'd set up on the floor had been extinguished by the stir of air as the column had opened.

Rashim snapped his torch back on.

Liam jumped. 'Jay-zus!'

'Sorry.'

Liam strode towards Adam. 'How did you close it, Adam? Which symbols did you touch?'

'I don't know. I was just hitting everything and anything.' He approached the column once again and looked at the symbols in front of him. 'I'm not even sure it was me that closed it.'

'Well then who?'

'Maybe . . . I dunno, maybe it's a built-in safety measure? If it stays open for too long, it closes by itself?'

Liam looked the column up and down. Once again a tall silent sentinel of obsidian-black material decorated with thousands of symbols. He wondered if that was a reassuring notion. A safety measure? Something built into the design of this structure, in case the primitives tasked with guarding this thing decided to mess around with it instead?

Or, on the other hand, was it vaguely disconcerting? Was this thing somehow aware of what was going on around it? Perhaps it had some kind of 'intelligence' built into it?

'At least we know it *does* close,' said Adam. He looked at Liam and puffed out air. The adrenalin making him grin like an idiot. 'That was pretty intense.'

'Aye.' Liam likewise puffed out his cheeks and blew. 'Still, I'd feel a lot safer if I knew it was *us* that had closed it and not something else.' He turned to Maddy. 'You OK?'

She shook her head silently.

'We've lost her, Liam. She's gone.'

CHAPTER 54

1937, 13 Hanover Terrace, Regent's Park, London

From the journal of H. G. Wells

We emerged into the waning light, through a knot of curious onlookers. The crowd allowed us a respectful distance, parting to let us pass. But I could sense a growing unease among them. It was as if they suspected that something had transpired. That we, uninvited guests, might not be gods returned to inspect our godly devices after all, but charlatans, impostors, meddling with machinery we couldn't possibly begin to understand.

We returned to our quarters in one of the high temples, and there, I remember, the American girl, Madelaine Carter, finally allowed herself some tears, mourning for Miss Saleena.

I must confess, that night, I too mourned for that beautiful and mysterious young lady. I recall I had so hoped our nascent acquaintance, our polite 'How do you do's might have had a chance to develop into a friendship. Perhaps something more than that . . .

CHAPTER 55

1479, the Lost City of the Windtalkers

'She is not necessarily . . .' Rashim chose the next word carefully, '. . . *gone*. She could be in there still. That, or she may have emerged into another time. Even as I speak, she might be walking around in Jerusalem, in the time of Jesus Christ.'

Liam watched as Rashim did his best to console them. But, like Maddy, he suspected that if Sal was *gone*, then she was gone for good.

It had felt like a part of her had already walked out on them long before now. She'd been quietly distancing herself from them both for a while now. At the beginning the three of them had felt like a tightly knit family, like siblings – *the Three Musketeers*, squaring up to danger together, a phalanx of trusted friendship. However, in recent weeks, she'd seemed so preoccupied, keeping her troubles wrapped up inside herself and letting slip nothing apart from the occasional moment when he'd caught her gazing sullenly at images from the future on their computer screens.

Liam realized they'd lost a part of Sal the day they'd learned exactly what they were.

He was certain she had stepped into that field deliberately. It hadn't been a mistake or an accident. Her discarded shirt lying on the floor of the chamber was as distinct and clear a message as a goodbye written carefully on a sheet of notepaper.

She was either looking for an escape, perhaps looking for her own answers – or maybe she was simply looking for an end? Either way, as far as Liam was concerned, that shirt was her telling them 'I'm not coming back'.

He wondered if he could have done more, if he could have made more of an effort to corner her and force her to talk to him. To stop brooding, open up and talk about what she was feeling instead of keeping it all bottled up inside her.

He'd tried that once. Back in that abandoned elementary school. It had been a hard and bitter conversation – for both of them that horrible revelation had still been so fresh, so raw – but she'd been honest with him then, he thought. They'd talked like a brother and a sister sharing some sort of a bereavement; the loss of their innocence, the loss of who they were.

At the very least, talking about it had reminded them both that they had each other. They weren't alone facing that awful truth.

Why hadn't he done that again, though? Had he really been far too busy to find time to really talk to her again?

Rashim was standing at the edge of the temple's walled terrace and looking out over the low stone wall down on to the moonlit plaza, talking quietly about something with Billy. And Liam noticed Maddy was being consoled by Adam. The young man had an arm stretched round her narrow shoulders, he was holding her, squeezing one of her hands gently in his. By the flickering light of the fire in the clay bowl, he saw Adam tenderly wipe tears from her cheek with the back of his hand.

There was something else he hadn't noticed. Adam and Maddy.

Jay-zus. When did they start . . . being like that?

H'ed suspected Maddy had some feelings for Adam. He'd asked her once and she'd done her best to laugh it off and tell him he was being ridiculous. But here, now, it was clear she and Adam were more than just 'colleagues'. At some point during the last few days they must have stepped over an invisible line.

He smiled. *Good*.

She needed Adam. Liam could hold her and tell her it wasn't her fault, it wasn't *anyone's* fault that Sal had finally buckled under pressure. He could do that, but it would merely be the comfort offered by a close colleague. The comfort offered by a loving brother at best.

He was glad she had Adam.

'What will we be doing now, Mr O'Connor?' Bertie warmed his hands over the fire, then sat down next to Liam. They both stared at the flickering flames for a while, Liam glancing occasionally over the top at Maddy and Adam beyond the shimmering ripples of heat haze. She was crying still. Liam had never seen her look so beaten, so broken and fragile.

So utterly spent.

She seemed like just an ordinary nineteen-year-old girl now. A girl who'd had enough and just wanted a home to go back to, trifling problems with boyfriends, college assignments, overdue library books and suffocating, nosey parents.

'I imagine we'll head back to London,' replied Liam. 'Drop you back home where you belong, Mr Wells.'

'And what will you do then?'

Liam nodded slowly. *What then, indeed?*

CHAPTER 56

White. A featureless white. A swirling milk-white soup of dimensions beyond any possible comprehension. Home to an infinity of bizarre planes of existence, creatures that mere human eyes cannot begin to interpret and find form. We cannot see these entities. Our minds turn what we do see into curls of fog, the closest our feeble brains can come to conjuring up an understandable image. And, while we cannot truly 'see' them, these entities that exist beyond three dimensions can certainly see us.

But we're unimportant, *uninteresting* to them.

As a person might look down on a child's drawing of a stick man and pity the scribbled wretch's limited world, the two dimensions of a sheet of paper, so these entities barely notice this pitifully limited universe of height, depth and width.

And yet one such entity *is* interested.

Very interested.

One such entity is drawn by the ebb and flow of energy somewhere in the mist, the foolish 'noisy' opening and closing of a small window – like a voice crying wolf far too loudly in a dark forest full of menace. The entity is drawn, like a shark idling in sun-warmed shallows, idling, then suddenly alert at the first faint ultra-diluted trace of blood.

This entity knows that foolish lower-dimension creatures

have recently acquired the habit of blundering through its plane of existence. Blundering so recklessly, ignorantly.

The entity follows the vibrations of recently stirred energy, like a spider feeling the subtlest tremble of a thread of web silk. Smelling the trail, sensing the vibrations.

Closing in on the foolish come-for-me cry.

Black. A featureless black. The darkness of the chamber was complete. A wave-a-hand-in-front-of-your-face-and-not-know-it's-there darkness. The chamber was vacant. With Maddy temporarily unable, unwilling, to maintain the role, as leader-by-default it fell to Liam to step in and make some decisions. He had considered posting Bob or Becks down here to keep an eye on the column overnight, just in case something happened – in case Sal emerged. But then he thought better of it. He wanted the support units close by tonight. The mood of the people in this city seemed to be shifting subtly. They were still being treated with cautious deference, looked after respectfully, but he sensed the *awe* with which they'd first been greeted was wearing off. Perhaps these people were beginning to suspect they were just human after all.

And if it did finally occur to them that Liam and the others were mere human visitors taking advantage of their hospitality, then what? Would they feel aggrieved that mere mortals had tried to pass themselves off as heavenly messengers? Would there be resentment? Anger? Revenge?

So the chamber sat empty. Thus there were no witnesses when the column silently opened and light momentarily filled the dark void. If either Bob or Becks had been standing there, not only would they have seen the shaft of light from the column sliding open from floor to ceiling, they would have registered the momentary surge of energy as something quite invisible to the naked eye emerged from the tachyon beam.

Something large and powerful.

It entered the dark cavernous space, invisible and silent, the only clue to its presence the stirring of static energy, the faintest odour of ozone. Moving slowly through the dark, the entity explored its surroundings. Somewhere in this invisible cloud of energy an animal-like mind processed simple destructive thoughts; thoughts that could almost be labelled 'hate'.

The undulating form finally encountered a claustrophobic stairwell and, curious about its surroundings, glided up the steps into a small chamber, then drifted through a narrow doorway into a larger, low-ceilinged chamber full of squat stone columns.

It sensed the presence of life not so very far away, simple beings that lived in their simple dimensional universe. It wondered what these life forms might look like on the inside. What they looked like turned completely inside out.

Its substance – rippling energy – phased in and out of solidity, one moment invisible and as intangible as tendrils of wind-swept smoke drifting away on a lively breeze from a bonfire. The next moment, just barely visible, the ghost of an outline of an incomprehensible form, yet as *solid* and material, as real, as any other object in this universe.

As it weaved through the squat pillars of the low-ceilinged chamber, phasing in and out of physical form, its momentarily material bulk bumped heavily against several pillars. One of them collapsed, bringing down with it several of the plaza's large stone slabs.

The entity found the exit and emerged into the weak grey-blue light of an overcast dawn sky. Heavy drops of rain came down and alternated between passing through the entity in its non-corporeal form, sizzling and turned to steam by the crackling energy within. Then, as the entity phased, the rain no longer passed through, but spattered against the ghostly outline of it, the spray of impact droplets giving a clearer sense of its shape.

It hesitated, trying to make sense of what it saw; even in this simple three-axis world the jumbled stone geometry was confusing. It could sense life forms all around it, thousands of them, all still, all at rest, complacent, not knowing a monster was stalking in their midst.

Something moved towards the entity. Small and noisy. It growled and snapped.

Simple life.

The entity was curious about the little snarling, barking animal, wanted to feel the texture of the creature, both inside and out.

Its invisible form materialized and a long 'arm' reached out.

CHAPTER 57

1479, the Lost City of the Windtalkers

'We have a bit of a problem,' said Rashim quietly.

Liam stirred from his sleep as Rashim shook his shoulder gently. 'Whuh? What is it?'

'I will tell you when I have awoken the others. I will meet you at the temple entrance downstairs in five minutes.'

Liam watched Rashim leave the room. He splashed cool water on to his face from the clay bowl placed beside his cot, then got up and got dressed. Before he headed down the stone stairwell to the floor below, he stepped out on to the terrace into the warming sun. He looked down at the plaza, and noted a knot of people standing around something dark. Was that a hole there? Had some of the plaza collapsed?

He then noticed another, much larger knot of people to one side of the plaza, not too far from the trench-entrance to the underground chambers. They were looking at something on the floor between them. He could hear their voices carrying up to him, a note of alarm and unrest quite clear in the timbre of their cries.

Downstairs in the temple's large entrance hall, the others were already assembled. 'What's going on down there on the plaza, Rashim? I saw loads of people looking at something.'

Maddy nodded. 'Yeah, what's going on?' To Liam's eyes she seemed better this morning. Not a complete return to her usual prickly, bad-tempered self. Just a step or two in the right direction. They might have lost Sal – they might get her back yet – it was hard to know whether to grieve or carry on hoping. At least Maddy seemed to have found her voice again.

'I was taking a morning stroll and I was confronted by a group of people.' Rashim pointed to a graze on his forehead. 'Young men. One of them threw a stone at me.' He shook his head. 'I am not so sure they consider us godly now.'

'What did you do to upset them, Rashim?'

He shook his head. 'Nothing!' He lowered his voice slightly. 'But I think they may be on to *us* now. I suggest it might be sensible to make our polite apologies and leave some time today.'

'I saw a commotion going on down on the plaza,' said Liam. 'Something's happened down there. Them Indians were looking at something.'

'Then we should go and take a look at that first,' said Maddy.

'What?' Rashim frowned at her. 'We should get our things and *leave*!'

'If we're supposed to be *godly*, then we can't afford to appear frightened of them! We can't just *run*!' She looked around at the others. 'We'll all walk down to the plaza together. We'll look calm, relaxed, confident . . . and we'll check out what's going on.'

'We should leave, now!'

'What's that, Rashim? Leave behind us that huge frikkin' tachyon beam and pretend we never found it? That what you're suggesting? Never come back here? Is that it? Just forget we found the biggest mystery of all and go back to joyriding our way around history?'

'I'd like to know more,' said Liam. 'I *think* at least some of our answers lie here . . .' He shrugged. 'Or if not here, then maybe right at the other end.' He smiled. 'Maybe Jesus has them.'

'Just a quick look, Rashim,' said Maddy. 'We'll show our faces, show them we're not afraid of them.' She offered him a consoling shrug. 'We can't just walk away from this. Not yet. Not until we've got *some* answers from it. Is that being stupid?'

He narrowed his eyes behind his glasses. Not an answer exactly.

'Come on, then. Just a quick look.'

They made their way downhill, along a narrow cobbled thoroughfare flanked on either side by small clay-brick homes stacked on top of each other. Faces peered suspiciously out at them from dark interiors. It seemed suspicion had quickly spread right across this city; these strangers' recent activities in their holiest place, below ground, were now beginning to cause concern.

They emerged on to the plaza and were very quickly spotted by the gathered crowd. They began to advance menacingly towards them.

'Get ready for trouble,' Maddy muttered from the side of her mouth to the support units.

'We are ready,' said Becks.

The people's elder, Pat-ishka, assisted at the arms by a young man on each side, led his people towards them. Presently, he drew up in front of them and began to berate them in a high-pitched voice, gesturing wildly behind him.

'Anyone any idea what he's saying?' asked Maddy.

'He not very happy,' said Billy.

'I guessed that.'

'Do you think he's angry about a hole in the plaza?' Liam nodded across the open space. 'See? There's a chunk of it that must have collapsed last night.'

Maddy craned her neck to see. Indeed, there was a hole several yards across. She guessed one of the support struts must have given way during the night. 'We didn't cause that to happen!' She looked uncertainly at the others. 'Did we?'

'That column made some very deep noises yesterday. The sonic vibrations may have caused some structural damage,' said Rashim.

She cursed under her breath. 'Then we'll offer to repair it.'

'The elder not angry,' said Billy. 'He afraid. Very afraid.'

'Afraid? Of what? That the whole plaza's going to collap–'

'No.' Billy nodded to the right. 'He use a word Tawahka use. Over there. Something over there.'

The old man noted the direction of Billy's gaze and beckoned them all to come with him. He seemed to want to show them something. It felt more like an order than an invitation.

'What's his problem?' Maddy uttered. Pat-ishka impatiently reached out and grabbed her forearm and pulled at her gently. Bob and Becks stirred uneasily. Maddy raised her free hand to indicate she was fine. 'OK! All right! Sure, we'll come and look.'

She walked alongside him awkwardly, his grip insistent on her arm. Her brisk step slowed down to account for his old man's shuffle.

Adam leaned towards her as he walked alongside. 'One doesn't manhandle a god like this,' he said quietly. 'Be very careful, Maddy. I think they're on to us.'

She nodded. Adam was right. *They've figured us out.*

Ahead of them a gap parted in the gathered crowd, allowing them passage through. Presently, the last of the Indians gave way to reveal what it was they had all been inspecting.

The stone slab floor was awash with dark sepia spatters and smears of drying blood. Among all of it – gallons of blood by the look – she picked out what appeared to be shreds of flesh and fur, nuggets and shards of shattered bone, a purple loop of glistening intestine, the round pink nub of some organ.

'What the hell . . . ?'

Liam drew up beside her. 'Jay-zus . . . something got shredded!'

It reminded Liam of the remains he'd once witnessed in the jungle of the late Cretaceous: the inside-out remains of a school kid. The uncontrolled energy of chaos space let loose on a mere child.

'Turned inside out and thrown around a bit,' added Adam. 'Looks like something bloody well exploded.'

'Good God!' Bertie gasped.

Maddy spotted the head of some animal, pink with shreds of attached muscle and flesh, but its skin flayed off. Bloodshot and glazed eyeballs glared accusingly at her from bone sockets. Teeth exposed by the lack of lips looked as if they were bared angrily.

'That was dog, I think,' said Billy. He pointed to another flayed animal's head. 'That one, goat.' He pointed to another. 'That one, llama.'

'Jay-zus 'n' mother Mary,' whispered Liam. 'It's like a goddamn abattoir.'

Billy pointed to another skull, bigger, round like a football and stripped clean of any flesh at all. 'That one –' his eyes met Maddy's – 'that one, *human*.'

CHAPTER 58

1479, the Lost City of the Windtalkers

'They want us to leave this place,' said Rashim. 'That much is very clear. We are not welcome here any more, Maddy!'

Maddy shook her head and looked out of the small square window of one of their temple rooms. Beads strung on twine clattered gently together as a soft breeze teased past them. They'd retired back to this building, high up on the city slopes. Keeping out of sight. Keeping a low profile. There were noises rising up to them, though, coming from outside. The people were gathered together in the plaza, a meeting of the elders watched by their people. Clearly they were discussing the fate of their – no longer welcome – guests, trying to determine who or what they were, what they were up to down in their holy chamber and what that meant for them. Voices sounding shrill and afraid and angry.

'You're asking me to walk away from Sal?'

'She is gone, Maddy. We may never find her.'

'But she left this place. She might just return here, at this time! If there's one place she's going to come back to, it's going to be right here! If we're gone when she does come back . . .' Maddy pointed to the crowd on the plaza. '. . . she'll be facing those people alone. And what do you think those people down there will do to her? Huh?'

'That is, *if* she *can* come back.' Rashim reached out for her hand. 'She may not even be alive now. Maddy, you have to accept that possibility.'

Maddy pulled her hand away. 'Well you go if you want to. But I'm staying.'

'I think Rashim may be right, Maddy,' said Adam. 'These people don't want us here. They're angry, they're frightened. They could easily turn on us. Billy, what was that word the elder was using? You said it was a Tawahka word?'

'*Tik m'hathla*.'

'And what does that mean?' asked Liam.

'It is not exact *same*, but *like* word old Tawahka holymen use. I not so sure in English. In Spanish . . . ?' He waggled his hand uncertainly. 'Perhaps you might say *diablo*.'

'*Diablo*?' Liam frowned. 'That means something like "devil", doesn't it?'

Billy nodded. 'Devil! Yes, this is English word.' He looked at Maddy. 'He say we bring Devil up from his Hell, the underworld. Very frightened now.'

'Because of those chewed-up animals?'

'And some person,' added Adam. 'Let's not forget that, there was a person died too.'

Maddy frowned. 'Some jungle predator! That's what it must have been. A jaguar or cougar or whatever animals they have in this jungle. It got into the city last night and . . .' Her voice trailed away. Nobody appeared to be convinced by that. Not even herself.

'Well, come on!' She looked exasperated. 'Obviously it's *not* the Devil,' she said.

Liam met her eyes. 'Come on, Maddy . . . you're thinking what I'm thinking.'

Maddy shook her head. She didn't want to say it . . . didn't even want to think it.

'Aye. What else could it be? Think about it! We had a bloody great window open on to chaos space for nearly ten minutes! It must be a seeker!'

Bertie turned sharply. 'A seeker?'

Neither Liam nor Maddy were inclined to explain just then, but Adam, Rashim and Billy seemed to want to know too.

'It's some kind of . . . parasite or something that lives in chaos space,' she explained. 'Mostly you don't see them when you jump through, or, if you do . . . you'll see them at a distance. They don't seem that interested in us.'

'Aye, but we think they might be attracted to open windows,' said Liam, 'just like a moth comes to a lamp. That's why you've seen us with portals – how we try an' close a window quickly after we're done with it.'

Rashim squinted as he thought back to yesterday. 'We did have that beam open for a long time . . .'

Maddy shook her head. 'I know where you're going with that, but if a seeker had come through we'd have known. Bob or Becks would have registered the energy field, right?'

Bob nodded. 'Affirmative. The information acquired on "seekers" suggests that they are phasing energy fields.'

'Where do they come from?' asked Adam. 'What *are* they?'

'There is currently no information on their origin,' replied Becks.

'They are energy, and they require additional energy to stay alive,' said Maddy. 'We know that about them. When we were first recruited, we encountered one. A weakened one. Without access to energy it just dwindled to nothing.'

'Aye, and that was scary.' Liam recalled what Foster had told them about it. It suddenly came back to him and his eyes rounded. 'Didn't Foster tell us that a seeker had killed the team before us? *Torn to pieces*, he said! Those were his exact words, so they were!'

Rashim's mouth dropped open. 'There was a team before you?' He stared from one of them to the other. 'You never mentioned that before! Why not?'

'Aye,' Liam flipped his hand to dismiss the subject. 'It's not a big detail, Rashim.'

'I thought I was a trusted member of your team!'

'It's not important, Rashim!' snapped Maddy. 'Not right now!'

'I'll second that,' said Adam. 'I'm kind of more focused on the "torn to pieces" bit.'

'Nothing came out, Adam.' She addressed all of them. '*Nothing* came out! We were right there! We were watching, we would have seen it! The support units would've sensed something! Jesus . . . *we'd* have been the ones ripped to shreds! Not a dog and some llamas.'

'Lest we forget, some poor hapless person as well,' added Bertie.

'Look! That bloody mess down there could just as easily have been the work of a witch-doctor or someone wanting us to go. They just slaughtered some animals and flung bits of gunk around and told everyone the gods were angry with us.'

'And sacrificed somebody too?' Adam pointed out.

She shrugged. 'That could've been the bones of somebody who already died.' She sighed. 'Look, there's no Devil! There's no seeker! More likely, that old guy, or some other witch-doctor whose thunder we're stealing, wants us gone. If these people are getting jittery or suspicious – or they want to start becoming threatening, then I say *screw it*! They're just a bunch of frightened, primitive savages! Let's fire a shot or two into the air, or Bob can go rip a goat in half or something. That'll give 'em something to be frightened about! They'll soon get off our backs and leave us alone.' She shook her head. 'But the one thing I'm not doing is running away and leaving Sal to come out here on her own.'

'So, what *are* you going to do?' asked Rashim.

'I'm going in.'

'*What?*'

'I'm going into the beam. If she's in there, I'll find her and I'll bring her back.'

CHAPTER 59

1479, the Lost City of the Windtalkers

This time round, making their way to the chambers, the atmosphere was wholly different. No longer thousands of pairs of eyes glistening with excitement and reverence. No longer people dropping to their knees as they passed by, offering tributes of fruit and meat.

There was now an almost palpable sense of hostility and fear. The crowd stepped aside in complete silence to allow them through; a couple of thousand pairs of eyes wordlessly warned them that they should turn and leave immediately or this was going to end badly for them.

The only sound was the gentle hiss of rain pattering down from an overcast sky.

Maddy wanted to call out to them and assure them that everything was going to be just fine, that they weren't going down there to open up the gates of the underworld and invite a horde of demons into their city. But, even if she could speak their tongue, the grisly scene of dismembered animals was so dark and horrific an omen to them, that her words wouldn't carry any meaningful weight.

The rain spattered on the shreds of flesh and tendon, the shards of bone, making them wet, glistening like the scene of a fresh slaughter. The rain made the congealed blood *fluid* once more so that it ran again, meandering in a crimson stream among the many sandal-clad feet. Hostile eyes, wide and warning, remained on the passing strangers.

They made their way through the crowd, all of them huddled closely together. Bob up front, gigantic and menacing with the rifle like a large club in his hands. Becks at the rear and equally intimidating with hers brandished in both hands. Billy walked beside her, his AK cocked and ready to fire. They descended into the trench, then ducked down as they entered the low stone arch of the entrance into the upper chamber.

Thick shards of grey light from the large gap in the ceiling pierced the darkness at an angle and rain spattered in noisily through the jagged hole, the sound of drips echoing around the chamber. They could see a dozen other angled beams of weak daylight piercing the dark where other support columns had been damaged or dislocated and cracks in the weakened stonework above had appeared.

'I can't believe deep bass vibrations from that device below did all this damage,' said Adam.

Maddy wasn't so sure. The throbbing had been deafening, they'd all felt it against their chests: the kind of ultra-deep frequency that can rattle cups in saucers, and cause brittle glass to shatter. She could well believe those vibrations, amplified by the shape of the chambers themselves, had caused this ancient stonework to rattle and loosen up.

This city, the upper chamber, all of the stonework had been built many, many centuries ago. Here and there, she'd noted the stonework appeared to be worn and old and beginning to show signs of attrition and fracture. Very little sign of recent repair work or any new structures. The city had the look of a place that was once far grander and better maintained. In other words, this micro-civilization had seen better days. This was a civilization on its way out – in the midst of a gradual and gentle decline.

Yeah, as far as she was concerned it was perfectly plausible that deep throbbing frequency had caused some of the plaza to cave in on the chamber below.

They made their way across to the narrow gap in the wall and the small antechamber beyond. Torches snapped on. Then down they went, down the narrow stairwell into the much bigger second chamber.

She was certain there were no *monsters* down here – damned if she was going to jump at shadows just because those primitive people up above were. All the same, she asked Bob and Becks if they were picking up any unexpected energy signatures.

'Negative. We are only detecting stray tachyon particles from the field.'

'There is still a significant surge of energy in progress,' added Becks.

They crossed the glass-smooth floor until they were standing close to the central column. Adam and Rashim approached its curved wall and started work on picking out the three glyphs Adam had touched last time to open the column.

'See? It's still closed, Liam,' she said, finally breaking the wordless silence. 'So if it was a seeker, it was rather decent of him to close the door behind himself.'

Liam laughed. It sounded forced and uncomfortable as it echoed back to them. She imagined he'd rather that particular echo hurried up and faded away.

'We should discuss a back-up plan, Maddy,' said Liam.

She knew what he was getting at. It was written all over his face: *what happens if you go through and you don't come back either?*

She dug into the pocket of her jeans, pulled out the transponder and handed it to him. 'Just in case, you know? If for some reason . . . ?'

'No.' He pushed her hand away. 'You should keep hold of

it. If you do find yourself coming out somewhere else, then we can use it to find you.'

She shook her head. 'This little thing would be about as useful as a needle in a haystack. It's no use to me unless you guys know pretty precisely where to look.' She offered it to him again. 'Take it, Liam. You're going to need it to signal computer-Bob . . . to get you all back home.'

Liam stared at the device in her hand. Unwilling to take it yet.

'And listen, if I don't come back out, you make sure you go back to London. OK? You take Adam and Bertie back to their times. And Rashim and that stupid bot of his can decide for themselves where they want to go.'

She held the transponder out. He took it off her reluctantly. 'You know, Mads, maybe this isn't such a great idea?'

'Maybe – maybe not. But it's the only idea I've got right now.'

'There is another way, Maddy. We could all just leave. We could just get out of here and go home!'

'Then what?' She shrugged. 'You know you and I – we'd end up coming back here eventually. You know that, don't you? We'd want to know what's happened to Sal. We'd want to know what this field is doing here. Who set it up here in the first place. We'd want to know what's waiting for us at the other end . . . and whether Sal is there, instead, patiently waiting for us.'

Liam conceded that with a slight nod. 'Aye, well. Perhaps we would.'

'No perhaps about it.' She tried on a brave smile. It looked shaky and uncertain. 'We're here right now. So we might as well get those answers now. Right?'

He nodded. 'Right.'

'Anyway,' she added, 'I think this is where we're meant to

be. We've been led here. This is what we were meant to discover.'

It seemed obvious to her, even if Liam wasn't seeing it yet, that everything since she'd discovered that handwritten note in San Francisco had been leading up to this. It was as if they'd been actors following an elaborate script, being carefully led by the nose, scene by scene, to this place and this moment. And it appeared that Sal had somehow read the script that bit faster than either of them, read ahead of them by a couple of scenes.

'Let me come along with you then,' said Liam.

'No. Just in case –' she lowered her voice just a fraction – 'just in case something happens, one of us needs to get this lot back home.'

'Rashim can do that,' he replied. 'He knows how the technology all works better than I do.'

'No. *We* were given this job, Liam. We were *made* for this job. We're the agency. We're all that's left of it. Not them. It's just you and me now.'

She patted his shoulder. 'It's gonna be fine. I'll bring her back.'

'For the record, I think this is a really bad idea, Mads,' he replied. 'Definitely not one of your best ones.'

She looked up at the imposing form of the column, something built by technicians from the far future; a future beyond the near-complete annihilation of mankind. Perhaps a future in which mankind had learned all the important lessons. Learned that this world was a fragile closed system of finite resources. Learned that war was not the best way to resolve difficult decisions. Learned that to wield technology like this, there was a duty, responsibility, a required level of cultural maturity.

She realized, digging deep down into the bedrock of her mind, this wasn't just about searching for Sal, this was about satisfying her own insatiable curiosity. This was about wanting to know if there really was a future worth fighting to preserve. Wanting to see for herself and wondering if, somewhere behind the smooth curved wall of the column, she would see what Waldstein once saw.

Perhaps she would emerge again, not only with Sal by her side, but finally with a clear understanding of why Waldstein had set up the agency and why they had the grim task of carefully steering mankind towards its own undoing.

She squeezed Liam's hand. 'I will come back, I promise you.'

Adam joined them. 'I've marked up the three symbols that open the door.' He pointed at the column. Three scraps of paper were stuck to the surface beside each symbol, stuck with gum. Numbers 1, 2 and 3 scrawled in biro on them to indicate the order in which they were to be touched.

He noted her hand clasping Liam's. 'I don't think this is such a great idea either.'

She let Liam's hand go and reached out for Adam. Curled a hand round the back of his neck. 'I know.'

Liam took a step back with a polite nod and a smile, allowed them a moment of privacy.

'I really need to do this, Adam,' she whispered.

'I overheard Liam suggest we could all just walk away from this. I just thought I'd add my tuppence worth and say I think he's right.'

'Don't you want to know why your name ended up a part of ancient history? Aren't you curious?'

'Sure.' He shook his head slowly. 'But not at the risk of you losing your life!'

She wondered if it would help him understand where her head was at if she told him that his own burning curiosity would ultimately lead him to New York and his death in one of the Twin Towers. She wanted to tell him that, in a way, every human life was a journey to have questions answered. It was a journey that inevitably ended with death.

We all die eventually. But the one thing we *can* do is seek answers along the way.

She squeezed the back of his neck. 'You answered some important things I needed to know, Adam.'

He offered her a puzzled look. 'I'm just the geek with the map. I'm just the hanger-on here.'

She pulled him closer and placed a tender kiss on his lips. 'In another universe you and me live together in a scruffy Manhattan apartment . . .' she whispered, 'with clothes tossed all over the floor and the cap left off the toothpaste in our bathroom.'

He smiled sadly. 'Lucky Adam Lewis.'

'I *will* come back.' She kissed him again.

And maybe we'll have that . . . one day.

She let him go and stepped back. A couple of deep breaths to steady her nerves and her voice. She nodded at Rashim, standing beside the wall of symbols. 'OK, open it up.'

He gently touched the three symbols in order.

A dazzling vertical white line suddenly appeared on the column, hairline thick, then it became a thick bar, flooding the chamber with light and the deep thrumming hum of energy. The bar widened until it was six feet across. Impatient energy crackled and fizzed before them. Maddy shielded her eyes, squinted at the glare until her vision adjusted to it, and then she found herself staring at the featureless white.

She picked out Bob and Becks standing to one side. 'Let it close up by itself, and then open it later like we agreed! OK?'

The support units nodded. They'd calculated a gap of a minimum of four hours between openings would allow the field energy surge time enough to die down and then spike again. If there were 'currents' or 'flows' of energy inside for her to try to follow, it would help to have a discernible tide-flow to look for and carry her back.

She nodded at Billy and Bertie, then at Rashim. 'Coffee, black, when I return.'

He saluted that.

Her eyes met Liam's and she mouthed, 'I'll be fine.'

He nodded. Cupped his mouth against the noise. 'You bring yourself back, Mads. You hear?'

And finally Adam. Her eyes met his.

You answered a question for me, Adam. And yes. Yes, I can do that. I can fall in love.

She turned towards the bar of brilliant white light and stepped forward. She could feel the build-up of escaping static electricity lifting the hairs on her arms. Stepping closer, chaos space was now just a yard away from her, the static stirring the hair on her head, tickling her scalp.

Directly in front of her now, a wall of chaos space. She closed her eyes, took a deep breath and took one, two, three steps forward.

CHAPTER 60

At once familiar – that featureless white. But slightly different in that there was no sensation of falling this time. She was not flailing with her arms. Instead there seemed to be something beneath her feet. Not firm floor, but soft and yielding, like the elastic of a trampoline.

As always, it was silent. The only noise she could hear was her own ragged breath, the rhythmic thud of her heart in her chest.

She cupped her hands round her eyes and narrowed them against the brilliant white, knowing from past experience that this seemingly blank, milky froth surrounding her did yield *some* form and detail when you shielded the glare a little. Now the empty white became a faint pattern, splotches, areas, slightly brighter and slightly darker. She thought she detected the faint movement of thin strands of something rising from the 'ground' and fading into the fog above her, like souls rising from cemetery dirt to the heavens above.

She wondered if she might just be seeing the faint ghostlike forms of future humans busy in transit along this projected conduit of chaos space. The Archaeologists, coming and going through history, quietly observing, cataloguing and archiving information about their long-lost ancestors.

'Helloo!' she called out. Her voice was deadened in here. No echo or reverberation. No hard surfaces off which sonic waves could bounce – indeed, no time or space in the normal sense for those sonic waves to travel through to find any hard surfaces to bounce off.

The smothered sound of her voice against the absolute silence was still alarmingly loud. She squinted at the ghostly forms rising from the ground around her. Some of them seemed to be only a few feet away from her. Curious, she was tempted to step towards the nearest and try wafting her hand through the denser mist. But what effect might such a careless act like that have? Would it cause some poor far-future human to emerge – on the way to or from an errand – completely mis-formed? To be turned inside out?

She'd said to the others that she wondered if this artificial tunnel of chaos space had some kind of flow, *direction*, that would carry her somewhere; that would decide on her behalf where she was to go. Perhaps these ghostly forms were showing the way, that she needed to travel upwards like them? Perhaps 'up' was the way to go? And what did *up* lead to? The future? The past?

Uncertain what to do, she tried calling out again. But this time calling for Sal.

'Sal! SAL!! You there?!'

None of these rising forms seemed to hesitate at the sound of her voice. She wondered if sound carried at all in this place anyway. She called again. And again.

And waited.

The 'wraiths' passed up around her, seemingly unaware of her – or, if they were aware, then they were utterly uninterested. She was about to cup her hands round her mouth and try again when she picked out the faintest sense of movement working against the uniform upwards motion.

Looking directly at it, it seemed to vanish, merged into the mist. But on the periphery of her vision she detected something curling down from above. Now it was on her level, at her height, moving slowly, horizontally, around her. Circling cautiously. Drawing nearer and now more distinct.

'Hello?' she called again.

The ghostly form seemed to hesitate for the briefest moment at the sound of her voice.

God, it heard me.

'Hello,' she said again. Her voice deadened and lifeless. 'Who is that? Is that you, Sal?'

The form remained motionless. Maddy tried to discern the outline of this silhouette. But it changed from moment to moment, as intangible as candle smoke caught in a draft. Whatever, whoever, it was – it seemed to have reacted to her voice. It had heard her. *Definitely* heard her, and now it seemed curious.

'Are you another . . . *traveller*?'

The form shifted slightly. Maddy thought she could see tendrils of smoke emerging from the densest area, tendrils that seemed to reach out and taste the air, then evaporate into disassociated curls of mist.

'Can you hear me?' she asked. 'Can you understand me?'

The form drifted closer to her. More distinct now, closer in fact to Maddy than any of these 'wraiths' they'd all admitted to seeing at one time or another had ever been.

Closer still.

Now she could see this thing was more than just a denser patch of mist. She could discern the faintest surface details, texture. And these details, the texture, seemed to be in a constant state of flux: patterns that suggested the creases of leather, the grain of wood, the scales of a fish, veins of marble . . . as if this thing was choosing what it wanted to be crafted from, second to second. It reminded her of how the pigment in a chameleon's skin cells can oscillate through colours and patterns and assume any camouflage in a matter of seconds.

She wondered, if this was another person, then this must be how she would appear to them, something equally mysterious, equally alien and disturbing. Perhaps sound, though, perhaps her voice, wouldn't be corrupted into something so weird by chaos space. Perhaps she would sound human to this thing.

'Hello,' she said again, her voice quieter and softer. It was close enough that she felt she didn't need to shout. 'Can you hear me?'

Yes.

She wasn't sure whether she actually heard that answer, or merely imagined it. It didn't seem to have come from any particular direction, certainly not from this undulating cloud of indecisive matter hovering just feet away from her.

'You can hear me?'

Yes.

'Understand me?'

I understand you.

Maddy struggled to not let out a yelp of relief. To be able to communicate with this thing – this *person*? – was somehow reassuring. Not some animalistic or unfathomable alien mind, but quite possibly another human, albeit in chaos-space form.

Incredible.

She wondered what question to ask this fellow traveller first. What question? What question?

'Are you . . . are you a person? A human?'

The form drifted around her, she sensed it was trying to understand her too, perhaps also seeing another amorphous form and frightened by it. She wished this thing had something analogous to eyes – eyes that she could meet, address her conversation towards.

Yes. It replied as it shifted form, tendrils spinning out like tissue strands in water.

Yes. Human. Once. The voice sounded sexless. Ageless. Emotionless. Like an averaging-out of all possible voices, the very definition of neutral, impossible to read . . . and yet, in its bland voice, Maddy thought she detected a hint of – grief? Sadness?

'Are you someone else . . . in transit? A time traveller?'

No answer.

'Are you one of the people who built this displacement field?'

The being shifted textures. In places its 'skin' thinned and became gossamer, a semi-opaque membrane revealing even deeper complexities of curling texture and form within. It reminded her just a little of the interior of a time wave.

Once, just once, she'd been up close and had her eyes open as a time wave had swept past her, just inches away. She'd witnessed the churning, roiling sea of possibilities inside: millions of souls seemingly screaming in torment at lives they would never lead; structures, cities that would never be built; kings that would never rule, empires that would never have a chance to rise and fall.

The entity answered her. *Travelled through time. Long ago.*

She shuddered as a thought suddenly occurred to her. Perhaps it was something like this entity that Waldstein had witnessed, perhaps even spoken with, on his very first trip through chaos space.

'Are you from the future?' she asked. She realized as soon as she voiced the question how stupid it was. How would this traveller know how to answer that? If it didn't know when Maddy came from, it couldn't say if it was from her future.

'Are you from beyond the event that wiped us all out? Beyond the year 2070?'

It drifted a little closer to her. She noted several bacilli-like tendrils of vapour reaching out towards her. She felt nothing as they seemed to touch her skin. Maybe this thing was seeing tendrils reaching out from her as well; perhaps these wisps of vapour were a visual representation of thought, curiosity expressed in an ethereal form?

Future, past, present, there is no difference. There is now. There is an eternity. That is all.

There seemed to be a bottomless, weary grief folded into that answer. She wondered if this could be a traveller who had got lost, some fool who had stupidly walked into a portal without having an exit window arranged.

A stupid fool just like her, she realized. No. She had an exit arranged. The others would open the column in four hours. Although she had no idea what four hours of 'real' time would be to her, stuck in this place.

'Are you lost? Are you trapped in here?'

Trapped? It shifted form and glided around her. *From here all possibilities can be seen. Seen so many things in here.*

She wanted to ask this creature about Sal. But how to ask and what to ask? *You seen my friend walking around? She's five foot two, about a hundred and twelve pounds, dark hair.* Perhaps she would ask about Sal soon. But first she needed to know *what* it was, even *who* it was, she was communicating with.

'What have you seen?'

Beginnings, endings and all between. Everything that could be, and never was.

'You mean alternative timelines?'

Yes.

'Have you seen what happens to us, to humanity after we destroy ourselves?'

The entity took its time answering that. *There is a future beyond that way.*

'We *do* survive then? We go on? We rebuild?'

Only on that way.

Maddy pondered that curious choice of words. '*That way . . .* you mean the timeline in which we wipe ourselves out?'

Other ways . . . it is dark. Nothing to be seen. Empty.

'Why?'

There can be only one way out.

'One way out?' What the hell did that mean? One way out of *what*? Chaos space?

We are all trapped. For eternity.

The entity's surface phased momentarily, revealing ghostly images within itself. She saw images she could comprehend – this thing was showing her pictures, *thoughts*, to help her understand: a dungeon, the padded cell of an insane asylum, a face locked behind an iron mask, a prisoner sealed in a buried coffin, screaming, scratching at the wood.

Were those metaphors it was showing her? Was this a warning? A caution of what might be? Or what already was?

'Are you showing those things to help me understand?'

No answer.

'What do those images mean?'

All trapped. Only one way to be free.

She thought of Waldstein again. 'We have to destroy ourselves? Is that what you're saying? To be free we have to destroy ourselves?'

It stirred, shape-shifted. She had a sense the question was confusing it. Distressing it.

'Are *you* trapped? Can you leave here? Can you leave this place?'

No answer.

'What about me, can I leave?'

Its membranous surface became opaque again, hiding the turmoil of images within. Somehow, *guarded*. She sensed it was becoming suspicious of her, wary.

'I came in here looking for someone. Another person like me – another traveller. She entered just before me.'

No before. No after. Only now. Only eternity.

The entity retreated from her. Becoming less detailed in the mist.

'Please!' she called out after it. 'Don't go away. Don't leave me alone.'

She tried to keep sight of it as it grew fainter. 'I can get out! I can come out the way I came in! There's an opening nearby. You could come with me!'

Out of the mist a long thin tendril of vapour rapidly coiled towards her, hovered just inches short of her face. Its thin end expanded, mushroomed, and then on its undulating surface she saw the fleeting images of tormented faces. Dozens morphing one after the other in quick succession.

Then one last face. One she recognized. Sal's face, contorted and stretched as her mouth opened impossibly wide with a dreadful scream that seemed to fill the space around them. In one shrill raw wail, there was rage, grief, insanity, agony . . . yearning.

'Sal?'

LET ME OUT.

Just then, Maddy felt the flow change. Something pulling at her softly, insistently. The thin and faint tissue-like forms, travelling upwards, stirred and spun like jellyfish, like water-borne debris tugged by a fresh current. As if a plug had been pulled from a bath tub, and all that was free-floating was now drawn along by the flow of vacating water.

Maddy backed away from the tendril as it retreated into the mist again. She could smell the ozone-like odour. Air charged with energy. *Rage* as pure energy.

She backed away in the direction that the current was pulling her. Quick step after quick step across the uncertain, giving surface of the 'floor'.

Then one foot settled on a hard, unyielding surface. She turned round and found herself staring into darkness. Her eyes adjusted to reveal a smooth floor, and emerging out of the gloom, several approaching figures . . .

CHAPTER 61

1479, the Lost City of the Windtalkers

'Maddy!' Adam reached out for her. He looked relieved. 'My God, you've been gone days! We didn't know whether to –!'

'Close it!' She gasped for air as she staggered past him, several yards away from the column, and then finally came to a halt, doubled over. 'Need to close it!'

He joined her, shook his head. 'Still haven't worked that out. It closes on its own –'

'Jesus! Then –' Her laboured breath came in wheezing, ragged gasps – 'we – got to – run!'

The others had gathered round her. Liam had a half-cocked smile stamped on his lips; utter relief and growing concern wrestling with each other. 'Mads! I thought we lost you! Two days we've been waiting! Did you see Sal?' He stopped himself and looked at her pale face. 'What is it? You look like you've seen a –'

She finally caught her breath. 'RUN!' she screamed. 'WE HAVE TO RUN!'

Behind them the white glow of the field began to ripple, deform, then bulge. The steady, deep, rhythmic throbbing gave way to a crackling sound.

'Good Lord,' gasped Bertie, 'what is going on there?'

They turned as one to look.

The air just outside the field now shimmered like the flame-heated air above a campfire. Something invisible, super-heating the area it occupied – a space twenty feet high and just as wide, was causing it to warp and dance.

Jagged forks of static electricity arced from the field, flickered round the edge of the mass of heated air, momentarily, fleetingly, describing an artist's sketch of its outline. In one blink of an eye, they had a lightning-strike depiction of its form: three thick elephant-like legs supporting the round mass of a giant head. A mouth that looked vaguely human but stretched impossibly, vertically, with a Munch-like scream, like a Halloween mask. A mouth filled with teeth. Above the gaping maw, two small coal-dark eyes that slanted with grief and pity. The mouth was all rage, the eyes were sadness.

Its roar filled the chamber. Not the roar of a predator, but the shrill scream of a chorus of human voices. It swayed, weight shifting from one thick leg to another, the giant head surveying the darkness around it, then turning to look down at them.

'What is that creature?!' screamed Bertie.

'Jay-zus,' Liam uttered. 'That's a – a seeker?'

Maddy wasn't sure what it was. Explanations could come later. 'RUN!'

She was the first to turn on her heels and flee, more than happy to lead from the front this time as they raced across the floor, then scrambled for the narrow stairwell that led to the upper chamber. Behind her she heard the crack of gunfire. She halted, turned to see who it was. Guns weren't going to stop this thing.

Twenty yards behind her she could see Billy shouldering his AK, his torch strapped to the barrel, the flicker of muzzle-flash as he fired shots out into the darkness.

'Billy! Forget it! Run!'

The seeker had stepped far enough away from the column that the arcing electricity was no longer leaping across from chaos space to hint at its outline. It was invisible now – the only thing giving its location away, the tell-tale shimmer of heated air. From where Billy was, closer, much closer, he had obviously picked out that faint outline and was now emptying rounds of ammo into it.

Liam stopped beside Maddy and looked back. 'Billy!' he cried. 'GET OVER HERE!'

Billy was shouting as he fired. Curses in Spanish or Tawahka or Zambu.

'BILLY!'

All of a sudden, their guide spasmed, dropped his gun and was lifted up. He thrashed around, mid-air, screaming with agony and fear. Maddy thought she could make out the fleeting, phasing form of a long arm ending with three claws holding him aloft. Then another one appeared out of nothingness, claws wrapping round the top half of Billy's torso. One savage twist and the guide was torn clean in half. His separated body hurled casually in two different directions, and the long arms of the monster phased out of sight once more.

'Jay-zus, help us!' cried Liam.

Maddy felt hands tugging at her shoulders, pulling her towards the stairwell. Adam. 'Come on!' He pushed her on to the stairs ahead of him.

She clambered up the slippery-smooth stone steps; steep steps that had her thighs burning by the top of them. Rashim, Bertie, Becks already there. Liam, Adam and finally Bob emerged from the stairwell behind her.

'Yes –' she was gasping for air again, answering Liam's question of a minute ago – 'it's a seeker. Or . . . maybe it's several . . . merged into one mega-seeker. I don't know.'

Adam looked at the stairwell descending down into the

darkness of the lower chamber. 'It can't follow us up that narrow space, can it?'

'It is constructed from pure energy,' said Bob. 'It can change form.'

'You are not safe staying here,' Becks added.

They heard something heavy impacting the steps below. Felt the vibration of it through the stone floor, through their feet. Followed by its mournful chorus-cry of tormented human voices echoing through the lower chamber.

Liam looked at Maddy. 'It's coming up.'

They headed for the narrow exit out of the small chamber. Bunched up, they tangled with each other.

'One at a time!' bellowed Liam. 'One at a time. Go! Go!' They squeezed through the narrow doorway, one after the other, an impatient queue to escape. Liam and Bob the last to go through. Liam turned to look over his shoulder, aiming his torch at the hole in the floor, and thought he detected a thin vapour of shimmering air coiling out of it.

'Go! Go! Go!' He pounded at Bob's fleshy shoulder, pushing him roughly through the gap, then stumbling through after him. 'IT'S UP THE STAIRS!' he shouted to the others waiting just outside the gap in the wall. 'RUN FOR IT!'

They turned on their heels and ran, all of them weaving their own paths through the forest of support columns.

Liam was about to do likewise when he noted Bob, unslinging his antique rifle.

'Bob? What're you doing? Come on!'

'I will be able to delay the seeker at this chokepoint.'

'Don't be a flippin' idiot, Bob. You won't win against *this* one!'

'I understand, Liam . . . but I will provide you with additional time to escape.'

'The hell with that, you big idiot. Just run!'

Bob shot a glance through the narrow gap in the wall. It was too dark to see anything clearly, but he could sense the energy building up inside that small room as the creature's distended cloud emerged from the confines of the stairwell and consolidated in the antechamber. The seeker's form had adapted to the narrow stairs, was now pouring into the room like liquid filling a bottle, breath filling a balloon.

'Bob? For Chrissake don't make me smack your big arse! RUN!'

The support unit nodded. Logic making a better decision than some badly timed notion of courage.

'Affirmative.'

They turned and ran, picking separate routes through the ranks of support columns. Up ahead Liam could see the others had converged on the exit. He saw their silhouettes as they stumbled out of the small doorway and on to the steps outside.

Behind Liam came a loud thump and the crash of shattering masonry. He chanced another hurried glance backwards, flinging his torch beam wildly behind him. The seeker had just exploded through the narrow gap, knocking blocks of sandstone out of the wall, creating a much wider opening. His torchlight pierced through a thick rolling cloud of dust that hung lazily in the still air for a moment, before suddenly it swirled, disturbed, as something unseen surged through it, pushing the billowing cloud to both sides.

A support column that lay between Liam and the ruined entrance to the antechamber suddenly seemed to explode into fragments, as if impacted by a heavy cannonball. Then a few seconds later another one, closer to him, lurched and toppled to one side as though rammed by a charging bull. Several large slabs of ceiling stone, now robbed of the support from the toppled column, collapsed to the floor.

Shards of salmon-pink evening light speared down through billowing clouds of dust.

The chamber was suddenly filled with a roar that sounded half like the trumpeting of an elephant and half like the mournful, echoing call of a humpback whale.

Panning the torch back behind him, the beam piercing the thickening dust, he picked out movement and, for a moment, the invisible monster phased into view. He caught a glimpse of its form changing shape: the giant head twisting and elongating, morphing from human to an almost boar-like extruded snout; spines and jagged protrusions erupting through its 'flesh'.

Dark-as-coal eyes settled on Liam, before the beast phased out of sight again. Then a moment later yet another column even closer to him erupted in a shower of dust and fragments.

The thing was heading directly towards him. He turned and resumed running for the faint glow of the exit.

Maddy and the others emerged from the trench into the wan glow of a setting sun. Long purple shadows and stripes of rose-pink sunlight striped the basin of the city. Around the entrance the people were gathered, thousands of them. At the first sight of them emerging from beneath the plaza, voices rose in unison into a shrill, deafening wail, drums stirred to life and beat a threatening rhythm among them.

The crowd surged forward.

'We have been holed up down below, the last two days,' said Rashim. 'Our hosts were getting very agitated outside. But they would not follow us down.'

Becks stood out front, using the butt of her Martini-Henry rifle as a club, jabbing and swinging at the pressing crowd to force them back, to create a space for them to escape through.

Bertie was doubled over by the entrance, one hand resting against the weathered stone, trying to get air into his lungs. 'What the Devil . . .' he called out, trying to be heard over the clamour of voices and the beating drums. 'What the Devil was that three-legged monster? That tripod beast?'

She shook her head. She didn't really know anything about it other than what Foster had once told them. 'It's what I told you before about seekers! *That's* a frikkin' seeker!'

Adam glanced back behind them. 'Do you think we've lost it?'

Just then, emerging from the low archway of the entrance, they heard a deep boom and felt the thump and vibration of some heavy impact occurring inside. Voices in the crowd cried out in alarm as several sections of the plaza floor collapsed, a column of dust mushrooming up into the sky.

'My God, it's followed us up,' cried Maddy. 'It's still coming for us!'

Another shudder, another boom of impact. More sections of the plaza floor collapsed. The belligerent crowd now suddenly seemed far less interested in pressing forward and getting their hands on their unwelcome guests. They began to back away from the entrance. Then they all heard it. The deafening roar of something huge, something tormented, echoing through the upper chamber.

The crowd's angry chanting disintegrated into thousands of individual cries of horror and panic. The drumming stopped. The press of people around them began to thin as they started to turn and flee in terror.

Maddy looked around at the others. 'Where's Liam?'

'He was right behind me,' said Rashim.

'And Bob?'

Another thump. Louder. Closer.

Rashim ducked down and peered back into the entrance, shining his torch into the darkness. 'I think there is someone coming this way!'

'Liam?'

Rashim squinted as he played his torch around. He could see the flicker of movement in there; rolling clouds of dust and something disturbing them. Something big. 'I don't think so.'

Another loud roar and Rashim turned to look at Maddy. 'RUN!'

He pushed past her, scrambled up the shallow steps of the trench and up on to the paved thoroughfare. Maddy beckoned at the others to follow.

They were up on the flagstones and now mingled among the few remaining city people. These onlookers were no longer determined to get their hands on the 'pretenders' who had deceitfully gained their trust and access to their holiest place, but, like them, their eyes were glued to the small arched entrance to the chamber below – both terrified and fascinated to see what was about to emerge from it.

The small stone blocks around the entrance suddenly erupted. As if propelled by an explosion, shards of stone arced into the sky, dust rolled upwards and outwards like a volcanic pyroclastic surge. The setting sun painted the thick cloud of dust a candy pink as it billowed out over the crowd of awestruck, horrified onlookers.

Amid the cloud, something large raged, stomping and swaying from foot to foot. It was only an outline in the cloud: the mass of the invisible beast displacing dust-thick air. An enormous bulk, twenty feet high and across, three elephantine legs stamping the ground.

From an open 'mouth' – if that's what it was – something long and sinewy shot out. An arm? A tentacle? It extended quickly and curled round a hapless young man who had remained too close for too long. He was yanked into the air kicking and screaming. The pall of dust had begun to thin and the entity's outline became harder to determine. Just the faintest edges of heat-seared air.

The young man now seemed to be flying from side to side thirty feet above the ground. A smoke trail followed him as his skin seared, burned; the smell of cooking flesh filled the air. His agonized screaming suddenly ended with a sickening crack. Then his body, ripped in two, was tossed into the fleeing crowd.

One half landed just a few yards from Maddy. The top half, smouldering and blackened by the intense energy; the open ragged ruin of the boy's torso was almost completely cauterized by the creature's furnace-like heat.

Oh, God help me . . . what did I bring back?

Maddy had seen more than enough. 'Come on! We've got to get out of here!'

They joined the people streaming away from the plaza, and quickly found themselves funnelled into a narrow street, all of them now united in terror, united in the direction they were running and the mindless imperative to escape.

Behind them there was another roar, amplified by the curved acoustics of the city, a roar that sounded as loud and all-encompassing as the forbidding rumble of an earthquake.

A section of the plaza floor had collapsed on to Liam as a column nearby had been casually knocked aside like a stack of poorly balanced books. The thing had been bearing down on him and he had been certain that this was *it*.

This is me done. Smoked like a kipper.

However, the debris from above – not just flagstones but a

trader's cart, several woven sacks of guavas, bushels of straw – had all but buried him.

He found himself hidden from view and watched, petrified, as the beast had stamped and swirled mere feet away from him. Where his skin was exposed and not covered in dirt and dust, he could feel the heat from this thing radiating like a blast furnace.

It was his first proper close-up glimpse. It was invisible mostly. But occasionally small portions here and there flickered into view, visible for a moment; blink and you'd miss it. Its form and texture seemed to be changing from one second to the next. Spines and bone-like protrusions extruded one moment, then collapsed inwards the next, as if the creature's form was in a constant state of wretched indecision.

A patch of the entity's 'skin' appeared, then turned semi-transparent, revealing a spinning, churning mulch of human body parts inside. A face was suddenly pressed up against the membranous 'skin', nose squashed, eyes wide, mouth far wider – an unheard scream of torment from within this beast. Then the next moment it was gone, whisked away.

Liam thought, lying here, trapped under the avalanche of debris, that he was certainly going to die. The thing would find him, *sniff him out*.

But it didn't.

It stamped angrily for a moment, then paused. The roaring ceased and Liam thought he could hear a muffled chorus of wailing voices coming from deep within its mass.

Then, invisible once again, just shimmering air, he heard it move off. Heavy booming footsteps taking it away from him. He saw another column, further away, lurch to one side like a pile of playschool building-blocks spitefully knocked over by a child's hand. It appeared to be heading towards the faint outline of the distant entrance.

A shadow loomed over him, blocking out the pink evening sky above, and he felt the pressing weight of fallen stone blocks lessen as Bob began to dig him out of the mound of debris.

'Are you damaged, Liam?'

'I don't think so.' Nothing seemed broken. 'I think I'm all right.'

Bob helped him up on to his feet. 'Where are the others?' asked Liam.

'The others left the chamber through the entrance.'

Liam shook his head, steadied himself. Pulled in a couple of breaths. 'How the hell are we going to fight this thing?'

'It is pure energy. There is no way to fight it, Liam.'

'Then what do we do?'

'Evade it.' Just then the entire chamber shuddered. Grit and dirt cascaded down from the low ceiling. The entrance on the far side, a second ago a pinprick of faint light, was now a much wider, ragged hole.

'We will have to evade it until its energy has been fully depleted.'

CHAPTER 62

1479, the Lost City of the Windtalkers

Becks suddenly became aware that she had lost visual contact with the others. She was being carried along by a press of fleeing bodies, up a narrow alleyway. Taller than most of the people around her, she craned her neck to be sure. But she could locate none of them.

'Enough,' she grunted.

She barged through the desperate natives until she was out of the 'flow', her back pressed up against a cool stone wall. Systematically, her eyes swept across the faces passing her, but none of them were Maddy, Liam or the others. She realized that in the turmoil of panic she'd become separated from the others, pushed up a different narrow alley. Her lips stiffened; if she'd had a decent enough database of profanities and curses, she might have tried one out. Instead she put her mind to something more useful – determining where she might locate them again. They needed her.

The only likely place they would try to head towards was surely the exit tunnel. The only way out of this natural basin. The highest probability: that would be where they'd make for.

She pushed her way back into the flow of people, against it this time, roughly shouldering fleeing men, women and children out of her way as she made her way back towards the plaza, to go round it and towards the tunnel exit on the far side.

★

The tide of terrified people carried Maddy and the others up the narrow stepped street. Many of them seemed determined to flood into the various temple buildings, either because they believed those stone structures with their thick wooden doors were robust enough to keep this thing at bay, or because they believed their gods and their priests would protect them. Others filtered off into narrow passageways, presumably hoping to hide in their small dark homes.

Maddy and the others went with the flow, with little choice in the matter, and finally felt themselves being carried, pushed and jostled through the large doorway of the main temple building. The sounds of screaming and wailing coming from the women and children now bounced off the high stone walls around them: a cacophony of panic and terror magnified tenfold.

Some men pulled the thick wooden door of the temple firmly shut. It slammed with a deep boom that silenced many of the voices inside.

We've just gone and sealed ourselves in. Maddy looked around at huddled family groups, mothers with babes-in-arms, holding the hands of petrified, ashen-faced children. Husbands and fathers convened in little groups, speaking in hurried, hushed tones. And eyes – so many pairs of suspicious eyes – settled on the strangers in their midst who'd brought this evil down upon them.

'This isn't good,' said Adam. He looked at Rashim. 'This isn't good! Remember all those bones you discovered . . . ?'

Pat-ishka, the city's shrivel-skinned elder and – as far as Maddy had been able to work out – spiritual leader, began to talk calmly to his frightened people. His thin, reedy voice and birdlike frame belied the hold he had over them. They instantly hushed and listened as he spoke. Maddy wished Billy was here with them. He'd had some vague understanding of the language, and while he might not have been able to tell her precisely what the old man was saying, he could have given her an impression of what was being said.

Through the thick reinforced wooden door they heard the entity rampage outside. They could hear the crashing and splintering of buildings, that chilling trumpeting roar of chorused inhuman voices raised in unified torment.

The elder hushed the frightened cries of his people with raised withered arms. He then turned round slowly to look at Maddy and the others as he resumed talking to his people.

'They are frightened,' said Rashim. 'They are blaming us for this.'

'Well, they're right to,' replied Maddy. 'We caused all of this to happen.'

'Rashim's right,' said Adam, 'he's blaming us. He's gonna use us . . .'

She could see where this was headed. Although these people were far less blood-thirsty and brutal than the sacrifice-addicted Aztecs, they had conducted several animal sacrifices in honour of their guests over the last week. And Adam had found, in their pictoral history, some evidence that in the past – on rare and extreme occasions – they had conducted one or two human sacrifices. Right now, she imagined, Pat-ishka was considering whether this might be a good time to have another one.

A sacrifice to flatter their gods or appease this monster. She looked around for Becks. At least with her they were safe from –

'*Where the hell's Becks?*'

The other three did the same look-around. 'She was just with us!' said Adam. 'I swear I saw her moments ago.'

'She must have got separated from us outside,' said Rashim.

Maddy felt her legs wobbling. Becks . . . she'd been sure she was right here, right beside her. *No Bob . . . now no Becks.*

Oh crap.

Pat-ishka was jabbing a finger towards them now, his voice finding a bit more strength and conviction. Only . . . not jabbing a finger at *them*, he was pointing his finger directly at *her*. He shrieked a command and a group of men, young and old, began to approach her. One of them pulled out a long sickle-like blade from beneath his poncho.

Even if she could speak their language and appeal to them, she'd be talking to men doing the only thing they could think of to protect their families, their loved ones.

All the same, she shook her head. 'No! Please . . . don't do this!'

Rashim raised his torch as a club. Adam reached for the hunting knife strapped to his belt. Bertie balled his fists. The three of them instinctively huddled close together, forming a protective phalanx in front of her.

Outside, the sound of destruction had suddenly ceased. Now a calm had descended upon them; the noise had suddenly reduced down to the ragged breathing of her three male protectors; three unconvincing musketeers facing up to the group of fifteen or twenty men standing before them.

'We – need – to – leave,' whispered Adam. He glanced over his shoulder at her. 'Is there another exit to this building?'

There was none. They all knew that. There was a narrow doorway that opened on to stone steps that led up to the floor above, to the rooms they had been allowed to stay in. Up there, the only way out of the building was the terrace, the low wall and a forty-foot drop over the side down on to cobblestone steps. The drop would undoubtedly result in broken legs.

The men began to fan out round Adam, Rashim and Bertie as they shielded Maddy. And the four of them backed up several steps to prevent the natives working their way behind them.

Backed up until they finally found themselves hemmed into a corner of the large temple room. Nowhere to go and now out of options other than a short, brutal fight that was only going to end one way.

The elder shuffled towards them, he began to speak again, one withered hand extended towards Maddy, imploring her to step forward. With his other hand he was gesturing back at the huddled groups of frightened women and children. Maddy could guess what he was saying. He was imploring her to do the right thing, the decent thing, to offer her life up in order to save all these others.

And perhaps she might have been prepared to sacrifice her life if it could have saved them all. But letting them gut her like a freshly caught fish, right here, right now with that large sickle-shaped blade – a grotesque and futile sacrificial ritual – wasn't going to make that thing outside go away.

Oh God, not like this . . . I don't want to die like this.

She felt her legs trembling beneath her. Her stomach churned, desperate to jettison its contents one way or the other.

A loud crash. Something large and heavy slammed against the door to the temple. The women and children answered with screams. The thick wooden door was already cracked and weakened, a shard of rosy evening light piercing through into the gloomy interior.

'The door will not hold long,' said Rashim.

Pat-ishka stepped further forward, eased his way through the younger men until he stood just in front of Adam. His feeble voice didn't sound angry – which, given the destruction Maddy and her colleagues had accidentally visited on them, would have been perfectly understandable. It was, instead, a plea.

Maddy could see that he could so easily order his group of men to charge down Rashim, Adam and Bertie. These were frightened men, frightened for their families. At a word they would rush forward and do the bloody necessary. But the old man clearly wanted Maddy to willingly offer herself up, for it not to be a forced sacrifice – but an offering.

The voluntary surrendering of one life to protect many.

Perhaps that was the way it worked with these people; a sacrifice had to be a gift from the 'victim'? Not something brutally taken by force.

Another crash. The wooden door rattled in its frame, its hinges working loose from the stone, freeing grit and sand on to the floor.

Maddy looked at the shafts of light piercing through the increasingly fragile door. The dying sunlight flickered as something large moved around outside, pacing the narrow street. She imagined the entity could sense the hundreds of frightened souls trapped inside this building. It was determined to find a way in. It was almost through. It wasn't going anywhere.

'I've already spoken with it,' she told Pat-ishka calmly.

The elder hushed. He narrowed his eyes. He seemed encouraged at the calm sound of her voice. He offered her a warm, paternal smile. The fingers on his extended hand twitched, beckoning her to step forward, to prevent her friends from dying needlessly.

'I spoke to it,' she said again, 'inside chaos space . . . I was talking with it.'

Adam glanced back at her. 'That thing speaks?'

She nodded. 'It might be . . . *reasoned* with.'

All three of them turned to look over their shoulders at her. 'Tell me you're not thinking of going out there,' said Adam.

The door crashed again, this time it bulged inwards, splinters of wood clattered on to the floor. Renewed screams of terror from those inside. The door was a shattered ruin now. Just one gentle nudge away from collapsing to the floor.

I may not actually need to go outside. Next bang – it's coming right in.

'I'm going to go talk to it,' she said.

'*Talk* to it?!' Rashim shook his head. 'The thing will tear you apart!'

'No! Maybe not! I think . . . I think Sal's in there!'

'*What?*'

'I think Sal's a part of that thing!'

CHAPTER 63

1479, the Lost City of the Windtalkers

'Where did they get to?' Liam surveyed the scene of panic around them. He and Bob were now standing beside the entrance to the tunnel out of the basin. People streamed past them into the darkness and the escape beyond that would take them out of the cave and down the narrow cliff-front trail into the jungle.

In the city below they could see a thick river of people pushing up the narrow stepped alleyway to the main temple building; a river of those with more faith in their gods' ability to protect them.

'I do not know.' Bob scanned the chaos of the city. Every terrace, every passageway, every rat run between buildings, seemed to be filled with fleeing people, a multicoloured storm of painted skin, flowing robes, rattling beads and flapping ponchos.

They listened to the din of terrified cries all around them, amplified by the bowl-like acoustics of the city. And in that cacophony somewhere they heard the distant roar of the beast and a deep echoing boom as it smashed its way into some building.

Liam had assumed the others would have made their way here. The obvious place for them to rendezvous. The only way out. But clearly they hadn't.

An old woman slammed into Liam, her brow decorated with

tattoos, her earlobes stretched with clay rings. She screamed something at his face. A curse? A warning? A plea? Or perhaps just raw fear-fuelled rage that he was impeding her exit from the end of her world. She side-stepped and bustled past him, several small children in tow behind her.

It was a true miracle, he mused, that so far, none of these people had been tempted to lash out at him as they'd passed by. A fist, the swipe of a sickle blade, the thrust of a spear tip. And why not? Their meddling down below had brought destruction upon this city.

Their thoughtless meddling.

These people had demonstrated their anxiety and fear over the forty-eight hours they'd waited for Maddy. There had been an angry crowd that had gathered and grown beside the plaza, and the atmosphere of hostility had become intimidating enough that they'd elected to stay out of sight and down in the lower chamber. These people seemed to consider that place either far too sacred or far too dangerous to enter.

Despite their anger, their fear, these people had refrained from attacking any of them. He suspected these poor, poor people, whose world they had just brought to a premature end, were normally a passive and contemplative people. With hindsight, Liam had realized this place had seemed more like a monastery than a city. A spiritual retreat.

They'd been here little more than a week – and look what their curiosity had done to this little piece of Eden. It now looked like the fall of Rome. Sodom and Gomorrah.

Jesus, what have we done to them?

'Becks is approaching!' said Bob.

He must be picking up her ident signal. Bob stood straight, alert, craning his neck one way then the other to look over the people flooding past, like a meerkat on predator-watch.

Liam scanned the passing faces, painted many different colours but all punctuated with the same wide white eyes and dark oval mouths stretched with terror. This was their version of the end, their apocalypse in miniature. Their Pandora.

And it was us that caused it. Jesus.

Just then, Bob pointed. 'There is Becks.'

Liam thrust his thoughts and regrets aside and followed the direction Bob was indicating. By the fading light of evening he just about managed to make out the distinct outline of her tall athletic frame striding up through the river of people evacuating the city. She casually pushed those in her way aside. Her icy glare met Bob's and she tipped a nod of greeting at him and Liam as she roughly shoved a small girl out of her path. The girl fell to her knees and would have been trampled to death had it not been for the helping hand of some old man scooping her up again. Becks was oblivious to that as she strode out of the flow of people and approached them.

What lay in her wake was irrelevant to her.

She was alone. The others weren't with her.

'Where are they?!' called out Liam.

'I do not know.' She frowned. 'I estimated a high probability they would attempt to rendezvous at this location.' She pursed her lips thoughtfully. 'It appears I was wrong.'

CHAPTER 64

1479, the Lost City of the Windtalkers

The wooden door crashed inwards into the temple hall, shards and splinters of wood skittering across the stone slab floor. A cloud of dust, rubble and grit filling the doorway.

A large shape pushed through the cloud. It was no more than an indistinct mass that seemed to glide in through the opening. Its animal-like roar filled the temple chamber. Pat-ishka turned and cried out in horror, his weak, reedy voice lost beneath the chorus of screams and wailing behind him.

But, trembling and frail and now fallen down on to his hands and knees, he had courage enough to crawl towards the swaying, roaring entity standing just inside the shattered doorway.

Half a dozen yards short of it he stopped, lifted himself up on to thin wobbling legs and spread his arms wide. He called out something – a challenge, a command, a plea? But it was drowned by the din of the beast's trumpeting cry. Something invisible and large swiped through the air, the only indication of mass in motion was the blur and ripple of heat. The elder seemed to explode. More precisely, his body appeared to suddenly separate of its own accord into four large pieces – legs, abdomen and pelvis, upper torso and head – each portion spinning, flailing along a bloody arc of their own direction.

'Oh, God Almighty, have mercy!' cried out Bertie.

Maddy pushed Adam's obstructing arm aside. 'It *knows* me! It'll listen to me!'

'No!' said Adam. 'Not you!' His lips trembled uncertainly. 'I'll talk to it. Let me –'

'No.' Maddy shook her head. 'She won't listen to you. It's got to be me!' She pushed past him and stepped forward, not entirely certain that this thing was quite the same entity or in the same frame of mind as it had been back in chaos space. Back there in the mist, it seemed to be able to reason, to think . . . and certainly able to communicate. But this terrifying apparition appeared to be nothing but energy and blind rage.

The entity surged forward into the temple room, now wholly invisible again and only detectable as a gliding cloud of shimmering super-heated air. She could feel the burning heat of its energy on her cheeks as she approached it; like the open coals of a furnace roused by a blacksmith's bellows, glowing fiercely and crackling as it fed on the fresh blast of oxygen.

Another roar from the beast. A chorus cry of tormented human voices filled the room. It seemed to her more a collective cry of anguish than an animal's territorial challenge.

Maddy waved her arms above her head. 'Look at me! Over here! It's me! Maddy!'

The entity's roar faded away and for a moment the energy phased and it became visible. It had changed form yet again. No longer a giant boar-like head with a snout, but now necks protruded, long, swan-like necks that emerged from the central mass, different human heads on each. Heads that constantly morphed from one face to another.

'It's Maddy . . . you saw me in chaos space!'

A head turned down to look at her, then the neck swung down. The head staring at her from its tip was human but not of human proportions, three times larger than her own. She thought she recognized one face that came and went in the blink of an eye – wasn't that the secret agent guy who'd found their archway? The one who'd been carefully looking after that fossilized piece of clay containing Liam's carved message? What was his name? She remembered.

Cartwright.

My God, was that deliberate? Was this beast signalling that it knew her? Deliberately presenting a face she might recognize?

'Yes! You *know* me!' Maddy called out again. 'YOU KNOW ME!'

The room had become quiet. The entity was no longer roaring. The men, women and children behind Maddy had quietened down. She could hear the whimper of one or two children, but the rest of the people seemed to be collectively holding their breaths.

More faces played across the giant head hovering in front of her, but no more that she recognized. Perhaps, as she'd imagined back in chaos space, they were the faces of other people who had become trapped in the mist. Lost souls. Ghosts.

Then – so sudden and unexpected it made her take an involuntary step backwards – Sal's face appeared. Her eyes narrowed, her head cocked slightly, just as Sal's used to do when something was puzzling her.

'My God! S-Sal!?' She gasped. 'Is – is that you?'

The entity, or at least this portion of it, seemed to stir with the faintest indication of recognition. '. . . *Maddy . . . ?*' The voice was many voices, old and young, male and female. But in there, somewhere, among the chorus, was Sal's voice.

'Yes! It's me! It's Maddy!' She wanted to reach out . . . she wanted to touch her friend. But the searing heat, even from feet away, was too intense. She could feel her skin prickling, the first sting of burning. She had to step back a little. 'Oh my God, Sal . . . what's happened to you?!'

Again, her friend's eyes narrowed. She looked as if she was fumbling to retrieve distant memories. '*. . . so long ago . . . we were friends, so long ago . . .*'

'No! We're still friends. You and me and Liam. The three of us. We always will be friends. Sal, we were so worried. You went missing. We tried to find you –'

'*. . . you abandoned me . . .*'

'No!' Maddy shook her head. 'That's not true. I came into the mist looking for you, hon. We –'

'*. . . waited . . . and waited . . . hundreds . . . thousands of years . . . you never came . . .*'

'Why, Sal? Why did you do it? Why did you step in?'

Her face became vague again. And so old. An ancient soul trawling a mind long ago wiped clean of childhood memories.

'*. . . I . . . I . . . don't remember . . .*'

Then her eyes suddenly widened. Some of her ancient past was coming back. '*. . . I remember . . .*'

Maddy nodded encouragement. 'Remember what?'

The entity phased and became invisible for a moment. Maddy could still see the shimmering air, and knew the head on the long neck was just there, still hovering a few feet away from her.

'Sal? You there? Remember what?'

Her face reappeared. '*. . . you wanted to kill her, destroy her . . .*'

'Kill her? Destroy *who*?'

'*. . . Saleena . . .*'

'What? I don't understand. That doesn't make any –'

'*You wanted to change history . . . make her life never happen . . .*'

Then it came to her. She understood. Sal had been convinced her memories were those of a real girl. Maddy remembered her telling her how she'd actually seen her 'real self' in New York.

Seen her with her father, young and happy even in a world full of portents of a dark and difficult soon-to-be future; there she'd been, wearing an impenetrable cloak of contentment. Happy seeing the sights alongside her father. Happy simply being in the company of her beloved father.

'We just want to know whether this is the *right* history, Sal! Can you remember? We all talked about it? That it *could* be wrong. It *could* be we weren't meant to wipe ourselves ou–'

'. . . *you envied me . . . I was once real . . .*' Sal's eyes narrowed again. Her face contorted, her jaw distended, grew longer. It became underslung and pointed like the jaw of a Punch and Judy hand-puppet. Cruel and clown-like.

'. . . *you were just patchwork lives . . . but I was real . . . once . . .*'

'Sal, this isn't how you are! Not before you stepped in. You weren't thinking things like that! You weren't –'

The neck curled backwards like a rattlesnake recoiling, preparing to strike. '. . . *YOU DON'T KNOW! . . . you NEVER cared! . . . you NEVER asked! . . .*'

'I did – I *do* care! We're friends! We're like sisters, for God's sake! I loved you!'

'. . . *you had love, didn't you? . . .*' Sal's eyes receded into her head, deepened until they were shadowed by her brow, lost dark pits on an ashen face. '. . . *not me . . . never me . . .*'

Maddy glanced over her shoulder. *Adam? She's talking about me and Adam?*

'. . . *Liam had adventure . . . and you found love . . . but me? I was spare . . . I had nothing . . . I WAS nothing . . .*'

'We had each other, Sal! God, we still do! We can still get you –'

Sal's mouth stretched long and wide, a smile like a gashed face, lips pulling back revealing gums, tendons, glistening bared muscle and sinew, skin peeling back beyond any possibility of returning her face to normal.

'*. . . all I had was her . . . Saleena. She was MY love . . .*'

The face was morphing beyond recognition. All that remained of what Maddy could recognize as Sal was a flap of grey membranous tissue that hung from above her forehead. It had been black and silky like her hair had been, but now the texture had changed to a sickening putrid flesh, like the jellied skin of an eel – a half-hearted attempt at replicating how her dark hair used to flop over one eye, hiding all but a mischievous glint.

'Sal?'

The long neck, bulging laces of tendon beneath a translucent skin, recoiled once more and the mockery of Sal's face lifted up and hovered above, looking down on Maddy. '*. . . you were going to take Saleena from me . . .*'

'No! Sal! That's not how it is! I'm not lying!'

The neck swung down low again, Sal's face looking more like a skull than anything else now: the skull of Mr Punch, Punchinello. The trickster. It hovered just a foot from Maddy, searing heat emanating from the glistening grey image of bone and rotten eel flesh.

'*. . . then let me open you and see what's inside your head . . .*'

CHAPTER 65

1479, the Lost City of the Windtalkers

Maddy felt a hand roughly grasp her shoulder and yank her back. She staggered backwards, lost her balance and fell to the floor. She looked up and saw that Adam was standing where she'd been.

'Adam! No!'

He shouted over his shoulder. 'GET HER BACK!'

Rashim and Bertie pulled her to her feet. 'Adam! What're you doing?!'

Adam turned to her quickly. 'Maddy . . . I get it! I know what happens! I'm dead already!'

'Adam! Get back from –'

'GO!' He looked at Rashim. 'GET HER OUT OF HERE!' He turned to face the entity. 'Sal!' he barked, his voice warbling with fear. 'I'm something you'll never have!'

The skeletal head that had been looking at Maddy, cocked and curious, now swung its attention to him.

'Love!' he cried. 'Somebody to love you!'

'Adam!' Maddy screamed at him. She struggled to free herself of Rashim's and Bertie's grasping hands. 'God! She'll kill you!'

He side-stepped across the room, away from Maddy and the others, drawing the attention of the seeker with him. 'It's me! This is all down to *me*! She loves me . . . she doesn't care about you any more! She doesn't give a damn about keeping your stupid future any more! Because she's got better things to do. She's in love. I changed her, Sal! You want to know who to blame? It's me! Me! ME!'

The creature roared: a chorus of voices high and shrill and feminine, all of them sounding achingly pitiful. Grief multiplied out over millennia. Sorrow, brittle and fragile, shattered mercilessly over a hard uncompromising knee. A keening moan that filled the room. Its energy surged and crackled, heating the room almost as if the gates to Hell itself had been flung wide open. The broiling heat threatened to render every last person in the temple a blackened, carbonized mannequin.

It surged forward after Adam, now invisible again except for a heat haze that glided towards him and away from the ruins of the doorway.

Rashim and Bertie dragged Maddy to the exit. She kicked, squirmed and screamed, desperately trying to free herself, to give it one last go – to call out after Sal – to try one more time to talk her – or what was left of her – out of doing this . . .

Adam was still shouting something at it, his voice lost beneath the wail of beast. Backing into the far corner of the room, the people behind him were immobilized with fear, too frightened to move and make a break for the door in case they attracted the attention of the creature.

'Adam!' Maddy screamed out for him. 'Get out of there! GET OUT OF THERE!'

They were scrambling through the doorway, stepping over shards of jagged wood, and stumbling out into the narrow alley – when Maddy caught her very last glimpse of him.

Alive. Still.

But certainly not for very much longer.

Her last sight of him was through the oily ripple of the intense heat haze. She could just make out his pale face, blotched pink by the intolerable heat, his untidy greasy rope-like dreadlocks, his scruffy tie-dyed shorts and shirt, arms frantically waving at Rashim and Bertie to get her away.

And then he was gone as they pulled her with them, down the now-deserted street. It was dark. Night had fallen quickly and the stars were patiently waiting for the moon to wake up. She was vaguely aware of the smells around her, the perfume of night-blooming flowers, the tang of wood smoke, the odour of seared human flesh.

The stepped flagstones beneath their feet were littered with shattered blocks and rubble knocked from the buildings either side and dozens of dark steaming humps – the charred husks of what were once people.

Liam decided they'd waited around here at the mouth of the tunnel long enough. 'Stuff this, I'm going back there to look for them.'

Bob reached out quickly and grasped his wrist in one giant fist. 'I advise against that decision, Liam,' he said. 'If they are still alive, they will know to meet us here.'

'Dammit! Let me go!'

'Negative. It is too dangerous.'

Becks nodded in agreement. 'Bob is correct. You are making a flawed and foolish tactical judgement, Liam.'

'I may be a fool, but I'm still the bloody operative! I'm the one in charge, last time I checked. So let me go!'

'As you wish.' Bob released his hold and Liam staggered forward. 'If that is your *command*.'

He rubbed his wrist. 'And the both of you are coming with me, so you are – *now*!'

The support units briefly looked at each other. Becks replied, 'It is better to be as far away as possible from any source of energy. We should allow this entity to simply deplete itself.'

'You understand, Liam,' added Bob, 'we will not be able to protect you from this seeker? It is pure energy.'

'Aye, well . . . we'll worry all about that if we bump into the bloody thing. Now come on!'

The three of them were about to set off down the sloping flagstone path towards the plaza when they heard the *clack* of footsteps hurrying uphill towards them. Distinct and clear: not the soft muffled slap of leather sandals but the hard *clack* of boot heels – and something more . . . the muffled sound of someone sobbing.

'Maddy? Is that you?'

'It is us, Liam!' Rashim replied. Moments later they all but bumped into each other in the moonless dark. 'Thank God,' said Rashim. 'I was worried you were gone. Tell me you have the transponder still?'

'Aye.' Liam felt for it in his pocket. He noticed Maddy was being held up by Bertie. 'Is she OK?'

Rashim shook his head. Not that the gesture was seen. 'We had a close encounter with the seeker. We just managed to escape. But Adam was not so fortunate, he . . .' Liam heard the words trail away and figured out what he was saying.

'All right,' he replied. Maddy's sobbing was intermittent and subdued, the tail end of an outpouring of grief. The tears might be slowing for the moment, but that meant nothing more than she'd cried herself dry for now.

'All right,' he said again, thinking aloud. 'All right. We should leave. There's nothing more we can do here and now.' He looked out across the dark city. Tonight there were no pinpricks of light, no cooking fires or oil lamps, no tallow candles. It was a dark, abandoned ghost town. He knew this was how this place would remain as nature slowly recovered its hold over it. Centuries quietly passing, vines and roots meshing with each other and covering weather-worn stonework beneath an emerald-coloured shroud.

And the bodies of the dead would decay to bones.

'That thing is out there somewhere,' he said finally.

'It is . . . it – it s-still is out there!' whispered Bertie. His quiet voice fluttered with fear. 'I . . . I saw it. The Devil h-himself! We should go. We should go. We should go!'

Liam nodded. Wherever Sal was, she was surely somewhere less dangerous than right here. 'We'd be bloody idiots standing around here a moment longer. Come on.' He started uphill towards the entrance to the tunnel. 'I'll turn on the transponder when we get to the cave.'

They made their way up the tunnel, feeling their way in the absolute dark, none of them daring to snap on their torches and all of them hoping the pitch black was covering their quiet escape.

CHAPTER 66

1479, the cave, Nicaragua

'Does – does it normally take so long?' whispered Bertie anxiously. 'Are you sure your d-device is working p-properly, Mr O'Connor?'

Liam nodded. 'Don't worry, it's working.'

The first faint grey stain of dawn was lighting the sky over the carpet of jungle below the cave. By the wan light, they watched mist gathering in ghostly pools far beneath them. Daylight couldn't arrive soon enough.

'Sometimes it's immediate, other times we might have to wait a few hours.' He offered Bertie a reassuring smile. 'Relax. The portal will open for us soon enough.'

He turned back to Rashim. 'I still can't believe what you said earlier. Sal? Are you sure you saw her? I mean really sure?' Liam shook his head. 'Maybe you're remembering it wrong –'

'I saw her face on the seeker, Liam!' His eyes looked haunted. 'It was definitely her face. She was that thing, or at least, she was *a part* of that thing.'

He felt something cold ride his spine. A shiver. Not from the cool breath of the pre-dawn breeze, nor was it like the pleasant shudder from a lover's whispered words or the touch of tender, feather-light fingers. Instead, it was the prickling sensation that accompanies a terrible and sudden understanding. He realized what had become of Sal.

'That thing was not Sal, not any more,' uttered Maddy. 'That thing – that monster wasn't her.' She looked at Liam with eyes raw and red from crying. 'It was . . . it was a *corruption* of her. A twisted version of her.' She rubbed at those red eyes. They looked painfully sore.

'Perhaps it was the "essence" of her,' said Rashim, 'a *borrowed* part of her consciousness. The darker side.' He looked up and out at the stars. 'We all have a dark side, a part of our mind that broods on matters, sometimes wishes upon others the very worst of things.' He rubbed his cold hands together. 'Is it possible that in chaos space not only can physical matter be fused together but also consciousness? Our thoughts? That thing could be an amalgamation of many, many people's minds. A manifestation of their darkest wishes and dreams.'

Liam struggled to believe that thoughts as dark as that might have existed in Sal's mind. 'She was troubled, for sure,' he said. 'I know she was finding it hard to accept what she was. But I can't believe she ever meant us any harm.'

Maddy nodded slowly. 'Not the Sal we knew. But . . .' Maddy was going to say more, but instead she fell silent.

'What? But what?'

'I think . . .' She closed her eyes, and a fresh tear leaked out on to her cheek. 'I think she was in there for a long time, Liam.' She opened her eyes and gazed out of the open mouth of the cave at the dark outline of the jungle and the subtly lightening sky, just that little bit paler now and closer to dawn.

'She . . . she said something about "thousands of years", Liam. *Thousands*. I don't know how chaos space works. But you know what it's like; time can feel distorted in there. Horribly distorted.'

He knew exactly what she meant by that. Sometimes, stepping into a portal and emerging out the other side seemed to occur in an instant. A heartbeat. Other times, it could seem like several minutes had passed. On those occasions, mercifully few, it was a profoundly disturbing experience; the cloying mist and that feeling of complete isolation, the deadened senses.

Alone . . . with nothing but yourself, floating in that featureless white soup.

For thousands of years? Thousands of years of that . . . *?*

'I think she went insane,' said Maddy. 'Long ago – centuries ago, in that white, she must have quietly gone insane. And all that was left of her mind was just vague memories of us. All twisted up and confused.'

'Jay-zus,' Liam uttered. All of a sudden he wasn't so sure he wanted the transponder to be working, for the portal to open up here in the cave. To step once again through that place.

Maddy met his gaze. Perhaps she was thinking the very same thing: what if this time while heading home something went wrong, left one of them stranded forever? Like one of those lost souls?

'We could stay here,' said Liam. 'Stay in 1479?'

Bertie looked alarmed. 'Oh no! I'll not stay here! Please! We must return to –'

'Information,' said Bob. 'Our current base of operations contains a fully functional displacement machine. This cannot be left behind intact.'

Bob didn't need to elaborate. There was no real choice. They had to go back. They couldn't leave things as they were. Eventually Delbert or someone else would kick the door in and discover what was inside. In the hands of Delbert, perhaps the conniving merchant would not know what to make of it? But then he might pass on his discovery to much smarter men who would understand what power they had at their fingertips.

What would the secretive ruling elite of Victorian England do with technology like that in their hands? The inquisitive minds of those learned gentlemen would want to explore it. Would want to visit the past with their hunting rifles and notebooks, pith helmets and magnifying glasses, to joyride the past, leaving their muddy footprints all over history and not care, probably not even understand, the damage they might be doing.

'Bob is right,' said Maddy. 'We do need to go back.'

'And s-soon – for the love of God! Soon!' whispered Bertie, hugging his knees. 'Before that monster finds us hiding away up here!'

'It is unlikely to follow us here,' said Rashim. 'I imagine it will want to stay near that beam, to replenish its energy.'

'If the column behaves as it did on previous occasions,' said Becks, 'it should have automatically closed itself after less than half an hour. The seeker will have no access to the tachyon beam and be unable to restore its energy level.' She shrugged. 'It will eventually . . . *die*.'

Liam hunched his shoulders. 'I think we're safe up here for the moment.' He turned to Bob and Becks. 'Sniffing any particles yet?'

Both silently shook their heads.

Liam sighed. 'What the hell's keeping computer-Bob?'

The conversation died to an uneasy silence and they sat for a long while, listening to the *tap*, *tap*, *tap* of moisture dripping from some fissure in the roof of the cave, and watching the sky gradually lighten and the faintest bloom of peach stain the far horizon as the sun, still unseen, raced to catch up to its appointment with dawn. Liam discreetly sneaked a look at Maddy. He could see moisture glint in her eyes, see her swiping tears silently from her cheeks. He wondered who she was thinking about, who she was crying for. Sal? Or Adam?

'I . . . I need to relieve myself,' said Bertie quietly.

Liam turned to look at him. 'Well go on, then. You don't need to announce it.'

'But where?'

Outside on the ledge it might be a little slippery with the morning dew. 'Back there somewhere.' Liam gestured into the cave. 'Where those wall paintings are is far back enough.'

Bertie swallowed anxiously and peered into the gloom. 'It's dark.'

Liam tossed a torch across to him. 'There you go. Button's on the top. Don't go too far.'

CHAPTER 67

1479, the Lost City of the Windtalkers

Its movements were governed by 'committee', by a community of mind fragments. Pieces of consciousness from so many tortured souls, all of them confused, frightened – but most of all, angry. One fragment, however, seemed to hold sway over the others. It had a vague recollection of who it once was, a girl. Incalculable years, centuries ago . . . it had been a girl.

A girl called Sal.

The instinct of the collective was to withdraw. The entity's rage had been spent, its desire for revenge sated. And now, feeling itself weakening, it needed to return from whence it came, to drink energy again, or else wither away to nothing.

But the one voice, the girl's, had a clearer goal. A far stronger imperative. What remained of her mind recalled those faces; once upon a time those faces belonged to the dearest of friends, almost like family . . . then, they became her betrayers.

She remembered them and how they wanted to take something from her. What it was that they'd wanted to take came and went, just like its form phased from energy to material. But she recalled again now. They wanted to erase the girl she'd once been.

Yes . . . I . . . was . . . once . . . real.

Her will called out above the fragmented noise of all the other confused voices. And drove the entity to leave behind the large room and the bloody carnage it had wrought there. To wander through the darkness, the silence of this abandoned city . . . *and find them!*

The entity could feel its energy seeping away, and with less energy its form was beginning to shrink. No longer a towering, seething cyclone, it was something smaller, yet still very much substantial. It drifted down an alleyway, finally hesitating at the edge of a large open area.

The voice guiding the collective retrieved fleeting age-old images from a distant past. From the time when she had been a girl.

A girl with 'friends'. She had been with those 'friends'; she recalled seeing this open area from some vantage point, from somewhere higher up.

They had emerged from a long, dark space. She remembered that. She dug deep into what was left of her tangled mind. She remembered darkness, and a light at the end. She remembered emerging from the dark and the pleasant sensation of the warmth of sunlight on her face.

A tunnel.

That dark space had been a tunnel. They'd stepped into sunlight and gazed in awe down upon this very place.

The entity drifted across the plaza, towards a low stone wall. It phased from a gliding cloud of energy to something material – a three-legged monstrosity that morphed form as it paced awkwardly, then back to drifting energy again. It began to ascend a narrow stepped walkway, littered with discarded belongings: sandals, necklaces of beads, robes, baskets of clay tablets . . . the detritus of a panicked departure.

More memories began to form in its consciousness. Nothing more than a confusing slide-show of images that made little sense to her. She saw a giant muscular man. Not human, but more like a simple automaton. She saw a dark home of bricks and crumbling mortar. She saw a young man with a plume of silver hair and a lopsided grin. She saw a menagerie of pitiful human-like creatures dressed in rags of clothing, brutally gunned down by a row of soldiers in crimson tunics. She saw two tall towers in a busy city, gushing plumes of dark smoke into a clear blue sky. She saw the very same city as ash and ruins, and pale creatures with weeping sores on their skin and milk-eyes glaring out at her from darkened spaces. A lifetime lived by someone that used to be her.

The entity drifted to a halt before an archway of darkness, the entrance to a tunnel. And she knew for certain that they, the faces she remembered, the ones she sought, had come this way.

She knew they were waiting for something to appear. Waiting for something to take them home. She recalled that's how it worked . . . as friends together, they'd travelled. Different places. Different times. And to do it they'd had to step through a window into Hell.

She couldn't quite remember why, but it's what they did.

Then her phasing memory finally reminded her why. Finally made sense of things.

They travelled through time . . . seeking the girl I once was . . . to find her. And kill her.

The entity's fading energy crackled and rippled once more, like dying fireplace embers revived by the gentle puff of a breath.

Then, silently, it glided forward into the dark hole in the rock wall.

CHAPTER 68

1479, the cave, Nicaragua

Bertie stared at the cave wall in front of him as he went about his business. One-handed, he panned the torch across the strange painted markings in front of him. Having spent a week in this long-lost city, some of these symbols he recognized now. He'd seen their distinct shapes in the decor of the temple buildings, in the colourful tapestries of beads that hung everywhere. Even in the designs these people had painted, and tattooed, on their faces.

The meanings of these symbols, however, were still no clearer to him.

He reflected for a moment on what Adam had told them – that this whole society had evolved around what their ancestors had once upon a time discovered beneath the ground. Their written language, their costumes, their art, even the city itself borrowed the circular design of that subterranean chamber.

The poor young fellow had posited two theories: that either these people had stumbled across the chamber and built their city around it; or, far more likely, they had been living here when the Archaeologists arrived, and had been in awe of them, perhaps even honoured by those 'gods' with the task of guarding the chamber, protecting it from prying eyes.

And for hundreds, perhaps even thousands, of years they had.

'Then we came along, roused an unspeakable creature from the depths

of Hell and let it destroy everything.' Those had been Adam's words.

His mind flashed images of what he'd witnessed in the last few hours and he bit his lip and tried to think of other things – homely, banal, *normal* things.

His unpleasant boss Delbert's ugly pug face.

The Fox and Firkin public house, down the bottom of Farringdon Street.

Mrs Chichester, his ample-bosomed and ruddy-faced landlady.

His small, bare bedroom.

His parents.

Somehow, all those images and memories seemed one step removed from him. No longer were they the images of a very familiar and wholly unexciting life. No. They were now glimpses of another young man's life.

In just these last few days, Bertie realized, everything about him had changed. Everything he thought he knew about this world was wrong. The ordered nature of things, the predictable Newtonian safety of a clockwork universe . . . all of that was wrong, wrong, wrong.

The universe was chaotic and incomprehensible to him now. Worse than that, the future wasn't the gleaming utopian dream he'd always imagined it might be: a world where the innovations of science would provide kingly comfort and luxury to every man, woman and child on the planet.

No. The future was a frightening place. In his lifetime, there would be things called 'world wars', where science would be leveraged to make terrible devices of wholesale destruction. Where murder would be conducted on an industrial scale.

And moreover, this terrifying future – if Miss Carter was to be believed – was ultimately doomed.

'Bertie . . . ?'

He turned to his left at the sound of the voice. Soft, female

. . . coming out of the darkness. He panned the torch round and, emerging out of the gloom, he saw a small figure.

Sal.

She took a tentative step towards him.

'What . . . how . . . ?' Bertie quickly buttoned up his flies and backed up one step. He swallowed nervously, all of a sudden his mouth was bone-dry. 'Miss V-Vikram – Saleena, how . . . how d-did you . . . !'

She shook her head, frowned. She looked lost. 'I . . . I don't know . . . I'm not sure. I remember stepping into that force field. Then it's all jumbled up. Things . . . nothing making sense to me. I'm a bit confused, to be honest.'

Bertie could see her face in the envelope of light. She looked afraid and very confused. Traumatized. Like a child.

A lost and frightened child.

Yet he had seen her just a few hours ago, her face as part of a monster. Seen that face become a snarling mockery of itself, a rictus on a deformed jackal-like skull. A head on a long, distended neck, one of many.

Bertie recalled a medieval engraving he'd seen once in a museum, 'The Whore of Babylon', picturing the beast on which she rode – a beast so similar, a beast with seven heads, each one depicting a different Catholic sin.

'Bertie . . .' She stepped closer, there were tears on her cheeks. 'I'm so frightened.'

The poor girl must have escaped the hell she was trapped in. Perhaps the monster had simply seen her face in that hellish dimension and decided to copy it.

Cruelly chosen to mimic her, to make a monster of her.

'You poor, poor thing,' he cooed softly. 'Come . . .' He stretched his arms out towards her, to hold her. She looked like she desperately needed that right now.

She smiled. 'Thank you for being so kind.' She reached towards him, and as she did, Bertie felt the knuckles and fingers of his extended hand prickle from an intense heat.

Instinctively, his hand recoiled before it burned.

And then he understood what he was sharing this small dark space with. He began to back up, one faltering step, then another.

'Don't go,' she pleaded softly. 'Don't leave me here alone.'

He shook his head. Prickles of sweat rolled down his waxen face. The heat was increasing, he could feel it burning his cheeks. He could feel it through his linen shirt. 'You . . . you . . . you're not her – you're n-not Saleena.'

'I don't want to be left all alone.' Her eyes spilled more tears, her lips curled. 'Not *alone*.' She cocked her head as she looked at him.

'You were so kind to me.' She gazed up at him with a face that ached with remorse, with grieving for what-might-have-beens. 'I remember . . . I remember you brought me such a lovely cake once . . .'

Her fingers brushed a clump of damp moss on the cave wall. It instantly smouldered, smoked, then burst into flames. 'Don't let me be all alone . . . in there . . . for eternity . . .' The flames flickered momentarily, sending shadow-puppets dancing across the painted wall.

'Come with me, Bertie . . . we could be together, you and me.'

Bertie whimpered. 'P-please . . . don't hurt me! Don't –'

'I'm not a monster.' Hot tears dripped from her jaw and spilled on to the floor. They hissed as they spattered on the cool stone. 'Don't leave me here.'

He turned and ran. 'IT'S HERE!'

CHAPTER 69

1479, the cave, Nicaragua

The portal shimmered before them. An eight-foot-wide orb that revealed the faint undulating, reassuring blue glow of computer screens and a flickering light bulb dangling on a flex from a low brick ceiling.

'About time!' Liam blew a sigh of relief. 'I was beginning to think that transponder of yours was broken,' he said to Rashim.

Rashim smiled. 'For a minute there, so was I.'

Liam reached out for Maddy and helped her to her feet. 'Come on, Mads, we're going home now.'

She nodded. Clasped his shoulder, then hugged him. 'It's just you and me now,' she whispered into his neck.

'Aye,' he replied softly. He knew what she was saying. They were leaving Sal behind, or what was left of her. She was gone. Gone for good. Leaving Adam behind too. Departing felt like an act of betrayal, abandonment. Cowardice.

'Aye, I know.' He sighed. 'But we still got each other.'

Just then they heard Bertie's voice echoing from the rear of the cave. And an unintelligible, high-pitched and lady-like scream.

Bob and Becks turned towards the sound. Both of them stepped into the gloom and stood side by side, a closed wall protecting the others.

'Caution!' barked Becks. 'I am detecting an energy surge approaching us. Twenty yards away.'

Bob looked back at them. 'You should leave. Now!'

They heard the clack and scrape of boot heels, then Bertie emerged out of the darkness, wide rolling eyes, his ashen face glistening with sweat. 'It's heeere!' he screamed. 'It's right behind me!'

He pushed his way past the support units.

'Go! Go through!' Liam yelled. He grabbed Bertie's arm and roughly shoved him towards the portal. Bertie tossed aside any reservations he'd had about stepping back into chaos space and leaped headfirst into the floating orb.

'You too,' Liam said to Maddy.

She shook her head and took him in her arms again. 'Not without you.'

'Don't worry, I'm not staying!'

'Fifteen yards and closing!' called out Becks.

'Go!' Liam stepped out of Maddy's embrace. 'Go! I'll be right behind you!'

She disappeared into the portal, her eyes staying locked on his until she vanished from view. Rashim followed her a second later.

Just then the sun finally breached the distant horizon, and the blood-red light of dawn flooded into the deepest recesses of the cave.

'Liam!' said Bob. 'You must leave now!'

He was standing right beside the portal. One small jump and he'd be through it. 'I'm not leaving without the pair of you.'

'We will protect you,' said Becks.

'Oh Jay-zus, stuff that! Just get back here and go through!'

The support units seemed to weigh that up for a second, then backed up towards the portal. The light of the sun reached further into the depths of the cave and Liam caught a glimpse of something moving slowly among the shifting shadows.

He slapped Bob's shoulder. 'Go!'

Bob scowled. 'I will protect –'

'I'm right here, right next to it!' He nodded at the portal. 'I'll be through straight after you two! Now for the love of God . . . GO! That's an order!'

Bob nodded and stepped through.

Becks looked at Liam sternly. 'Do not delay unnecessarily.' Then she too stepped into the shimmering displacement field.

Liam planted his feet, ready to leap into the sphere, but something caused him to pause. Perhaps it was curiosity. He'd heard Rashim's and Bertie's descriptions of the manifestation the seeker had assumed in the temple hall: Sal's head on the end of a long snake-like neck. A head that had turned into a skull.

He couldn't bring himself to believe that. They must have been mistaken – perhaps it was a face similar to hers. Maybe the seeker was simply copying faces it had seen.

He couldn't believe that this thing was actually her, or even partially her. And if it really was . . . maybe he might be able to get through to her.

Then he saw her. Sal, in the flesh, the crimson light of the rising sun picking her head and one bare shoulder out of the dark.

'Hello, Liam,' she said. A casual greeting. Just as if she'd wandered into their Brooklyn archway with a basket of laundry under one arm.

He tried to offer her a smile to hide the fact he was trembling. 'Hey, Sal.' His voice warbled uncontrollably. 'How're you doing there?'

She cocked her head. Her dark fringe flopped down over one eye. 'It's been a long while. I almost forgot what you looked like.'

'You've only been gone days, Sal.'

She laughed. The sound was a dry rattle, little more than a bitter sneer. The one eye he could see rolled up until only the white of it was visible. She closed her eyes. 'Far longer than a few days, Liam. Far longer.'

She remained silent for a few moments, remained standing in the darkness. The sun continued to rise, its warming rays reaching back into the gloom and causing the shadows to chase each other in slow motion across craggy rock surfaces.

'I'm dying, Liam,' she whispered. 'As I stand here . . . I'm slowly dying.'

Energy. He realized her energy was draining away with every second she existed outside of chaos space.

'I know.' He turned to look at the portal. The others would be anxiously waiting for him. 'Is that what you want, Sal? To die?'

Her eyes still closed, she frowned. Her lips twitched, emotions chasing each other across her face like the shadows behind her.

'I wish I could help you,' he said, his voice catching. 'Why did you do it? Why did you step in?'

'I . . . I don't remember. So long ago now.'

Her body was gone. She was just energy. A ghost. What was once Sal for real was gone. What stood before him was an echo of her, a facsimile constructed from energy.

'Sal?'

'Yes . . . Liam?'

'You know, you have a choice.'

'Choice.' Her eyes opened. All-white. An unsettling sight. He realized it wasn't that her eyes were still rolled upwards, but instead the pupils had become a frosted, opaque, milky colour.

'You don't have to be stuck in chaos space forevermore.'

She cocked her head again, smiled. 'If I stand here? Is that what you're saying?'

'If you stay right there –' Liam nodded – 'you'll fade away to nothing. You'll be at peace.'

She nodded. That seemed to be a comforting prospect.

'Is that what you want, Sal?' He took a tentative step forward. 'If you'd like, I could stay with you . . . until the very end.'

For a moment she considered that. A fleeting smile played across her lips as she imagined the possibility; an end to the sadness, an end to the torment. But the voices of others in her head cried out angrily that their say in the matter was just as valid as hers.

To be outside of the torment of chaos space was a blessed relief to them all. To be standing on firm ground, to be in a space of three comprehensible dimensions was a joy. To touch, to feel the flesh of real living beings was an addictive sensation.

But to remain outside indefinitely, like this – and not return to replenish their strength? Only one trapped soul in this colony of diminished form was ready to end its existence like that.

'Sal?' said Liam softly. 'Is that what you want? Do you want to go?'

She felt the control that she'd exercised over the others begin to slip. She felt her mind fading away, her internal voice becoming lost in the cacophony of voices screaming inside her.

'Sal? Is that what you want?'

Yes . . . Liam . . . that's what I want . . .

But her reply was a whisper. A chorus of voices shouted it down. An angry chorus that wanted to rip this living thing to pieces. To feel the texture of its flesh, its bones, its blood. To feel it singe, crisp and curl like cooked meat. Then . . . then, to step into the glow of that shimmering orb behind. They could feel the energy emanating from it, like the warmth of a campfire on a cold night.

Needed, so *needed* that energy. But before that . . . one last taste of something alive.

'*We want you . . .*'

The slight shape of the girl phased out of view and became an amorphous cloud of energy. Liam realized the rippling air in front of him was now no longer his friend. Whatever part of Sal had been standing there was now gone, swallowed up inside this malevolent form. It began to move, slowly gliding towards him.

One touch of it, one gentle brush against it and he was dead.

'Oh, bugger this,' he whispered.

He turned round and leaped for the portal.

1899, London

Liam landed heavily on the brick floor of the dungeon, a drop of several feet that knocked the air flat out of his lungs.

Maddy and Rashim were anxiously waiting for him right beside the portal. 'Oh, thank God!' cried Maddy. She swiped at her cheeks with the heel of her hand as she dropped down to her knees and reached out towards Liam, to get a hold of him. To be sure he was the real thing and not some apparition.

'God! I thought I'd lost you as well –'

Liam managed to get some air in his lungs. 'CLOSE THE PORTAL!' he screamed. 'CLOSE IT NOW!'

All eyes in the dungeon rose to look at the liquid image of the sphere hovering above Liam. The orb revealed the pleasant crimson tint of sunrise warming ridges of weather-worn rust-coloured sandstone. The dark outline of a distant jungle horizon; pools of mist coloured candyfloss pink by the rays of sunlight; creamy combed-out clouds in the sky above, lit from beneath.

Amid this swirling scene of beautiful serenity, something suddenly moved into view. A dark and indefinable form: like a murder of crows fluttering far too closely together and merging into one; like a school of fish constantly changing form as they evade the jaws of a circling predator.

The dark shape quickly filled the spherical image and for a moment it seemed like it might emerge from the orb and step out into the dungeon among them, but then the portal suddenly collapsed down to a pinprick of light and vanished.

In the dim electric-blue glow of the array of computer screens across the room, and the unblinking glare of the solitary bulb in its wire cage dangling from the low ceiling, they silently stared at each other. Ragged breathing filling the space between them; no words were necessary, and anyway, right then, none would have sufficed in helping them make any sense of what they'd just been through and all that they'd witnessed.

All the same, the silence was eventually broken.

'I think I might just go now,' said Bertie. He nodded politely at the others as if he was excusing himself from a rather uneventful game of cribbage. He turned and walked across the room, ducking as he stepped through the low archway. He looked back at them and offered another polite nod, before walking out of the dungeon and gently pulling the oak door shut behind him.

CHAPTER 70

1937, 13 Hanover Terrace, Regent's Park, London

From the journal of H. G. Wells

I will admit I never cast eyes on those people again. Every night after our return to London – for weeks, perhaps even for months afterwards – I recall I was awoken with the most dreadful night frights.

Awoken by my own screams.

So it was that I avoided them. I admit I even had trouble entering the premises of Delbert Hook's business for the knowledge that only several brick walls separated me from their device that opened a doorway on to Hell itself. I became haunted by imagined visions of that demon stalking the dark corridors and archways of the viaduct.

I recall that I managed to last but a few days before I finally left a note for Delbert informing him that I would be seeking employment elsewhere, with immediate effect. I do believe now that that was the only course of action I could take.

Over the intervening years I have often wondered if those young ladies and gentlemen ever truly existed, and what became of them. Whether they remained as subtenants of Mr Hook and his so-called import/export business. Or whether they eventually found other premises more suitable to their goals and plans.

I moved from Holborn to Kilburn in London, where I took up a teaching post at Henley House. Although I think I made the move more to distance myself from those haunting memories, to distance myself from their Hellish device. And I recall for many months after leaving Holborn I hungrily scoured the morning newspapers for fear of reading a ghastly report of giant three-legged monsters emerging from beneath the ground to burn us all to ashes.

With every year that has passed, I have managed to convince myself better that those memories were the product of an excitable young mind, an imagination run wild with no outlet of expression for it. Thus, I do believe my writing of works of fiction in later years has helped me in this respect.

Helped me to accept that in all likelihood those things never in fact happened to me.

That they were perhaps the side effects of a fever, most probably caused by food poisoning. A hallucination that lasted a few days. Or a particularly vivid dream that has stayed with me.

I believe I have finally managed to convince myself that none of those things were real. That they were imagined and that I am safe. That this – fortunately – is a very mundane world. That there are no such things as machines that travel through time or open doorways on to Hell. That there are no demons and monsters waiting patiently for such doors to open. That maybe, after all, mankind's future will not be as dire and dark and war-torn as the girl (what was her name, now? Maggie?) described it to be.

Such notions now seem to me to be too ridiculous and far-fetched for truth.

They have, however, proven to be particularly profitable to me, treated as ideas I have used for my fiction.

CHAPTER 71

1889, Brighton

The trip away from the smoke and fog of London down the line to Brighton for a few days turned out to be one of Liam's better ideas.

Maddy's mood was lifted by the sight of so many fine dresses and elaborate *chapeaux*, by the warmth of the unfolding spring bringing summer unseasonably early. Her spirits were raised by the sight of families playing bat-and-ball games together on the wide beach, by the jaunty sound of brass bands competing with each other for applause from the bandstands along the promenade.

Warm evenings filled with tea and cupcakes and the soothing draw and hiss of a gentle sea across sand and shingle. He noticed every now and then that her gaze was off somewhere far away, wistful, seeing other possibilities, other could-have-beens. But when he spoke to her she came back to him with a quick smile accompanied, he now noticed, by the first faint hairlines of crow's feet beside her green eyes.

We're both ageing.

The attrition of so much time travelling, of so much exposure to that misty hell, was finally making itself apparent. Even though he knew they'd both been engineered to have a greater resistance to the corrosive effects of stepping through time, it was, inevitably, going to catch up with them. Eventually. And as he studied her now – as she stared at seagulls swooping and bullying a hapless child throwing out breadcrumbs – he also saw the faint lines of silver in her hair and a purse line on her upper lip, subtle indicators of what she might one day look like.

Not old. Not even close just yet . . . but the signposts were all there.

Rashim too was showing the signs of this attrition. Liam had noticed the heavy folds in his brow, the grey highlights in his beard, a subtly mottled tone to his dark skin. He most certainly looked ten years older now than the man they'd first encountered in a remote field outside Ancient Rome.

And Bob and Becks? Liam smiled as he regarded them. They sat stiffly at the tea table, both slurping a lamb broth from soup spoons. They of course never seemed to change. At some point tachyon damage would surely reach too high a level for their cells to repair. At some point they too would start to age. However, he suspected that he, Maddy and Rashim would be long gone before either support unit began to grumble about aching hips or creaking knees.

He knew Maddy was still quietly grieving for Adam. He hadn't realized until now how strongly she'd felt for him. That it was, quite possibly . . . *love*. Or maybe he'd just been some kind of a lifeline: a last chance for her to feel like a normal girl. She'd told him the other day how Adam had pulled her away from the seeker and offered himself up as bait at the last moment. And how she'd only just now figured out what he'd meant with his last words to her. She said Adam must have worked out that he was going to die in 2001. He was going to die *anyway*, whatever happened. Either now or be one of the victims who died in the World Trade Center – he wasn't going to be in the world for much longer.

She'd told him she reckoned Adam had decided he might as well die for something. To save her.

'I'm not done with this,' said Maddy presently. Her eyes returned from the child, now backing nervously away from the gulls massing at her feet. 'I've been thinking about things.'

'About what?' asked Rashim.

'That column field.'

She was quiet for a while. Thoughtful. Fiddling with a coil of her hair, wrapped round a finger. 'What if, as you suggested back at that city, Rashim, the column was some sort of a marker? An end date for mankind?'

'A marker?'

'Like one of your tachyon beacons. But, you know, on a much, much grander scale.'

'Indeed.' He stroked his beard thoughtfully. 'It is highly conceivable that it had that function.'

'And you suggested that perhaps . . . this is all, like, some big *experiment*?'

'Experiment?' Liam finished his tea and set the cup back down on its saucer. 'You're actually taking his idea seriously?'

She nodded.

'You are in a strange mood this afternoon, Maddy.'

'No, listen to me . . . what if he's right? What if that's all we've ever been. Us humans? An experiment? A grand experiment? And experiments have a cut-off point. Right? When you've gathered enough data, you close the whole thing down.'

Rashim shifted in his seat. 'It was just an idle theory, Maddy. Just a –'

'What if you're right and all of Earth and the last – I dunno – the last, say, two thousand years of history have been like a giant Petri dish?' She looked at him. 'And us humans are like the bacteria sitting in it, being studied?'

Rashim returned her gaze over the rim of his glasses.

Maddy continued. 'Rashim, didn't you say that there was something really odd about why we never, *ever*, intercepted a single radio signal from aliens, even all the way up to 2070? Despite all our powerful radio telescopes and stuff, combing the frequencies, searching the skies for decades. Do you remember saying that?'

'The Fermi Paradox,' he uttered. 'Yes.'

'And you agree that the math is stacked against us being the only intelligence in the universe? That it's highly improbable that we are alone here?'

'Yes, of course, that would be the Drake Equation you are talking about.'

'You also agree that, in theory, at any given moment in time, given the infinite size of the universe there should be *thousands* of intelligent –'

'*Tens* of thousands.'

She looked at him. 'And yet in over seventy years of radio astronomy we pick up not even one single, solitary, radio signal?'

'And therein lies the Fermi Paradox, yes.'

She carefully unwound the coil of hair from her finger and looked at him. 'So, I know you were only theorizing, but maybe you've got it exactly right. We're in some kind of "quarantine". Some isolated dimension?' She glanced at Liam. 'Maybe his Petri dish theory isn't so stupid-sounding?'

'What are you gettin' at there, Mads? I'm not sure I –'

'So, my point is this . . . what if Waldstein knows something more? What if somehow he knows what's going on? What if he really is trying to do the *right* thing?'

'The right thing?'

'For us. For everyone!' She shrugged. 'I dunno . . . I guess what I'm saying is that maybe if we steer history the way he wants it to go – to the *place* he wants it to end up, to the day where humans nearly wipe themselves out with that Kosong-ni virus . . .' She looked up at her two friends. 'Maybe that's the only way we get out of this Petri dish? Maybe it's the end condition of this "experiment"?'

'You think it might be just like Adam thought?' said Liam, instantly regretting his words. He noticed the slightest stiffening of her lips. He knew the mention of his name was a painful jab for her. And it probably would be for a long while yet. He blundered on, keen to quickly move on from the mention of Adam's name. 'That those visitors in the jungle, the Archaeologists, came from the far-future? From beyond 2070?'

She nodded. 'But they're not observing us discreetly, like anthropologists. No, they've taken us and put us into this – this isolated pocket of space, just like we're all a bunch of lab rats.'

It sounded ridiculous to her and she decided to let it go. 'It's the only explanation I can think of.' She shrugged. 'Or maybe I'm just losing it.'

'No,' Rashim was nodding slowly. 'Who knows how advanced humans become in the far-future.'

Maddy also nodded thoughtfully. 'So maybe all of our answers lie in the far-future – lie beyond the year 2070?'

Liam met her eyes; they both shared the slightest smile. 'Aye. You thinking what I'm thinking, Mads?'

She turned and looked back out over the low promenade wall at the sea gently lapping across the broad beach, at distant scudding clouds in a warm and clement evening sky, at seagulls dipping and swooping, hovering on the breeze like untethered kites.

'Yeah . . . maybe . . .'

EPILOGUE

1379, the Lost City of the Windtalkers

The holy man dipped the bristles of his brush into the clay pot full of dark brown paint and then daubed some more on to the cave wall. Carefully. He needed to get the symbols exactly right, to faithfully reproduce them.

They of course meant nothing to him. An incomprehensible series of markings, but clearly they meant *something*. A message from the heavens that perhaps wiser men, more deserving men than he, would be able to fathom out.

Again he picked his way forward through the cave to remind himself of how the markings on the very next symbol went. The light of the day was bright. The midday monsoon had been and gone and cleared the sky, leaving the sun sitting in clear blue, warming up the jungle below.

The old man emerged from the mouth of the cave on to the lip. To his right a merchant was leading a tethered line of heavily laden llamas up the trail, oblivious to, or perhaps used to, the drop to their side. The merchant hesitated, and turned and looked at the same thing as the old man. A spectacular sight. Then he returned to the task of ensuring his animals carried on into the cave and through the access way to the city at the rear of it.

The holy man stepped to one side to let him pass, and the cave behind him soon echoed with the snorting, scraping, clopping of the beasts as the merchant guided inside and towards the rear.

His eyes returned to the jungle before him; below, moisture steamed up from the thick velvet carpet of tree tops, like the ghosts of the forefathers rising from Deep Mother Dirt to gaze curiously at the enormous object in the sky.

It hung there, over the jungle, like a solitary storm-cloud, casting its shadow over much of it. The Visitors came from it and returned to it each night from their labours in the village. They were hard at work on something beneath the ground.

Something godly, something wonderful. Something his people's ancestors had discovered centuries ago and now protected, kept safe for the Visitors. Its purpose was mysterious and yet the Visitors were not secretive; they were happy for the villagers to watch them as they set about their work.

The holy man once again looked out at the vast structure hanging in the sky. *Vast*, and circular in shape, topped with ridges and spikes and convolutions that made no sense to him. It glistened in the sunlight, as smooth as a polished riverbed pebble.

Along the surface of this floating heavenly chariot, as large as a mountain top, were giant markings – symbols. The old man studied the next symbol carefully, making sure he had it in his mind correctly before finally turning and heading back into the cave to daub it on the wall beside the last one he'd painted. As he stepped back inside, he reminded himself again that perhaps, one day, wiser, far more deserving minds would determine their actual meaning.

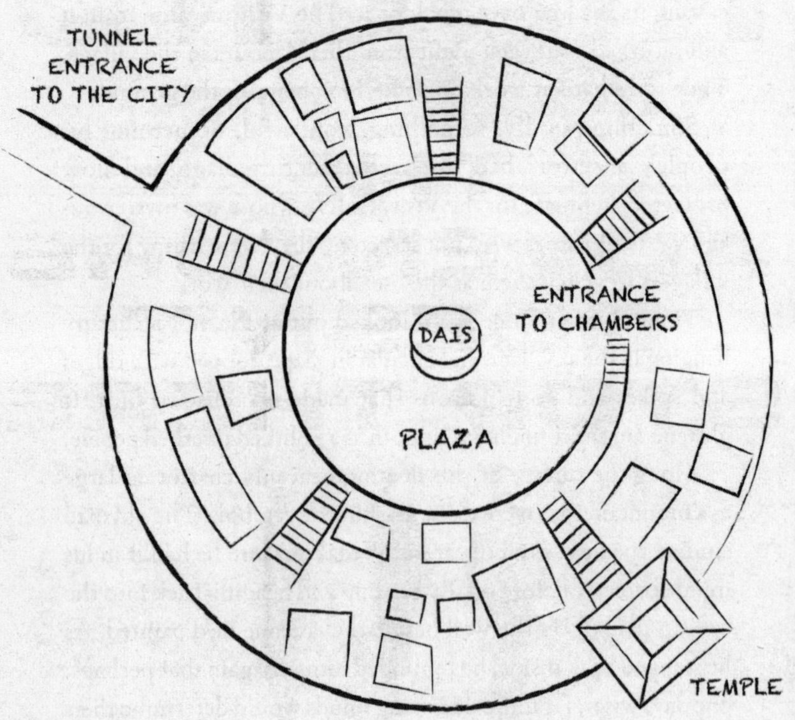
THE LOST CITY
OF THE WINDTALKERS
TUNNEL
ENTRANCE
TO THE CITY
ENTRANCE
TO CHAMBERS
DAIS
PLAZA
TEMPLE

TIME
RIDERS
2001
1957
1941
1912